DARKBEAM 1

ADRIENNE WOODS

PART I

THE RUBICON'S STORY

ADRIENNE WOODS

Fire Quill Publishing
First publish in the USA by Fire Quill Publishing.
This is the first Edition published in 2017

CONDITION OF SALE

DEDICATION

To everyone who wanted more.

ACKNOWLEDGEMENTS

First and most importantly, as always, thank you to our Father in Heaven, for blessing me still every day.

Without Your guidance, I wouldn't have finished another novel. You were involved in this every day. You are my purpose of life and i will love You till the end of time.

For the endless support of my family; my husband, Heinrich, and my two beautiful daughter. i would be lost without your loving support and your ability to keep me pursuing a new project each and every time.

It takes a village to get a novel ready and a special thanks to everyone that helped me to get this novel ready.

My editors; Hillery and Jess. Hillery you are still a true Paegeian and Jess, I fell in love with the love you have for your work. It shows in every manuscript you work on. I've learned so much as a writer from your guidance. Thank you for giving Darkbeam the wings it needed to soar.

To Monique. Thank you for always delving head first into my novels. For the beautiful words you add and for all the reference checks and making sure that my characters do not stray from who they truly are.

To Joemel Requeza for your beautiful design to another one of my covers. Your talent cannot be put into words to describe what your covers make me feel. I don't have a favorite as all of them are perfect and unique in their own way.

To Carlyle. I couldn't have done this without you, as you always took a lot on your plate and never disappoint. You give me the amount of time to finish every one of my novels. You are my sister in a world filled with books.

To Anika. My limbs. I cannot say enough thanks to you. You are the best assistant anyone could ask for and for taking care of anything I throw in your way with a smile and a positive attitude. I couldn't have done any of this if you were not involved in my daily life. Thank you, thank you, thank you.

And last, but certainly not the least. My readers. I truly hope that you are going to love Blake's story. I hope I do the big guy justice.

Thank you all for being part of my journey.

Adrienne.

PART I

PART II

PART I

ONE

Darkness or Light,
The Rubicon will fight.
He will succeed,
But a rider he needs.
Rider be brave and fierce,
strongest bond in all these years,
of Royal blood they be born;
Fate of Paegeia is forewarned.

I HEARD the words whispered above me and then a small ray of golden light seeped through.

That moment had happened sixteen years ago. Why I'd thought about it today, I still didn't know. Those few words or prophecy were what had been spoken when my egg hatched. But they had been a lie. Why the words were still black in the Book of Shadows, none of us knew, but they had given me hope, hope that maybe, just maybe, my true rider existed somewhere. Those words were all I had to hold on to now. They were what my mother held on to. And Irene.

I remembered her words, ringing inside my skull as if they were spoken yesterday. I remembered them just like I could remember the temperature of my egg as my mother lay on it. Why she didn't just trample on it and end all of this, I will never know. She knew what I was: a Rubicon. Only one was born every era. Two of us would annihilate this world, because we craved dominance. I'd been born almost a thousand years after Quitto, the last Rubicon, finally died.

We were just so different from the other dragon races, all ten dragons combined, or so they'd told me.

I had ten abilities, but I only knew of five. Or better said, only five had shown themselves to me. It was with these five abilities that I would fight the person who used to be my best friend later today. I had known him since I'd shed my first scales and he was in diapers. But the innocence of childhood never lasts.

It had all changed three summers ago, when the darkness started speaking to me. It didn't use words like humans did. It had no language. It was a darkness that stirred and boiled inside my core. It had wants foreign to me. It awoke a monstrous beast that wanted to kill. Thoughts, dark thoughts, erupted in my mind incessantly. It would drive me insane until I did its deeds. Then the beast would go quiet and I could breathe again, fight again, but those dark deeds would haunt my soul.

No one could pull me from this. The beast that had awoken three summers ago was now too strong. Too strong for anyone but one person. A dark sorcerer trapped behind deadly snatchers. He was the only one who would be able to control me, to make me do things that would make every living soul fear him, and I would rejoice doing that. I would know that as every second ticked by, the beast would be growing stronger.

Lucian told me to fight it. That I was stronger than this. That I was good. But that was a long time ago.

As I sat consumed in my own thoughts, a note landed on my table. I looked up and saw the Snow Dragon, Tabitha, a few tables away sitting next to the Green-Vapor and giving me her dashing smile. *What does she want from me now?* I'd thought my actions from a few weeks back would have made her back off, but some girls were pathetic. It was a known fact that Snow Dragons fell into that department. Still, her beauty somehow turned her cowardly streak into something I couldn't put my finger on. I wasn't in love with her; it wasn't even lust. I was no longer capable of anything like that. Maybe I never was.

I opened the note.

Her handwriting was practically illegible, but I managed.

"Tell you what, meet me in the Colosseum's changing room before your claim, and you can show me how sorry you are."

How sorry I am? I wasn't sorry about anything. My lips curled. Some girls would do anything not to be ignored.

Fine, whatever. It would fulfill one of the beast's carnal needs and maybe, just maybe, Lucian wouldn't die today.

Not many knew that the Prince of Tith and the Rubicon used to be best friends, except for my younger sister, Samantha Leaf, a Fire Tail and the biggest pain in the ass a brother could be cursed with. She would attend the Academy in two years and I was dreading it. She was also a Metallic—one of the good dragons who didn't have to suffer beatings on a monthly basis to stay good. Those stung like hell, and I felt sorry for my father, as there would come a time when even he wouldn't be able to tame my beast.

It was one of the things I feared, killing my loved ones. I knew when the time came I wouldn't care anymore, as even this part of me would be completely dark too. But I feared for him now. Just like I feared for this afternoon when I was going to face my first claim with the Prince of Tith.

I'd had many claims, ever since I'd turned sixteen. Others had tried to claim me, but they'd failed. One almost died.

The Prince of Tith, well, he'd just come of age and was keeping the promise he'd made three years ago.

The memory of that day was an ever-present flicker in the back of my mind.

It was right after a beating. We were both sitting on the stone wall back at the castle in Tith. It overlooked parts of Tith, and you could see the Creepers writhing in the distance.

The beating was horrible. I remembered the fatigue that

came with it, my two weeks of silence. The beast inside me was raving mad, but I was in control. In pain, yes, but in control.

It was twilight. I gazed at a stellar sunset, colors of red, pink, and orange melting over a glow of purple. It was peaceful.

My back stung.

"If I were a dragon, I would give you my oath," Lucian said.

"Oath for what, to stop my father whenever I needed a beating?"

"No, to find a way to claim you."

I stared at him. Was he deranged?

He was grave. "I guess my promise will do."

"Lucian, you don't know what you're saying. Nobody can take part in a claim before their sixteenth birthday."

"Then I'll wait."

"You have no idea what I will be like three years from now."

"Doesn't matter. I know who you are now, and that is enough. I'm not going to lose you to darkness, Blake."

He dangled his arm around me. "You're like my brother. Brothers don't give up on one another."

That was then. We'd been tight like brothers. But that was before the light came. His light.

I'd had no choice but to push him away. That pure goodness inside him clashed with my darkness, a darkness that was slightly stronger than his light. It made me sick.

The best way to explain it was when someone eats too much salty and sweet at the same time. It was like that. A nauseating feeling that I couldn't handle.

I had no choice but to stay as far as I could from him. Today I was going to face that inside the Colosseum. It was going to rile up the beast while I had to deal with the nauseated feeling and try my best to not let the beast rip his head off.

He had no idea what he was putting me through, and for what? A promise he'd made me that summer when that first glimpse of darkness had showed itself.

He was going to die in that ring. I just hoped it wasn't going to be this afternoon.

❧

THE CROWDS WERE ALREADY CHEERING in the Colosseum, as I was busy feeding the beast. The Snow Dragon kept to her word. I found her wearing only her robe in my changing area where I would exit into the ring.

It happened so fast. I wanted to fill a need, one of the beast's needs. I kissed her fiercely. Her back connected hard with the wall as her legs curled around my waist.

Her body was sculpted to perfection. Her white skin brought to mind an ice queen. She reminded me of winter; she calmed my yearning, and her cold touch calmed my own stirring flame deep inside.

Her complaints filled my ears. It pleased the beast. When she begged for more, I gave her what she wanted.

Lust and satisfaction numbed both the beast and myself. When we reached climax, my brain temporarily exploded into fireworks, blinding the darkness.

Her laughter filled my ears, tired laughter. I could hear my name being called outside.

"Ru-bi-con, Ru-bi-con, Ru-bi-con." I didn't know how long it had been carrying on. It was time to go.

"Give him hell. Make him regret that he ever decided to try and claim you." She touched my lips. The beast was calm. He was at peace. "You are untamable," she said softly.

My lips curved. I kissed her on the lips and left.

The crowd was going insane. The Dragonians and the dragons. And of course the press.

My eyes snagged on King Helmut. There was a warning in them.

Don't hurt my son. No, don't kill my son.

Your son shouldn't have done this.

Our gaze broke and I turned slowly around to see how packed the Colosseum was. Everyone was here because it was me and the Prince of Tith.

I wasn't a show pony like some of the other dragons. I didn't rile up the crowds or put on a show for them. I was the Rubicon. A mere lift of my arms made them go wild.

The song played.

It was something stupid Dragonians did. And the one

Lucian had chosen only amped me up more. Whether it was too much bass or the effect the electric guitar had on me. It rippled through my bones, clawed on my scales.

The Dragonians hummed with the tune. The ground vibrated under my feet as they stomped in unison.

My gaze found Lucian's.

He looked determined, with a rope wrapped around his arms and a shield in his hands. His eyes were narrow. Wearing his safety vest with combat boots reaching his calves, he looked more like a soldier who belonged in a futuristic story than a modern-day knight trying to tame a dragon. Especially a dragon who didn't belong to him.

Why the hell are you doing this, you fool? You haven't even ascended yet!

His light streamed out of him as he stared at me with so much compassion, it made me want to throw up. The beast was starting to reawaken.

The Snow Dragon hadn't been enough.

I jumped into the air. The first part that broke out of my human flesh was my wings. The rest followed as if it was the most natural thing in the world.

Deep, dark red and purple scales replaced human skin.

A deadly tail.

Four paws with sharp talons replaced my limbs.

Rows and rows of pointy teeth and a mane of thick tendrils flapped with a shake of my head.

I roared.

Lucian stood his ground.

I tuned in and found his heartbeat. It was elevated but not from fear. From adrenaline, admiration, and anticipation. He was ready.

He steadied his shield in front of him and placed his free hand on the rope over his shoulder. "Let's show them a claiming they will never forget!" he yelled in Latin.

I started to chuckle. The beast was taking over. Nothing I did would protect Lucian from its wrath.

"There will never be a claiming. You are not the royal the Viden prophesied."

I changed the scenery of the Colosseum to a swamp. I loved swamps; you could do and be so many things in a swamp. Set booby traps, drown enemies in mud, and they wouldn't even see it coming. The beast was already clouding my mind.

Remember who that is. No killing him! I roared. The beast gave a roar back; it sent shivers down my spine and straight into my soul. It was letting me know who was in charge. Today was going to be a fight I could have never prepared myself for. The one inside myself.

Lucian looked dazed by the swamp that had suddenly appeared around us. Fresh terror lit his eyes.

I stayed still, concealed like a boulder right in front of him. Then the beast took over completely. I was in way over my head.

Don't kill him. I'll give you what you want. Just don't kill him.

The fight was hard. Not just against Lucian, but against myself too.

I almost gave in. I hung on by a thread. Killing Lucian wasn't an option.

I had to stay in control.

Lucian fought well.

The swamp didn't last long. He was really good, the only one truly worthy of being inside this ring with me, If I was honest.

He finally lost his balance as I shook the ground stomping my feet.

It carried on like that for a long time. Like a stupid game. Lucian struggled to regain his balance and bounced hard against the floor.

The beast thought it was comical.

Enough! I put a stop to it.

The beast went for Lucian. Lucian rolled around; my paws just missed squashing him by inches.

I didn't want to look, but I had no choice.

I was scared. Yet at the same time, I loved everything about it. I was getting angry as he slipped through my paws.

The battle raged.

Lucian refused to give up. Every tiny breadth of space he found, every second of reprieve, he used to gain the upper hand.

At one stage, I thought he had me. It was so intense. The way the crowd cheered. Their chants coursed through the ground and drilled into my scales.

And then he used his rope.

I didn't even see him coming.

The bastard had just been on the ground, rolling to dodge my lethal paws, and then he was gone, just like that.

I heard his scream from behind as he leaped onto my back.

I was too late to attack him with an ability. He landed on my spine hard. The rope looped around one of my horns. One that I couldn't reach.

He'd done his homework. He swung from the rope.

I tried to squash him in the process of climbing off my back, but he was thumping and throwing my body in all directions. I only did exactly what he'd hoped.

I got myself tangled in the ropes, half-strangled.

He was bringing me down. "Yield, Blake, for the both of us! Just yield!"

This was it. He was going to win. Whether he was the foretold royal or not. Lucian always believed it didn't matter what people said, that as long as you believed it with your heart and you confessed it with your mind, you could make anything happen. And this was it. The proof behind his faith.

But the beast in me refused to yield.

I wasn't anyone's lamb. *I am the Rubicon! I cannot be tamed!*

The strength that had waned a few minutes ago came back, amplified exponentially. My body shredded through the rope that had trapped me.

Lucian yelled out of frustration and ducked, diving again to escape my wrath.

I wasn't thinking clearly anymore.

I didn't remember our friendship and how close we'd been.

I spat my acid at him. The spots where my acid orbs landed disintegrated. Rocks melted and shattered, giving him less and less hiding spaces. But the weasel still escaped me. My wrath became darker.

ENOUGH!

He rolled out from hiding, ready to jump again, but this time the beast was ready. Before I could control it, a flash of lightning left my mouth.

He wasn't supposed to be here in the first place.

The lightning struck him.

He flew back and convulsed violently on the floor. He shook as volts of electricity ran through him.

Then it stopped.

Lucian's body lay lifeless on the cold, unforgiving floor of the Colosseum. I wanted to attack him again. He would always come back if I didn't finish him off and I couldn't have that.

A Sun-Blast dragon flew in, followed by a Fin-Tail and a Copper-Horn. All of them were so fast.

I wanted to scorch their asses.

I growled and screeched. They ducked and dove, avoiding my lightning and acid.

One of them connected hard with me. I staggered a few

feet, but kept my balance. They pummeled me. They came again and again.

I growled.

"Blake, calm down," Professor Mia said as a Fin-Tail crashed into me this time.

"Remember who you are," she commanded.

The Fin-Tail rammed the other side of my body.

It took four of them to make me remember who I truly was and the guy I'd almost killed.

I pulled back.

"He's calming down," she said. "Give him some room."

The beast inside me still growled.

STOP IT! JUST STOP! the human part of me yelled as I disconnected from the hatred, the darkness, and the irrepressible drive to kill. The beast's constant thirst for blood.

I morphed back into my human form and lay on the ground. Someone scurried up from the sidelines and covered me with a robe, then disappeared before I had a chance to attack.

I took huge breaths to calm my soul, my mind, and my heart, even though I couldn't feel it beating. My entire being was on edge.

"Blake?" Mia asked. I looked up at her. She was in her human form too, draped hastily in a robe from somewhere, crouching next to me. I pushed myself up, resting with my elbows on my knees, just taking deep breaths, steadying myself.

"I thought we'd lost you for a second."

I shook my head. "It's getting stronger. I don't know how much longer I can hold on, Mia." And then it hit me. "Lucian!"

I jumped up from the floor and bolted to the one of the gates. The one that led to Lucian's changing room. The gate was locked but I could see Constance working on his limp body.

"Lucian!"

"Blake, calm down." One of the other professors said through the gate.

"Lucian!" Tears streamed down my cheeks. *What have I done?*

"Lucian!"

Mia got hold of me. "Let them do their job."

"Get off me," I said through gritted teeth. Hot, shameful tears rolled down my cheeks. "I did that to him, Mia. Me."

"Calm down. Lucian knows the risks, Blake. He knows."

"No, don't." I needed to get out of there. There was no escape. I looked at the sky.

"Lower the shield!" Mia yelled and pulled my chin down to look at her.

Our eyes met.

The shimmer started to soften and then the shield vanished.

"Just go." Mia's eyebrows knitted together, her eyes soft. I hated that look. Pity.

Thank you. I wanted to say it so badly, but the words just didn't form in my mouth.

I shifted back into the beast and flapped my huge wings. I flew like I'd never flown before. Away from the atrocity I'd committed this day.

TWO

I FLEW straight to View Top Mountain. It was the closest to Dragonia Academy and also one of Paegeia's highest peaks.

I couldn't control my anger and frustration anymore and just let it all out. My abilities shook the ground as wrath poured out of me.

I screamed.

Why me? Why him? Why couldn't this just be a fucked-up dream?

When was I going to wake up?

At length, I wore myself out. I felt empty. I started to calm down.

The nearby trees were scorched. *This isn't me!*

Minutes crept past. I sat on a boulder and watched Paegeia spread beneath me from a safe distance.

The stars were already starting to light up the night.

I focused and played a counting game with the shimmer of the shield that protected Paegeia from the rest of the world.

I wished I could just fly through that wall and disappear,

but it wasn't going to be that easy. They would send hordes after me, and I'd been warned on numerous occasions that they would take me down if I lost control.

I didn't want to push my luck with the beast. I didn't want to kill more innocent people. A shudder racked my body at the thought.

So I stayed. Wishing I didn't care anymore.

Since the day I'd taken my first breath, a predestined evil hung over me. Without my true rider, I would turn dark.

Even if Lucian found a way to claim me, I would keep growing stronger. There would come a time when I would destroy him—or he would have to kill me.

It was just who I was. Who we all were.

All the Rubicons before me had turned evil, dark. The last one was felled by a brave Viking called William. They'd made him king of Paegeia the day he slew Quitto.

They said that we used to be part of the outside world. Paegeia wasn't always hidden. But humans got greedy when it came to dragon blood and magic. Therefore, the best sorcerers of that time wielded the Wall.

The Wall only dragons could pass through.

I had a theory about why it was only dragons, but what was the use of sharing it with everyone? They would just give me more responsibilities if they knew I had any brains. I already had too much to deal with as is. I wasn't a scientist, and I wasn't a philosopher. Maybe it was the Crown-Tail in me.

It was so obvious; I didn't know why no one had

thought of it before.

The Wall fed off essence.

A dragon's heart beat way softer than humans' hearts. The Wall didn't detect dragon heartbeats, but it did pick up on humans'.

Even if one tried to transform oneself into a dragon through some kind of crazy impossible magic, it could never change the heart. One would still be human inside.

It was why humans got incinerated when they tried to leave. It was why dragons could come and go as they pleased. Well, that was just my theory.

I gazed down at my world.

I doubted I would ever want to leave, even if they granted me permission to do so. But I'd always wanted to know more about the other side.

The only place I'd seen beyond the confines of Paegeia was China. It had been a long time ago. I still hadn't received my human form yet. The people of China nurtured a great love for Paegeia. Even in the present, our existence was evident in their art and architecture.

The truce between China and us was strong. We still engaged in commerce with them—well, dragons disguised as humans did. They wanted to show their respects to the new Rubicon who would save both worlds if it came to that.

It had been a real ego booster.

Others knew about us too. Dragons lived among humans; they registered with a council on the other side.

Plus, the leaders of each nation were informed of our existence. Elected leaders and monarchies alike all kept Paegeia a secret.

They assisted us when we needed it, and we reciprocated with secret missions.

I knew this because I was the Rubicon.

The rest of the other side had no idea that our world existed. It was sad, but it was the only way to keep Paegeia safe.

The humans who discovered our world by mistake, well, most of them couldn't deal with our reality. They lost their minds. Went insane. Many of them got locked up at institutions in Paegeia, drugged and incoherent. That was how they would remain until they died.

The few who fought the madness—not many—could never go back because of the Wall.

I was one of the lucky ones, born a dragon and because of what I was, I would die here too. Though I knew that my life would be over soon.

Rubicons didn't live long.

It was a constant battle I had with myself. I wanted to be good. I wanted to win this fight. But good didn't always win in the end.

I needed my rider. Not just someone who could claim me. I needed my true rider.

It was the only way I could win.

My true rider doesn't exist. The foretold bloodline had

died 15 years ago. The bloodline my rider would've been born from.

Paegeia had three kingdoms. Etan, Tith, and Areeth. The king of Etan, King Albert, had been the greatest ruler of all time and the true king. The King of Tith and Areeth were granted kingships by King Albert's father. He did so to strengthen Paegeia.

My father was the true king's dragon, so I'd known the guy quite well. But he'd been betrayed by his best friend, Goran, an evil Dragonian who became one of the most powerful sorcerers the world had ever seen.

The night he took the king and queen of Etan's lives, giant creepers that had the ability to attack and shred intruders sprouted from the ground.

Many said the king's dying breath had conjured them. His love for his people had been that magical. He protected us from evil still.

Irene, the Viden, gave the foretelling when my egg hatched that King Albert and Queen Catherine's bloodline would produce an heir who was destined to be my rider, my true rider.

That heir was never born.

So it didn't matter who claimed me.

I would turn evil.

I would die young.

Perhaps that was why I hated the Colosseum so much. What hope it gave didn't apply to me. To me it was a waste of time.

Still, I fought.

Why did I fight? Because of the foretelling. Foretellings were like a fortune. Some were pure bullshit, but now and then you really got those who truly saw the future.

Irene was our era's Viden. Many private Videns were employed by the rich, but she was Paegeia's. She'd lived in one of the Dragon Cities, but a few years ago, she'd moved to Dragonia Academy because of me.

I saw her almost daily now.

When Irene had a vision, something really magical happened .Her eyes became silver and she spoke in a thousand tongues. They always came out in riddles, but what she saw was quite different, albeit confusing.

It was the gift of all Moon-Bolts. The older they got, the clearer their visions become.

Irene's visions and foretellings were connected to the Book of Shadows. If they were important to Paegeia's survival, her visions magically appeared in black ink on the pages of the Book of Shadows for all to see.

Most of mine were in there.

When a foretelling was fulfilled, the words turned red. But if the time came and the foretelling was not fulfilled, the ink turned blue. The black foretellings still needed to be fulfilled.

All of mine were still black.

That was the main reason why I fought against the darkness. Even though my rider didn't exit, there was still hope.

How big or small, I didn't know.

But lately it has gotten harder. I was losing hope. My eyes were finally opening to the bleak reality of my situation.

Dragons didn't always have riders. It wasn't natural for them to share our gifts.

The Metallics had no problem with that, but we Chromatics… we were different. We used to despise humans until King Albert changed our minds.

I hadn't hatched when they took place, but my father recounted breathless stories about the wars that had raged across the land. I'd grown up with so many possibilities, but they were all starting to fade.

The Colosseum was one of them. It wasn't a place of hope to me. Inside that ring, riders broke us. It was where they tamed and took the wild out of us. A life sentence to serve and protect someone else.

I sighed.

I was meant to do so many great things. Yet all I was good at was destroying.

My destiny was that I was supposed to free Etan with the help of King Albert's spawn. A destiny I'd never fulfill.

That wasn't the worst part, though. The worst part was that if I didn't get claimed before my darkness got too strong, I would go fully dark. Then I would destroy everything I loved, everything I needed.

The only rider with a fighting chance to tame me was the one haunting my dreams. He was stronger than the beast, more evil than the beast. Part of me couldn't wait for our union to come to pass. He was the sorcerer who had betrayed the king.

Goran.

It was obvious, when I considered what had just happened today, with Lucian. My best friend. I'd almost killed him. If he wasn't dead already.

I stared at nothing. Sightless. Hopeless.

He shouldn't have been in that ring today; he shouldn't have tried to keep his promise. Blood promises had been broken before. It wasn't like I'd even accepted his pledge when he made it.

Nothing would hurt him, nothing. Yet I had.

Just then, I felt words I hadn't felt in a long time.

> *I am power and I am might.*
> *I am flame and fury.*
> *I have no need for man nor beast.*
> *I am judge and jury.*

Stars twinkled in the night sky. I lay on my back, watching them. How I wanted to be able to fly up to one. Just fly until I couldn't anymore.

The night was my only friend. The night and the darkness.

> *Friend of the night, I've now become.*
> *Anticipating him made me succumb...*

Words started to pour out.

Sparring Lucian was never easy. And this went way beyond sparring. It had been life or death. Did I kill him?

It wasn't meant to be. Still, he wouldn't give up.

I gave in to my words and kept reciting the poem until it was in my head.

> *Tired of fighting the beast inside.*
> *Mirrored reflection I cannot hide…*

I should've never fucked the Snow Dragon. It was stupid. After that, she thought we had this bond, a thing between us. She pretended as if I belonged to her.

I belonged to no one.

I needed to call Phil. Phil was full of schemes, more like a Crown-Tail instead of the Night Villain he was.

He was scaly, though, and not just his skin. Phil's kind would stab anyone in the back to save his own tail.

But I needed to calm the beast. And his schemes always managed to do that.

❦

ONLY AFTER MIDNIGHT did I return to the Academy. I landed gently in the courtyard by the infirmary.

It was quiet.

Is he okay?

I tuned in, trying to listen for a heartbeat, but all I heard in the infirmary was a dragon's heart beating soft and calm. No human heart.

Tears welled up in my eyes. I stalked in the opposite direction toward the castle, back to the dorms.

I'd almost reached the staircase, almost out of danger when...

"Blake," Master Longwei said in his strong Chinese accent. He was the headmaster of Dragonia and one of the best Fin-Tail dragons I'd ever known. He was slightly weird though. Always wearing knee-length shorts with flip-flops and ugly, colorful shirts with big loud flowers on them.

I sighed and stopped.

"Lucian is okay," he assured me. "King Helmut picked him up a few hours ago."

Relief flooded me, though I didn't reveal it to him. I nodded, as my back faced him. I sniffed, pulling myself together.

"Is that all?" I said, as if *thank you for putting my soul at ease for the night* was forbidden to say out loud.

"That's all. You can go," he said.

I walked up the stairs to my room. I didn't get far, though. A great, bottomless sadness and vast loneliness rose up and overwhelmed me.

My knees buckled beneath my weight and I slid down the wall to the floor. I sobbed.

When will this struggle end? I feared that I was fighting

a battle that I could never win. *Why do I even try to hold on?*

To what? A stupid foretelling? There was no hope. Not in Lucian. The beast inside me destroyed hope.

That was all it had ever done.

Destroy everyone I'd ever loved.

THREE

THE CLAIMING and Lucian's absence took a tremendous toll on me. The claim had been a victory for the beast, but I had lost.

Lucian was one of my best friends—still was, in a way. Even though I couldn't come near him.

That light.

I was the only one who could see it. What caused the light? Lucian had a good heart and a kind soul. He would never give up on his friends. He saw me as a brother, so yes, his persistence was amplified because of that.

That purity in his soul was magical all by itself. I would put it in the same category as a mother's love, a father's protection, a brother's promise... They all left a mark.

That mark of pure love didn't mesh so well with my darkness. It made me recoil every time I came within a few feet of him. It made me sick. Made me nauseous.

I blamed the beast.

It was doing this on purpose. It knew how much Lucian

hated the darkness. The beast knew I would do anything for my brother, at least that small part that was still holding on deep inside of me.

I must be such a huge disappointment to Lucian. What did he think? That I was going to roll over and give up?

It wasn't that easy.

If he was strong enough, he would earn it.

With all the thoughts swirling in my head, I skipped class and went back to View Top Mountain. I had to plant trees to replace the ones I had destroyed the day before.

As my wings furled and I landed, shame flooded me. My temper tantrum had done this. A strong pine smell used to linger in the air. In the beginning, the forest would calm my soul. A sedative to the darkness. But now it did nothing. The pine smell was gone and in its place was a sooty, charred smell.

I did this.

"I am what I am, Blake: you. Nothing more. Stop treating me like an independent entity, because I'm not."

The voice in my head was like honey. A voice I could never trust. The voice of darkness. My darkness, also known as the beast.

I would always think of it as an entity. It wasn't me. Well, not yet anyway. I would never embrace it, never think of it as me. For now that was the only way to cope.

Evil laughter echoed inside my head and chilled me to the bone. It threatened to drive me to the brink of insanity. I covered my ears to no avail.

I thought about Lucian's promise again. When we were thirteen.

That time it had been so easy, easy to hold on.

Now, it was nearly impossible, but I couldn't give up. I had to hold on. I had to keep fighting. Had to for my mother, for my sister, and for Lucian.

My father? I didn't want to think about him.

Those were the only people who really meant anything to me, really. Yet they were the ones I pushed away the hardest.

I wished none of this was so damn complicated, but this was my life.

I'd been thinking back to my foretelling, the one Irene had made when my egg hatched. Why did she see that, and not the guy who betrayed my true rider's parents? Was it because it was mostly about me, and not them?

She'd been seeing funny things lately. Things that made absolutely no sense. Some sort of a search was happening, a killing spree. She couldn't tell me where or when the search was taking place, or who was committing the bloodshed. She just saw victims, all perished. For what cause, I don't know. Why was it linked to me? Was this killer my future self, united with the beast at last?

It only awakened the beast more.

The Viden saw the killings so clearly.

A part of me loved it. The danger, the chase, the death. To be truly free from what I was fighting against. Not to feel so tired anymore.

Another part of me was terrified of how much I liked it.

It scared the living crap out of her too.

ஃ

I KNOCKED on the Viden's door. The tower was behind the boys' tower but separate, off to one side of the castle.

Vines with dainty purple flowers ran up to the lone window that overlooked Dragonia Academy.

This was where Irene met with all the students at least once a month. Except for me. I was the Rubicon; I was required to see her up to three times a week.

Irene was a three-hundred-year-old Moon-Bolt dragon. She could see into the future and had guided a multitude of humans, dragons, and other magical beings to their true destinies.

But in person, she appeared the opposite of someone who was three hundred years old.

Because of dragons' magical essence, we aged slowly. Part of that essence could be transferred to humans. The precise ins and outs of the process had never triggered my curiosity.

Her essence made her look like she was in her late twenties, tops. It drove students nuts. She was gorgeous with long black hair, big cerulean eyes, and a skin that made me think of caramel, or something else I wanted to taste.

I was fucked if she saw even a glint of lust.

She opened the door.

Something always changed inside of me, rippled through my being whenever I came to see her.

"Good afternoon, Blake." Her lips fanned out and revealed the whitest pearls and deepest dimple in her left cheek. "Come in."

I entered, wiping my hands on my jeans. *Sweaty palms?*

What was it about this creature that put me on edge? She wasn't intimidating. No, this was something I couldn't put words to. *Why did she make me so nervous?*

I sat down at a spindly table with an orb resting in the center. I'd never seen her use it; I truly wondered if it wasn't just for show.

She disappeared into the kitchen. The sound of a kettle whistling on a hot plate filled the room. She loved her tea. Her voice floated out from the kitchen. "So, how do you feel after our last session?"

"Okay, I guess. Have you seen any more killings?"

Seen. She knew what I meant. I doubted she had; I needed to be in her immediate vicinity for her to see a glimpse of visions related to me.

She laughed. My own lips curved slightly at the sound of her sweet laughter.

"You know that's not how it works." She came out of the kitchen with a tray that held two cups and a plate of cookies. She put the tray down and handed me a cup of tea.

I'd never drank a cup before and wondered why she kept offering. The same with the cookies. She put the plate in front of me, and I shook my head.

She smiled and left the plate in front of me. Silence filled the room as she prepared her tea. It was that awkward, suffocating kind of silence. She sat in the chair diagonal to me.

"So," she started, pinning me with those big blue eyes of hers.

It was hard to think of her as a three-hundred-year-old dragon when she looked just a few years older than me.

"How are you feeling?"

"Same," I mumbled. She would know before anyone else did if there had been a drastic change in my darkness. That was how potent her ability was. Her connection to me was strong, and the beast felt something for her too. *Of course he did.* The only problem was that I didn't know if it was good or bad.

"I've tried to channel other tools to see. The cards were no help." Her eyebrows rose. "And the tea leaves are all over the place. It's hard to make out what they show."

"What do they say?" I had to know.

You won't be claimed, boy! The beast said.

She shook her head. "It's better to leave it."

"What do they say, Irene?" I was adamant.

She looked at me. "What do you want me to tell you? That the only thing your cards indicate me is darkness and death? Only destruction, not an ounce of hope? The leaves give me omens, dark omens, and…" She shook her head and closed her eyes. A breath left her lips and she sank lower in her chair.

"And what?"

"I get headaches, Blake." She rested with her head on her hand and stared at me through thick, dark eyelashes that went on for days.

I looked away. "Headaches?"

"It's like the darkness is starting to block me from your future. I can still see bits here and there, but when I truly do see something connected with you, it leaves me with a mother of a headache."

"I'm sorry."

She touched my arm. It felt good. As if I needed her touch.

Hungry thoughts filled my head, visions of taking things further with Irene. Taking *her*. Things I shouldn't have ever thought to begin with. I jumped up "I've got to go."

"Blake, you just got here."

"You said it yourself, Irene." I paused at the door. "It's only darkness and bad omens." I left.

What was happening? *Why her?* What does it want with her? The way her touch felt on my skin, it was innocent. Yet the beast made it feel different.

Why her?

Because it's forbidden, it whispered.

The muscles of my jaw clenched. I hated how it always got exactly what it wanted. But not this time. No, I would fight.

I was still in control

FUR

I USED to get an overwhelming nauseated feeling whenever I entered my dorm.

I'd recently moved up to the seventh floor. Lucian had demanded it. He'd ordered Master Longwei and the rest of the board to make the room change the minute he set foot on Dragonia Academy soil. He wanted me to be his room-mate. Wanted me close.

Yay me.

It was hard to get used to at first. Most of the time, I wasn't okay being that close to him. His light. I doubted I would ever get used to it.

The one good thing from my failed claiming was that I could breathe in my room for this first time in ages. My stomach didn't churn, and I didn't feel like I was going to throw up my organs.

I'd just returned from View Top Mountain. I had to check and see if the trees I'd planted were taking root.

I needed a shower. It was where I could think, where I could be myself, and where I drowned out its voice. Most of the time.

Today was different, though. I struggled to calm down. Knowing what the beast was after this time... It was insane.

She was three hundred years old. She would probably just laugh in my face if I tried anything.

"Dude," I spoke to myself softly in the mirror. "C'mon. Focus."

It had been going on like this the entire fucking day. I couldn't stop thinking about Irene. She was what the beast wanted now. Given enough time, I would soon see things its way.

I took my shirt off and turned on the faucet. I crawled out of the rest of my clothes and stepped into the shower.

Water cascaded over my head and bare back. It felt warm, but it wasn't. My body ran exceptionally hot; cold showers were the key to regulating my temperature.

My snow ability hadn't manifested yet. I don't know when it would.

The only abilities that had shown themselves were my lightning, fire, acid, and a tiny bit of healing. It was the weakest one of them all.

Constance, my mother's identical twin, was the Academy doctor. She predicted that gas would be next.

But it wasn't mine just yet.

My throat felt thick and sore. At times it felt as if I was breathing fire. But I wasn't. My fire wasn't like the Sun-Blast or Fire-Tail's flame. When my fire touched living things, they died. It was like a disease; it spread and didn't stop. No cure. No hope to survive. The only thing it targets could do was turn into piles of ash.

When I first received the ability, I struggled to control it. Whenever I sneezed, flames would shoot out of my throat. It had felt as if I swallowed lava on a daily basis.

I had that same burning feeling in my throat, now. The gas. It was like chloroform. People who weren't immune to it would suffocate and die.

It had a green shine to it. When contained or if it was trapped in a room it actually formed a thick green smoky substance.

It was the only ability that could cause this sort of pain within me.

The snow had other qualities; I couldn't wait for it to show itself. Then maybe I wouldn't feel this hot on a daily basis.

A longing crept into my soul. It was starting to suffocate me.

Without Lucian my room was too quiet. I didn't want to think about him. I pushed him to the back of my mind.

I had the urge to stretch my wings and feel the wind in my face. I had to get out of here. If only for a few hours.

I got out of the shower, didn't even properly dry myself, and opened the window. I stepped onto the ledge and leaped into the night.

The pull always came first. Like a shift in personality, anatomy, and DNA, all together. Whatever kept me human was shoved back, and the dragon moved into place. It didn't hurt like it had the first time I transformed into my human form and back to my dragon self.

It was now just a pull.

Then the crackling of bones. The rip was next. The flesh didn't really tear; it just morphed and stretched until it took the form of scales and wings.

The entire world shifted from big to actually kind of small in less than five seconds.

My dragon lungs opened and I breathed in the fresh air. For a second, everything was good.

"Kiiiillllllll."

My nightmare just started.

⚜

I USUALLY DIDN'T REMEMBER what I did when I was in my dragon from. But lately I'd been aware of a lot of things while the scales were still out.

The beast was letting me see more. As if I needed to see more. I didn't know how this worked. A part of me wanted the beast; another hated who I was when it came out.

But right now, I felt free. So alive. My need for darkness and evil, my need for blood, drove me forward.

I didn't care anymore. My conscience was switched off. I had my needs and they needed to be fulfilled.

All I knew, the way I felt in this moment was one reason I hated shifting into a dragon.

The Dragonians had a great way of explaining us. Our human sides and dragon sides. *Dr. Jekyll and Mr. Hyde.*

We weren't exactly like the literary characters they referred to us as, but it was pretty close.

I was now Mr. Hyde. I liked the control, liked to make havoc, liked to take what wasn't mine, liked all things dangerous and evil, and just being free... If that meant Hyde must come out to play, then so be it.

Dr. Jekyll was long gone.

Still, that analogy wasn't spot-on. Dr. Jekyll was still in the same room; he just didn't care. Or maybe he was equally evil. I didn't know which theory was true, and at this moment, I really didn't care.

I was the beast, whether I wanted it or not. I did love everything I was and everything I did when in dragon form.

The switch that connected my moral soul to my conscious self was off. And nothing could switch it back on. Not until the human shifted back.

I knew what would happen when the human returned. Everything I was going to do tonight would hit me full in the face and I would drown in a pool of guilt, regret, and emotions. Or as the beast liked to call it, weakness.

Morality would come back, right and wrong, all the basic crap of life and the regret over what I was about to do. Knowing this was never enough for me to control my behavior as a dragon.

That was why I started mentally separating the human from the beast. Sure, it wasn't healthy, referring to my true self as a separate entity. But it was the only way to deal with my shit whenever I was in human form, the weaker form.

A part of me wanted to stay in this form forever. Another, well, it didn't matter which form I was in. I still loved my family. I didn't want my mother to lose the last bit of hope she had left.

My father? I gave up on him the day he gave up on us. Ever since his rider's death he hadn't been the same man. It was like all life left him, like part of him died with the king. He was dark, and he had taken it out on his family one too many times.

I was done pretending he was still the dragon he used to be. So I didn't pretend anymore.

My thoughts sometimes wandered back to the night everything changed.

How did my father escape? Did King Albert force him to leave, or did he flee like a coward?

I doubted the latter. My father was many things, scaly and deceitful among them, but he was no coward. He'd loved King Albert. He would've done anything for his rider, even died.

Thoughts of my father aside, if it weren't for my mother, I would've given up a long time ago. Her love and fervent belief in my redemption was what made me keep fighting.

Plus my sister's kindness and big heart. I hadn't seen her in such a long time.

My family made me want to fight, made me want to be good.

The glint of a knife caught my eyes. The moon gleamed on Baldarian steel, and it blinded me for a microsecond. Even though the blade was miles and miles below me, my vision was sharp.

Two people on a pier extending over a lake.

They were fighting.

One was stronger than the other. They were quarreling about some moral standard that had gone shit-ways.

I started to rejoice as I saw the first stab. Blood pooled onto the ground. The weaker one cried for help. The one with the knife clamped his hand tightly over his mouth.

The loser's arms waved vigorously, in and out, in and out. He was still fighting, trying to block every blow but eventually couldn't fend off the attacks anymore.

His arm fell limply on the pier.

The thud vibrated through my bones, even at such a great distance. My hearing was just as perfect as my vision.

The other, still gripping the bloody knife, dropped the corpse of his vanquished enemy into the water. He threw in the knife afterward.

I finally darted down to the docks.

A voice from deep inside begged me to stop one last time. But my conscience was gone.

Game on.

Kiiiilllllll.

FIVE

Destruction and mayhem you cannot hide.
Darkness coiled deep inside.
The monster no longer under the bed.
He's always lived inside my head.
Screaming and aching to be set free.
The temptation so strong it won't let me be.
A hope deep inside so light struggles to shine.
A bond so promising, but yet not mine.
Good and evil, both I know
Which is friend and which is foe.

I SAT with my journal open in my lap, rereading one of the entries I had written before Lucian came. It was penned right before I got the news about what he was planning to do. He'd celebrated his sixteenth birthday with a claiming. Mine.

I didn't think the Council would give it to him, but they had. They'd granted it.

After a dark few days, I felt semi-normal again. All thanks to that night on the docks.

The darkness was satisfied... for now.

But my mind was reliving the nightmare, the horror of it, over and over again.

I'd killed that man.

I didn't even flinch. *No, Blake, the* beast *didn't flinch.*

I was Mr. Hyde when the wings and the scales came out, and Dr. Jekyll had to live with the consequences of what he had done.

It hadn't always been like this. There was a time when the beast had been good. A time before the clock started ticking down.

Sometimes I wished that I'd never gotten my human form. It was a curse; it had been at that exact moment that the first grain in the hourglass fell. The hourglass that ticked off the time until I was fully dark.

I took another long drag on my cigarette. Sometimes, I liked to sit on the roof and gaze at the stars. Gaze until I couldn't focus on them anymore. Until my mind was numb.

Tonight was such a night.

I tried to soothe my mind, clear my thoughts away from the blood and murder that had taken place a few nights ago.

The beast slept like a baby, but I couldn't.

The hatch to the roof opened and snow-white hair appeared, almost glowing in the moonlight.

I sighed deeply and hoped that my irritation wouldn't show too much.

What the hell is the Snow Dragon doing here again? Why did she always come back? I treated her like shit each time I was done with her. Still, a few days later, she would hunt me down and beg for whatever she needed from me like a lost little puppy.

"Shouldn't you be sleeping?"

"I couldn't," I answered. She was lucky to get that out of me.

"You know, I have the perfect thing for that."

I already knew what she was going to offer me, and she usually did on a silver platter. "Oh yeah?"

"You have such a dirty mind. I'm talking about milk and a shot of vodka. It's really good at soothing tired minds and nerves. You'd be asleep in no time." She gave me her dazzling smile.

I couldn't help but laugh. Okay, so my mind went to only one thing when it came to the Snow Dragon.

"Okay, if you say so," I finally said.

She lay down next to me and watched the stars too.

"Ever wonder if what they say is true?"

"If what is true?"

"You know, about our ancestors and when they die."

I squinted. She was one of the smartest girls at Dragonia and she was asking me about the supernatural.

"I know logic and science don't back that theory, but I always wondered. Of all the things we don't know yet... Could our ancestors really be among the stars, watching over us?"

Okay, now I was really wondering if Snow Dragons were actually the smartest dragons out there.

She slapped me playfully. "Don't look at me like that. I'm serious."

"No, it's not possible. That would mean there's a higher power and I don't believe in that."

"You don't believe in a higher power?"

"No, 'cause if there was, he would never make something as dark and evil as me."

Compassion filled her eyes. I didn't like that look. It reminded me too much of pity.

"You are not that dark and evil. Not yet. And King Albert always believed that with the right influence, Blake, you might be surprised at how good you are, deep down."

"With the right influence?" I humored her even though I already knew where this was going. "Oh? And who do you think that right influence could be?"

"No idea," she played along. "I'm way too naughty so it has to be someone who is truly good. You might try that book nerd, the one who always sits in the library. You know, with the glasses and long brown hair."

I roared with laughter; I knew exactly who she was talking about. "Brittainy?"

"Yes," she smiled. She propped herself up on one arm. Her face was inches from mine.

"You might have a point with her, though. Maybe her goodness will rub off on me and maybe, just maybe, I might rub off on her, and then we're back to square one."

"Ah, man, and here I thought I was setting up a match made in heaven."

I shook my head. "Yeah, sorry. I would lead poor Brittainy to hell."

She laughed. "Damn."

Our conversation meandered. She mused about her life, her worries about her brother and that he had a man crush on me.

I laughed again, but I knew that wasn't why he kept asking Tabitha to tell me he needed to see me. He wanted me for something.

"He either owes someone a shitload of money, or he has a bunch of illegal money."

I huffed, a small smile tugging at my lips. "There's nothing wrong with breaking the rules a little bit."

She squinted. "Did you even hear a single word I said about my brother, or were you busy staring at my eyes?" The way she said eyes, told me she didn't actually mean her eyes.

"I'm not three years old anymore, Tabitha. If I want ass, I get ass, as easy as that."

She swallowed hard and bit her lower lip. It was sexy in an unwanted way. "So you want ass?" She asked in a seductive smile.

"I thought you'd never ask." I pushed her down and rolled on top of her.

She laughed as I pinned her tightly to the ground and our lips touched.

The kiss was vigorous. Her cold essence lodged deep inside her cooled my boiling fire. Her hands were always cold. Her entire body an ice sculpture. It made mine feel absolutely perfect.

She was wearing a skirt and I ripped off her panties as she fiddled with my jeans.

When she touched me, it felt for a second like I was going to die. The cold touch on my sizzling skin felt like ecstasy.

"You like that?" she asked as she moved her hands up and down my shaft.

"You know I do." I growled in her ear. I opened her legs with one hand as I pushed myself inside of her.

I grunted. I really didn't want to wake up the beast, but the way Tabitha was moaning in my ear, it was only a matter of time. She complained harder. I covered her mouth with my own again, trying to drown out the sounds.

"You're really loud," I spoke against her lips.

"Sorry." She laughed. Then she waved her hand. A soft tingling sensation sparkled around us.

My thrusting stopped. I squinted. *What the hell?* Okay, so that was impressive.

"How did you do that?"

"What, the shield? It's not just the Dragonians who can wield them, Blake. We are superior to them. You think we don't have the gift to enchant things like shields?"

"Teach me," I said.

She laughed again. "Oh, I will, if you promise to be super nice to me."

I thought about it for a second. "Done." I kissed her once more.

The rest of the night was one long fuck session.

🐉

I woke up at nine the next morning. "Ugh." It had to be at least third period or something. Thank heavens I was alone.

My body ached from last night. Who would have thought that the Snow Dragon had it all along?

I was positive that last night had broken a world record for the longest fuck.

My mind was filled with her smell still. But it wasn't really about what she'd done to me; it was all about what she could do. She'd found a way to wield a spell that only Dragonians could do. I needed that spell for hiding who knew what shit I would do later on.

I pulled myself out of bed and got dressed. For the first time in a long time, I had a purpose. I was driven to learn something new. Driven to master it.

And master it I would.

🐉

The next two weeks flew by. Tabitha kept her word. She taught me the enchantment, and I'd practiced every single day.

The first few days, nothing happened.

She just smiled, and said of course it wouldn't. "We aren't meant to be the ones casting spells. You need to take it. See it like you're stealing something you really want."

If I could kill, well, then I was certain that I could steal too.

The next four days were quite different.

The enchantment wasn't hard to speak, but what mattered were the intentions as I spoke it. That was what made magic spells so difficult to begin with.

I couldn't be pathetic or needy, and that was why I struggled.

It kept backfiring on me. It would either throw me ten paces from where I stood, or send a rush of pain that forced me to my knees, grinding my teeth. The worst was when a jolt broke my arm.

I pushed it back, and it took a day to heal. But the next day, I tried again.

I had to learn.

Tabitha was a natural, because she was a Snow Dragon. If there was a scale from one to ten that listed which species were the closest to humans, Snow Dragons would be a twelve.

No doubt that was why she had all these spells. She had the key.

"I really pretend that I'm in danger, and it happens. I have to *feel* it. That night I had the urge to hide and..." She smiled and shrugged. "It's like breathing to me now."

"Breathing." My tone was annoyed.

"Your problem isn't that you can't do this. It's that you don't need it, Blake. Need it and take it." She got up. "As much as I enjoyed you that night, I didn't want to get caught. It's why I could wield it. You don't care if you get caught. Everything is a breeze to you."

"A breeze." I was starting to get pissed off.

"You don't get what I'm saying. You don't need it, Blake. It won't come if you don't really *need* it."

Then what the fuck was I doing with her?

I got what she was saying. I wasn't the type to be scared. The Rubicon wasn't built to be afraid of anything. I usually instilled the fear.

She bent down and kissed me softly on my lips.

I didn't return the kiss and she smiled at me.

"You know where to find me," she said and sauntered away.

I watched her go.

I wasn't going to give up.

Around the tenth day, I worried this was all a waste of my time.

She had said she went through this difficult phase too. Tabitha's voice kept playing over in my head. *Magic wasn't meant for dragons. It was meant for the ones who wanted to tame us. The ones who were born with the mark.*

Dragonians. I hated everything about them. The way they thought they could just walk into that ring and we would yield.

Never.

It wasn't in me to yield. Not inside my human body, and definitely not inside my dragon.

And on the fourteenth day, exactly two weeks of working my ass off, something finally happened.

I had it. Only for a few seconds, but I had it. I couldn't see it, but I could hear it. I could feel its tiny pricks in the air. I heard it coming, too—a click and then a zing. The same sort of sound that bugs made as they baked in the sun.

A faint popping noise surrounded me. But it became difficult to hold on to that need and it disappeared.

"You did it!" Tabitha yelled.

I didn't even know that she was close by. She was a bit of a stalker.

She ran into my arms. I had to catch her as she literally jumped onto me.

"Hardly," I said, more agitated than anything else. I let her go.

"Hardly?" Her smile still sprawled over her lips. Damn, she had a beautiful smile. "It took me almost three months to master just that, Blake."

I frowned. "Three months?"

"Yeah," she nodded. "Guess you are a hell of a dragon."

"I'm the shit," I joked and she laughed.

I tried again.

It was weird how easy it was for me to get used to the idea of spending time with Tabitha. At least I wasn't calling her Snow Dragon anymore.

It took an entire year for me to call her by her name.

Still, as beautiful as she was, and as dazzling as her smile, she wasn't the one the beast wanted.

She would never satisfy his needs.

&

I PRACTICED EVERY DAY, every minute I could. Even in my room.

I didn't like being in my room that much, though. Without Lucian's presence, even though his light still made me feel sick, I felt guilty for what I'd done.

Why wasn't he back yet?

They had Swallow Annexes.

I hoped that whatever he was going through had taught him never to try and claim me again. But I knew him too well. In a few months, after a gazillion trainers prepped him again, he would stand before that Council once more, begging for another chance to face me inside the Colosseum.

Just thinking about that made my skin crawl.

The popping sound came quicker now. It lasted a few seconds longer than the first time. A minute was the longest I'd held on before it disappeared.

It made me wonder how many other spells I could learn. There were so many. I could use them to protect myself, not that I would ever need them. My fire was my protection, the Pink Kiss as I called it.

I wanted this kind of protection badly.

It didn't come.

$\bullet$

"WHY ARE YOU IGNORING MY BROTHER?" Tabitha asked. "He's driving me insane."

I huffed at the way she said it.

"Please, just call him."

"I'm not ignoring him. I just don't have the time to speak to him right now, okay?"

"Seriously? What does he want with you, anyway?"

"Your guess is as good as mine."

"Well, if Phil is calling me to get a hold of you, all I know is that he's desperate. Be careful. His gigs can cost you your life."

His gigs? I laughed. "Sweetheart." *Wrong. I shouldn't call her that.* "The only gig I have is with my band members. At the moment, we're not doing so well. So when your brother calls, tell him I will call when I'm damn good and ready."

I turned around and walked the opposite way.

"I'm just the messenger! No need to bite my head off."

I shook my head and put on my hood.

What does that Night Villain want from me this time?

I still felt fear. That was the only thing that kept me fighting. My fear was a good sign.

As evil as some of his schemes were, Phil did help the

darkness. He fed it and it would stay away for a long time. So of course I was intrigued.

But it was the idea of feeding my darkness that scared me a little. There would come a time when he was not going to be able to satisfy it.

Then what?

I couldn't call Phil, no matter what schemes he had.

I found myself in the Colosseum. I hated the fucking place. *What am I doing here?*

I could still hear the chants from the crowd, cheering Lucian's name that day. Cameras flashing. More chants and a pissed-off dragon.

I still smelled fear, his adrenaline mixed with excitement. He'd really thought he would get me on the first try.

He was in many ways my perfect match; both of us would never give up. But I wished he would; one day, he wasn't going to walk out of the Colosseum alive.

They wouldn't prosecute me. Everyone knew that what happened in the ring, died in the ring. If a Dragonian wanted to be stupid and claim a dragon that didn't belong to him for starters, then the idiot must be ready to die.

Still, it was Lucian.

Although he had this strange effect on me at times, he was still my very best friend in so many ways. But I needed him to back off, not just for my own good, but for his too.

He would never be ready.

 SIX

"WAKEY, WAKEY." A voice spoke my name. I couldn't place the voice, but it was familiar. *Fucking weird.*

I opened my eyes and found a redhead staring at me. Her hair reached her shoulders. For some reason, she reminded me of King Albert. I frowned.

"What's up?" I said.

What's up? It doesn't even sound like me. Way too chirpy.

"You need to get dressed. Otherwise we're going to be late."

Late for what? Who the fuck are you? "Do we have to go?" I asked instead.

"Blake, yes. My mother and father will be there."

Your mother? "Fine. Give me a minute."

I got up against my will and walked to the bathroom. I saw myself in the mirror. I was smiling, and I started to whistle. I touched my torso, but the Blake in the mirror did not mimic me.

This was fucking weird.

Was I high? Had I called Phil? What the fuck was going on?

The girl's arms wrapped around me from behind. I knew one thing: I liked her. She felt familiar, like home. She was where I was meant to be.

My hand glided over hers. "Let's just stay." I turned around. My arms wrapped around her tiny waist. She was sort of beautiful. Freckles sprinkled her face under vibrant green eyes. "My bed has been very lonely."

"Your bed is always lonely, Mr. Leaf," she teased. "If my mother catches us, she'll pull all your scales off and use them in her potions. Don't tempt her. Get dressed."

She kissed me. It was nice.

Then I woke up.

I was in my dorm room. It was still dark. I lifted my head and saw Lucian's empty bed.

What the fuck was that?

It couldn't have been my Moon-Bolt ability to foresee things. No way. My rider didn't exist. The queen was dead. Unless… no.

I'd never thought my rider could've been a she. I always assumed it would've been male. The Prince of Paegeia, and I his mighty Rubicon. It was always a him. But that dream…

It felt so real.

It was just a dream, Blake. The beast inside me spoke softly. *You have no rider, no one to tame you. Darkness is our only friend.*

"So, are you going to come with?" Tabitha plunged down onto the pillow next to me.

The cafeteria was almost full for lunch. George stared at me, and Brian lifted his left eyebrow. He wanted to say something, obviously. I quickly shook my head.

"Sweetheart." I smiled. "Now why would I come home with you?"

The guys chuckled. Tabitha shook her head and left.

Nobody knew that we were doing it, and I didn't want them to know, either. I had cultivated the mystique of the Rubicon as a solitary creature, someone who wouldn't be spoken for by a mere Snow Dragon.

I watched her leave. A part of me felt bad as Brian and George high-fived one another, trash-talking Tabitha.

I felt stupid.

This meant that I had to go back home. My mom was there. She was always hovering, always wanting to know about my dark side. What if I told her about the guy I killed, about both of them? She would never understand.

The bell rang and I left for Latin. I didn't really need the stupid language; it came naturally to me as a dragon. But I had to go; I desperately needed to assure Tabitha that it had been a joke.

Going home with her was the only way out of breaking my mother's heart. Mom wasn't going to be happy that I wasn't coming home yet again, but was better this way.

Tabitha sat a few rows in front of me. She was pissed off, that much I could tell. I would probably be pissed off, too, if she had just dissed me like that.

I tore out a page from my notepad and scribbled a few words. *Sorry, I'll make it up to you. I'm stupid. It was all just a dumb joke.* I rolled it up in a wad. My aim was perfect as the ball flew through the air and landed perfectly on her desk.

Professor Gregory turned around just as Tabitha grabbed the little ball of paper and quickly hid her hands underneath the desk. He didn't suspect a thing, but it was horrendous just imagining the outcome of being caught by him this time.

How would I explain that to the boys?

She read my note as the lecture droned on. I watched her expression. She didn't think much of my note.

I had really done it this time.

When the bell rang, I ran up to her and put my arm around her shoulder.

"Don't even try it." She shrugged my arm off.

"It was a joke, Tabitha." I forced a laugh. "C'mon."

She threw me a middle finger. "Ha," she said sarcastically and stalked away.

I shook my head. Her loss. She'd come around. She had to come around.

ON THURSDAY, a knock came at my door. I sighed as I looked at the empty bed. When was Lucian coming back?

I went to the door and found Tabitha.

"You'd better make it up to me, big time," she announced. She turned on her heel without waiting for my response.

"You don't want to come in for a drink?"

"No," she stated. She disappeared into the elevator.

I smiled. I knew how to handle Snow Dragons.

I closed the door and thanked my lucky stars. I needed a break away from all the eyes. The glares and pitiful looks.

I needed to just feel free again.

I hadn't been to see Irene in a while. I couldn't, not while the beast craved her.

I must resist. It wasn't just my ass on the line if things got out of hand. *Jeez, Blake, listen to yourself. Irene is three hundred years old. She would never go for a young dragon like you.*

I needed a break.

Friday flew by. I skipped Transformations and went to pack a bag.

Still no sign of Lucian. Why did his empty bed wrench my insides? I'd never told him to keep his promise to claim me.

A knock on the door drew me back from my thoughts. I grabbed my bag and left.

❦

WE REACHED the dragon city closest to Tith later that night.

Tabitha's parents didn't like humans and had never changed into their human form before. Only Phil and Tabitha embraced their human form in that family.

They weren't rich, but they weren't poor either. They lived in a huge cavern. They hunted like dragons and slept in a pack. It was customary in the wild, not unheard of, but I wasn't used to it. My family was the opposite. The only time my mom and dad had transformed into dragons in our presence was when we were little.

Tabitha's father loved the prospect of housing the Rubicon for the weekend.

I needed to speak to Phil.

"Tonight, Ruby," Phil joked. "We'll go to Longbottom and then we can have a proper chat."

By proper, I knew he meant out of our dragon scales and away from parental ears. But the fact that he'd picked Jimmy's semi club wasn't comforting.

What if Isaac and the band were there? We hadn't left things well the last time we'd spoken, and I wasn't ready to drop it.

I could've easily hurt Isaac. He was part of the shifter race, a giant eagle. We'd fought viciously in our true forms. It had been all over the news. My father didn't understand; my mother had just given me a look. It was the last time I'd gone home and was one of the reasons I hadn't gone back since.

The beast pushed everyone away, everyone who mattered.

Around nine, we grabbed our backpacks and flew to one of his friend's houses.

The guy was filthy rich. His name was Samuel, and he owned a powerful corporation that traded illegally in things I didn't even want to know about. He was a Spaniard and comported himself like a drug lord. If I wasn't mistaken, Sam was Phil's contact when it came to Fire-Cain. He'd given it to me once, and I had to admit, the high was amazing—though the low was shit.

We got dressed in front of everyone who was there. They treated me as if I was made from gold.

The girls gave me kisses and offered me a couple minutes on the side. Tabitha growled at them. Vulgar curses were exchanged. Girls fighting over me should've been my thing, but for some reason it wasn't. I didn't want to be spoken for.

Phil shook his head and we left. We reached Long-bottom around ten. Relief flooded me; no one from the band was in sight. We went to the VIP room upstairs.

Everyone who was anyone greeted me with either a slap-shake or an arm press. It was a dragon thing. The girls just stared. It wasn't as hostile as it had been in the mansion.

"So," I started. "Why the urgency to meet? What do you want, Phil?"

The sides of Phil's mouth tugged. "Ruby, it sounds like you're not really interested in what I have to say."

"Just spit it out!"

"Fine. Sam is sponsoring the resurgence of a sport that died out a very long time ago."

"What sport?"

"Slay the dragon."

I narrowed my eyes and put two and two together. Had a sport like that ever existed? "You want me to kill." The beast inside of me relished every word. The human, not so much. My stomach twisted and turned.

"Not humans, Blake. There's not a lot of money in sponsoring dragons. And the Rubicon can't participate in the tournament. It's against an old set of rules."

"Seriously, then why even mention it?"

"Because Sam thinks we might be able to get away with a potion and a very dark spell performed by a really good magic wielder."

I wanted to tell him that magic didn't work on dragons but he interrupt.

"It works on dragons, it will make you appear as someone completely different. We'd have to bind a few abilities; that's going to be a bit harder than your appearance, but the money is good, Ruby. The money and perks are really good, and who knows?" He slapped me hard on the shoulder. "Maybe you can hold on just a tad bit longer."

"A tad longer." I said sarcastically. I was pissed off, pissed at myself for ever telling Phil I was losing control over the beast. "So you want me to become a human who kills dragons in a sick tournament?"

A cold finger rushed up my spine. I didn't like this. Not one bit.

"Think about it. It will be completely new for you." He got up and left before I could say anything.

I just stared at his back as he went over to the nearest group of guys and greeted everyone.

"So," Tabitha plopped down on the couch next to me. "What did he want?"

"Nothing." I pushed myself up from the couch. I needed to get the hell away from all of them.

I couldn't do this. I couldn't kill my own kind.

I put my hood over my head and skipped down the steps. I should've never come. I didn't even want to go back to Tabitha. I didn't want to be in another evil presence. I was already trying my best just to hold on. I didn't need the temptation.

"Hey, bud," a familiar voice said, inches away from me. On my left, there stood Isaac, smiling mischievously. "How are you? I haven't seen you in such a long time."

"Isaac, please, I can't."

"It's okay. I'm okay. Can we just talk?"

I hated when he begged.

He was like Lucian in so many ways. Except, well, he didn't make me sick, for one thing, and he didn't want to claim me, either. But he was a great friend whenever I was in trouble, and the most amazing thing of all, his eagle form was just as big as my Rubicon form. Which was saying something.

"Can we please just grab a beer and talk? I haven't seen you for such a long time."

He really did look sincere. *He isn't angry?*

I nodded and followed him to the bar. I bent my head low as girls bombarded Isaac. The shifters were famous; they could make it big if it weren't for the lead singer being bound to this world.

Dragons could never live a life of fame. Our essence made us stay young for centuries and centuries. The oldest dragon was King Albert's nanny. She'd raised more kings than anyone in this world. She was twelve thousand years old. The king had thrown her a mother of a birthday party for that one. Nobody else had beaten her milestone yet.

I doubted it would be me. It wasn't in my destiny to live more than a hundred years. I'd be lucky if I made it to my thirtieth.

I didn't want to think about it.

I walked past Isaac as he signed a couple of shirts and boobs. If they knew I was here... well, it would turn into something I didn't want to be a part of right now.

I took an open barstool .

"What will it be?" Jimmy asked. I barely looked up and he froze. "You sure it's safe to sit there?"

I thought he was going to throw me out because of what had happened the last time I was here.

"Nothing I don't deserve," I joked back.

"You guys going to kiss and make up?" he cajoled. He

wanted me to get back with the band. On the nights we played, his bar was packed.

"We'll see."

"Please do, Blake. Battle of the Bands is coming up soon."

I smiled as he handed me a beer with an ounce of Fire Powder—the drug of all fire-breathers.

He dropped the matter.

Isaac finally made it to the bar in one piece. He put on his hood, too, and we started to talk.

§

THE NIGHT FLEW BY. I hadn't laughed like this in a long time. Isaac, Ty, Jamie, and the rest of the guys just knew how to lift each other's spirits.

"Come back, dude. The guys miss you and to be honest, we could do with a few gigs."

"You don't need me for that."

Isaac slugged me. "You're fucking with me right now? Nobody wants to book us without you. Please, I'll get on my knees."

"I can't," I sighed. "The same thing will happen, just like last time."

"Dude, then let it happen. We know what you are, who you are. You losing your head is bound to happen from time to time. Just come back. At least think about it, please."

I nodded. My eyes caught on Phil. I looked away immediately as he was searching for someone—probably me.

Isaac picked it up. "You know him?"

"Yeah, it was a mistake to come with him. I'm staying with the Snow Dragon this weekend. I just want to go back to Dragonia."

"Not going to see your mom?"

"She's too much right now," I lied. That wasn't the reason I didn't want to see her.

"Then come crash at my place. My father is dying to know how you are. Been asking me so many fucking times it makes me want to puke."

We both laughed.

I peeked to the right again and saw Tabitha and Phil leave.

"Okay," I said. It was only for a night. I'd just see how it went.

SEVEN

CLOUDS DANCED in the sky above. I squinted. Weird clouds. They were actual shapes—clowns juggling, horses galloping, a lion roaring, and a rabbit jumping.

"Oh, look at that one," said a female voice. I looked to my left.

She was lying in the crook of my arm, pointing at the sky. It was the redhead with freckles again. I stared as her lips moved, describing the cloud.

She was kind of beautiful, in an unconventional way. The feeling came. It crept into my soul. It warmed my ever-freezing bones. I was addicted to this feeling, yet I had no idea what it was.

All my emotions had been smashed into a big ball; I felt everything at once.

Her eyes caught on mine.

"Blake, the point of this game is, you actually have to make pictures by staring at the clouds, not at me."

I laughed and my face turned automatically toward the clouds. "Fine. That one looks like a baboon." I laughed softly. This Blake sucked at the game. "That one looks like a guy getting a blow job."

The redhead laughed. "You are such a pig." Despite her words, she climbed on top of me. "But I absolutely love every ounce of you." Her face neared mine. A shift in my body told me my heart was beating faster. I couldn't breathe, but it wasn't the scary kind of suffocating; this... this was amazing. And then our lips touched.

My eyes opened. It was dark. The clouds were gone, the redhead was gone.

Who is she?

Was I going to meet her? Was she supposed to be my rider?

If she was, I was so screwed. I would never get a chance with her. She'd never get to take that first breath.

A title stuck with me: "Never-Breath."

Words started flowing through my mind again. I got up. I needed a pen and paper.

§

I COULDN'T FIND ANY, so I left. The funny part was that I didn't care about anything anymore. Not about Isaac and what he might think when he found his couch empty. Not Phil or Tabitha, when I saw her on Monday again.

Not my mother.

Getting these words on paper was more important than anything else.

I just had to hold on to them.

I found myself in front of our creaky old house. It was a wonder that the thing was still standing. Termites holding hands.

It made me upset just thinking about everything again. We owned a shitload of land behind those Creepers, plus a mansion, which probably had burned to the ground. A cave stuffed with gold that we could never get to. It probably was the first place those assholes raided, the dragon caves.

The Council hold no value in our lives. My father had been King Albert's dragon, for crying out loud. I was the Rubicon. I guessed the Council already knew my fate and didn't see us as assets anymore. They didn't care about what King Albert had wanted.

We became nothing the day he died.

I climbed the wall and jumped into my room.

When I got in, I opened my drawer and found an old notepad. I wrote down words to a song that was probably going to end up again on an album. Well, maybe not this one.

The door opened and my mother stood in the frame, clutching a golf club.

I raised my eyebrow.

"You bloody gave me a heart attack," she said in that strong British accent of hers.

"Sorry." I didn't even bother to sound sorry. "Why do you have a golf club?"

She started to laugh uncontrollably.

I joined in. I'd missed her.

"You want some breakfast? Of course you do. You're always hungry." She closed the door behind her and headed toward the kitchen.

I went back to thinking about the words again, how I'd felt. But I couldn't get my mother standing with a golf club in the doorway out of my head.

The door flew open again, and a figure with a very loud, shrill voice ran into my room. Her body connected hard with mine. My sister's floral scent filled my nostrils.

"You finally came back. You know how much I missed you? This house is so empty without you. Why didn't you come home? Where were you just now?"

"Stop with the million questions. I needed a pen and paper."

She squinted. "You came home for a pen and paper."

"Yeah." I sighed audibly. "Crazy, huh?"

She shrugged. "Are you at least going to stay for breakfast? She'll make me crazy if you just disappear again."

"Yeah, I'll stay." I smiled.

She smiled back. Her dimples dented deep into her cheeks. She got up and walked to my door. "It's really great to see you again, Blake." The door closed behind her.

This was one of the reasons I didn't want to come back. I didn't want to hurt them, or worse—I didn't want the beast to hurt them.

They were the only people who still looked up to me. I didn't know what I would do if that ever changed.

੩

I STAYED FOR BREAKFAST. My mother kept talking about the Council, the things they'd promised her, but there was a shallow pool of deceit clinging to her face. She was trying to dodge my questions about my father.

I hadn't seen him yet.

I sighed. She knew how I felt and I wasn't going to spoil today because of his disappearance. For all I knew he was stuck in a bar or some casino.

Then, the conversation took a drastic turn and we started speaking about Lucian's claiming.

"Maybe you should go and see him," my mother suggested.

I shook my head. "I almost killed him. Believe me, he is the last guy on the planet who wants to see me."

He'd been out for who knew how long. As far as I knew, he was still recovering.

I ended up staying for lunch. It was good to be back home again.

That night, I went back to Longbottoms. I thanked the heavens that Phil wasn't there. I still couldn't come to terms with what he wanted from me.

It was so evil, so vile. Killing my own kind. Yet the beast inside wanted nothing more. It was as if I'd opened a box full of possibilities. One that could push my humanity over the edge, that could make me give in to the darkness.

I sat in a corner, trying to figure out more words to the

song. I had two sentences down. Just two, and yet when I read them, they encapsulated exactly how I felt.

Who was she?

"Can I get you something else to drink?" a girl asked and I looked up.

Her eyes grew slightly when she saw me. Mine did, too, but not enough to make her uncomfortable.

She had red hair and her skin was dusted with freckles. But she wasn't even close to the dream girl. Her features were just similar. The exact same hair color.

"Sorry." I chuckled. "Um, yeah, another beer with fire-powder."

"Sure," she said briskly.

Smiling, I tuned in to her. Her heart was stammering in her chest. "Am I seeing things?" she asked the bartender under her breath, unaware of my excellent hearing.

"I don't know, Lesley. You *are* kind of weird."

"Ha ha." She sounded sarcastic. "I think the Rubicon is here." She leaned over the bar and I looked away as the bartender peered in my direction.

"Is it just my imagination? I doubt he would come here. He's at Dragonia, right?"

The bartender laughed. "Lesley, he is free to go places. You know Dragonia is only in the sky. It's not a prison."

"So it's really him!"

"Why so surprised? He used to play with the Shifters all the time."

"Are you serious?"

"How did you not know that he was the lead singer?"

"My mom never let me listen to the Shifters, okay?" She sounded embarrassed. "It's a dragon thing."

Her mom didn't like dragons.

I chuckled. In less than five minutes, she was back, handing me my beer.

"I'm Blake," I introduced myself. At her hesitancy, I continued, "I promise I won't eat you."

She laughed. "Lesley."

"Sit." I put away my notepad.

She looked around at the bartender.

"Just sit. I know Jimmy well."

"I bet you do." She put down her tray and followed me to sit on the couch next to me.

I couldn't help but feel the distance between us. But I had to find out if Lesley was the girl from my dreams or not. So I started talking to her about ordinary things.

She went to one of the human schools. She was okay with the fact that the dragons ruled the skies, but she'd never been near one. Her mother was too scared that we might turn tail and kill them.

"Your mother does know that we have human forms, right?"

She laughed. "I really don't know. I'm too scared to ask her."

I chuckled too.

"You're not that bad," she blurted out. "Everyone says how evil you are, but you're not."

"You wouldn't say that if you truly knew me, Lesley."

She kept quiet for a second and then someone called her name. "I've got to go. Work is calling again."

Longbottom's was exceptionally quiet again tonight. I felt bad for Jimmy.

So I went and took the stage without asking anyone.

"Hey, that is not for..." Jimmy said and I looked over my shoulder. He backed away immediately. With his hands in the air he retreated to the bar without a single word.

I sat in a chair and looked at the few occupied booths. I strummed the house guitar that had gone from sitting disregarded at the back of the stage to be cradled in my arms like there was nowhere else it wanted to be.

The microphone was in front of my face, and before I knew it, a tune burst out of me. My hoodie was still on but when I opened my mouth, I could hear the twitters of the meager crowd.

They all mumbled similar things: *You've got to be kidding me. No way, it's not him. Fuck, I need to tell Sandy.*

I smiled. Jimmy could thank me later.

SINGING AND PLAYING FELT GOOD. I'd missed it. I'd been performing for about half an hour and Longbottom's was already filling up.

Even Isaac and the band had come. They just picked up the other instruments without saying a word and we jammed a few of our songs we'd written before the band had broken up.

An hour later, it was packed. I sang my heart out. The crowd was cheering like crazy. Lines formed outside. Long-bottom's probably hadn't been full like this in a fucking long time.

I had fun, the band had fun, and I thought maybe, just maybe, we should get back together.

Then it was over. My voice was raw and fading. "Thank you all. You have no idea how much I needed that." I did the polite thing of thanking the amazing crowd. They all screamed for more and I tapped on my throat, telling them it was fucked.

They laughed and the band went upstairs.

"Dude, you back?" Ty asked. He was brawny like me; the girls loved him. He had this army thing going on and was a Shifter like Isaac. A panther. He used to pull off all his clothes at the end of our gigs and shift into a panther, growling at the crowds. They loved him.

"Maybe." I slap-shook his hand.

"Maybe is not good enough, dude. Tell me that wasn't the fucking shit."

"Yeah, it was the fucking shit."

We all laughed as Jamie and the others greeted me with handshakes.

"What happened last night?" Isaac said.

"Sorry, I went home."

His eyebrows raised. "Home, as in *home*?"

I nodded.

"Then it's all okay." He smiled.

I shook my head. It was unbelievable how they just forgot so easily.

The last time I saw them, I almost tore Ty apart, Isaac had jumped in between, and we'd fought in our true forms. The last thing I remembered seeing was Isaac falling. I hadn't even followed. I'd just flown away.

"Stop thinking about that." Isaac was handing me a beer.

I squinted. "How'd you know?"

"It's written all over your face. Look." He pointed at Ty. "Not a fucking scar. No missing limbs. We're tougher than you think, Blake. Let us help you. Please."

"You'll get hurt."

"It's our choice, all of us. Don't push us away, bud. Just sing your heart out, like tonight. You needed this as much as we did. The band needs you, and from what it looks like, you need us."

I laughed as Lesley gaped at everyone.

"You know her?" Isaac asked.

"It's a long story."

"Won't ask. Just one thing: she's not really your type."

"Like I said, long story."

Isaac laughed and that was where we left it.

❦

LESLEY HAD HER HANDS FULL. Plenty of the girls who had

VIP access flirted with the band. Isaac found his girl for the night, and so did Ty. Well, he had like three.

Panthers.

It was a bit too much for me, being overpowered by female hormones. I had to get away, get fresh air. So I climbed onto the roof and found Lesley smoking a cigarette.

She had a semi–heart attack when I accidentally startled her.

"Sorry, I really didn't mean that." My voice was still fucked.

"I didn't know you were part of the Shifters. Wow."

I shook my head. "So explain why your mother never let you listen to us." She squinted and I tapped my ears. "Enhanced hearing."

"You were spying on me earlier," she sounded embarrassed.

"Sorry, I didn't mean to."

"It's because she thought they were dragons," she said.

"No, I'm the only dragon. And look." I moved my hands up and down my body. "No scales."

"Yeah, I see that. It's what happens when the scales come out that makes me worry."

"Does it help if I tell you I don't like it either?"

She squinted. "But dragon is what you truly are."

"Yep. And it feels as if I have no control when I am one. So how can it be who I truly am?"

She sighed. "I'm learning so much about dragons tonight, it's scary."

She laughed and I smiled.

Then, before I could stop myself, my lips touched hers and one thing quickly led to another.

❦

I LOOKED at the sticky note in my pocket as I stood in my room back at Dragonia.

Her name wasn't even written on it. I wouldn't remember who she was in the next few weeks. So I'd written Redhead, her phone number, and one word: Coincidence.

She wasn't the girl from my dreams. That much I now knew. I felt bad that I was never going to call her. *Then why the hell am I keeping her number? I don't know. I really don't know.*

Lucian still hadn't returned. I was glad that Tabitha hadn't come over tonight to scream at me. I just couldn't go home with her. I couldn't. I was glad, though, that I'd gotten a chance to jam last night. The tabloids buzzed about our potential reunion. Some even had pictures of last night at Longbottom's.

Maybe it was time for us to get back together and jump back on that horse again. I couldn't believe none of them were angry at me for what had happened. I couldn't even remember what'd triggered it. It was something stupid, that much I knew.

I wrote a few more sentences in my journal about my

dream. It was hardly a verse, but it was what I felt.

My voice was still fucked and my healing ability still sucked. I laughed at my rhyme. Why was I was like that? Why was the artist in me so strong?

I closed my eyes when I couldn't keep them open anymore.

I found myself in a maze.

It was the same kind of maze that was in Lucian's back-yard. The kind that shifted in the full moon. Purple flowers blossomed everywhere.

I was chasing something, or someone.

"Marco!" I yelled.

"Polo!" She yelled back from somewhere on my left.

I changed direction. As I ran the maze changed. I still couldn't see her. "Marco!" I yelled again.

"Polo!" She was on the other side this time. How the hell was she doing this?

I grunted but changed directions. The maze changed a few times. When I yelled "Marco!" again, no "Polo" came.

Shockingly bone-deep worry welled up inside me. Why was I so scared?

Then a body connected hard with mine and I lost my balance.

The redhead was wearing a mask. She wore a beautiful poufy dress. Her body was dusted with freckles. She laughed softly. "Why are you staring at me like that? It's as if you're only seeing me for the first time."

"Who are you?" It came out just like that.

She frowned. "What do you mean, who am I?" She sounded afraid. I could hear it when her voice broke. "You're scaring me. What's going on?"

I shook my head and kissed her. I didn't want to stop, but I had no choice. Everything stopped when my alarm went off.

She was gone and I was left with a longing for something I didn't even understand.

IGHT

FOR THE NEXT few nights I dreamed about the redhead. I didn't mention anything about who I suspected she was or ask what her name was. I just enjoyed our time together. We were close. I just wanted to spend more time with her.

These dreams were dangerous. So dangerous.

When I woke up, I felt terribly alone, sad even. I badly wanted her to be real. After a while, I didn't want to feel any of this anymore and the fights that Phil mentioned started to... No. That was inhuman and I would just tumble into the darkness more quickly.

I had to fight the darkness, anything that could lead to the darkness. I couldn't succumb.

That night, I found myself at Longbottom's again.

It was a weeknight. I'd slipped out, as the room was getting too quiet.

I just couldn't stand Lucian's empty bed. I wondered about him a lot.

Maybe my mom was right. Maybe I should go and see him. See how he was doing, ask what was taking so long. Why hadn't he returned yet?

But then the nauseated feeling jumped into my head again and I pushed him to the back of my mind. I doubted he wanted to see me anyway.

"Blakey." Phil's voice came from behind me. I flinched when his scaly paw touched my shoulder.

He was in his human form.

I took another sip of my beer. "What do you want, Phil?"

"You know what I want. Samuel is waiting for your answer."

"Tell Sam to go fuck himself. He can be glad I'm not reporting this."

Phil laughed. "We're trying to help you."

"By pushing more darkness into me, Phil? You must be cleverer than that."

He just stared at me. A faint smile on his face.

"Don't say I didn't try."

I couldn't help but feel this was a threat.

I ordered another beer and watched Phil leave.

"What was that about?" Charlie, one of the bartenders asked.

"Nothing," I muttered. "He's an idiot."

I stayed till about midnight and then flew back to the Academy.

🐾

A COUPLE OF DAYS LATER, my father showed up at school. He was with one of Samuel's goons.

I closed my eyes. *Dad, what did you do?* I walked with huge strides to the entrance.

Master Longwei was speaking to my father.

My father pretended that everything was okay, that the man next to him was one of *his* men.

Little did Master Longwei know what a drunk and useless piece of shit he'd turned out to be. All the traces of the king's dragon were gone.

"A word, son."

Master Longwei looked at me. I nodded.

The dude wielded a shield the minute Master Longwei disappeared into the castle.

"What do you want?" I grunted at my father. "What are you doing with this idiot?"

"I'm in trouble, Blake. Samuel is going to..."

"I don't care. I'm not fixing your mess."

The big guy put his hand on my shoulder. I looked at it and back at him, eyes narrowing.

"Your father borrowed money from Samuel and claims he cannot pay it back. The offer still stands, Blake. If not, we will take our pound of flesh another way."

I laughed. "You're barking up the wrong tree. Take your pound of flesh. It might just do him some good." I spat that last word in my father's face.

"Blake, you don't know what you're saying!" my father yelled after me.

I didn't give a shit.

"Please. I'll get help."

"If you knew what they wanted from me, you would rather take the beating, Dad." I whirled. As much as I hated what my father was about to go through, I couldn't do what they asked. Killing my own kind? It would push me over the edge.

I entered the castle and found Master Longwei at the foot of the stairs. I pretended not to see him and vaulted up two steps at a time.

"Blake, is everything okay?" He asked in his strong Chinese accent.

I nodded and went to my room.

The next few days, I kept an eye on the tabloids. They hadn't posted anything about my father for such a long time. But a beating like this was newsworthy, front page even.

He was still King Albert's dragon, even though many had forgotten that, including himself. I used to look up to him. He was so big but now, he'd become so small.

The old Sir Robert would never ask anyone to sort his shit out. Not to mention asking his own son who he knew was predestined for evil. I had no idea who this Robert was.

I'd even considered changing my mind, but all I could think about was holding on. Doing everything in my power to hold on longer, this game, tournament that Samuel wanted me to compete in...

I couldn't. I had to stay strong.

I took another midnight flight when my room started to feel cramped.

As I flew, I came across a colony of dragons. About five or six of them.

"A word, Blake," one of them said. I recognized his voice; it was one of Samuel's guys.

"What don't you get? I told him to take his pound of flesh. Believe me, my father needs it more than you think."

The dragon laughed. "You don't know Samuel."

"Not interested." I cut him off. I flapped my wings faster.

"Your mother might think otherwise."

I stopped in midair. "What did you just say?" I felt the beast starting to lose it.

"Samuel always gets what he wants, Blake. Fight and everyone wins. If not, I see hard times ahead for your mother and that fetching sister of yours."

I growled.

The colony dove away from each other. Every single one of them took a different course.

So I followed the messenger. He was fast, really fast and I struggled to keep up.

I blew some thunder his way, but he dodged it.

My fury knew no bounds. *How dare they?* Samuel was going to learn the hard way that one should never, ever cross the Rubicon. I didn't care how famous his father was. He would die a slow and gruesome death for just thinking about laying a finger on my mother and sister.

His mansion came into view. Almost all the lights were on. I tuned in immediately. His walls were soundproofed. I had no idea if my mom and sister were there or not. I had no choice but to land.

The minute my paws touch the path that led into the mansion, I shifted back. It wasn't a willing shift; this was magic.

I ached all over as my wings were forced back into my human form. My tail felt as if it was being pulled in by machines.

I tried to leave. Hell, Mom and Sammy weren't here. But I couldn't leave. I grunted. My bones felt like they were going to shatter. I collapsed.

And then just like that, the pain was gone. I took huge breaths.

The door opened and I saw the hem of his white trousers and bare feet approaching me on the perfectly manicured lawn. He stopped right next to me, his big toe inches from my eyes.

"Do you always have to put up such a big fight, Ruby?" Samuel said in his thick Spanish accent.

My gaze lifted to him. I hated him.

I got up and prepared to rip off his head—when I froze solid.

I couldn't move. It hurt like hell.

I found a filthy-looking thug staring at me. He had long, dark hair, pale blue eyes, and tattoos from head to toe.

His lips were moving so fast, I couldn't make out the

words he was saying, though his voice filled the air around me. It increased the pressure on my body.

Still I fought. Harder. Magic didn't work on dragons, but here I was feeling every bit of it.

Samuel laughed. "Ruby, give it up. You can't beat me. I need this, this fire, this passion. I need it in the ring. If you comply, I promise, your mother and sister will go home unharmed."

"Where are they?" I grunted.

"You don't believe me?" He touched my face. His hands felt like they might scorch the skin off my face. He nodded over his shoulder. Two water orbs appeared.

They wobbled in midair. Then they took form. One was my mother. The other, Samantha.

I knew what this was. This sort of magic was an ancient incantation. Only a formidable sorcerer could pull this off.

Where had Samuel found such a powerful sorcerer?

My eyes fell on the guy with dirty hair and tattoos. *Is it him?*

The magic—the ability to show my mom and sister like this—required the DNA of the hosts. Samuel had my family.

Where my father fit into all this, I had no idea.

"Fight, and I will let them go."

I capitulated. "You have a deal. Now release them. Please."

He laughed again. "Not so fast, Ruby. You see, I don't trust you. We have that in common, you and I."

I was nothing like him. But he had my family and I wasn't going to egg him on. I was useless against this magic anyway.

"I'll call for you soon. We'll sign a contract, the kind dragons are compelled to obey."

I didn't like how he said that. A blood contract. He was going to revoke my free will.

"Now go."

"Samuel!" I roared. "If you hurt them!" A strong gust of air blew me back. I struggled to control it. To gain my strength over whatever spell and magic I was up against. I had to find a way to save my mother and sister without selling my soul to the devil himself.

But it was no use. The magic was too strong.

When the wind stopped blowing, I found myself in my room. On my bed. I looked around. Lucian's bed was still empty.

Was that a dream?

I got out of bed and without thinking jumped out my window. Dragon limbs replaced my human ones and in two flaps, I was in the air.

I needed to go home, to Mom. I needed to find her and Sammy safe in their beds. I flapped like I'd never flapped before and pushed forward harder.

The sun came up as I was en route.

Eventually the old house came into view. I tuned in. No sounds came from the house, not a peep.

I landed and transformed back as I raced up the steps in

my human form, buck naked and not giving a damn. I flung open the door.

"Mom! Sammy!" I yelled. No answer came.

I yelled again.

"Blake." Phil. I threw myself at him, ready to strangle him, but the minute I touched his neck, my hands disappeared into his flesh.

A hologram.

I grunted.

Phil laughed. "I warned you. Don't fuck this up, Ruby. Your sister and mother are depending on you."

"Where?"

"Be patient. I'll send word with my sister."

I growled as his hologram disappeared. I was going to kill my father if anything happened to them. That was my dragon oath.

⚜

THE NEXT MORNING, Monday, Tabitha showed up in my doorway. She still wasn't happy that I'd never returned that weekend. Without a word, she finally dropped my bag of clothes from that weekend on the floor.

I was furious with her, with Phil. If I didn't know her, Phil would've never met me.

"My brother wants you to call him." She handed me her Cammy. "What does he want, Blake?" She sounded sincere.

"Don't. The less you know, the better," I mumbled. I

couldn't help thinking that she was just the unlucky egg that had been laid in their family.

She handed me her phone. "Be careful. I love him to bits, but he is really not good company to keep."

I took her phone and grunted a thank you. Phil's contact was easy to find. I dialed his number.

"Where?" I said as his hologram appeared. His expression changed real fast when he saw it was me.

"Nine. Tonight at the docks. Don't be late, Blake. And don't ever threaten Samuel like that again."

I almost choked. Threaten him! He was the one who had captured my family and was holding them hostage.

The beast inside me acted weird. It should be angry that Samuel had taken his family, but it wasn't. It loved the idea around me killing dragons.

I, on the other hand, was livid.

As crazy as that sounded. I truly felt sometimes like I carried two entities in my body.

I put the phone down. Phil's hologram disappeared. I handed the Cammy back to Tabitha. She didn't say a thing, just put the Cammy in her bag and left.

I felt bad that she was in the middle of all this. She wasn't a bad dragon; I just didn't care as much as she did.

Nine. Tonight at the docks. I couldn't be late.

❧

I LEFT DRAGONIA AROUND EIGHT. The flight to the docks

was a bit of a push, but I landed at five-to-nine near the water's edge.

As I pulled on the clothes I'd packed in my pouch, I saw a black limo parked in a shadowy corner.

Phil climbed out. "You're late."

"Sue me." I climbed into the limo.

Samuel was sitting in the backseat and right next to him was the same guy who had wielded dark magic the other night.

"Where are my mother and sister?"

"You will see them soon." Samuel took out a folder.

I could feel the magic vibrating off the papers. I didn't like it one bit.

Samuel grabbed me behind my neck and pulled me toward him. Our faces were inches apart. His breath, which smelled of champagne, tickled my cheek.

Easy. I calmed myself down.

"You know I don't like to wait, Blake," he grunted.

"I got here as fast as I could. Technically, I'm on time, you know. I have people watching me," I said through gritted teeth.

He let me go.

He had no idea who he was dealing with. He should be careful. If he didn't have the only two people I cared about in his custody, that would've been his last touch.

"This is Dimi, short for Dimitri Ramakof."

Ramakof... I'd heard that name before. He was a sorcerer. Not as good as Goran, but he loved to tamper with the dark arts. I looked away; letting people know that you are wary of them isn't always a good thing.

"As you know by now, Dimi is a master of more than simple spells, Blake. One of them can make you pass as a human if you do your part."

"My part?" I asked. "You do know that I'm a dragon, right? We don't have magic strong enough to enchant things and protect ourselves with spells."

"It's just a small dose of magic," Samuel said. "One that dragons can master after taking one of Dimi's potions."

"A potion?"

"One that will bind your other gifts, Blake. You must choose one right now and stick with that one. During the fights, you will only be able to harness that one ability."

I started to chuckle. "You can bind my abilities?"

"Just for a few hours. We can't allow anyone to figure out your identity. If they do, well, let's just say you don't want them to find out."

I nodded. I didn't want to die. "If I do this, you'll allow my mother and sister to go free?"

"Sign the contract and it will be as if this never happened."

I squinted. "What do you mean?"

"They won't remember a thing. We'll make sure nobody remembers a thing. And to toss in a freebie, we'll take your father's addiction away, give a little bit of him back to your mother and sister. But he won't remember what he's done, Blake."

A forgetting spell. Heaven knew I wanted just a bit of the old Sir Robert back. I hated the dragon my father had become. I would never trust him again. But my mother and sister needed him.

I nodded.

"I never wanted it to turn out this way, Blake," Samuel said. "Believe it or not, I actually like you—and I don't like many people. You should've just said yes the first time and that would've been it. Indeed, you might have even achieved a better bargain than just paying off your father's debt and protecting your mother and sister. See what stubbornness gets you?"

I didn't answer.

"I want them released tonight. And if you ever come near them…"

"Sign the contract and I won't be able to come near them."

Dragon magic. This guy was an idiot.

He handed me the papers and a pen with a razor-sharp end. It was the kind fashioned to slice skin so you could dip the pen in dragon's blood straight from the veins. I did it. Without even wincing, I dabbed the point of the pen into the blood that formed in the palm of my hand.

I signed the first page and initialed everywhere he pointed.

I could feel the magic of this contract binding me to his tournament. To fight for this asshole and to do my best at slaying my own kind. It hurt to write, and it hurt even more to think about. I stopped reading and just signed where I was told.

When it was done, I grunted.

The pain that came with it was unbearable. When the deal was sealed with his blood, the pain vanished.

He picked up his Cammy. A hologram of one of his men appeared. He gave a signal and dropped the Cammy.

"Arrive at my mansion on Saturday morning. Nine sharp. Dimi has a lot of work to do to hide all of that," he sneered.

"Fine. Anything else?"

He nodded at Dimi. He dug into his back pocket and handed me a slip of paper. "Recite this over and over until it becomes like breathing. All of our lives depend on you not revealing yourself."

I took the piece of paper. "Got it."

The door opened and I climbed out. I hated everything about that limo.

Samuel had another thing coming if he thought he owned the Rubicon. *Nobody owns the Rubicon.* He would've found out tonight if I hadn't needed to negotiate for my mother and sister's release.

I hated this feeling. I was bound to magic, to the terms that monster wielded on that contract. It was going to last until the dark magic ran out.

The limo drove off. The minute Samuel was out of sight, I jumped into the air, transformed, and flew as fast as I could back home.

I needed to make sure that my family was there. My father, my mother, and my sister. I finally reached the house and hovered high in the air. I tuned in.

My father's laughter pierced through the kitchen.

"Dad, what is that? It looks like some sort of rodent," Sammy asked.

"Is it a bunny?" my mother asked in her high-pitched English accent.

Dad laughed again.

They were playing a game.

It sounded like the old Sir Robert. The pathetic Robert was gone. My family finally had some of him back.

As scaly as Samuel was, I had to give it to him. He was a man of his word.

I didn't want to stay, so I turned around and flew back to the Academy.

FOR THE REST of the week I said those words over and over again.

I found a book in the restricted area explaining how to use this certain spell. It was exceedingly dangerous. They'd used it in the olden days to interrogate dragons. It was right after they'd discovered we had human forms.

The potion bound their abilities and then they would do horrendous things to dragons to study them.

I closed the book.

I was the Rubicon. I had to be stronger than this.

But I'd heard things about Dimitri Ramakof. He was as evil and as scaly as they came, putting Samuel in a completely different type of dangerous category.

Still, I wasn't scared of him. I needed to be more careful, though. He could become the cage that cost me my freedom.

I kept saying the words over and over in my mind until they became a part of me.

Every ounce of my human body told me not to do this, but I needed it. It was what the beast wanted. I had to satisfy its needs at least somewhat, so I could hold on longer.

Saturday came faster than I thought possible.

I reached Samuel's house around half past eight and found Dimitri already busy with the potion.

Samuel acted the opposite of the night in the limo. He was friendly again. He patted my cheek and brought my head closer to his. "I love punctuality, Blake," he said, his Spanish accent sharpening the consonants. "You know the spell?"

I recited it word for word in perfect Latin.

"Music to my ears."

"So when are we going to do this? What time is the fight?"

Samuel laughed. "That eager? I like."

Everyone laughed, Phil included.

I saw a couple girls passed out on the couch. They were high; white powder dusted the tips of their noses. It didn't surprise me anymore, but a part of me felt sorry for them.

I knew the feeling. I'd tasted it once. The high was amazing, the low not so much.

"When?" I asked again.

"Your first fight is at three."

I frowned. "How many fights do I have today?"

"Easy, Blake." Phil got off the couch.

"Are we having a problem, Blake?" Samuel asked.

This guy was starting to piss me off. "No, just wanted to know how many times you want me to kill my own fucking kind."

His eye twitched. "Okay," he said. "Five times. Today is an entrance for you. Five times and that is it."

I nodded. "That's all I want to know. Now where do we begin?"

❦

IT TOOK Dimitri five hours to get me ready, to hide from the world who I was.

The guy looking back in the mirror wasn't me, but he did everything I did. He had blonde hair and dark eyes that looked evil. His body was covered in tattoos. My birthmark was even gone.

The stuff Dimi gave me to drink was disgusting and broke my body, or at least that was how it felt.

I only had access to my acid. The other abilities were bound tight.

The Mark of the Dragonians was plastered on my lower left abdomen. I hated that mark with a passion because of what it represented.

"You look ready, Hansel."

"You going to go with that?" I looked at Samuel in the mirror.

"You look like a Hansel. Don't disappoint me, Blake."

"You too," I spoke back to him. It wasn't just his ass on the line, it was my ass too. And something told me that not even royalty could get me out of this if things went south.

Especially since no one knew I was here.

☙

THE ARENA WAS deep in the Abysmal. It was where thugs and lowlife scum hung out. My eyes caught on a little girl—five, maybe six—scraping for food in a garbage can.

Dimi's eyes were on me. He grunted. I didn't want him to know that I had a weakness for the poor. He already knew about my weakness for my family.

The limo drove into what looked like a sprawling storage facility. Inside was a parking lot.

We were directed to a private parking zone and parked among other cars—Ferraris, Porsches, and SUVs—that cost more than our home.

Samuel handed Phil papers that I assumed were forged

and probably carried the name of Hansel Borgendorf—my false identity for the tournament.

Dimitri came with us. Phil went to register me.

I was taken the area where competitors' identities and qualifications were vetted. Dimitri was close by and I was surprised that they picked up a strong heartbeat and human anatomy in me.

He was that good.

Then we went to the fighting rooms.

There were athletes of all shapes and sizes. Some shorter than me and some even bigger.

The hair on my body stood on end; I could tell they truly hated dragons.

These people never wanted a treaty with the dragons. They'd never wanted to rule alongside them. This was the sort of place King Albert and my father tried to burn down to the ground.

The black market wasn't far from here. My scales, the Rubicon scales, were worth more than some of these cars. Yet I wouldn't trade them for anything. Every spell they were used for if removed from me would reverberate through my being. It was my curse; I would never sell a single scale or the tiniest slice of my organs to the black market.

My leg started to tap fast as I got dressed and waited for the next part. I looked at my watch. It was a quarter to three. My first fight was at three.

A part of me was scared. I only had my acid to rely on. I couldn't even transform.

Who knew what Dimi had put into that potion. I didn't want to think about it.

The time ticked off slowly as the Dragonians or the ones meant to slay dragons chanted and got each other worked up.

I looked at Phil, who was sitting next to me, staring at them. He didn't like it any more than I did.

But I was human now, for all they knew. I had to act human. I could hear a human screaming outside. The crowd went crazy.

Something told me that the dragons were exactly like the bunch of idiots in front of me. They hated every ounce of humans too.

Caught between two groups blinded by mutual prejudice and hatred.

Then Hansel's name was called.

THE SECOND I climbed into that ring, every part of me wanted to escape.

I didn't want to be there anymore, but the beast loved every bit of it.

It was a massive cage. The beams would be charged with electricity when the fight started.

Blood, new and old, was splattered on the ground. They were disposing of an arm and some guts as I walked in.

"It ain't a good day for dragon slayers," one of the guys remarked in a redneck accent.

I didn't reply.

Phil pinched my shoulders. "Remember, Hansel. Fast kill and get the fuck out of this ring. It gives me the creeps to see you in here."

"Then why the fuck did you drag me into this?" I sneered and shrugged his massage away. *Fucking idiot.*

Second thoughts were spooling in my brain when a voice over a speaker announced the fight. He called out my name and told the crowd that I owned the acid ability. He gave everyone my stats. My heart raced—not that I could hear it, but I could feel it in my entire being. My body felt wrong. I felt sick. What if the potion was defective? What if Dimitri... *Calm down, Blake. Deep breaths.*

Then he called Skull Crusher. *What the fuck?*

A huge mother of a Sun-Blast walked into the ring. Usually they could sense the Alpha in me, but this one didn't.

He just kept banging on his chest, still in his human form. He wore a leather garment wrapped around his torso, with bare feet and a bare chest. He had bright red hair, like Brian.

He couldn't even smell the Rubicon on me.

I looked at Dimitri again. He was standing at the gate,

controlling his part of the spell. Mine was playing in the back of my mind like a record stuck on a few lines.

I had to concentrate on how to kill the Sun-Blast really quickly.

The crowd cheered as the Sun-Blast stats were called out. He'd won 45 fights. Fuck, that was a lot. I couldn't believe he was matched up against a newbie.

This was so wrong. No wonder the humans didn't last.

As I was thinking, he suddenly exploded into a gigantic dragon. Limbs popped out like giant tree stumps. Scales erupted everywhere.

He growled in my face. I just turned my head and looked in Dimitri's direction again.

You'd better not fail; otherwise, it's not just me you have to deal with, but all these fucking dragons.

And then the siren went off.

I ducked and dove out of the way of the first fireball that came out of the dragon's mouth.

They were so predictable.

The second one I ducked and then I leaped onto his back.

He didn't like that much. I reached down with both hands. I would've given anything to test my fire. To see if it did spread like a virus..

The crowd cheered wildly and I reached for his jaw, releasing my acid into his mouth.

He was immune to fire, but not acid.

Liters and liters of acid dripped down his throat. His

body started to disintegrate; holes burned him from the inside out.

The crowd went wild.

Gore and blood splattered on the floor as he teetered.

I rolled out of the way, covered with dragon blood.

The fight was over before it even began. And that was just the beginning.

I became an instantaneous favorite. Everybody here knew my name, or at least Hansel's.

It was ten according to my watch. I felt tired but I had two more fights to go.

Next up: the Night Villain against a fire slayer.

Human screams filled the air one more time. It was no wonder that the odds for bets on humans were lower than dragons.

 NINE

THE LAST FIGHT WAS HARD.

Dimitri's potion worked well.

I screamed as the wing of the Night Villain ripped off. Its blood, mixed with mine, pooled on the floor.

The emcee lifted up my arm.

I could only see part of the crowd. The rest was black. My vision was fucked.

I needed to fly, but this enchantment Dimi conjured still clung to me.

I felt trapped. Suffocated.

The crowd was cheering.

Phil and Samuel were too. I pushed Phil away the minute he laid his hands on me.

"Careful. The crowd."

"Fuck your crowd!"

"Easy, Hansel."

"Let him go," Samuel said. "He'll be back. He has no choice."

I needed the spell to release. I got a lift with a group of strangers. It was a couple of students.

The spell started to wear off while we were driving. I told them to let me out. At first they didn't want to listen, but I barked, "If you knew what's good for you, you'll let me out."

"Okay, man. Jeez, relax," the one guy said and stopped the sportster. I ran as fast as I could in the opposite direction, toward the dark docks.

At last the spell wore off. I dove into the ocean and stayed there for a long time. I could finally breathe. Even underwater, I finally breathed.

I swam to Dragonia Academy.

My eye was still swollen, my knuckles were raw. So was my body.

Purple bruises, whether from tonight's fight or the enchantment, covered my body. I felt broken.

Once in my room, I took a long bath. When I was done, I crashed on my bed. I felt as if I could sleep for days.

At first I dreamed of nothing, then it shifted.

I was in in the air. The stars shone brightly.

Her laughter came from above me. She was on my back, enjoying our midnight flight.

Who was she?

She knew my name, yet I didn't know hers. She was my breath. She was the one that'd never had her first breath. Tonight's dream made that clear. Reality seeped into the dream. My lungs grew tighter and tighter. I struggled to breathe. She didn't exist, and she never would.

I woke up gasping for air. I couldn't breathe.

ON MONDAY, I was almost healed. Thanks to my healing ability. The only signs of me fighting was the shiner.

I wasn't going to be able to dodge the questions this time.

I hadn't dreamt about the girl again.

Now I was left with screams, haunted by the horror that I had killed my own kind.

My body shuddered each time I heard a dragon wail, and the last screech that each had made before the blow of death.

I decided to lay low and skipped class.

I worked on the "Never-Breath" poem some more.

It was coming along nicely and slowly turning into a song. I could see it being sung, but I struggled to hear the tune.

Knocks came around two-thirty. In the hall, Tabitha stood frozen.

I didn't wait for her to say anything, just left the door open. She could either come in or fuck off. It didn't bother me which one she chose. She came in.

"What the fuck, Blake? What happened?"

"It's nothing for you to worry about."

"Does my brother have anything to do with this?" she wanted to know. "I'm so calling his ass."

"Don't." I got up and grabbed her phone. "Nobody tells

me what I can and cannot do, you get that? I don't need you to worry about me. I can take care of myself."

"Yeah, I can see that. Look at you."

"Just leave."

She didn't.

The damage was already done.

Still the beast was calm. I had to deal with the consequences now. All of them.

She sat in front of me. "Talk to me. What the hell is going on?"

"I can't," I said. I didn't know why I said that.

"Fine, if you are not ready, I won't push."

She took my head in both her hands. They were so cold. Her touch calmed down the burning in my core.

It was soothing. But then something else entirely happened. It was at first a zinging sensation on my swollen face. Then, it felt warm.

I tried to pull away, but she wouldn't let me. Her lips moved softly. I could barely hear what she was saying. Another spell.

A healing one.

How the hell did she do this?

"There," she said. "I told you to be careful, Blake."

"I know." I knew if I went to the mirror I wouldn't find a black eye anymore. Somehow she'd healed me. How, I had no idea.

SHE STAYED with me the rest of the day. We watched movies and hardly spoke a word.

There was something about Tabitha that I couldn't put my finger on. She calmed my soul. I still didn't feel the way she did, but it wasn't bad having her around either.

She could be good for me.

We fell asleep on the couch and instead of dreaming about the redhead, I dreamed about dragons screaming and dying. I killed all of them.

I startled awake and almost punched Tabitha when she put her hands softly on me.

"Easy," she murmured.

"I'm sorry. I think you should leave," I said and walked to the bathroom. I closed the door and struggled to fill my lungs with air.

I should've never fought. But what choice did I have? I had to for my family.

Who was I kidding?

I was born predestined for evil.

It was never going to be any easier, only harder. This would've happened eventually.

I succumbed to imaginary growls and screeches. I could understand why King Albert and my father tried so hard to bring down the Black Market. It was pure evil and it catered to pure evil.

I'd somehow fallen asleep again. I woke up and found the sun streaming into the bathroom. Relief washed over me. I hadn't dreamed about the dragons again.

I opened the bathroom door and found a plate of food on my table.

She was too good for me.

I should tell her that, at least.

⚜

DURING THE DAY I worked on "Never-Breath."

Around six that night, I was finished.

The words took a lot out of me. Words that had the potential of a great song if I could find the right tune.

Isaac jumped into my head. I should give this to him.

The thought was hardly formed when I found myself standing on the ledge of my window.

I dove and transformed.

I felt free. The only time I really did.

I landed with a thud a few hours later at his house in the Shifters' village. They reminded me of the Pilgrims, but they had tribes too. It was a mixture of old traditions. It boiled down to just them being plain and simple folk.

Isaac's dad was the chief. He was a Chimera, like his daughter.

Isaac was the last giant eagle. His father wanted badly for him to take over one day.

Isaac was surprised when I turned up on his doorstep. "Blake, what the hell are you doing here?"

"That's how you greet a bud?"

"Sorry, not what I meant, just surprised."

"Who is it, son?" Isaac's father's voice came from the kitchen.

"You wouldn't believe it if I told you. Come in."

The minute I entered the door I felt her. Isaacs's sister. Ever since she was little, she did this thing whenever I came to visit. She would try to surprise attack me.

My lips curved slightly. She was good, but I always detected her hiding place right before the attack.

She leapt out and I jumped out of the way. She crashed into the staircase.

Isaac laughed. "Next time, sis."

"Dammit." In place of the Chimera appeared a fifteen-year-old blonde.

"Really, still?"

"Sorry… I can smell you a mile away."

"Oh, that is not good," Isaac teased as she ran up the stairs to get dressed.

"She has been a pain in my ass too, Blake. Wanting to know when you were going to come."

"Well, better late than never, or so I've been told."

"Blake," Isaacs's dad said as we entered the kitchen. "Is that you?"

"Sorry for popping in unexpectedly."

"I just asked Isaac the other day how you were."

"Well..." I tapped on my chest. "As you can see, I'm fine."

"So you are. Your mother good, father?"

I nodded. Last time I checked they were.

"We'll be in my room," Isaac said led me to the basement, which he'd turned into his room.

It looked the same as ever, with a king-size bed in the middle of the room and a couple of instruments in the corner. His half-assed job of trying to soundproof was still evident on his walls.

I should really help him with that.

"So, to what do I owe the pleasure of this visit?"

"This." I handed him the words scribbled on a second sheet of paper—"Never-Breath."

For the next few minutes, Isaac was quiet as he read the words. Then he shook his head. "Dude, this is deep. Who is she?"

"Nobody. She doesn't exist."

"Is this how you feel?"

I shrugged. I didn't want to tell him how pathetic I truly was. To admit that I was in love with a figment of my imagination.

"Do you think it might be linked to your Moon-Bolt?"

I laughed. "It's just a song, Isaac. You think we'd be able to give it a tune?"

"Sure," he said. "I need some time, though."

"Cool. I need to get back to Dragonia. I slipped out. If Longwei catches me, he'll never let me out of his sight again."

Isaac chuckled. "I'll have something for you, say, in the next week or so?"

"Got it."

"You have a new Cammy yet?" he asked.

"Nope." I waved goodbye.

"I will tell my sis to practice for next week."

I chuckled and nodded. "See you soon." I rushed up the stairs and let myself out. If there was one guy who would be able to give a tune to "Never-Breath," it was Isaac

TEN

IT WAS LATE when I got back to Dragonia Academy.

The school was quiet and everyone was asleep, apart from a few rooms. I could only hear hollow sounds as their rooms were actually soundproofed.

I found a silver piece of paper on the floor outside my door. I knew who that paper belonged too. Irene.

I knew what it was going to say. She wanted to see me and I couldn't. I'd ended up giving the beast everything he wanted.

I couldn't give him that too. They would definitely expel me.

I picked up the note. Scribbled in elegant cursive letters, she demanded to see me. There wasn't just one date, but time slots for the rest of the week and the next one.

Every day. She wanted to see me every day. *WHY?*

I chucked the note in my drawer and rubbed my face hard.

Lucian's bed was still empty. How long did he need to recover? Was he even going to come back? The beast loved that, but I hated not knowing if he was okay or not.

I took a shower and forced myself to sleep, praying that the nightmares would stay away.

THE NEXT MORNING, I went to the cafeteria. Every single person's eyes were on me as I walked up to the buffet line.

I got a couple of greetings from girls as I dished up.

"Blake," Chef said. "Nice to see you up again."

I grunted, resenting his insinuation. *Copper-Horns.*

I found an open table outside and in less than thirty seconds, George, Brian, Tabitha, and everyone who was everyone joined me.

I wanted to explode but I ate my breakfast and went to class the minute the bell rang.

Time flew today; I dreaded seeing Irene. My palms were sweaty. What was she doing to me?

Professor Edward called my name. "You can go," he said in his brisk Irish accent.

I packed my bag and went for Irene's tower. I should've just skipped her today, but she would report my absence to Master Longwei and that would lead to more questions. I didn't have all the answers right now.

So I wiped my sweaty palms against my trousers and trudged up the steps that led to her room high in the tower.

I reached out to knock.

"Enter!" she yelled out before my fist even connected with the wood.

I opened the door.

Her face lit up and she gave me her brilliant smile. I was glad for the first time that my heart couldn't be heard; this would've been embarrassing.

"I didn't think you were going to show." she said in her honey-sweet voice.

"I wasn't sure if I should." I was being honest, too honest.

"Well, I'm glad you did. Sit." She smiled.

I dropped my backpack and took a seat. I lay on my back and closed my eyes.

I missed this tower, the formality of it. I missed talking to her.

"What is it?"

"I don't know. You tell me, Irene. What am I doing here?"

"You know it's mandatory to see me as the Rubicon. You've missed quite a few sessions."

I chuckled at her word choice. If only she knew the sessions I had in mind, she wouldn't say that to me.

"Something funny?" she asked.

"No, quite the opposite." My tone was gloomy.

"Then talk to me. What has been going on with you lately?"

"I'm having dreams, dreams I don't know how to interpret. Whether they're my imagination or something to come."

"Tell me about the dreams."

I looked at her with one raised eyebrow.

"Give it a shot."

"Fine. I think I'm having dreams of my rider."

She squinted. "I don't understand."

"I think it's my rider or what she would've been like if she was alive."

"She?" Irene said.

"Yeah, I was always under the impression that it was a he until the dreams."

"Tell me about them. What do you feel? What do you do? How do you know it's about your rider?"

"I know how it sounds, okay? My rider doesn't exist. They're just stupid dreams."

"Nothing is stupid, Blake. Try me."

It was silent for a moment and then I just opened up. The words poured out of me and I told Irene about every single dream. She listened eagerly without saying a single word. So I kept talking. "And that's that. It's the last dream I had." I looked at her. "Do you know what it could possibly mean?"

She squinted thinking hard. "I know you want me to tell you that it's about your future, that it's your Moon-Bolt side awakening within you. But I don't think it's that. I think it's what you think it is. Wishful thinking."

"Wishful thinking." I rubbed my face hard. "What about what I feel in this dream? Does that sound remotely like anything real?"

"I don't know. I wish I had the answer, but you know I hardly see anything good when it comes to you."

I nodded, feeling sad. "Yeah, my curse. Everything I try to accomplish is completely hopeless. I might as well just give in."

"Don't say that. It's not hopeless, okay?" She got up and came to sit next to me. She'd never sat this close to me before.

She rubbed my arm. If she knew what was good for her, she wouldn't touch me like this.

The beast was awakening. It wanted more.

Don't, Blake, just don't.

It took a deep breath. I should be going. Now was a good time, but I couldn't. I didn't have the strength to fight anymore.

She came closer to me then and her lips brushed against mine.

I froze. *What the fuck?*

She kissed me full on the lips. The beast took over and pulled her closer. Her body was warm against mine. I grunted softly as her hands twirled in my hair and her kiss deepened.

She tasted amazing. I wanted more.

She finally stopped. "We shouldn't do this."

"Shut the fuck up." It didn't even sound like me. Before I knew it, she was pinned against the wall and my shirt was off.

My lips trailed all over her skin. Her breathing grew faster and our clothes disappeared.

She moaned softly in my ear as I thrust myself inside her again and again. She tasted amazing and being inside her was worth every single forbidden second.

I didn't care anymore. It felt great when the beast got what it wanted. It was rejoicing. Maybe I could hold on just a tad bit longer.

❦

SHE OFFERED ME A CIGARETTE AFTERWARD. I didn't want to leave, but she probably had another student soon.

We'd somehow made it to her bedroom.

Who knew sleeping with a three-hundred-year-old Moon-Bolt would feel this way. She... tamed a part of me.

I hadn't felt so free in a long time. So rested. Ready for whatever faced me next.

She took the cigarette away from me. I rested with my head on her belly and she looked down at me.

"You don't regret this?"

"You're the Moon-Bolt. Do you see me regretting this?"

She laughed.

"No, I don't," I said and kissed her. "But I do need to go unless you want others to know."

"Oh, damn," she said. "Why do you have to be a student?"

I laughed. "Just a few more years and then I'm finished."

"Still," she said.

I got up. I slipped on my pants and looked for my t-shirt.

"So, same time tomorrow?"

"You bet," I said and bent over the bed, kissing her goodbye. "And I'm quite possessive, Irene, so I'd better be your only."

She blushed. She didn't say a single word, just shook her head.

I pulled on my shirt and blew her another kiss as I slipped on my shoes. I left before her next appointment.

I still couldn't believe what the fuck just happened. I didn't even have to kiss her, she'd gone for me. Me.

I took a deep breath as I left her tower. For the first time in a very long time, I was looking forward to tomorrow.

§

I COULDN'T GET Irene out of my head. Her smell overpowered my senses. The beast inside was purring. It wasn't a real sound, just what it felt like. It was at peace and so was I.

I was glad that this sensation resulted from something as simple as Irene, and not murder. Those were the hardest to deal with. I couldn't do the nightmares anymore.

I doubted the dreams about the redhead would come again.

I felt sad about something I never really had to begin with. It showed just how fucked up dreams in Paegeia were.

They were so real.

The Shifters believed that the strong ones guided people on the right path, the path to their destinies.

I chuckled. I guessed it was one of the reasons why Isaac wasn't ready to take over from his father.

He didn't believe in any of that crap.

I closed my eyes and slipped into a rare, blissfully dreamless sleep.

§

A TAP on the window woke me. At first I thought I was hearing things, but the tap persisted. I opened my eyes and went to the window.

Huge wings flapped outside in the dark. A giant eagle hovered just beyond my reach.

Isaac? What was he doing here?

I opened the window. The wings disappeared instantly as a pair of strong arms grabbed the ledge.

I hauled him into my room. He immediately pulled on the jeans that were in his other hand. I tossed him one of my shirts.

"You know it's late, right?" I asked.

"Dude." He smiled. Something was different about him. "Dude," he said again. "'Never-Breath' is one of the best songs you've ever fucking written."

I started to laugh. "Please tell me that's not why you came."

"I had to. You don't have a fucking phone and I need us to record this. The song, the tune. It's brilliant."

"Okay, calm down." He plopped onto the couch and I flipped on the lights.

"You want a beer?"

"Sure," Isaac said. "Your room is the shit. Fuck, dude, this is the first time I've been here."

We both laughed.

"How did you find my room?" I grabbed a beer from the mini fridge.

"Your smell."

"My smell?" My eyebrow arched.

"Not like that," he said and accepted his beer from me.

I sat on the couch opposite him. "You keeping me hanging? Hum the melody."

"Better. I'll sing you the fucking song."

Isaac had a brilliant voice and it was weird how they couldn't get booked without me being the lead singer.

He started to sing the tune and made the beat, which was soft and low, with his mouth. Goosebumps crawled over my arms and neck when he started singing the lyrics.

He closed his eyes. His voice went up in just the right places. He felt each word exactly the way I did.

In the chorus, it was as if he was begging death himself to put him out of his misery. Just how I felt. Whom did I need to see to turn her into a reality?

I wiped tears from my eyes as Isaac finished the last verse. I shook my head. "I think you got it."

"Yeah, it just fits so fucking perfectly. Don't you think?"

"It does."

"Is that how you truly feel?" he asked.

I really didn't want to think about the dreams anymore. "I did. I hate the darkness. The constant fighting, not knowing where I'll be and what shit I'll do tomorrow."

Sympathetic sadness cloaked his expression. "You really imagine her as a girl?"

I chuckled. "Actually, no, I actually think it would've been a guy. But this industry needs a good take-me-back type of song, don't you think?"

"Fuck yeah." He fiddled with a loose thread in his jeans. "So are we going to record it?"

"Sure." I shrugged. "Why not?"

"Yes," Isaac pumped his first. "Oh, before I forget—the phone is ringing nonstop, dude. We have gigs lined up. Please tell me you can do this."

"I'll try. I can't promise anything, Isaac."

"That's all I want. Well, I'd better get going." He finished his beer. "Before the old man discovers I'm gone."

"Yeah, who knows what he would do this time?"

We both laughed. Isaac had slept many a night in jail because he hadn't told his father where he was. So the police came looking for him and when they found him drunk out of his wits, they locked him up.

I was never around to bail him out or beg the officers not to take him. Some friend I was.

He put down the empty bottle. "See you, dude. Don't forget, five o'clock Friday, my place. And get yourself a fucking phone." He took off his shirt and jumped on the ledge. "Bye." he pulled off his jeans and dove.

An eagle burst out of Isaacs form and I watched him fly away as I closed my window.

I felt happy and sad at the same time.

He'd done an amazing job with "Never-Breath." I couldn't write music without him.

Life for now was good. And that was all I needed at this moment.

ELEVEN

Perched in the bathroom, I had no idea why I was so fucking nervous. I'd done this a million times, yet I was dreading getting back on that stage.

My stomach turned at a knock on the door.

"Dude, you okay?" Isaac asked.

"Give me a few seconds."

Was this because we were going to sing "Never-Breath" for the first time?

I took deep breaths. More than a few, actually. Finally I opened the door.

Ty was resting against the wall and raised his eyebrow. "Yeah, yeah, I know."

Isaac laughed and handed me a shot. "For the nerves."

"I need an entire fucking bottle."

"Blake," James said. "You've done this a million times."

"I know. It's that song, man."

"The song is perfect," Isaac said.

"We need to do that song." Ty was adamant.

"You scared to show people what really goes on inside you?" Mathew joked.

"Ha, ha." I said sarcastically.

As we approached the stage, the guys kept teasing that all I was made of was mush and heart.

If only they knew the truth.

I shoved aside the curtain and the crowd roared like crazy.

Twenty-five bands had already played tonight. They always did something for Independence Day. I was obligated to come anyway. But since the band got together, it was completely different.

They chanted our name and I chuckled.

"Nothing new, Blake!" Isaac yelled.

Still, I was nervous as hell.

The hall was packed. Thousands upon thousands were here for this feast.

We waited for Jeremy Scwhile, a famous actor, to call our name.

"You are going to be okay, dude," Isaac said.

"The next band... Oh man, we've all been waiting for this," Jeremy exclaimed into the mic.

They cheered until Ty jumped out and lifted his arms. Then they went ballistic. Isaac and I just laughed. He had no self-preservation.

"We've all been waiting for them to finally get back together and blow us out of the park."

"So lame," Isaac said.

"I give you the Shifters!"

Ty ran out to his drums, then James on the keyboard,

Mathew and Isaac took the guitars and last, it was my turn.

The crowd churned and screamed. I smiled, shaking my head as I took the microphone.

"You guys ready?" I asked Isaac.

"Oh hell yeah!" Isaac said.

"Ty?" I prompted.

Ty beat the living crap out of the drums nonstop. I started bouncing up and down until he finally stopped and screamed, "Yeah, motherfuckers!"

Mathew did a small intro on the guitar, playing his heart out for a few seconds.

I counted down and we launched into our first song of the evening.

Isaac was right. I was fine.

Each band got four songs in between intervals, so two now and then one later and our last song would be the introduction to "Never-Breath."

I still felt nervous about how the crowd would take it.

It was an extremely personal song. Not that the others weren't personal... But this one was deeper.

It made me feel vulnerable. It was a side of me I really didn't want to be associated with. But it was a fucking good song.

When the second song was over, we left the stage and everyone demanded more. Jeremy struggled to get in a few words.

It was hard to imagine that this was just because of me. The entire band was brilliant.

We walked into the VIP section where everyone waited and listened to the banter of all the other bands.

I dashed to the bathroom, wash my face, and cool down from the oppressive heat of the stage. I splashed cold water on my neck and dried it with a towel. When I opened my eyes, Irene had appeared behind me.

I smiled. "What the hell are you doing here?"

"You always ask so many questions," she said. She was wearing a short skirt with a button-up shirt. Her breasts filled her shirt near to bursting. Boots came up to her knees. Before I knew it, her legs were wrapped around my waist and our lips smashed vigorously together.

I pushed her into the stall she'd just exited and peppered every bit of her skin with kisses.

I went down on her, showing her that dragons my age could be just as brilliant lovers as dragons her age.

She complained and had to suppress her noises. "Fuck, Blake," she gasped and pulled me up to kiss her again.

Her hands fiddled with my jeans buttons. She pushed them off. My boxers were discarded next.

In less than a minute I was inside her. The beast growled in pleasure. It loved every single moment. I was lost inside of her. Not wondering or caring about anything in this fucked-up world.

She was my antidote. And as long as the beast needed it, I would kill whoever stood in our way.

The door opened and my name rang out. It was time to stop this wild over-the-top screwing session and go sing.

"Sorry, I really don't want to leave, but..."

"Go. Sing." She pushed me away as I hitched up my boxers and jeans. She gave me another kiss. "Has anyone ever told you how amazing you are?" Her blue eyes penetrated mine as if staring into my soul.

"No, lately I only hear about what a shit-head I am. But I'll take that compliment anytime." I slapped her perfectly sculpted ass, hard.

"Go," she pushed my hand away.

I ran out of the stall. I found Isaac outside at the bar asking someone if he had seen me.

"I'm here," I said distractedly, still buckling my belt.

"Dude, what the fuck? You already had sex?"

Laughing, I ran my hands through my hair and tugged my shirt until it sat perfectly.

"Yeah you look fine," Isaac growled. He strutted onstage to the guitar.

I sauntered out and the crowds went insane again.

"What is it with you and crowds?" Isaac's voice came over the speaker.

"It's a Rubicon thing," I joked. They cheered again. "Only a Rubicon thing."

The crowd laughed as Isaac pretended to be pissed off. I looked at them for a while and introduced our next song.

Ty beat the intro on his drums. The rest of the band joined in. The first few notes wailed on the guitars and it was my turn.

The crowd sang the chorus with us. I bent down with the

mic in my hand and everyone sang as loud as they could with Ty and Isaac on backup.

I laughed, got up, and took over, finishing the song perfectly.

The crowd chanted for more as Jeremy reclaimed the stage.

I returned to the bathroom, hoping Irene was still there, but the stall was empty. She really just knew how to keep a guy on his toes, wanting more.

I found Isaac by the bar.

"She's gone?"

"Shut up."

"Only you can get sex before the gig is fucking over."

I chuckled. "I'm not so sure about that." I sipped the drink the barman put in front of me as Isaac's eyes followed mine toward Ty.

"So fucking unfair." Isaac shook his head.

"You're too nice. I told you, treat a few like shit. I mean, just ask Ty." We watched him, sitting on a couch with four girls. "They'll eat out of your hand in no time."

"Yeah, no. I don't possess that talent."

I couldn't help but wonder where the hell Irene had disappeared to. I couldn't even call her. I really should get myself a new fucking Cammy. Soon.

❦

OUR TURN WAS up one last time. This was it. I was nervous, but it was time. The big one.

"You ready?" Isaac slapped me on the back as I downed my beer.

"To pour my guts out? No." I got up from the barstool.

Jeremy was already introducing us. The crowd seriously had a thing for the Shifters.

"Break a leg," Fred from Downstairs Octavius said. He was their lead singer, and man, he had pipes.

"You fucking wish!" I yelled back and he laughed.

My heart stammered as I grabbed the microphone. Just listening to the crowd cheer and soaking it up made me rocketed me to the top of the world again.

The stage manager brought a high chair. I took a seat.

"It's one of those songs," I joked and the audience chuckled indulgently. "I'm pouring my heart out, so be gentle."

The crowed *ahh*ed.

"We love you, Blake!" someone yelled.

"I'm bad news, sweetheart," I joked to general titters.

Isaac started strumming the guitar. I took another deep breath as the tune picked up, soft as a dove's wings. The drums and the keyboard joined in. I closed my eyes and started to sing "Never-Breath."

It was seriously over before it even began, but in that moment, I completely lost myself. My heart, my guts, I poured out my everything.

When the last word was sung, the crowd fell silent. I felt as if I was going to die.

A few seconds later cheers and chants brought the house down. Goosebumps flushed over my skin; it carried on for thirty seconds, a minute, longer.

They absolutely loved it.

"Thank you very much. You've been great," I said and waved at the crowd.

We left as they chanted for more.

"What the fuck was that?" Milly from Two Steps Up asked. "How the hell am I going to beat that?"

"Sorry," I mouthed.

"I hate going on after you." She threw a playful fit.

"I told you, Milly, you should've stuck with us."

"Suck my dick, Isaac," she joked and disappeared.

Everyone congratulated us. They loved "Never-Breath." They'd soaked it up.

I was on top of the world again and this time I didn't need a snort of Fire-Cain to get me there.

❧

I STAYED the night at Isaac's and celebrated. I needed to buy myself a phone with my cut of the prize money we'd won. The rest, well, my mom needed it more than I did.

Isaac had already gotten a few calls from studios wanting to record "Never-Breath."

I hated when that happened. It was hard to choose.

Although the money was good, I would find a way to spend it on bullshit.

But not this time. The house needed it more than I did.

On Monday, I was in Irene's tower again. More specifically, her bed up in her tower.

She was driving me insane. Our time was limited whenever she summoned me for our sessions.

"Have you decided who you are going to use to record 'Never-Breath'?"

I shook my head. "I don't know if I should. The record labels always find a way to screw you over."

"C'mon, Blake, it can't be that bad."

"Shows how little you know about the entertainment business. We need to fix that." I forced her on her back and kissed the soft flesh of her neck. She smelled great, fresh. It was addictive.

Gazing into those bright blue eyes, I asked, "Why do you never tell me about your past?"

"You never asked."

"So if I ask you anything you'll just tell me?"

"I will."

I squinted. "Okay, how did Tansee die?"

"Long story. One I'll need a few bottles of gin for before we get into that conversation."

"You were Dents?"

"No, but after a while it felt like that. She was my everything."

"Your everything?"

"What, you didn't know?"

"Know what?" I squinted.

"I'm not just into boys, Blake." She bent over and kissed my lips softly.

"You like girls too?"

"Oh, women are the best damn lovers one can get."

"Excuse me?" I felt intimidated.

She laughed. "You are quite impressive yourself, but if you don't leave soon, I'm afraid someone will find you. Then all this will be over."

"Yeah? Let them try."

She laughed just before my lips kissed hers one last time. She took a strand of my hair and played with it. "Do you have any idea how beautiful you are?"

"I've heard that one a couple of times," I joked.

"Well, you are. I can tell you this. If your father finds out, he will literally kill me."

I squinted. "Why does he hate you so much?"

"Easy. I couldn't see who was going to betray Al. He lost his rider. He lost everything that night. And he blames me."

"It's not your fault."

"I know, but…" She sighed.

"It's not your fault." I kissed her again and that was that. The nail in my coffin. Irene was starting to become more than just a tool to calm the beast.

She was starting to become my everything too.

TWELVE

THE NEXT FEW weeks flew by. I became more and more content with my life. I was starting to feel like the old me.

Isaac selected one of the recording labels. He didn't go with Frank this time. He was a fucking sleaze-ball, good with his mouth but with very short arms when it came to money.

So Isaac chose a boutique record label that was treating us like kings. It took an entire weekend to record "Never-Breath."

For the music video, they got a blonde and used a spell to transform her hair and dust her with freckles. She didn't look anything like the girl from my dreams, even when her brown eyes became green.

Another Dragonian played the part meant for a dragon, but the less they knew, the better.

It came out great. It was fun. Even though the hole in my gut tore each time we did another take. I didn't want to feel it. The darkness would return again soon. I was sure of it.

We wrapped up on Sunday. Now we just had to wait for the single to come out.

I snuck off again and spent the day with Irene. I quickly forgot about the hole the weekend had left me with. Irene's presence healed me. I forgot about the redhead, about the dreams and how I felt.

Maybe Irene was enough…

The next week our sessions became longer, but because of that, more people started to notice.

Master Longwei asked her if there was any change when it came to me since she was seeing me so many times. She was worried. She needed me just as much as I needed her.

She handed me a joint. The sex I had with Irene was like a drug, but the joint just sealed it somehow. It was as if she knew my darkness needed everything she offered.

"What do you suggest? What are you going to tell him?" I had to know.

"I don't know. I cannot lie, Blake. And I have no idea what he wants me to say to him."

"You told him about my messed-up dreams?"

"Believe me, I used that one first. It has to stop eventually."

"No!" I was adamant.

She smiled. "I meant using the dream as the reason. Dreams usually stop and the reasons do too."

"I'll think of something."

"Blake, you already have too much on your plate."

"I need this, Irene. I need you."

Her cheeks became a darker pink. I couldn't believe she was still blushing from my compliments. She was so beautiful. She gave me a soft kiss and took the joint from me again. "You need to leave. I'm seeing Stephanie at noon."

I looked at her clock. It was five minutes till.

"Okay." I kissed her once and slid out of her bed. I jumped into my jeans and pulled on my shirt. "Same time tomorrow?"

"Not tomorrow, Blake. It's getting dangerous. We need to be careful."

"Then when?" I demanded.

"Two days from now, okay?"

I huffed.

"We have to be careful," she pleaded.

"Fine, whatever." I turned around and left.

"Don't be like that," she called after me, but I didn't slow. I had no idea how the fuck I was going to last two days.

As I left I almost knocked Stephanie out of the way.

"Sorry," she said.

"It's fine. She's in a terrible mood. Just a heads up," I mumbled.

"Okay." She sounded really confused. I got it. I'd probably never spoken a word to her before now.

I didn't look back. Just slung my backpack over my shoulder and strode back to my room.

I OPENED my door and froze. Lucian stood in the bathroom.

He looked fine until he started to walk. He had a limp. How was that possible? He was the Prince of Tith. Swallow Annexes could heal him.

"I'm back," he said.

I nodded and frowned.

"You're wondering about the limp?" He smiled. "You and everyone else."

"Why?" It was all I could get out.

"I healed the normal way. No Swallow Annexes, Blake."

"Why would you do that to yourself?" I was upset. Not just with myself for putting him through it, but with him too. He could have been healed easily. It wasn't that easy for us dragons. A Swallow Annex's touch couldn't heal dragons. Only humans. And here he was refusing it. Why? To make me feel shittier.

"To remember how it was, how it felt. Each time I turned, that pain. It's my fuel."

"Fuel for what?" I roared.

"To do better next time, Blake."

I huffed. "Are you insane?"

"I made you a promise, Blake. And I'm going to keep it. I don't need you to understand why I do things the way I do. But you're like my brother. I will find a way to claim you."

I closed my eyes, took a deep breath, and opened them. "We were thirteen years old. I don't expect you to keep that promise."

"I am a man of my word. Just think what sort of king I would be if I cannot keep my word."

"You're wasting your time."

Lucian chuckled. It made me feel small. It was as if I didn't see the bigger picture of why he must claim me. "If I don't claim you, then I must kill you, Blake. I don't think I can live with that. So that is why I chose to heal normally. I need the pain. It fuels me to do better."

I got what he was talking about. Nobody would ever be brave enough to face me if I turned. Nobody except him.

This was a fucked-up world.

I swallowed hard and left.

⬥

OVER THE NEXT FEW DAYS, everything came crashing down. Not being able to see Irene took its toll on me.

Master Longwei was doing more harm than good with his constant questions. My family got that I needed certain things in order to stay good. Why didn't he?

Lucian's return only added more weight. If felt as though I was descending from high among the clouds to the earth.

Heal normally? What a joke. As much as I wanted to believe that he was going to be the one to claim me, I couldn't. I didn't.

He wasn't the royal Irene saw when my egg hatched.

His heart and head were in the right place, but he was from the wrong bloodline.

I'd just taken a drag from my cigarette when the hatch of the roof opened.

The first thing I saw through the corner of my eye was snow-white hair. She wouldn't give up. Weird trait for a Snow Dragon.

"Thought I'd find you here," she said, taking the cigarette from me.

I just stared at her. What was her deal?

"So, how is it going?"

"Fine, I guess."

"My brother is looking for you. I told him you were occupied," she said.

"Occupied?" I asked.

"Yeah, that was all I could think of. You are extremely hard to track down. It's a wonder I found you here. Oh," she said, handing me back my cigarette as she reached for her pocket. "Before I forget." She took out our new album out a pen. "Mind if I get your autograph?" She said. "Pleeeease."

I huffed. The corners of my lips tugged up softly. "Sure, what's your name again, honey?"

"Ha, ha," she said.

I didn't leave a sweet message or anything like that, but signed her name in a heart with "Blake" and placed my signature below before handing it back to her.

She considered it. "Didn't think you were the heart type

of guy," she observed. "But I do love 'Never-Breath.' Are you sure she had red hair and green eyes?"

I chuckled. "Let me guess. Her hair is supposed to be snow-white and eyes bright blue?"

"Oh, that would've been perfect."

A strong urge to kiss her seared through me. I acted on it, not giving it two thoughts as I pulled her in by her jersey.

She smacked into me and our lips touched.

One thing led to another and I wielded my shield.

She stopped at the small popping sound. "I'm impressed, Mr. Leaf."

"Finally, someone is impressed," I flirted. She kissed me again.

&.

I FELT LIKE A DOG AFTERWARD. Even the beast did. I thought cheating would be something it loved, but I was wrong. It didn't want Tabitha. Did my human side want her?

No, I wanted Irene. Then it hit me.

What if Tabitha was just a cover-up? Sure, I would pretend that I was okay with her constantly in my company, but I could fool Master Longwei and get some of the spotlight off Irene and me.

It will work. It has to work.

I couldn't wait for tomorrow to tell Irene. But what if she didn't buy it? What if she thought I wanted to butter my bread on both sides?

No, I'd make her see it. I had to.

Lucian was snoring. I pulled the pillow over my head.

It didn't work.

I wished I could call Irene, but with Lucian back, it was no use. A lost cause. He would tell Master Longwei in a jiff and that would be it. They would lock me up and throw away the key.

No, I had to be patient. I would see her tomorrow.

❦

MY SESSION with her was at noon, right after lunch. I found her standing at the window. She was smoking a cigarette. I closed the door, locked it, and went to her.

"Don't touch me." She pushed me away.

"Seriously?" I was pissed off. First she insisted on taking a two-day break and now this shit.

"You and the Snow Dragon?" she asked.

My body inflated. "How did you find out?" There was no hiding this shit.

"Seriously?" she asked. "I'm a Moon-Bolt, Blake."

"It's not what…"

"Stop." She laughed. "I'm three hundred years old. I've been through all this shit. I thought we had something."

"We do. Can you please just listen?"

"NO!" she yelled. "It was fun, but it's over."

"NO!" I grabbed her.

She pushed me away before I could kiss her. "Get out, or I will scream."

"Just let me…"

"Out!" She pointed at the door.

I couldn't talk to her when she was like this, so I did what she said and left.

I had known that my deeds were going to backfire sooner or later. I just didn't think this would happen. I had been sure that she would hear me out, but I was wrong.

My mind rested then on something else.

If she saw me on that roof, then why the hell didn't she see what I was planning? That Tabitha was just a cover-up.

THIRTEEN

THE NEXT FEW days were shit. There were no other words for it. Irene made me feel like shit. Lucian made that feeling ten times worse.

I had finally gotten my Cammy. Isaac called one day; his number was the first one I paired with. We had another gig in about three weeks.

I told him that I don't know what I would be in three weeks. I told him about the darkness.

He wanted to come over, but I said no.

Not this time.

I put the phone down and didn't speak to anyone. I found myself on Table View mountain a lot. All the shit I'd done lately was just making the crash harder.

Starting a relationship with a much older dragon, not to mention the Viden and one of the school staff... It was fucked up. But I missed her. The beast inside still ached for her.

Over the past few days, I'd written down some words. At first they didn't make much sense, but then they started to form another poem. I called it "Forever Lost."

It was how I felt at this moment. Lost and no matter what I did to get out of it, I just ended up feeling more lost.

Mind, heart and soul.
Should be good, pure as gold.
Darkness free was my forecast.
But because I'm evil, I'm fading fast.
I'm forever lost.
I'll be forever last.

Aw, are we going to cry? The beast mocked me.

"Shut the fuck up!" I replied but its laughter just echoed through my mind.

He was always pushing, always showing me the truth, how it was.

Why should I hold on? To what? If this was my destiny, why not just give in now? Why put myself through all this shit?

❧

I was inside the ring again. The sides of the cage sparkled with electricity.

In front of me stood the Rubicon. He was an ugly motherfucker.

This was it.

I was finally facing him.

We fought. No matter how hard I tried to get the upper

hand, he would just do the unexpected and throw me against the wall. The electricity would jolt through me each time.

It hurt like hell.

My energy drained, but still I refused to quit.

I tried again, failed again, and tried something else. Failed, again, failed, again, failed.

I was at my last breath when he picked me up.

His mouth was wide open, just about to swallow, when he started to laugh. The mocking kind.

"When are you going to get it, boy? I *am* you."

I woke up with a jolt. Sweat dripped off my forehead. I could still hear his laughter echoing. Echoing from deep within.

Lucian was asleep. The entire Academy was asleep. I needed air.

I found myself on Table View again.

There, I roared until my throat felt shredded. I just needed to not feel dead. "Alive" was maybe asking too much. Just... not dead. I need to know I was holding on for something. My life couldn't end like this. I wasn't ready.

I screamed until I couldn't scream anymore.

I knew what I had to do. I knew how to hang on for a little longer.

I took out the Cammy from my pants pocket where they lay crumpled on the ground and punched Phil's number in manually.

"Blakey," Phil's hologram appeared. "You are late."

❧

"BACK BY POPULAR DEMAND!" The emcee yelled. "Hansel Borgendorf."

The crowds cheered. I was in the ring again and this time it wasn't a fucked-up dream.

The Green-Vapor hulked over me like a house. He was huge, but size never scared me. The bell went off and this fight was over faster than a ten-count.

The night was over in a flash. I fought three times. The last dragon was a bit more difficult than the other two and was also a Green-Vapor named Henry. When I finally got hold of his wings, he squealed like a pig.

The sound of flesh tearing, the spilling of guts and blood against the floor, the taste of it against my lips.

My acid burning in between.

Some spectators vomited. It was the most gruesome fight they had ever seen. It was replayed on the big screens endlessly.

I knew that when Samuel phoned again, I would come. Samuel wasn't happy about my taking so long to contact him. If it weren't for that contract, Samuel would've known that I was nobody's pet.

But without Irene, the darkness would come soon enough. I needed this.

I got dressed in the locker room. On my way out, I signed a couple of girls' body parts, shirts, shorts, and pieces of paper adorned with Hansel's face. I climbed into the limo with Samuel, Dimi, and Phil.

We went straight to Sam's house and partied all night.

Phil handed me my cut. It was a packet of Fire-Cain.

"Phil," I looked at him.

"I'm not trying to get you hooked on this, Blake." He came to sit down on the couch. "You know how calm the darkness is when you use. I'm trying to help you hold on."

I nodded.

I didn't want to get hooked either, but he was right. The beast wanted me to fail. It was its plan from the beginning. It had tricked me into doing all sorts of shit so I would think that was what it needed to stay calm. And then it snatched it away.

Using a dirty razor blade from his wallet, Phil neatly cut us each two thin lines on the coffee table in front of us.

"To better times, Blake."

"To better times."

Then we snorted.

·❦·

I CRASHED in one of Sam's guest rooms. When I woke, I couldn't remember much from the night before. My head wanted to explode.

A girl with long, red hair and plenty of curls had caught my eyes. She didn't have one freckle, but there was a huge purple bruise on her shoulder.

A brunette was on my other side; she had a bruised arm. I lifted up the sheet and found a third girl sleeping under the covers.

Three?

Her neck carried the imprint of my hand.

A cold finger rushed up my spine and my stomach turned. I had to get out of this bed, but my head was about to split in two.

The high was one hell of a rush, a rush where I didn't give a shit about who got hurt and who didn't. But the low? The low was bad.

I pushed my legs off the bed and could feel in my muscles that I'd had sex last night. Rough sex. A lot of it.

I closed my eyes. Images jumped in front of my eyelids. Naked bodies everywhere.

What the fuck happened?

I pushed myself up and found my pair of jeans mixed up with leather pants, dresses, and fancy tops. I found my button-down shirt and almost tumbled over. I literally saw double.

The room stopped spinning eventually and I forced myself up and put on my shirt.

I kept glancing at the naked girl's bruises.

I did that.

I was a monster on the high.

I opened the door, my shoes were in my hands and the house was quiet. I had no idea how I was going to get back to the Academy, but I couldn't stay there. I had to get out of this place.

_

I LAY low for the next few weeks.

I felt stupid that I hadn't accepted his offer. Remembering what Samuel said to me in the limo... it was all biting me in the ass right now.

I could've gotten something out of this. I could've saved and maybe bought that beauty in the window of Andy's bike shop. It was the most gorgeous piece I'd ever laid eyes on. Some called them sex on wheels. For me they represented freedom. The more exhilarating the better.

I could've.

I shouldn't think about the what-ifs. They didn't exist. No matter how vivid the dreams were, they would never become real because she didn't exist.

She couldn't.

I pushed the freckled face to the back of my mind when Lucian came in.

He didn't limp anymore. I hated the fact that he had opted not to heal like the rest of the humans did in Paegeia. It was stupid, the way he spoke about the pain, remembering it.

He was never going to tame me.

The nausea was present again but I could handle it slightly better. Thinking of it as a weakness had done the trick. My darkness didn't like weakness. After that, it was easier to get closer to Lucian for short periods of time.

I still barked at him a lot, a conversation style that couldn't be easy for him.

"Hey," he greeted.

I barely looked at him.

He didn't take any notice of it anymore. There wasn't disappointment in his eyes like before and he didn't ponder or huff each time I attempted to ignore him.

He was sort of growing up. Maybe King Helmut had a weighty conversation with him about thinking twice about claiming me.

He was the crown prince of Tith. His future was more important than a thirteen-year-old's promise.

I took a deep breath and my stomach turned slightly. I closed my eyes and make a mental note. *No deep breaths when he is close.* I let it out slowly. Trying to ease the roiling of my stomach.

One could hope that Lucian would break his promise and never try and claim me again.

I went to bed well past midnight. I struggled to sleep. When I woke up the next day, I found a silver envelope on the floor.

Lucian was still sleeping. It could be for him, but it didn't stop me from getting off the bed and picking it up.

My heart flipped as I saw my name on it.

She was summoning me again.

I still felt like a shit for what I'd done to her. I hadn't even spoken to Tabitha since that day.

Master Longwei could've easily forced her to meet with me. I hoped that it wasn't that, but it was possible.

Time crawled. I hated my sweaty palms and lack of concentration. Not that I really had any concentration to begin with, but I felt so wired. I didn't know if it was seeing Irene again or the darkness creeping back.

When the time finally came, I packed up my books and walked out of the classroom before the professor could say anything.

I reached the tower, dreading each step. Why was I so nervous?

It was times like this that I wished I already had my sight—my Moon-Bolt ability. To know what was going to happen.

I reached out to knock on the door.

"Enter," she said before my fist connected with the door.

She always knew. It was scary yet amazing at the same time, how strong her sight was.

I opened the door.

Her eyes immediately found mine and I looked away, back to the door as I closed it.

Please, no more fighting.

Neither of us said a word as I skulked toward the chair.

She grabbed her pipe and lit it. She didn't do that in front of others; the pipe held weed. You could smell it a mile away.

She took a few drags as she took the opposite chair at the table.

My eyes fixed on her.

The smoke blew out in a big white puffs. The smell of weed filled her room, it made the hair on my arms rise as I inhaled.

She put the pipe down and looked at me. "I'm sorry I acted like a little girl." She pinched her nose.

"You okay?" I asked.

"Slight headache." She frowned slightly and looked at me again. "I don't want to fight."

I got up from my chair and sat on top of the table in front of her. I bent down and hugged her. Her hair smelled like strawberries mixed with honey or vanilla. This sweet scent had become one of my favorite smells.

"I'm sorry, too. It was stupid and I thought maybe Master Longwei wouldn't get suspicious if I was with a girl my own age. It meant nothing."

"I got that through the little visions I do catch of you. It's so hard to see where you are going lately."

Why couldn't she see my fate? It didn't make any sense.

"Is it the reason why you are getting the headaches?"

She shrugged. "I have to force it lately."

"Why?"

"I don't know. I guess it's got to do with who you were created for, Blake. Even though your true rider doesn't exist, their blood is attached to yours. They still protect you, like Al used to protect your father. And I guess the more peril your soul is in, the harder it becomes to see."

I nodded. Why was I even trying?

She stroked my arm. Then her hand touched mine and our fingers intertwined.

Silence filled the tower.

Finally, Irene stood up in front of me. I stared at her for a few moments and then our lips touched. The kiss was soft and gentle at first, but soon it turned into something much stronger, a hunger I couldn't ignore.

FOURTEEN

WE SHARED A CIGARETTE AFTERWARD. The beast was satisfied again. Finally.

I couldn't believe how lucky I was to get another chance with Irene. She wasn't the type of woman who gave those out easily. I knew Moon-Bolts, and giving second chances was one of the hardest things for them.

"I need to go." I pushed myself upright. I swung my legs off her bed and grabbed my boxers from the floor by my feet.

As I pulled them on, her hands traced whorls on my back. Her soft lips caressed my skin. Goosebumps flushed over my body.

I smiled.

"You were right about the girl." She was resting on one arm, the linen covering her perfect breasts.

"I don't follow."

"She's a great distraction when it comes to Master Longwei, Blake. We'll need that if you want this relationship to succeed."

What? Was I hearing her correctly? "You want me to see Tabitha?"

She smiled. "Yes, I guess that would make you the luckiest guy under this sun. Having two girls to do whatever you want with."

I chuckled disbelievingly. "You're insane."

"No, I mean it. He cannot know, Blake. If he thinks you're dating the Snow Dragon, it'll be much easier to see one another."

I squinted.

"She's going to expect certain things from me, Irene, if I'm going to pretend to be her boyfriend." I pushed out the hated word.

"Then give it to her. I'm not the jealous type, as long as you promise that you know where you belong."

The beast liked that. She didn't say to whom I belonged; she said where. She wasn't possessive. The fact that this was so forbidden heightened everything times ten.

"Okay, but I swear if you get upset with…"

She lay her finger on my lips and brought her face real close to mine. "I won't fight." She kissed my lips while her finger was still there.

This was so hot. She was hot. I wanted more. I growled as I pushed her on the bed and pinned her down again. My boxers disappeared instantly and in a few seconds, I groaned. Pure euphoria.

I FINALLY MADE my way out of her tower.

Today had been insane. It seemed too good to be true.

Sure, Tabitha was by far the most beautiful girl in school, but not on the school grounds. Irene was way above her.

I entered my room to my Cammy's light flashing. I had like twenty missed calls from Isaac. I listened to the voice-mails. He sounded desperate to get a hold of me. A gig.

I sure could use the money and wouldn't say no to the high of performing, either.

He picked up on the first ring.

"Hey bud, you looking for me?"

"It's a big one, some rich kid's eighteenth at Jimmy's. The theme is vampires and werewolves, some book or movie that's the big thing right now."

"Seriously, vampires?"

"You're a dragon, I'm sure vampires won't be that difficult."

I shook my head.

"Money is really good. What you say?"

"Yeah, sure."

We said goodbye after he gave me the date: this Friday.

৻৶

IT WAS nice to be back with Irene. She made me feel less dark. More worth saving. Friday came fast and before I knew it we were getting ready in the VIP section of Jimmy's club. I knew this pub like the back of my hand, with its booths, small kitchen, the stage, and one mother of a dance floor. We owed a lot to Jimmy; everyone knew us because of him—that and the fact that I was the Rubicon.

"I look like shit," I muttered to Isaac, staring at myself in the mirror. My fangs were fake, my clothes were costume-ish, my hair was teased to ridiculous heights.

"You look like Count Dracula mixed with Elvis," Isaac joked.

"Suck your blood, blah, blah, blah," I joked. The band laughed. "It's time."

We walked out of the VIP room, down the stairs, and onto the stage.

Longbottom's was packed. The banners that hung on the walls all read "Happy Birthday Lee." *It must be nice to have a rich daddy.*

"Are you ready?" My voice boomed over the speakers. They cheered and Isaac counted down with Ty hitting the drums.

The first song burst into life.

We sang about eight, then took a break. My voice wasn't used to full gigs anymore.

It was nice to finally be back with the band.

We downed a few shots to get our throats all nice and warm.

Then a knock came on the VIP door. Ron, one of Jimmy's bouncers, opened it.

"Hi." A guy's voice.

Ron grunted something.

"I'm Lee, the birthday boy. May I please speak to Blake?"

A weird feeling, almost like déjà vu, crept into my gut. I'd heard that voice before, but I don't know where.

He walked in. He had stubble on his chin and ruffed-up hair. He extended a hand to me.

I hesitated. Where did I know him from? My memory was great, but this guy was a walking mystery. Yet I got the feeling that I knew him.

"Do I know you?" I asked.

"I don't think so. This is the first time we've met. I'm Lee. It's my birthday today. Thank you so much for playing, dude."

"Part of the job," I said.

"I was wondering if a few of us could, you know, hang with you guys for a few hours."

"Hang with us?" I repeated.

"Sure," Ty said. "As long as you bring girls."

I looked at Ty and then at Isaac.

"Blake?" Isaac asked.

"Fine, whatever." I took another shot as Isaac chatted with Lee. I knew him from somewhere but I had no idea where. I never forgot a face and this was going to haunt me.

Lee left as our break ended. Time for act two.

❧

I FOUND myself on the back of a yacht. It was a beautiful evening. A warm breeze blew against my face. I felt different. Content, happy... over-the-top happy. Shit, I knew what this was. It was one of those dreams.

She wasn't here though.

I looked around. A party unfolding. I could hear Ty and Isaac's voices, even Lucian's and others I didn't know.

In the corner of my eyes, I caught a figure.

"Blake." Lee looked different.

"You shouldn't have come back. She's doing great without you."

She? Without me? What was he talking about? But dream Blake didn't share these questions; he knew exactly what was going on here.

"And yet she is spending all her time with me." I sounded so cocky even to my own ears.

The dream faded.

I woke up as the sunlight peeked through the curtains. My dreams couldn't be where I knew Lee from. That didn't happen? Did it?

Reality seeped through. Although I didn't see the redhead at all this most recent dream, I felt achingly lonely. My dreams were so messed up.

Still, last night wasn't so bad. After the show, we drank a lot and I ended up crashing at Isaac's.

Missy was sitting next to my bed. I could feel her yellow eyes on me before I even opened mine.

"You know it's rude to watch people sleep. Creepy too."

"I really don't care. You know you're hot, right?"

I chuckled. That was Missy for you. No filter whatsoever. She was intimidating in a good way. If she hadn't been Isaac's sister, it would've been a completely different story.

I got up and asked her to hand me the sweater by her feet.

She picked it up and tossed it at me. "My dad made breakfast. Food's getting cold."

She left as I pulled my arms into the sweater. I stepped into my jeans and went upstairs to the kitchen.

That dream about Lee still occupied my thoughts. For the love of me I couldn't place where I knew him from. Maybe Irene would be able to help.

Isaac and Missy's banter came from the kitchen.

"Good morning Blake," Yuri, Isaac's dad, said.

"Morning, sir."

"Long night, I presume."

"Hard one." My voice cracked.

He laughed as Missy handed me a plate. Isaac was frying eggs. Balancing an egg on the spatula, he walked to where I sat and plopped it onto my plate. "Five more?" he asked and chuckled.

I dished up some bacon, hash browns and sausages. Isaac's dad knew how to serve a mean breakfast. The kind that clogged arteries for sure. The best kind.

We ate as Yuri kept throwing around topics. Only then did I realize how long ago we'd actually talked.

I missed my father. He hadn't been one for a long time. Would this wedge between us ever disappear?

We finished, washed up, and went back down to Isaac's room.

He picked up his guitar and strummed it. I smiled. He always played—didn't matter if it was for fun or for a gig, Isaac always had a guitar in his hands.

He was born to play.

He fell onto a beanbag with the guitar still secure in his arms. "So, have you thought about an album for 'Never-Breath'?"

I looked at the floor. "Inspiration is dry, Isaac. We have the single. It should do great for a while, don't you think?"

"The people want an album, Blake. We've got three great deals if we can just whip up ten more songs."

"Whip up? You make it sound as if I just have to drink water, pore over a dictionary, and *voila*! You have ten new songs."

Isaac laughed. "Think about it. That's all I want. We need at least one more album, dude."

Need. Before what? I got what he was saying, though. Before I became dark.

"Fine, I'll think about more songs. Speaking of, I actually do have the beginnings of one. It's called 'Forever Last.' I only have a few verses, but if you want to hear it…"

His eyes lit up. "Fuck, sure. Hit me."

I closed my eyes as I tried to arrange my memory to the words I'd written in my journal.

Mind, heart, and soul.
Should be good, pure as gold.
Darkness free was my forecast.
Because I'm evil, I'm fading fast.
I'm forever lost.
I'll be forever last.

We jammed all morning. Around noon, I left Isaac to tinker with the song. He was in seventh heaven.

Music was his life.

It used to be mine too, but too much bad shit had replaced it.

I could only imagine what he would think if he knew the truth. How would he look at me if he knew I was a killer? A druggie? I didn't want to think about it.

I reached the Academy just before nightfall.

I hated the elevators. They were unnatural. I'd taken them once when I was younger and said never again. I'd felt off balance for almost two weeks after. If I really thought about the way they transported people, sure it was magic, but mixed with science too. Science that broke a body up in code, like sending an email, and rebuilt the code on the other side. But the rebuild had its flaws too.

So now, I trusted only the things I could see and feel: my wings.

TABITHA FOUND me in the cafeteria.

I suddenly remembered what Irene said.

"May I?" she asked.

"Sure, it's a free world—if you don't count the Wall."

She smiled. "Getting technical again?"

I gave her a lopsided grin.

"So..." She set her tray filled with salad and steamed fish on the table. "Are you done ignoring me?"

"Ignoring you?" I frowned.

"Yeah, you always do it right after we have sex."

I felt... not bad. It was weird. "Sorry," I lied. "I've been a bit occupied lately."

"Does it have to do with my brother?"

I shook my head. "No, it's me and my shit."

"Blake, you don't have that much shit. But you have something else that is irresistible to a Snow Dragon, that much I know. My mind screams that I should just back off. It even fights with me now." She pulled a face that made me laugh. "But I can't. There's just something about you I can't stay away from."

I always knew that she was a bit pathetic, but she'd never been this open with me before.

"So that's why I keep coming back." She started eating.

She was a suitable cover-up. "I'm no good for you, Tabitha."

"Nobody is good for anyone." She shook her head and scooped another forkful of leafy greens into her mouth.

I huffed. "Okay, but don't say I didn't warn you."

She stared at me wordlessly for a minute. "What?"

I shrugged. "I can't seem to lose you, so I'm giving in, if that's what you want."

She smiled. "I have to think about it first. Having you as a boyfriend does have more disadvantages than perks, so you don't mind, do you?" There was that joke in her voice.

"Not at all. I'm not going anywhere."

"That's good to know. Cause I'm not going anywhere either."

I smiled. At least the cover-up was done. It was easier than I thought it would be.

FIFTEEN

IT WAS hard to get used to Tabitha. I constantly had to remind myself why I was doing this. She was just a cover-up so Irene and I could keep our secret.

But I didn't like how everyone twittered that the Snow Dragon had finally tamed the Rubicon. It was working on my nerves. And the guys didn't help.

"Dude, you seriously settling for the Snow Queen?" George asked.

We were playing a preorder game. Perks of being the Rubicon: if a gamer could get an endorsement from me, they made a lot of money. So most of the programmers who had games releasing soon sent me the first copy.

George was a gaming whiz. If he could play something for more than a day, it was a good game. If not, we tossed it.

"I just go with the flow. I can't seem to get rid of her, so…"

"That's your reason?" George didn't buy it.

"Okay fine, she fucks like a wildling. That better?"

"Much," he smiled.

Our fingers were proclaiming war as the game's intensity ratcheted up.

"It's not bad. Better than the other one." George changed the subject, for which I was grateful.

He winked lewdly. "Still, she couldn't be a better fuck then Ashley."

"Ashley who?" I asked.

"Seriously? She's a fifth year."

"Fifth year?" My eyebrows climbed.

"She's hot too. You'd never say it."

"So, you and this Ashley?"

"Don't," he said. "No bitch will tame me."

"Oh, excuse me." I tried to sound unimpressed about that last statement, that his words didn't bother me as much as they had, but they did.

When he finally left, I felt irritated with George. I knew what was going to happen. I was going to track down Ashley and find out if the rumors were true.

&.

"HOLY FUCK," she moaned in my ear as we both came to climax.

She turned out to be a dragon too. Huge bonus points; she wouldn't get pregnant in her human form, and because of my awesome healing ability, STD's and other sickness weren't a concern, so no condoms required.

I bit my lip. George had no idea what a great fuck was.

Ashley was just easy, nothing more. Her brown hair and dark eyes glinted. I let go of her, scooted away, and zipped up my trousers.

"You are one heck of a dragon. Pity they only make one of you."

I smiled.

"Great sense of humor too. I guess I was wrong about that."

"Oh, I'm sure you're wrong about plenty of things."

She gave me her panties and put them in my pocket. "Don't forget me, Rubicon."

The library would never be the same again.

I shook my thoughts away. Irene would probably be furious. I'd used my shield, in case it had any effect on her sight. Hardly heard it this time. I didn't even think Ashley heard it.

I was getting really good.

I sauntered out of the library a few minutes after Ashley and went straight to my room.

⚜

RUMORS SPREAD fast and within two days, everyone knew that Ashley and I had sex in the library.

She found me in my room after she heard. "Is this true?" Tabitha yelled.

"Would you keep your fucking voice down?" I asked through gritted teeth but she kept shrieking like a banshee.

"Just answer me!"

I rolled my eyes. "Is what true, Tabitha?"

"Did you have sex with Ashley in the library?"

I shook my head in annoyance.

"Answer me!" she yelled again.

"You are not my mother!" I yelled back without looking at her.

"You are a fucking asshole, Blake." Her voice broke. Part me felt a tiny bit sorry for her.

GETTING AROUND IRENE, however, wasn't so easy.

"Why?" Irene asked. Hurt shone in her eyes.

"She doesn't mean a thing to me." My hands itched to cup her face; my lips wanted to kiss her.

"Don't touch me." She pushed me away.

"Irene, c'mon." Frustration built in me.

"Why do you do that, why do you keep on doing it?"

"I don't know, okay? It's what the beast wants."

She narrowed her eyes. "What the beast wants?"

I fixated on the ceiling for a moment. "I know it sounds stupid, but if I don't think of it as a separate entity from myself, I'll lose my mind. It's the only way not to give in." My eyesight blurred. I wiped my face hard with the palms of my hands.

I hated this sign of weakness, but it happened every time

I hurt someone I cared for. "I'm sorry. I don't know how else to hold on."

Her arms wrapped around me. "It's okay," she whispered close to my cheek. "I don't want to fight with you, but you have to tell me when something like that happens. I'm more understanding then you think, Blake. I'm not twenty years old anymore, darling." She forced me to meet her eyes.

"We'll deal with your darkness together, okay?"

I nodded and it seemed as if I was out of the doghouse.

The sex was amazing as always. I drifted away to another dimension of pleasure. Irene was one heck of a lover. I could just love her forever.

She lay in my arms afterward as we both took turns dragging on her pipe. It didn't soothe the darkness as much as the Fire-Cain did, but it was settling nicely.

"You have to go. I see Cheng in thirty minutes."

"Cheng, the geek?"

"Yes, he's actually one of the few dragons whose futures I see clearly. Lately he's showing things that I don't understand."

"What things?"

"I'm not allowed to share them, Blake. Unless they end up in the Book of Shadows. You know the rules." She smiled. "But I've got a feeling that somehow they are linked to you."

"What?" Did I hear her right?

"I don't understand yet what I'm seeing. My vision

works strangely. What I say doesn't have anything to do with what I see. And somehow the two are connected."

"So what do you see?"

"Blake?"

"I'm not referring to Cheng. Use me. When you speak mumbo jumbo, what do you see?"

"With you, it's only darkness. It scares me at times. I feel suffocated. Defeated."

I didn't like it. I was going to turn dark and there was nothing I could do to stop it.

She touched my cheek. "I know it sounds scary, but don't give up. I'm not. Someone will claim you in the end, Blake."

"You've seen it? Or is it something you hope for?"

"Hope is sometimes much stronger than what I see. Wars have been won with only hope."

"Yeah, sure." I blew out a gust of air and rooted around for my boxers under the covers.

"Don't lose hope, Blake. You can't, you hear me?"

I didn't reply, just dressed, kissed her on the cheek, and left.

She saw darkness. That was it.

I was a goner.

෧

FOR THE NEXT few days it was all I could think about.

The darkness Irene saw.

When it was going to happen, I had no idea. That was worse than knowing it would happen.

I wanted more time, and I didn't know how much was still left.

I didn't want to destroy my world. I didn't want to kill everyone I loved. I didn't want to want to belong to *him*.

Goran. The source of evil himself.

Why had his dragon ever given him her essence? My dad didn't speak much about that time, but I remembered.

She had been a Swallow Annex. He was a frost wielder. That time nobody knew about the bonds or Dents. Sarafina was her name and she'd just perished from a poisoned arrow that had struck her during flight.

Goran was broken for months, she'd given him her essence. I was unclear about what the procedure was, but I doubted I would give my essence to anyone.

Not even Lucian.

It wasn't normal for the human race to grow that old. Sure, in biblical times they had, but only because dragons still roamed on their side. Before the Wall and before the wars.

The Metallics just loved helping humans.

They were so stupid.

"Blake?" Tabitha's voice broke through my string of concerns. I was in the cafeteria having lunch, or actually, ignoring my lunch.

"What?" I snapped at her.

"May I have a word?"

"Tabitha, I don't think it's going to…"

"Just hear me out before you think that." She put an emphasis on the word *that*.

Snow Dragons. Pathetic. "Fine, what do you want?"

She looked at Brian and George, who were sitting around the table.

"In private, please," she murmured.

Brian got up first. "Whatever the Snow Queen wants, Brian shall give." He mimicked a stupid bow and grabbed George by the collar, literally pulling him off his chair too.

"Why do we always have to leave?" I knew he was still pissed off about the Ashley thing, but if he thought I was going to leave, he had another thing coming.

I watched both figures retreat to the other side of the cafeteria and plunge down at another table.

"What do you want, Tabitha?"

"I want you to stop fucking other girls. Am I not enough?" Tears glistened in her eyes.

"Don't cry. We were never an item. It is what it is, Tabitha. I need certain things and I don't always want them from you. I mean, where is the fun in that?"

She shook her head. "Fun. Is that all this is to you, fun?"

"Don't start. If you can't handle it, then stop. Stop trying to get whatever it is you think you'll get from me, cause I promise you, I'm not that kind of dragon."

She didn't say anything, just shook her head, wiped her face, and got up. "You do know that I'm crazy in love with you, right?"

"Tabitha," I sat back into the pillow that served as my chair. "I don't…"

"Stop saying that you don't care or you don't feel the same way. Loving and caring for someone doesn't make you weak, Blake—it gives you a reason to hold on, to fight. And if you can't see it that way, then you're weak."

She spat that word, and I actually flinched as if it was spittle. She stalked away.

I grunted. For the rest of the day, her words haunted me.

I didn't want to pull more people in. I didn't want so many to get hurt when things went south. I wanted as few casualties as possible.

But Tabitha refused to give up.

Later that night, as I lay in bed, I stroked my face hard. Lucian was already fast asleep.

Pondering all these things today had drained me. Yet I didn't feel tired. I felt wired, frustrated.

I was actually looking forward to another fight.

SIXTEEN

"HANSEL! HANSEL! HANSEL!"

The crowd cheered my name. Technically not my name, but who I was at the moment.

A Green-Vapor named Patrick was filling the cage full of chlorine gas.

I held my breath. The chlorine did no harm, but I pretended it was a bitch. My eyes watered slightly because of the gas, but that was about it. Phil threw me a fake mask and I pulled it over my face.

I stopped pretending when the prop was on my face. It was time. Time for the Green-Vapor to stop breathing altogether. I leapt and found myself at the end of one of his wings. I ran up toward his back and grabbed hold of his mane. Acid poured from my hands. Acid they thought belonged to my dragon.

Dimi was in fact hiding my true appearance with his dark incantations. Nobody even saw his lips move.

I could feel the magic holding who I was in place.

Kiiiillllll, the beast rejoiced inside me.

The acid ran over the fin-like mane on his head and he shrieked.

The sounds coming from him were deafening. They seeped deep into my soul. This wasn't going to be like the others. Jeff, one of the guys at Dragonia, was a Green-Vapor, for crying out loud.

I could just as well kill him too.

Kill! the beast roared again. My acid ran stronger.

I tore his mane. The sight through the mask was as gruesome as it was without. Nothing was hidden. Blood spilled from his neck where his mane had been.

Nausea crept into my gut.

Kill him now, you idiot! the beast roared.

My hands, dripping with acid, traced his wings. Balls and balls of acid.

He tried to grab me with his claws and teeth, but they just snapped at air.

I was way too fast for him in my human form, and he wouldn't have stood a chance in my true form.

The sound of his wings being incinerated from his body would become my new nightmare.

It was that deep, tearing through flesh sound.

I lost it.

I couldn't contain it anymore. For a few seconds, I went crazy. Acid mixed with blood and guts spilled onto the floor. I slipped and fell, but it didn't matter. It was over.

The Green-Vapor was no more.

"Hansel! Hansel! Hansel!" the crowd chanted. It did

something to me. The sound of their voices. I screamed and lifted my arms in victory.

I was a monster, killing my own kind.

Killing Patrick was the last fight for the weekend.

The prize was once again my stash: Fire-Cain.

Phil hesitated. "I know my sister can be a pain in the ass sometimes, Blake, but she does care about you."

I stared at him. He was *not* giving me relationship advice.

"Treat her nice."

I didn't say anything. The beast was satisfied. He loved Phil and all his schemes that fed my darkness.

I hated every single damn thing that came out of his mouth.

I wasn't hers to begin with.

I was nobody's.

Not even Irene's.

I took my stash as Dimi approached.

"Samuel wants to see you."

Samuel. That sadistic fucker. I couldn't protest, even though I wanted to, because of that stupid contract. He could have my balls on a plate if I didn't do what he said. I hated being tied to someone. It wasn't who I was, what I was built for. The magic that he had over me compelled me to follow Dimitri to the locker rooms. If I didn't, he would force me. The grip he had on me was tight. Real tight.

I changed quickly. Getting to the limo was a mission. Everyone clamored for my attention, an autograph, a stolen kiss, a gleeful embrace. I liked the attention; it wasn't as overpowering as the Rubicon's.

The limo finally came into sight. Dimi opened the door. I waved before climbing in.

Inside, Samuel was staring out of the window. I'd learned the hard way not to speak or show any signs of life when he went silent like this.

The limo purred away.

"Why did you take so long?" Samuel asked.

I didn't understand the question.

"Answer me, Blake."

"I don't know. Maybe fighting isn't as easy as you think."

"Next time keep under half an hour. I thought that you might lose this time. Don't play with my money like that, Blake. If you die, nobody will protect your family."

I ground my teeth. I'd kill him myself if he ever tried.

"Do you understand?" His hands encircled my neck and jerked me to face him, inches away, his breath hot on my chin. He slapped me hard on the cheek. "I've got way too much money on this, boy. Don't fuck with me. You hear?"

I nodded. As pathetic as it was, these were the beast's friends. This was where he wanted me to be, even if I didn't agree.

He took something out of his pocket and threw it at me. It was a small packet of bills.

I look at him, uncomprehending.

"For next time. To kill them faster."

I thumbed the money.

He spoke in Spanish to the driver and nodded at Dimi. The limo stopped in the middle of nowhere as I felt Dimi's magic slowly evaporating.

"Get out."

I gaped at Samuel.

"Out, boy!" he shouted.

I had no choice but to get out and watch him shut the door behind me. The limo drove away.

I gritted my teeth as the real me returned. The Rubicon was at peace. I stretched out my arms and pushed myself up into the air.

I'd never felt so pathetic in my life.

⁊

"BLAKE?" my mother said. "Where did you get this money?"

"Does it matter? Just take it."

She gave me that look. The one filled with concern and fear.

"Don't worry. I didn't steal it, if that is what you're afraid of."

She flung her arms around me. "You know I'm grateful, right?"

"Yeah, I know." I kissed her on the head.

"Your father is just…"

"Don't make excuses for him, Mom. He should know better."

She nodded. "You don't know what it's like for him. He had everything…"

"He still has us! Look what he is doing. I don't want to hear how he lost everything. It was almost fifteen years ago. He should get over it and move on."

"Please!" She raised her voice. "I don't want to fight."

"Then stop defending him." I looked around. "Where is he anyway?"

"He took Samantha to Warbel practice at the club. He is trying, Blake."

I hope it sticks this time. I really did.

"You aren't staying?"

"No, I have other arrangements," I said and saw the disappointment on her face. I hugged my mom.

"I miss you."

"I know you do. I just cannot deal with him right now. I've gotta go. I'll speak to you soon."

She nodded. "You still here?" She was referring to the darkness.

"I'm still here, Mom." *For now.*

I walked out the front door.

I was glad Samantha wasn't there. She would find a way to convince me to stay.

I took to the sky again and flew back to the Academy. All the while, fears chased me like ghosts. Images of my mother finding out what I'd done to get that money haunted me.

Was I still here? Was I truly trying to hold on, or was I starting to give in?

I hoped I didn't exist when my mother discovered the truth about who I really was.

᪥

I WAS in the ring again. Patrick the Green-Vapor was overpowering me.

"I know it's you, Rubicon."

He was stronger.

He ripped at my arm. The screams were deafening. I didn't know how this fight could've gone so wrong so quickly.

I killed him. I knew I had. But somehow here he was. Beating me. Calling me out.

"You are a monster, Blake Leaf!" he kept yelling.

I grew smaller and smaller as the crowd chanted, "Monster! Monster! Monster!"

The words took the shape of an invisible force and it started to grip my neck. Suffocating me. I couldn't breathe.

"Monster! Monster! Monster...."

I shot upright in bed, panting heavily.

For a few seconds, I tried to get the invisible grip around my neck to loosen until I realized I was in my own room.

Reality dawned on me. What I had done, truly had done.

Bile rose in my throat. I ran to the bathroom and barely made it to the toilet. I barfed.

Thank God Lucian wasn't here. He'd gone home like he always did on weekends.

I could still hear Patrick's screams, still smell his insides spilled all over the floor, hear his flesh incinerating and ripping from his body.

I couldn't deal with this, not now.

I grabbed the bag of Fire-Cain that Phil had given me and poured a bit onto the palm of my hand, snorting it up. It burned my nostrils and set my brain on fire. It only lasted for a few seconds. Then, everything changed, the world fuzzy and clouded.

The high was everything I ever needed. It felt good to be free. To not feel or care or hear anything I didn't want to hear.

I was at peace.

And that was how I wanted it to be.

❧

THE NEXT FEW WEEKS, I dreamed about Patrick every night.

I didn't dream that he broke me anymore. My mind was too strong and even in dreams I knew the truth. I dreamed about the horrible deeds that had actually happened. Which were worse.

"Blake what is going on with you?" Lucian asked one morning. "Who is Patrick?"

"Leave me alone," I mumbled and stalked out the door.

Irene asked me who Patrick was, too. Apparently I cried out his name in my sleep. I lied to her, told her it was an old friend who'd died a long time ago. Whether she believed me or not, I didn't know. It wasn't as if she could see my future anyway. All she saw was darkness upon darkness.

I tried to deal with it as best as I could. I didn't want to fight anymore and I was literally counting the days until my contract ended.

❧

THEN ONE NIGHT SOMETHING ELSE, something totally different, happened.

I found myself standing in the ring. A different kind of ring. The Colosseum.

The crowds were chanting. I looked at each spectator. They all took Lucian's form. Every single one of them was Lucian. Icy fingers of fear snatched my spine, immobilized me.

The earth vibrated. I felt it underneath my feet. I couldn't shift. I tried, but my true form just didn't want to come.

Wake up, Blake.

Nothing happened.

I choked and gasped for air.

I wanted to run. I never ran. I was no coward. But whatever was making the earth vibrate was big—and unfriendly.

I couldn't get away. My feet became lead. They didn't want to move.

Lucian, every single one of him, pointed in my direction. Then everything just stopped. There was no more vibration, no sound. Just all the Lucians pointing at me and the sickening taste of silence.

The gate of the Colosseum creaked open. A drum beat rose, a tattoo of terror. It grew louder and louder until I realized what it was.

Not a drum.

When it came out, I had to cover my eyes as the sun reflected off armor. A thousand knights, all of them were wearing platinum—no, white, pure white—armor.

They marched to the same beat. Toward me.

A thousand knights couldn't claim me. It was against dragon law.

I finally shifted but I wasn't as big as I accustomed to being. In fact, the closer the knights came, the smaller I grew.

No, this wasn't right.

No.

No.

No! I woke up.

My breath was rapid.

Why the fuck did I just dream that?

"It's just a dream, Blake." Lucian was at my side.

His hand touched my shoulder. "Just a dream."

SEVENTEEN

THE DREAM about knights claiming me haunted my subconscious for the next few days.

Irene was incapable of discerning its significance. It couldn't be about my future. Lucian wasn't the white knight; he was in the crowd, pointing. Who or what represented the white knight? Goran? He was everything but light. He was evil and should be dark in the dream, but he was also the only one strong enough to be able to handle me when I turned.

No matter how hard I tried to figure this one out, all roads led to the one thing I didn't want: a rider.

I didn't care how brave or how worthy of me they were, I wasn't one of those dragons who could belong to someone.

The redhead popped into my mind again. Why did I dream about her, my Never-Breath? Why? It all started with her occupying my dreams.

I MET Isaac and the band on Friday for rehearsal. We'd put a few songs together and were tinkering with the rest. Getting another album out there might not be such a bad thing. We could record it during our summer break that was coming up soon.

We practiced "Forever Last," and Isaac's additions brought it to life.

The "Never-Breath" single had been performing great on the charts. Royalties from its sales went straight to Mom.

Hearing my mother telling me that he took my sister to Warbel practice made me wonder. Maybe he was really different this time.

Singing "Never-Breath" at practice added more pressure instead of lessening the darkness. The song was just for her. The girl who didn't exist, that would never exist.

I was an emotional wreck by the fourth time. I threw the mic to the ground, causing a shrill feedback loop that made the band members clap their hands over their ears.

"Blake!" Isaac yelled.

I ignored him. I needed to get away.

"Is he okay?" I heard Ty ask as I stripped and took flight.

"Just let him go. He'll be fine," I heard Isaac say before I was gone, headed to my mountain.

I screamed a lot that night.

I was so frustrated.

Frustrated about my past, frustrated with *what-ifs*, frustrated that I couldn't be normal no matter how hard I tried.

There would always be a dark underline in my life. Even if Lucian claimed me, which he wouldn't... I would always be dark.

I needed to make peace with it, but for some reason I still held on.

That night I dreamt again about the knights; they seemed to multiply and the fear became more real with each repetition.

I woke with a startle again and used. I had no choice. Nobody was here to calm my soul. To tell me it was just a dream.

Or maybe it was just an excuse.

Maybe I was already too addicted that I was going to find excuses now to use whenever I could. My worst fear just became reality. I was an addict.

⚜

A RAMPAGE of killing went on during the high. Everything the beast wanted. The human was gone, drugged out of his mind. No protesting, just giving the beast free range to do as he pleased.

Was it my imagination? Hallucinations? I couldn't be sure. But it haunt me on the lows.

The only thing I did feel on the lows was a mother of a headache and utter loneliness. Loneliness that made it hard to breathe.

I felt someone tapping on the floor. A hollow sound. *Tap, tap, tap*, fast.

Then I felt a tug against my cheek. It became harder, faster, until I realized that the tapping wasn't on the floor. Someone was hitting my face.

My eyes opened. The headache threatened to split my head in two. A body hovered over me.

It wasn't Tabitha, the smell was masculine.

Lucian. He was back. "Fuck, Blake. What the hell?" It felt as if he was screaming into my ears.

I saw the bag of Fire-Cain in his hand. He emptied the packet over the toilet. My reflexes were too slow.

"Are you insane!" I roared at him. "I NEED THAT!"

"You need that? You fucking need that?" Lucian wasn't much for cussing. No, he was too good for that. He flushed the toilet, face bright red.

"You need help."

"No, I need to stay sane. This was helping me."

"It's Fire-Cain, Blake. It's a drug that will put you into the ground faster than the darkness."

"Fuck you! You have no idea what it's like!" I yelled at him. "To have this darkness…" I chose my words with care. I didn't want to sound like a loon. I tapped my temple hard. "Stuck inside of you; wanting you to do shit you don't want to, and if you don't, it would kill everything you love."

His eyes were hard. Anger rolled off him in waves. "Fire-Cain was never the plan, Blake."

"The plan changed a long time ago, Lucian. You are the

only one who doesn't seem to be getting that."

"I'm working my ass off to claim you."

"You're wasting your fucking time. You aren't the royal fated to claim me!" I screamed. When would this idiot get it?

"I don't fucking care. You will not use again. Otherwise I will go to the authorities."

"Authorities? Are you threatening me?" I grabbed his collar.

He pushed back hard. "I will do whatever it takes to keep the Rubicon sane."

"Is that what blood brothers do? You would betray me?" The beast inside was furious. Furious with his fucking skinny ass thinking he could just snap his little fingers and get what he wanted.

"Blake, stop this," he said.

My fist connected hard with his jaw. The second punch was air as he rolled out of the way and then dove into me. I crashed with him on top of me.

"You want to use fists?" He knocked one out of the park. His blow burned on my face.

Another blow. My teeth scraped against the inside of my lip and I spat blood. My fist connected hard with his and he toppled to the ground. I got up and my foot connected hard with his stomach.

A pair of arms grabbed me from behind.

I growled at whoever was holding me back.

"Calm down, Blake," George said.

I pushed forward again but another pair of hands yanked me back.

Brian. "Dude, Brian doesn't approve. He is royalty."

"Brian," Lucian grunted still on all fours. "Shut the fuck up." He lunged, but Brian let go and took the blow instead.

"Calm down, both of you!" Brian yelled. No longer speaking in third person.

"Blake, snap out of it. That is *Lucian*."

I spat blood on the floor.

Blood poured out of Lucian's nose.

"I'll see you in the ring soon," Lucian grunted and walked out of the room, shoulders straight, chin high.

"Seriously, dude," George said. "You will fucking kill him."

"Get the fuck out of my room!" I yelled.

When they didn't move, I was tempted to beat the living crap out of them too. I decided it was best to go myself. I jumped out of the window and allowed my wings to take shape.

Calm down, Blake. Calm down. I repeated to myself.

That wasn't the beast who had gone off on him.

It had been the human. That was me.

&.

SUMMER ARRIVED, slow and sticky and hot.

Lucian and I hadn't spoken after the that last fight.

He trained every second he could with Mia in the

Parthenon and at night he crashed wordlessly into bed.

I hated him so much for trying.

I didn't want to think about the brotherhood we'd shared so long ago, about the blood promise he'd made. I was going to be the death of him. That I did know.

I wanted to spend the summer at Dragonia, but I was forced to go home.

The first day wasn't easy. My father was always there. We didn't speak much. I didn't even want to look at him. He was a coward, even if he didn't remember any of that. The old Sir Robert would never hide behind his family.

My mother often tried to get some sort of a conversation going around the table, but the minute my plate was finished, I would get up and leave.

I found myself in the park numerous times, sitting in the swings.

When it got dark and late, I would work on my songs. Sometimes a few sentences would pop up; other days I would sit for hours hearing nothing.

The tabloids were filled with Lucian and Arianna one morning.

Arianna was the Princess of Areeth. She wasn't what I thought of as beautiful. Not that she was ugly or anything; she was a looker in her own messed-up way. She had long strawberry curls flowing down her back and an oval face. I never cared for her or her family. Not the way I cared for Lucian.

Their budding relationship had been arranged from day

one. I wondered if he really loved her or if he was just giving his father what he demanded. Being a good son.

I couldn't identify with that.

The kingdoms wanted one ruler for Paegeia again. And this was their way. So sixteenth-century. I actually felt bad for the guy.

"So they're, like, an item now?" my sister asked over her orange juice, fluttering a newspaper over her eggs.

"I think it's lovely," Mom said. "They fit together."

"Fit together? Mom, it's Arianna."

"She is still your princess, Sammy."

"I don't know. Lucian is too good for her. He always has been."

"Do we really need to listen to this now? It's so not our department," my father said, pointing at me and him. He smiled.

I tried. I really tried to see what my mom and sister did, but it was so hard, remembering the bad.

"You need to get ready, sweetheart. Warbel tryouts don't wait for anyone."

"I'll take you," I said and got up.

"Seriously?!" Sammy sounded excited.

"Seriously," I mocked her, making my voice deeper and raising my eyebrows softly.

She clapped her hands and jumped up. "Let me go get my bag."

She ran up the stairs and I found my mother smiling after her. She kissed my head and took my plate.

My father got up and left the room.

"He's trying, Blake."

"Don't push this. We'll make peace when we do, okay?"

She nodded with a faint smile. I was worried about her speaking of the trying part. What did Samuel took away and what did he leave behind.

"Let's go!"

Sammy babbled all the way to the crevice. It was the only place big enough for Warbel practice.

I would have given anything to be on a team. But the Council refused. Being the Rubicon wasn't always all it was cracked out to be.

I watched Samantha play. She was fast, but her reflexes were slow.

I knew the coach. He'd played professionally and was on Blaze's team. She'd tried to get me on their team but it was no use.

She offered Lucian a spot, too, but he'd refused it because of another stupid promise; that one day we would both play on the same team. He tried to pull strings for me, to no avail.

Maybe I should have asked Arianna; her father was one of the asses who kept denying my request. She was going to attend Dragonia next year, and I was sure that she would be in our room often now that she and Lucian were a couple.

Finally the three-week break was over and the new year started. Everyone made a fuss about the Princess of Areeth finally starting at Dragonia Academy.

There were so many cameras, I wanted to fly away. I hated the press. They always showed up at the most annoying times for their pictures.

"Blake!" Some of them ran in my direction. I put my shades on my face and my hand in their lenses.

"Tell us, how does it feel to know that the Princess of Areeth is going to try and claim you?"

I stopped. Turned and stared at the woman asking the question. I laughed. "She what?"

More rapid-fire questions about Arianna and me. I walked away, laughing and shaking my head.

Lucian didn't stand a chance, and there was no way in hell Arianna Kingsley was going to tame me either.

❧

I SNUCK up to the tower later that night. I missed Irene. I had to see her.

She opened the door as I was still climbing up the stairs and then suddenly she was in my arms. Our lips met greedily. Grunts came from deep within. I was hungry, hungry for her, hungry to be inside of her. I was starving.

I kicked the door shut and took her right there on the floor.

Her nails dented deep in my skin as I pounded her hard. The sounds from her lips were music to my ears. I could fuck Irene forever and ever. It would never get boring.

We ended up on her bed sharing her pipe.

"She could easily claim you, Blake."

"It's Arianna, for crying out loud."

"You have no idea who she is. You don't know her fears. You don't know anything. Lucian is another story. Him you still know."

I got what she was saying. I don't know Arianna and I had no idea what she needed to hear to back off. "What do you suggest?"

"I shouldn't even think this, but she isn't worthy of you."

I liked the way she said it.

"It's not a jealousy thing. I would give anything for someone to claim you, but that girl…" She huffed.

"Yeah, my sister isn't fond of her, either."

"Discover her fears."

I chuckled. "Believe me, she wouldn't tell me, not this close to a claiming. She is a fashion doll, but not stupid."

She traced a lazy circle around my hardening nipple. "Not what I meant. There's something about you. I don't know if it's the Green-Vapor coming out."

I frowned. The ability had finally come during Summer and it was strong. If I wasn't the Rubicon, the I would've been a Green-Vapor.

"People tend to spill things around you they normally wouldn't. You'd be surprised at what she might tell you."

"Tell me?" I didn't follow where Irene was going with this.

"In bed."

My eyebrows rose. "You want me to sleep with Arianna? She's with Lucian."

"Blake, like you said. You are the Rubicon. You'll need to do whatever it is to not get claimed.

I was speechless. "You're serious."

"It's the only way she will spill her worst fears. They used the tactic a lot during war."

"I can't do that to Lucian."

"Why? Because he's such a great friend to you? He *used* to be. It's over. You need to think about yourself now. Do you want Arianna to be your rider?"

"No," I said, way too fast.

"Then do this."

"And you're okay with this?"

She touched my cheek and it was as if her touch just put everything into perspective. "I only care for you."

I nodded and gave her another kiss. It lead to another wild session, after which I literally passed out in her arms. Sleeping in Irene's bed was always blissful. No dreams came, no nightmares, no knights, no redheaded girls. Just serenity.

❧

THE ANNOUNCEMENT of the ridiculous claiming came over the school PA system the next Thursday.

I couldn't help but laugh.

"Something funny, Blake?" Sir Edward asked.

"Yes, Arianna does *not* have what it takes to claim me."

He nodded. "And you think her trying is hilarious?"

"Come on, Eddie, seriously. It's Arianna. The fashion princess."

"Just think how hilarious it would be if that fashion princess became your rider."

Students sniggered. I shook my head. This was a ridiculous claim. I didn't care what they said.

I found Lucian in our room doing some homework. I felt bad about what Irene had suggested, but the beast was enthralled.

"You should tell your girlfriend she is going to get hurt. It is not too late to take back her claiming."

Lucian laughed. "Oh, I told her that many times. But Arianna has a strong mind. She's not far from believing what I do. One of us will claim you. That is a promise."

I laughed. "You don't know what you're talking about. None of you do. Don't say I didn't warn you, Lucian."

🐚

LATER, I found the two lovebirds in the cafeteria.

They couldn't keep their hands off one another.

I shouldn't do this. *It's Arianna.* She wouldn't have what it took anyway. But Irene's words kept pounding in my mind.

What if she found a way to get the upper hand? I

couldn't show her hell, or whatever her fears were, because I didn't know.

It was the only way to get it out of Arianna.

§

THE NEXT DAY I found her having breakfast with some other girls.

I plunged down on the pillow opposite to her.

I met her eyes and held them in my gaze.

"What do you want, Blake?"

"Oh, you know. Just getting acquainted a bit, Arianna. If you're going to be my rider, I need to know a few things about you first."

She gloated. Of course she would. "Like what?"

"I don't know... what you like, what you don't like, that type of thing?" My voice was as sweet as honey.

She blushed but flirted back. "Well, knowing someone that intimately, Blake, takes time. Patience is the key. I'll show you everything in due time."

"Is that a promise?" I flirted.

"You bet," she said.

I got up and left.

This was going to be easy. Arianna didn't give a crap about Lucian. I would do him a huge favor.

§

"WHAT'S YOUR WORST FEAR?" I whispered in her ear as I slid in and out of her slowly.

Getting Arianna to follow me all the way to the library wasn't hard. It was actually the opposite. Less than two days and she was eating out of my palm.

She wasn't a virgin, but she wasn't an experienced lover, either. She was lazy.

"Being naked," she whispered back through deep breaths. "Scorpions, spiders," she laughed. "Being poor. Being a nobody. I need to claim you. You are mine."

She started to get rough, and so did I.

She didn't have what it took. Not one bit. She was shallow. Her possessions were what she feared losing, her status. Not the ones she loved—or pretended to love.

I finished and kissed her one more time as I buckled up my trousers. I had to wear a condom this time because she was human. She could get pregnant and that was the last thing I wanted. "I'll see you in the ring."

She chuckled. "You bet your sexy ass."

"Oh and another thing," I said before I left. "I'm a very jealous dragon."

She narrowed her eyes. She'd get it. Hopefully she would tell Lucian the truth.

I actually felt sorry for her. She was going to learn the hard way just how dark and twisted the Rubicon was.

I went back to Irene. I used her shower to get rid of Arianna's scent, which still clung to me.

"It's done, what is her fear?" Irene asked near the bathroom door.

"She's shallow. It's her possessions. Scorpions, spiders. But the first is her worst."

"See? I told you it would work."

"I hope so. I felt bad for Lucian though. He really liked her."

"He'll meet someone else. I've seen it."

"What?"

She left the bathroom. I finished my shower. I needed to know what she'd seen. Was he really going to be happy with another?

I wrapped the towel around my waist. No need to get fully robed; it would just disappear in a few minutes anyway. I walked out and found Irene's eyes lingering on my body with lust.

"He's really going to find someone?" I had to know and she snapped out of it.

"He will. Not anytime soon, but I've seen him happy. Like true love, making others sick, type of happy." She came toward me and put her hand gently on my cheek. "I promise."

Our lips touched again. The kiss was passionate.

I knew what Arianna's fear was. I'd done my friend a favor by showing him how little he meant to her, and I had this amazing dragon to call my own.

Her robe disappeared and so did my towel. The rest was one hell of a trip.

EIGHTEEN

THE DAY of Arianna's claim drew near. She hadn't told Lucian yet what she'd done. What *we'd* done.

I left her a note, reminding her what I was. She ignored it, so I took matters into my own hands. Lucian needed to know.

"You are a dragon," she said.

I smiled and pretended not to hear a word that she was saying and just wanted to kiss her. She wasn't just a fashion doll. She was a snake. Lucian needed to know about her snaky ways.

"Blake, stop." She chuckled. "I'm the Princess of Areeth. I have to marry…" I didn't let her finish and planted my lips on hers.

We were by the staircase that led to the gym. It was a dark corner.

"You drive me insane." She started to unbuckle my pants.

I had to admit, this was actually fun. I lifted her skirt and dispensed of her lace panties as I pushed myself inside her again and again.

"What the fuck?" I heard Tabitha's voice.

A small smile tugged at the corner of my mouth. Mission complete. I raised my voice in defense. "This isn't what you think."

"Arianna?" Tabitha asked.

"Tabitha, wait!" I feigned panic. I buttoned my pants and buckled my belt as Tabitha stormed off.

"This is *not* happening." Tears filled Arianna's eyes.

"You going to cry?"

"No offense, but I am dating the Prince of Tith," she snapped.

"Well he didn't mean that much to you a few seconds ago, now, did he?"

She spun around with her finger in my face. "I swear to you, Blake Leaf, if you planned this, I will skin off all your scales."

I laughed. "You and what army, sweetheart?" I strode past her up the stairs.

"Tabitha!" I yelled. She needed to throw a scene and Lucian needed to find out the truth.

I found her in the cafeteria. Tears were pouring out of her eyes. I pulled her back by her arm and she hit me in the face.

"I fucking hate you. When is this going to stop, Blake? Why her? She is shallow and only cares about the fashion tip of the week."

"I know. I'm sorry."

"Is it because she is royalty?" she yelled.

Okay, that I didn't expect. This scene was a bit too much.

"What?" Lucian's voice.

I turned my head to where his voice came from and only saw his fist. It connected hard with my face.

"Not again," George grunted as Lucian lunged.

"You did what?" he yelled.

"I did you a fucking favor." I blocked his kick.

"Lucian, don't." Arianna's voice came from the door. "It was a mistake. He's nothing to me."

"Don't touch me. I gave you everything." His voice broke and tears glistened in his eyes. "I thought you were different."

"I am different," she cried.

"No, you're not!" He curled his lip at me, shaking his fist, then whirled and stomped out.

"Lucian, please!" She went after him, her hair and blouse still askew.

"You've got to be fucking kidding me." Tabitha wiped her tears away. "That's why you did it?"

"Enough." I got up. "I told you before. If you cannot handle my needs, leave."

I rushed out the door, and as soon as I was outside, my wings tore through my flesh and the beast took over.

I'd just broken my best friend. I hoped Irene really did see someone in his life, someone worthy of him.

THE DAY of the claiming finally arrived.

Lucian had crashed in Dean's room the past few days. He hadn't spoken to me since that day.

I hadn't tried either, but Arianna wasn't right for him.

Tabitha came with me to the waiting area. I didn't want to calm the beast this time, to reign in the potential destruction. Arianna was going to learn the hard way that she should stick to fashion tips instead of claiming me. If she died... well. Maybe I didn't care.

"It's time," Tabitha said and she gave me a tender kiss that I didn't really want to return. "I said I was sorry."

I wasn't doing this right. What was wrong with this chick? I shook my head and remembered what she was. Cover. I kissed her back.

I walked out into the Colosseum. It was a royal claiming, so it was choked with cameras and flashing bulbs.

King Caleb was sitting next to Queen Gabriella. I hated them.

King Helmut and Queen Magerite were also there, with Lucian seated next to his mother. His eyes found mine. He was still pissed.

I was not sorry. She didn't deserve him. She would never deserve him. Even though it hurt, he would get over it and thank me later.

The crowd cheered as I lifted my hands.

Then she came out.

She was wearing a vest and a short gladiator skirt with long boots that reached her knees. Even I could see she was built to last. Her hair was tied back into a bun, sharpening her long, oval face. She was beautiful, but still a snake, and no snake was worthy of me.

"You and me, let's get this over with." A song started to play. Everything about this girl was corny. The song, who she was, all of it was a big joke.

I transformed. She backed away, eyes widening.

I doubted she'd really thought this through. According to the size of the last Rubicon, I wasn't even close to what I would be eventually. But I could see the fear that it instilled in Arianna.

"There is no you and me," I spoke in Latin. "But you are right about the *let's get it over* part."

She screamed and charged.

I closed my eyes and gave her, her worst fear. The image in my head was easy. One second Arianna was in the ring, the next she was in City Hall. She was in handcuffs. Standing beside her were her mother and father, their hands cuffed too.

"What is this?" she asked her father.

"I'm sorry, sweetheart," I spoke for King Caleb. "I fucked up."

Her eye twitched. Maybe he didn't talk like that, but I maintained the strength of the illusion.

"Daddy, where are we?"

"They have sentenced me to death."

"No, no!" she yelled. "Please, whatever it is you think my father did, Your Honor, he is innocent."

I laughed. So easy. I lay down. This was going to be so much fun.

The real King Caleb clamped the bridge of his nose as if he didn't want to watch the scene unfold.

The queen's expression was priceless. Gabriella was beautiful but she wasn't the brightest. Arianna was so much like her mother. She was confused by what was going on with Arianna.

Arianna was still begging. Everyone tittered. King Helmut and Queen Magerite started looking mutinous.

"Stop this now," King Helmut commanded. The professors came in.

"Enough, Blake," Mia said as I spoke the verdict.

"Just when I was having fun." I let go of the vision in my mind.

Arianna found herself on her knees begging. She stopped as she looked around.

I changed back. "A tip," I said. "Stay with fashion. Don't ever try to claim me again, and never reveal your worst fears to anyone."

She shot me a look of hurt and disgust. Her eyes filled with tears. She didn't say anything as I sauntered out of the Colosseum, victorious.

I actually expected a little more from her. Part of me was actually disappointed.

Arianna simply wasn't a match. And I hurt my best friend in the process.

❧

LUCIAN FINALLY CAME BACK. It took him a week to look at me again.

"I'm sorry for what I did," I said.

"Are you? You have no idea what you have done, Blake."

"C'mon, she's not worthy of you."

He chuckled. "Worthy of me?" He shook his head as if defeated. "I have no fucking choice, Blake. I have to marry her. You just annihilated what little affection for her I had. I could've made this work, but you just had to destroy everything."

I got what he was saying. It wasn't about whether Arianna was worthy of him. He had to marry her whether he wanted to or not. And he really wanted to love her.

My actions weighed more all of a sudden. "I'm sorry. I didn't think."

"No you never do. But it's done. I'll find a way to move on."

I wanted to tell him what Irene told me, but what good would that do? He had to marry Arianna. It wouldn't be welcome news, so I kept my mouth shut.

For the next few weeks, I had to make peace with the fact that Lucian didn't want to speak to me.

But I also knew he wasn't going anywhere. He was planning another claim.

I didn't know if it was because he was pissed at me. I hated it either way. He refused to hear that he wasn't the royal Irene had foreseen.

He was blind and believed in his heart that he didn't need to be my true rider to claim me. His friendship and promise was enough. But he would never be enough.

He trained hard again. Every day a new trainer came. They closed off the Parthenon just for him and he trained for eight hours a day.

Part of me wanted him to succeed. I didn't want to end up as Goran's dragon. But I knew that no matter how hard I hoped, the beast would be ready too. Something was going to happen, another ability, maybe. Or perhaps I would just kill him this time.

That last part didn't bother me as much as it used to. It scared me. It was as if the human part, the sane part, was slowly giving up this.

I couldn't. Who I was now, I must keep going. I had to fight. I needed to hold on.

I ended up in Irene's tower again. It was late at night and a storm was acting up. It felt amazing to have her in my arms as lightning lit up the sky. Irene got riled up from each bolt. Moon-Bolts were suckers for lightning storms. She was such a great distraction.

"Blake." She lay on my shoulder.

"Yeah?" My chest shifted her weight fractionally with the word.

"I know about the Fire-Cain. Lucian…" I closed my eyes and ground my teeth.

"Stop doing that. He's just worried. I'm worried. How long have you been using?"

"I can handle it." I got up and pulled on my pants.

"Said every junkie in this world."

"Irene, don't."

"I'm concerned."

"It's the only way I can hold on."

"Where do you get it?"

I pursed my lips. "It doesn't matter."

"It does to me!" Her voice broke and she grabbed my hand. "Don't go, please."

"I can't stay." I pulled on my shirt.

"Please, I'm not here to judge you." She got up and touched my cheek. I pulled her hand away. "I just need you to look after yourself. Fire-Cain isn't…"

"I know, Irene," I said. I knew why Lucian had told her. Payback.

I couldn't meet her eyes. I let go of her hand and walked to the door. I didn't even say goodbye or look back. I just left. I couldn't stay. That look in her eyes. I didn't want anything to change. She was the last person who ground my balls about anything.

But the fact was that I felt the darkness within the storm.

I felt every lightning strike vibrating through my scales. It made me scared. Too close.

I need more Fire-Cain.

Otherwise I was going to kill Lucian.

᪥

MY KNUCKLES WERE raw and I felt Dimi's hold finally disappearing.

My pocket was filled with Fire-Cain. I didn't even care about cash anymore. I needed the Fire-Cain. I was still in control and I didn't care if Lucian understood that or not.

I wasn't a junkie, not yet. This was mainly for me to hold on.

Right?

I reached the Academy around three in the morning and took a long shower.

The echoes of screams and vivid images of what I'd done to that Moon-Bolt played in my mind.

Guilt. I was their alpha, I was the one who was supposed to protect them. And I was the one tearing off their limbs, ripping them apart.

My body shook as I sobbed. Where was this going to end? When? When I was dead, when I lost, when the darkness won?

It wasn't going to end. It would never end.

When I got out, I lined up three thin rows of Fire-Cain

nicely next to each other and rolled a piece of paper into a tube and snorted them one after another.

The burn came as the last line disappeared. I screamed and clutched my head.

It only lasted for five seconds and then it was gone. My head spun before my entire body relaxed.

The last thing I remembered was laughter. My own. I sounded so evil.

NINETEEN

Lucian's date was set. Two weeks from now.

As the days went by and the Fire-Cain wreaked its work on my body, a second claiming, Lucian's claiming, became real. Each morning when my eyes opened, more pressure rested on my chest.

Do not kill him. Do not kill him.

The days sped by. Fourteen days became twelve. Twelve became nine.

His claiming brought on the dreams again.

I tried. I tried not to use anymore, but I needed the Fire-Cain. I needed my demons tamed.

Still, I needed the human to be in control and I wasn't when the Fire-Cain took over.

I found myself in the cage again. I was in my dragon form. The dragons I'd killed were all begging me. I was their leader, their protector, the only one they would give their lives for, and here I was taking their lives.

It filled me with rage. Not at them, at myself. I breathed fire.

It consumed me.

I deserved it.

I woke with a startle. Sweat dripped off my face as my breathing came fast. I couldn't hear my heart, but the tingling sensation and the nausea told me its pace was fast.

I tried to calm down. I went to the bathroom and looked into the mirror.

I was becoming hollow. My eyes weren't as bright as they were even a year ago. My soul was deteriorating. Nobody could help me, not even Irene.

I didn't think. I opened the loose tile in the bathroom wall by the sink, took out the packet of white powder, and closed it before Lucian woke up. I cut out a line on the basin and snorted it. The fire burned through my skull.

I started seeing it as burning the darkness out of me. That was why it hurt so fucking much. Plenty of darkness

It spread to my core. I doubled over but no sound left my mouth. And then everything slowed down. I saw clearly again, even though I knew I was not in control. I saw everything as it was.

I was the evil that the night brought. No matter how hard I tried, or how much I didn't want it. *It is who I am.*

I am the darkness that evil brings.

My skull throbbed as if someone was banging on the inside.

I heard the sunlight before I saw it. It streamed in through the window. I struggled to open my eyes.

I was still on the floor with a mother of a headache and the banging wasn't coming from my head; it was coming from the door.

Lucian was banging on the door.

"Give me a second," I growled.

"What the hell are you doing in there?" he yelled.

"None of your business." I got up and washed the powder off my face.

When I opened the door, he faced me off with defiance. I ignored him and pushed him hard with my shoulder as I passed. He closed the door.

I went to get dressed. My head throbbed and the loneliness took over. Why was I doing this? I should just cash in now and get it over with. If I weren't the Rubicon, I would've killed myself a long time ago, but I *was* the Rubicon and it wasn't going to be that easy to check out.

The Academy was filled with Lucian's banners again. There were a few of me, too, but it was more a Dragonian sport than it was a dragon one. No, if we dragons wanted our fun, it happened in the dark hours of the night and underground.

I ignored people who tried to start conversations with me and slept in most of my classes. I didn't care anymore.

One afternoon, the loneliness really set in and I found myself in the library, fucking Ash. She really wasn't that great, but Irene wasn't on the premises, and Tabitha was just crazy.

"Seriously, Blake," she spoke when I was done and buckling my pants. "We should make this a bit more exclusive, don't you think?"

"No, I don't," I said flatly.

I wasn't exclusive with anyone, not even Irene.

§

I FOUND myself leaning against the wall.

Lucian was training in the Colosseum. They usually kept his moves a secret, but I guessed this was a different tactic. A tactic to what, scare me?

He should have been the scared one. He wasn't close to being ready. The beast was going to eat him alive in seven days

My Cammy rang and I saw Phil's name. I picked it up and his figure appeared.

"Blakey," he sang.

"When?" I sounded empty.

"This Friday. It's the last day of the tournament."

What? It had been that long already?

Phil smiled. "Everything comes to an end. Eventually."

I nodded.

"Don't be late. Be at Sam's around four."

The connection broke.

I turned to watch Lucian again.

This call came just at the right time. I had the option of killing someone I didn't know, as opposed to killing someone who mattered to my world.

The only way Lucian would get out of that ring alive would be after a fight that calmed the beast. Maybe it would be so calm that Lucian could stand a chance to claim me.

§

"MY BROTHER SAID you should remember not to be late." Tabitha sat down on the pillow next to mine in the cafeteria.

"Noted." I smiled stiffly.

She frowned. "Where are you going this Friday?"

"Thank you for the message, but the rest is none of your business," I said and got up.

"Okay, sorry. I get it. I don't want to fight."

"Noted."

"There's a party on Thursday night in my room. A little get-together. Will I see you there?"

"I'll see," I said and walked away.

Back in my room I took a fingernail of Fire-Cain. It was every day now, but a little bit didn't cause too many problems.

The human was still in control.

It was just enough to get me through the day.

❧

THURSDAY NIGHT, I stood in front of Tabitha's room. I didn't know what I was doing there, but a party might be what I needed before the big fight.

I knew the tournament was coming to an end and Hansel was among the favorites.

She opened the door, looking exceptionally hot in her too-short skirt and fishnet stockings. She wore calf-high boots and a plunging V-neck shirt.

"My eyes are up here, Blake," she said. "They are pretty, blue, and not blind."

I gave her my lopsided smile and pinched my nose as she stepped out of the way.

I hated the feeling that the Fire-Cain left me with. Too little made me feel weird, like the tip of my nose was numb. I'd developed this stupid habit of pinching my nose every few minutes. Too much made me do fucked-up things I couldn't remember.

The door closed behind me and George greeted me with a beer. Brian was bouncing around like an idiot. The music was loud and the curtains were drawn shut.

Longwei sure hadn't had this in mind when he built the soundproof rooms.

I downed my beer and grabbed another.

"This is going to be fun," I said in a dull voice. Tabitha grabbed my arm and pulled me toward the bathroom.

I hated that a part of me was weak when I was alone with her.

She didn't grab me when she closed the door but took out a joint from the cupboard against the wall. She lit it and took a deep drag.

Weed.

It was doing little to nothing for me anymore, but seeing Tabitha taking chances like this, well, that was a first for the Snow Dragon. Usually she sat out things like this.

I accepted the joint and took a deep drag. With the Fire-

Cain flowing in my veins, the weed enhanced my high nicely. I chuckled.

"What?"

I shook my head as I blew out smoke. "Nothing." I smiled and pushed her against the wall.

Our lips met. I knew later on I was going to regret this, but that was later Blake's problem.

"I'm glad that you made up with Tabitha, Blake," Irene said as I shared a cigarette with her.

I chewed on my lip. She made me so confused and I didn't know why it bothered me so much.

She pushed herself up onto her elbow. "We need her and if you occasionally have to sleep with her to make her feel special, then so be it."

"You're not jealous?"

"Not as much as I used to be. Oh, believe me, two hundred years ago, the Snow Dragon would've been ashes by now." She bent over and kissed me.

I chuckled against her lips. She was so hot.

The kiss escalated to another round. I could feel her energy like an electric storm. It didn't hurt, though. It just made me want more.

Sex with her was out of this world.

I slept over that night.

I'd slept with two girls on the same day. That thought wasn't that awesome anymore. I wondered why.

Why did I feel like the biggest asshole on the planet? Sleeping around had never bothered me until now.

What did it mean?

Did I love someone other than myself?

WENTY

I OPENED my eyes and was in the Colosseum again. The wind howled. I had to cover my eyes as insidious particles of sand attacked and pricked my skin, my face, my mouth, everywhere.

The sky rumbled with thunder. Flashes of lightning lit the inky sky. I'd never realized how creepy the Colosseum was in the darkness of night.

My eyes caught on someone in the crowd. Just one. Then another appeared. It seemed to be the same guy. The first figure sat on the sidelines to my left and met the gaze of the one on my far right.

He was either fast, which made me think of a Night Seeker, or he was multiplying.

A third one popped up in front of me.

Then they appeared all over the place. It seemed to be the same person.

What was this?

The wind shredded at my being and a soft drumming vibrated against my feet. Something was coming.

I closed my eyes. *Wake up, Blake.*

The fear weighed me down to my core. It was heavy. My breathing quickened.

I searched at the crowd again. The crowd of Lucians. They all lifted their arms and pointed in my direction.

What did this mean?

The vibration grew stronger. A humming noise droned in my ear. My skin crawled; I hated feeling so afraid and vulnerable.

The gates opened and as one, a legion of knights in white armor came marching out. They poured straight for me, a sinuous, bristling serpent. They struck their shields and the ground in perfect tempo.

I drowned in their presence. I couldn't breathe.

I woke up to my own screaming.

My senses were alert. Sweat soaked my body. I breathed hard and fast.

A cold hand touched me. I startled.

"It's just me," Irene said and our eyes met.

Mine welled up.

"It's just a dream, Blake. It's not real."

I didn't know if she saw it, or if she just said those words to calm my soul, but she held me tight as I succumbed.

I didn't want to be dark. I didn't want to be claimed. I was stuck in the middle and it seemed life was pulling me inexorably in all directions.

❦

FRIDAY NIGHT, I was in the ring again.

I made it to the final round.

We'd been fighting the entire night, with the finale being a gruesome last-man-or-dragon-standing.

Three remained. Two humans (me included, so not in reality) and a dragon.

He was a Night Villain and had been a favorite for years. He was huge, old, and undefeated.

The humans who went up against him had all failed. It looked like I might have to face him.

I didn't want to kill my kind anymore, but I needed to hold on. What I was going to do when the tournament was over?

At least the limelight was diminished. Only the crowd here knew my name—or the one I had portrayed. One I could shed.

I could hear the officiator, the crowd cheering. It was a hard fight. They'd been grappling viciously for the past hour. It exhausted me just watching them.

I tried my hardest not to get involved with the Dragonians. This particular group loathed dragons. I could swear sometimes they smelled me.

Then it was as if Luke, the dragon, had enough. I heard Syd's screams. I heard how his bones crushed and limbs shredded.

Half the crowd cheered; the others screamed in agony.

Like Samuel said, no money was bet on the dragons. Many gamblers had lost big tonight on Syd.

I tuned out and could hear the officiator announcing Luke as the winner.

He must have blown acid or something, because the crowd went mad again.

They started cheering my name: "Hansel! Hansel! Hansel!"

Dimi and Samuel entered the changing rooms.

"Kill him fast. Don't try to wear him out. That Night Villain has no off button. The more he kills, the stronger he grows."

I nodded.

He touched the back of my neck hard. "Do this, and everything is over. No more debt. Nothing."

"You will leave my family alone."

"It's in the contract Blake. I can't touch them every again. You will be free."

I squinted.

"You have my word. Just kill him fast."

Dimitri was close by.

They were giving me another half an hour.

Kill him fast, Blake.

LATER, I'd wish that I could say it was an easy fight. It should've been easy. I was the Rubicon. But this turned out to be the hardest battle I've ever fought.

Part of me knew I wasn't going to escape this ring alive.

I was scratched many times. Blood poured in rivers down my body. I was tired and sticky and slowing down.

No matter what I did, Luke was like a machine. He didn't fail and he didn't weaken.

I was tiring myself out.

He gripped me tight around the waist and I could feel my bones crushing like chalk. I was blacking out and then, suddenly, the darkness inside me roared. The beast woke up.

I wasn't conscious for what happened next. I was, how did people put it, out of body. I didn't know if I gave up and the darkness took over, or whether the beast just came out to play, but my human part checked out.

Luke didn't stand a chance.

Only when I was sputtering, literally drowning, in his blood did I come to. I was covered in it. I was panting hard and my body ached immeasurably. I wanted to burst and I wanted to get away.

The crowd went crazy.

They screamed and cheered.

I was tired, but I got up. I focused in on Dimitri for the first time.

His nose was bleeding. He'd struggled.

Seemed fair.

The officiator lifted up my hand as I held the a gash closed on my stomach.

I didn't know which blood was mine and which was my enemy's.

Soon, I found myself in the showers. Even this far

removed, the crowd's distant cheers echoed painfully in my eardrums. Nobody in the victory room but me. We'd started out as twenty-four players. I was the only one still standing.

I'd killed my own kind. I'd damaged my soul. I'd given into the darkness. But why did I still feel like me? Why did I still *grieve* like me?

The contract was finished.

No more fighting. No more.

❦

I HAD enough stash to last me a good while. I just had to pace myself. A tiny bit whenever I needed it. That was the plan.

I partied Saturday. We stayed over at Samuel's mansion. Tabitha even came. She hated it at Samuel's because of all the drugs and girls.

Everyone was having a great time, including me. We were in the study on the top floor. It was off-limits and Tabitha had to stay below.

Samuel was different. Someone I could actually see as a friend. Maybe what he'd done was just business.

We used, and after that I didn't remember much.

When I woke, I was with girls who weren't Tabitha next to me. I knew whatever happened last night, I was going to hear about it till doomsday came.

My head was killing me. The loneliness was so bad this time, I just wanted to cash out again.

The rest was a blur. I didn't know how I got back to the Academy or how I got through Monday.

The cut on my stomach throbbed, but my healing ability seem to be kicking in and when I woke up on Tuesday I was healed. I really hoped that it would've lasted longer. It would've given Lucian a fair chance to claim me, to succeed. But it seemed that it wasn't in me to yield.

The darkness was just too strong. My mother was wrong. She had this saying: no matter how dark things seemed, hope was just around the corner.

Hope wasn't meant for guys like me.

&

MEMBERS of the press interviewed Lucian, a steady stream of cameras and journalists. Somehow I managed to escape all of them. I hated the limelight, even though I loved the stage. I felt different up there, like someone else and not this evil being who had to fight to stay good.

Staying good shouldn't be so hard.

My family had arrived. My father was hopefully somewhere in the crowd. Why I was even hoping for it, I didn't know.

Tabitha wasn't there. She was pissed off with me for whatever happened at Samuel's. I couldn't help it. I couldn't help anything when I was drugged out of my mind.

I got up. I stood in front of the gate, waiting for it to open.

For a split second, that dream about the legion of white-armored knights flashed through my mind. The scales beneath my skin shivered.

The beast wanted to get out. It needed to stretch its wings.

I doubted another ability would show itself today.

The gate creaked open.

"The Rubicon!" Alex's voice echoed over the microphone and bounced off the walls.

I stepped out and the crowd cheered like crazy, especially the dragons. The dragons. I was a dragon killer.

I lifted up my arms when I felt I couldn't breathe and air filled my lungs.

You want to sit this one out? the beast offered.

No, I thought. *You are not taking his life.*

Then stop being a pussy, Blake.

I hated these confrontations.

I growled. The crowd misunderstood, thinking I was trying to get them excited. I wasn't; I was furious. He shouldn't try to claim me.

His father and mother sat on two thrones right next to Arianna's parents. The rulers of Paegeia. A pity that none of them were royal enough to claim me, none worthy enough to walk out of that gate and face me.

Lucian was brave, but not the right one.

His name was called, and like clockwork, when he stepped out, so did the beast.

His form grew small in a matter of seconds, and I felt myself slip away.

Hang on, Blake. You can't kill Lucian.

"Thunderstruck" started to play and the crowd sang along.

I hated that fucking song.

&.

STOP! I yelled. My internal voice sounded deranged to me. Lucian's lifeless body lay on the floor. He had dodged countless acid balls, but it was the chlorine that ended it. It poured out of me, suffocating him.

I could still smell it.

The beast loved every single moment.

Enough! I yelled again and forced my human form to appear as the beast went to spit out another acid ball.

You weakling. He doesn't deserve… I pushed his rantings to the back of my mind.

"Lucian!" I cried.

Still, he didn't say a thing. I heard ribs cracking and bones breaking. Flesh almost tearing.

"Lucian!"

"Blake!" Mia was one of the professors holding me back. "Go calm down. Now!"

I frowned. But I listened to her and ran through the gate and out the door to my dressing room.

I ran until my lungs felt as if they were going to burst before I jumped into the air.

My wings took over and took me straight to my mountain.

I think I just killed the Prince of Tith.

WENTY-1

I WENT straight to Irene when I came back. She was waiting for me.

I broke down. "I killed him," I said over and over again. "I killed my best friend."

"Blake, calm down. You haven't killed him. It's just his lungs. The chlorine burned his lungs, but Constance was close. He will be fine."

I started to laugh. It wasn't because of relief. I was hanging on by a thread. I was close to losing it, to joining the darkness, to giving up.

Why me?

"Why not make anyone else the Rubicon? Why my egg?"

"Cause you are the only one strong enough to carry this burden." She got up and went into her bathroom. She came back with a blue velvet coin purse. She opened it and took out a silver tool. At the end it was a tiny spoon. "I know about the fights."

My body froze.

Tears glistened in her eyes. "No more, Blake, please. It's only going to destroy you faster."

A tear traced the length of my cheek.

She put the spoon-like tool into the bag and scooped up a fine white powder. "This is the only way. I will monitor it, and you will get through this. Just promise you won't go back into that ring."

She must have seen it. But she didn't see the contract. It was no longer. I nodded.

She held the spoon to my nose and I snorted. Fire burned into my head. I grunted and doubled over.

I felt her lips on the back on my neck. They scorched my skin. It didn't took long before the tingling sensation took over and I found myself lost in Irene's arms.

❧

LUCIAN WASN'T DEAD, but his lungs suffered badly.

The Green-Vapor in me was strong. Green-Vapors were liars and loved to play games. I despised lies, yet it was all I'd been doing the past few months.

I lied to everyone. Maybe it was why the part of me was so strong.

The coolest part of a Green-Vapor's gift wasn't breathing chlorine gas, but being able to persuade humans. They said the older the dragon became, the better this gift of persuasion got.

Henry was a Green-Vapor. Jeff too. He was more Brian's buddy than mine and had the ability to irritate me even worse than Brian did.

Still, none of them had the persuasion gift yet. I had a feeling that mine wasn't going to work quite the same as anyone else's. I had to figure it out, how to persuade someone's mind.

Thoughts of animals flashed through my mind. It was cruel, but the safest way.

I need to learn how to harness all my abilities. It had to become like breathing air.

The acid of the Night-Villain used to scare me. I was sixteen when it appeared. Then the lightning showed. The Pink Kiss was after that and in between all of the above, somewhere, I started to heal preternaturally fast.

How long was he going to take to heal?

I had really hoped he would forget about it, and never try to claim me again. Now we were back here. When was he going to stop thinking that he had it in him to claim me? I didn't know how long he'd be out this time. His lungs had been scorched from the inside.

The gas had almost suffocated me too, but after the sixth time inhaling it, I couldn't tell the difference between breathing in fresh air and chlorine. I was immune to it.

The abilities came to me in stages. I wasn't like the other dragons. Sure, I was born one, but I didn't get my abilities at the age of thirteen like they do.

I got my first one at the age of sixteen. And here I was at nineteen. With the ones I have.

The worst part was that I had to keep my fire as far away from claimings as possible.

My pink fire, the Rubicon's fire, or what I like to call the Pink Kiss, was different from the other dragons' fire. It carried a pink flame. It was like a virus. Once it touched its victim, it destroyed them.

My flame scared me at times. I didn't want it. It only made me indestructible.

✿

TWO WEEKS LATER, Lucian was still MIA.

I hated how long he took to recover. It had been stupid to argue like that. Another mountain had risen to stand in front of me.

An acid wielder had sought the Council's permission to try and claim me. They had approved his petition, and I was going to face him inside the ring. I didn't know why these idiots kept trying. They always failed, would always fail.

It was going to be held in the Colosseum of Tith.

It wasn't as big as the one in Dragonia Academy, but it was upper-class and the total opposite of the one in Dragonia.

They said that the one in Etan was a combination of the one in Dragonia and Tith.

I felt a bit of unease at the prospect.

This wasn't Lucian, and I didn't really care for the guy. I saw his name: Aaron Mendez. I shouldn't look at it. It was like naming a dog; you get attached and you wouldn't want to kill it.

Kiiiilllllll, the beast said. The beast hated the fact that Aaron Mendez had the guts to even consider this.

I spent the night before the claiming up in Irene's tower. I used again. She monitored me. At length I passed out in her tower.

She was my salvation. But I knew Master Longwei would make sure that she never told foretellings ever again if he caught us in the act. I couldn't let that happen. The fear of it chased me in the unsettled recesses of my mind. Getting caught.

❦

I FLEW ALL the way to Tith while Master Longwei, Irene, and Tabitha took the elevators. It took me more than six hours to get there. I had to leave early in the morning. My head was still a bit clouded, but at least I felt better than I had yesterday.

I went to the hotel that Master Longwei had booked for us and crashed on one of the beds. I needed some sleep before this evening.

❦

TABITHA, Irene, and Master Longwei waited with me in the dressing room. The chamber wasn't as cold and unforgiving as the one in Dragonia Academy, which resembled something ancient.

No this one was revamped. Lush red carpet lined the walls and the floor. An ornate steel gate showed parts of the arena. It was highlighted with huge spotlights.

Tabitha sat next to me and Irene was sitting right next to Master Longwei.

"You'll be fine." Tabitha patted my hand. I really didn't want her to hold it, not with Irene watching, but I had no choice with Master Longwei here. My fingers were entwined with hers.

I took a deep breath without looking at Irene. It was weird having both women in my life in the same room.

My mother had wanted to come so badly, but I'd told her no. She shouldn't. I didn't want her or my sister to see the day I killed a Dragonian.

"You ready?" Master Longwei asked.

"No," I replied. I was never ready for this. We dragons didn't have a choice.

He touched my shoulder. Probably trying to show some encouragement.

Then a voice echoed my name.

The door opened.

"Good luck," Irene said.

I wished I could grab her. Instead, I pulled my hand through my hair.

"Go get 'em," Tabitha wrapped her arms around my neck and kissed me before I even realized she was zeroing in.

I felt bad for Irene, but Master Longwei had to believe that Tabitha was my girl. So I pretend it was Irene and I kissed her back.

I walked out onto the arena. Bright lights shone in my face. It was a covered Colosseum. Big affairs and big claimings had been held here since it was constructed.

After Etan was lost to us, they had used this one more for the adult claimings and the one in Dragonia for the students.

The crowd cheered.

Déjà vu rested heavily on my shoulders, images from the tournament haunting me.

I wasn't the Dragonian this time. I took a few deep breaths. I lifted my arms and the crowd cheered. I wasn't much of a show pony.

I came here to do one thing: not get claimed. This Aaron was going to discover that, fast.

I could feel my limbs stretching. Deep red and purplish scales formed on my arms and ran all across my body as I grew. Horns and tendrils sprouted around my face. The crowd grew smaller. I was growing. I was already taller than I had been the day of Lucian's claiming. I was getting indestructible.

It wasn't good, but the dark in me loved it. It wanted it.

You idiot, you're going to end up with Goran if you don't stop.

Then the dream flashed through my mind. The one about the thousand knights. I didn't know why I was having these thoughts.

The beast was going to take over. I could feel it.

A song played.

The darkness started to laugh. It was some stupid metal song, nothing scary or anything. This wasn't the day.

My scales started to vibrate. They made that funny rattle sound. I hated it.

Then Aaron walked out. He was at least ten years older than me.

The darkness in me just sized his ass up. *Not worthy*, it surmised.

"You and me, let's give them something to remember," he said as he threw an acid ball my way.

You want the crowd to remember this? They won't.

I struck.

***

IT WAS over in less than half an hour. It could've been more.

It showed up. My fire. I'd never used it before now. I didn't want it to and the minute it had, the cameras flashed like crazy. Nobody alive had seen the pink flame except in history books. So seeing it tonight was a huge deal.

A speck of it touched Aaron and he screamed. We all watched in horror as it spread like a virus.

Numerous doctors rushed into the arena, but none of them could stop it. His screams rushed deep into my soul to the black recess where all the other screams of my victims had lodged themselves.

Master Longwei came out and I pushed myself back into my human form. At the horror-struck look on my face, he said, "Blake, it's okay. It's a claim. It's not murder. Calm your mind."

I tore my gaze off Aaron's body. It was starting to disintegrate. As I watched, Aaron turned to ash.

"It's a claim. He wasn't your Dragonian."

I felt empty. He misunderstood my emotion. I was slowly losing the battle. And I knew new nightmares were on the horizon.

The crowd was silent.

Flashes of the dream came again.

My throat was dry.

Then someone screamed, more horror voiced.

Master Longwei was already guiding me back to the locker room.

I killed him.

The thought should make me feel a bit guilty at least... but it didn't. He should've never tried to claim me.

Irene didn't say anything, but Tabitha just had to open her mouth.

I didn't focus on what she said. In my mind's eye, I was

fixated on the pile of empty clothes and the ashes of what was left of Aaron Mendez blowing away.

"He wasn't your Dragonian, Blake. It happens. You did nothing wrong." Master Longwei's voice was close by. I nodded mutely.

I'd killed the first Dragonian who had faced me with my Pink Kiss. I feared it wouldn't be the last.

PART II

TWENTY-2

MONTH'S FLEW by and Summer was around the corner.

Lucian didn't try to claim me again. He kept his distance. I guessed I'd really broken a part of him when I'd slept with Arianna. How big of a part, I didn't know. Not to mention the whole almost-killing-him thing.

I didn't want to go home. I managed to avoid it since Aaron Mendez's claim. This would be the first time that I would see my family again.

My mom had tried to call me a couple of times, but I couldn't face her. To see that disappointment in my mother's eyes and watch her trying to hide it would have been unbearable.

I'd already seen it in my aunt's eyes. I'd gotten a little bit of a preview.

I wouldn't be able to see Irene this summer. She lived in one of the dragon cities in Areeth. It was so far; to be honest, I had no idea where she lived. All I knew was that I would be caught and I would have nothing to say. What would my excuse be for visiting her in Areeth, or, hell, going to Areeth at all?

All I knew was that I was going to miss her like crazy.

When Tabitha asked if she could visit over the summer, I reluctantly nodded. Even though it was Irene I wanted.

A knock came at the door. George's figure stood in the frame. "See you next term."

I nodded, gave him a faint smile.

"Have a good one, and say hi to Sammy."

"Really?"

He laughed.

When it came to my family, I was like a dog. Their watchdog. I had been since King Albert died, rendering my father useless. He'd forced me to step up and be a man. Well, maybe now he would be a little bit better. Maybe not. Like I said, I hadn't spoken to my mom in ages.

I had to admit, I missed the way my dad used to be. He had been so majestic. When I closed my eyes, I could still see him with the king on his back.

They used to come to the manor, our first home, before missions. I would look up in awe and want that bond so badly.

What did I know?

It was one of the worst things that could happen to a dragon. I'd learned that the hard way. I was still learning it.

With their riders, dragons were perfect. The shit came when the riders didn't make it, and that was why I hated the Dragonians so much.

We turned to nothing the day our riders died. It was why dragons did stupid things like bequeath them their essence. I didn't know what the process was, other than the fact that it wasn't easy.

No, it was one of the hardest things dragons could do, presenting their riders with their essences. But the bond didn't make it look that hard.

They gave it without thinking twice.

That scared me. I was glad that I didn't have a true rider.

The redhead flashed through my mind. I hadn't thought about her for such a long time. She was my Never-Breath. A figment of my imagination. A wish that I'd conjured to, what, cope with all this?

I struggled to hold on. It was getting harder by the day.

Part of me wanted her to ease everything, to make all of this go away. But she didn't exist and I had to make peace with it.

&.

"YOU'RE HERE!" Sammy jumped into my arms.

I frowned as she'd grown at least a head taller since the last time I had seen her and yep, her boobs had gotten a size bigger too. She'd blossomed.

I pushed her away.

"What?" she asked.

I shook my head. "You look different."

"As in how?" She squinted.

"You're hot, Sammy."

"Ew, ew, ew," she said and I laughed. "You're my

brother."

"I didn't mean it like that. I'm just saying, I'm going to have a hard time at Dragonia keeping the guys off you."

She blushed and hooked her arm with mine. "I missed you."

"Yeah, I haven't been around lately, have I?"

She shook her head and clung to my arm as we walked to the house.

I dragged my feet. I still feared the look on my mother's face.

"Mom," Sammy said. "Look who's here."

My mother walked out of the kitchen. Her face was inscrutable for a moment. Then a huge smile covered her face and she ran to me. Her arms folded around me. "I missed you," she whispered.

"I'm here," I spoke softly too.

She didn't mention the Dragonian or try to coddle my feelings with empty observations that he wasn't my true rider. As if that somehow changed what I had done. I hated when people told me that. It reminded me how not guilty I felt about killing him. How vacant and inhuman I really was.

There wasn't an ounce of disappointment in my mother's eyes. This was one of the reasons I loved my mother so much. I should have known. She never saw the darkness. It wasn't because she was naive or anything; it just didn't matter with her. There had been no reason to avoid her all these months after all.

"Want some coffee?" Sammy asked and I nodded.

"I got a job," my mother sang.

"You did?" I asked.

She nodded. "It's not as glamorous as Constance, but I'm teaching little ones at daycare."

"You're a teacher?"

"It's a job, Blake. And I never thought I would enjoy it so much."

"I'm working too, believe it or not," Sammy said.

"Who would give you a job?" I teased.

"Ha, ha. The coffee shop at the mall."

"I see. They're lucky to have you, Sam."

"I know, and I make good tips, so stop worrying about us, okay? I know you want that little purple number at Andy's."

I roared. "That is not just 100 pagoleans, Sam. I'm fine. Besides, the only thing I care about is you and Mom."

"See?" She looked at my mother. "Still fine."

I laughed. It was sure good to be home.

❦

SUMMER TURNED out to be a really good time. The darkness was still there, but I'd made peace with it, sort of. It had backed off, just a little.

Maybe this was like my goodbye summer. I was giving my family something to remember me by. Before I drowned in darkness.

I hadn't seen my father. Mom told me that he had gone to see a shaman, to help him cope with his demons and to be a better man. I hoped he wasn't going to turn into one of those tree huggers who loved to eat only from their own harvests and found inner peace and shit. It didn't fit with Night-Villains.

Tabitha spent some time with us.

It was no surprise that Sammy didn't like her.

She wasn't that bad. I got why Phil didn't want his sister to get hurt. She was funny, made us laugh. She only stayed for like four days and then went back to her parents.

I had mixed feelings for the Snow Queen.

I reflected on the poem I'd written for her. Those words were still as real now as they were then.

Before I knew it, it was time to return to Dragonia Academy. I was in my fourth year, and Lucian was starting his third. I hoped that this trying-to-claim-me bullshit was over.

§

SAMMY TURNED some heads on her first day.

"Brian likes." He sniffed the air.

"Don't even fucking dream about it," I said.

"Blake, c'mon."

"That Fire-Tail is off limits, Brian."

His eyebrows rose as I walked faster. "No way, that's your sister?"

I didn't answer. George chortled.

"Fuck, she's hot!" Brian exclaimed. I shook my head. He would listen; all of them would listen. My sister's virtue was so not going to belong to any of these fuckers.

Sammy waved at me as I passed her.

They were standing right in front of the stairs waiting for orientation and were being sorted into their rooms.

George growled softly as we walked past them. I frowned as a huge smile sprawled on his face. What was that about?

We went up to my room.

"Hey," Lucian said. He was already unpacking his clothes.

Guilt washed over me, but I didn't dare ask him how his summer was. Instead I stalked in to the bathroom and splashed cold water on my face.

Brian greeted Lucian. "Your Highness, how was your summer?"

"Fuck off," Lucian said. George and Brian burst out laughing.

"So when is the next claiming date, Your Highness?" George teased.

"Soon."

I sighed as I stared at myself in the bathroom mirror. Water droplets clung to my dark eyelashes, making my peacock-blue eyes pop. Lucian was going to lose his life.

"The Pink Kiss doesn't scare you?"

"The Pink Kiss?" Lucian asked as I hadn't shared my

nickname with many people. "No. Losing him scares me. It should scare all of you."

Nobody said a word and I saw Lucian's figure pass the bathroom door. He'd left.

⁂

WE ALL ASSEMBLED in the auditorium.

Lucian was greeting Sammy. She looked at him with admiration, desire. Everyone looked at Lucian that way.

His heart was still broken, though. Thanks to me. He'd really loved Arianna. I'd tried to forget it. Neither of us had mentioned it.

I watched the fond way he said goodbye to Sammy to find his own seat.

One of the girls next to her asked how she knew him. I tuned out as she told the girl who she was. I hated the way they said my name. Like I was her sun and moon.

George plunged into the chair next to me. He was tense, the hair on his arms raised.

"What is with you?"

He looked at me, his facial features draining. Concealing his thoughts. "Nothing."

Tabitha moved past me as I stared at George. "Hey you," she said and kissed me once on my lips.

I smiled without saying anything. My eyes stayed on George. I could've sworn I just heard him growl softly. *What is George hiding?*

TWENTY-3

I SPENT that first night back with Irene. I'd missed her so much. The way her fingernails scratched my back told me that I was missed too.

I slipped out of her tower early the next day before anyone awoke. Lucian was still sleeping. I went to take a shower. I needed to get Irene's scent off me. If anyone discovered the truth, I would never be able to cope.

First period was bullshit. It was with Professor Pheizer. She thought she knew everything about dragons and their riders, bonds, and ascensions.

She was a joke.

We got new journals again. I wanted to incinerate mine, but she'd just give me another.

The Metallics loved her. They all asked her stupid fucking questions. Every dragon in this class hadn't found their riders yet, and she was supposed to help them.

They thought Irene was making up bullshit.

When the bell rang she spoke my name. "Please, just try this year, Blake."

"Why?"

"You never know."

I chuckled and shook my head as I walked out of her class. So fake. She wouldn't see my rider if they were standing in front of me.

But for some reason, I sat with both my journals that night. I just scribbled in hers, colors that made no sense. I wrote a little in mine.

What was the use of anything?

I closed my journal and shoved it under my pillow. I lay on my stomach and closed my eyes.

"MY BROTHER WANTS you to call him," Tabitha said. "I thought you were done with Samuel."

"I am," I said.

She hated them so much. I did too.

I had no debt to pay off this time and he couldn't threaten my family again. That contract saved his life till the day I die.

But the darkness... Irene was right. The Fire-Cain had to be enough this time.

Around six, my Cammy rang for the umpteenth time. I ignored Phil's call. He would eventually stop. I switched off my Cammy just as Lucian walked in.

He went to the kitchen in our room. Perks of rooming with the Prince of Tith. He came back with a cup of coffee and flopped down on the sofa, switching on the TV. Still not saying a word.

֍

THAT NIGHT I found myself in the ring again. It wasn't the Colosseum. It was the tournament.

I wasn't Hansel this time. I was Blake.

The crowd cheered my name. I loved every moment of it and paraded around like a show pony.

My eyes caught on my father. He was here. He looked different. Like he used to when King Albert was still alive.

Next to him was King Helmut. He looked different too. His eyes in particular. I thought I saw a slit, even though King Helmut wasn't a dragon. He was Lucian's father and owned a dragon.

What did this dream mean?

Then my opponent, a dragon, came out. It was huge. Looked purple. I frowned. I'd seen this dragon before. It was called a Thunderlight. They were extinct. They didn't exist anymore. What was one doing in the tournament?

Lightning shot out and struck me. I didn't feel a thing. I looked down at my hands and found my own lightning sparking from my palm and fingertips. It wasn't purple like the Thunderlight's.

The dragon went for me again. It taunted me. Toyed with me.

"Kill it," I heard Samuel's voice and found him in place of my father.

He had my mother in his arms. "Kill or she's dead."

"No!" I whirled the Thunderlight.

I blacked out and the darkness took over. I ripped off the dragon's wings. Thick, dark crimson liquid splashed into my face, all over my body. The dragon teetered on the brink of death when I finished.

I could see the shift happening and my gut fell.

Lucian.

Lucian was the Thunderlight.

"Why?" Blood poured out of his mouth. "Where the fuck were you?"

I squinted at him. I tried to get to him but I couldn't. It was as if my feet were tied back with weights.

"No, no, no, no!" I yelled.

How had Lucian become a dragon? What was he doing here? What was I doing here? When did all of this happen?

I fell on my knees and couldn't breathe as I clutched my head. The room started to spin as I lost control.

I found myself on a ledge. I was no longer in the ring. Lucian's body was gone.

I was somewhere in the desert. The wind gusted. Surrounding me was nothingness.

An edge. The edge of what? My sanity. I didn't understand.

The wind pushed and pushed. I couldn't hold on.

"It's time Blake," my own voice said.

"What?" To my own ears I sounded weak. Nothing like me.

"It's time," I said again, but it wasn't me.

He walked to me. His eyes were dark, everything in him was dark. This was him. The beast in his human form.

"It's time!" he roared. "You had your fun."

He yelled in my ear and then he crawled into me. I screamed. The pain was so real. I toppled over the edge.

I blacked out just as I hit the ground. When I awoke, I found myself on a cold wooden floor, surrounded by four nondescript walls.

Where the hell am I?

To my left was another room. I heard a baby cry. I went toward that room. I saw the bundle. It was moving. I bent down to pick it up and as I unwrapped the blanket, the creature inside jumped at me. I flicked it away, grabbed it in mid-air around its throat.

What was it?

Its talons and tendrils with and numerous eyes were all focused on me. There was foam around an opening, what I assumed was its mouth.

It spoke in a weird, raspy voice. "Blake, what the hell?"

One tendril smacked my wrist hard.

Then light through and the creature turned into Lucian, red in his face. My hand around his neck. The tendril that that had hit my wrist had been Lucian's arm.

I let go immediately. It fell and coughed. For a second I

was in our kitchen. Then it all vanished and I was back in the cabin with the barren walls.

The wind blew hard against the structure. It made a racket. I thought it was going to cave in, or blow away with me in it.

What was this?

My hands tucked in my hair. I closed my eyes. I didn't know what was real and what wasn't anymore. I succumbed and knelt on my knees.

Wake up, wake up!

Then silence.

I opened my eyes. I was still in the cabin.

I wrestled with the creature again that could or could not be Lucian. It became fast, but my reflexes was faster. I got the upper hand, and for some reason my abilities didn't want to come. I tried everything. Nothing.

But somehow I managed to be faster. Was it Lucian? Was it a demon? I was so scared that it was Lucian. But when it spit acid at me and burned my skin, I knew it wasn't.

I squeezed, but it refused to budge. Its tendrils flailed against my stomach hard.

It felt like a whip. I held on and took it to the only window. It squirmed in my hands. I managed to open the window and chuck the thing out.

The window grew smaller and smaller and then it vanished.

The wind still howled and the door burst open. A huge figure with long legs and a long torso walked in.

I roared. What the fuck was this?

It grabbed me. I tried to get free as it squeezed tight.

I couldn't hold on. It was going to rip me apart.

As I thought it, it happened. Like the exact moment, as if it was linked to me. It threw me hard against the wall, pulled me back, and ripped off my arm and my leg.

I screamed in white-hot agony.

It tore my body in half.

Guts and blood spilled everywhere. I waited for death as it split my skull, but it didn't come. My limbs and guts and shit scattered across the floor.

Tears welled up in my eyes.

The thing bent down and stared at me with dark eyes. "I told you before. It's time."

It happened. I'd finally died.

❧

WHEN I WOKE UP AGAIN, I was in a bed. It didn't look familiar.

The wind howled. Every inch of me ached. I found myself sown together. I was a freak, a real-life cubist painting. A second head was attached right next to mine. It looked like me. I screamed.

My leg was sewn on my arm socket, my dick on the other side. My arm was my torso and my torso took up space on one side of my leg. It was wrong. All of it was wrong.

I was a freak.

I screamed, cried, cussed, yelled, and laughed. I was losing my mind.

The eyes of the second head flew open. It stared right at me. They were dark and full of evil. He started to laugh and I screamed again.

"Don't, please," I begged. I tried to inch away, but I couldn't.

"It's time, Blake. Just say the words."

"Whatever you want. Just make it stop."

"Blake!" He yelled my name. Loud.

"Stop, please," I begged.

"Blake!" Mocking me.

I felt a punch on my arm that was now my leg.

"I'm not losing him." I heard another voice.

"Blake!" Another yell and a hard fucking punch.

"Noooooo!" The head yelled. "You are mine!" It sank its teeth into my neck.

I screamed and everything disappeared.

&

I WOKE UP WITH A JOLT. I took a gasping breath. A bright light blinded me. I was ready to fight.

But I heard someone break down, sobbing, crying in agony. I found my aunt staring at me with round, blinking eyes. The person that had broken down look just like her. She wrapped her arms around me.

It didn't feel right. Nothing did.

I looked at myself. I was me again. Every limb in its place. My hands, my legs, my torso. I had one head. I lifted up my pants suspiciously. It was there. Everything was in place.

"Issy, don't," Constance said. "We don't know if we are dealing with Blake yet."

I squinted.

"Blake?"

I looked to my right. The woman who had broken down had tears in her eyes. The realization of who she was came back. She was my mother. "How long was I out?"

"Three days. Blake, what happened?"

"I'm fine, Constance."

"Let me be the judge of that."

I started to laugh but it disappeared. "It's still me. I'm fine." Okay, so that wasn't entirely true, but I was not going to be treated like a lost cause.

She nodded. "I need to do a thorough inspection."

"Don't touch me." My voice broke.

Her lips started to vibrate. "Where were you, Blake?"

I don't know. "I'm fine."

TWENTY-4

Constance finally released me from the infirmary when she saw that I wasn't going to talk about the dream.

I needed Fire-Cain. That was fucking messed up, but I wasn't going to cry about it.

What happened in that dream cabin changed me. I didn't think it was possible to succumb completely. My aunt brought me back before it happened, but that darkness left a mark.

One that would spread like a virus. I would become dark. It was time to just accept it. To look forward to finally being free. The dark wasn't so bad. I just had to make peace with it.

For the next few days, the students and all the professors were wary around me.

I didn't understand why.

I thought I'd just dreamt, until I discovered the truth from Irene.

"You sure?" I asked.

She nodded. "What did you dream about, Blake?"

I shook my head.

"Talk to me, please."

"Stop pushing!" I yelled. "I didn't know it was him, okay?"

"Who did you think it was?"

"Don't." I stormed out of her tower.

The old me would've been terrified. The new wasn't. I was worried for sure, but not because of what I'd done—because I didn't care.

As it turned out, when I chucked the creature out of the cabin window, in real life I'd thrown Lucian out of our window.

Constance and everyone were already on alert.

Master Longwei and a couple of the other professors had already been on their way, while Constance and Julia waited for me. That was when they saw Lucian being hurled out of the window.

Julia didn't think twice; she transformed and caught Lucian in her dragon paws. He was unharmed, but my screams made my aunt worry and she called my mom.

Apparently they'd had to fix our room. My abilities that didn't want to come in the dream, exploded against everything and wrecked everything. Lucian was lucky to be alive.

Irene was worried. Everyone was worried. Master Longwei the most. I saw it constantly on all the professor's faces. Some of them thought I'd turned for the worst.

If this was what they were afraid of, then it was my turn now to yell at the beast. He was the weak one.

I just wanted to grab someone and squeeze, make them

feel what I had in that dream. Maybe then they would fucking back off.

I found myself on Tabitha again. We were fucking in my room. She complained loudly.

Lucian just left. I didn't give a shit.

I pounded her harder and harder. My hands grabbed her throat. I squeezed. Her eyes bugged out and her lips drained of color. She started to hit me against the arm. I let go.

She was pissed off at me. Tears filled her eyes. She called me a psycho and fled.

I watched her run out of my room. I was so going to have to see a therapist. Yet, it didn't bother me one bit. I should try, even if it was only pretend.

I got up and took a shower as the dream replayed through my mind for the zillionth time.

It had been more than a week since the incident.

I got out of the bathroom, took my Fire-Cain out of the lose tile and snorted at least four lines. My head burned and I fell down. I didn't know who I was succumbing to this time.

The beast... or the human?

❦

SHIT CARRIED on like that for two months.

I didn't go home for the first break. I stayed at school.

My sister begged me to come with her.

"Fuck Sammy, get out! I'm not going home. Leave me alone."

She held her face, eyes widened in shock.

I only realized what I'd done then. My hand throbbed. If she wasn't a dragon her head would've rolled off her neck from the force with which I had slapped her.

"I'm so...."

"Don't you fucking dare. If you ever hit me like that again..." Her voice broke. "You will regret it." She ran out.

Before the dreams, I'd never struck a woman before, or choked one, or hurt one on purpose. Now? I was a monster. I stomped to the window and jumped out. The ground grew nearer and nearer. A few girls shrieked as my body connected hard with the ground.

I started to laugh. The pain washed away as if nothing had happened.

"You are a fucking asshole, Blake!" one of the girls yelled at me as I tried to get up.

"That was fun." I laughed more.

I was insane. I needed to be locked up.

It never reached Master Longwei, though. Maybe he didn't really care. It wasn't as if I'd died.

I used that night. I was out for like four days. Breaks were the only time that no one really knew what was going on in my room, and using was the only thing that calmed me down.

I doubted that this would be the death of me.

I feared that nothing could be.

No doubt everyone wondered when the turning point was. When did my shit come together again?

The answer was simple. A huge fucking Night-Villain finally got his shit together.

Just as I lost mine, my father regained his.

When school started, I had another incident with Samantha. She heard what I'd done.

"Why didn't you fly, Blake? What, are you trying to kill yourself?" She kept pushing and yapping like a little dog. She was driving me insane.

I pushed back and she hit her head hard against the floor.

At once Lucian was on me. So was his pathetic little friend, Dean. They all tried to knock me down, hold me back. They all end up with bloody noses and almost-broken limbs. Then George and Brian stepped in with Jeff and a couple other dragons.

I was sedated afterward. When I woke up, there was still someone I had to deal with. He waited for me in the chair beside my bed.

"Seriously?" I grumbled. "They sent you? The man who can't even take care of his own family?"

One second my father stared at me; the next I was facing him. His hand gripped my neck. "I fertilized your egg when your mother laid you. I will crush you, boy."

I couldn't breathe. But he didn't let go.

"I'm not afraid of the Rubicon. Hit your sister one more time, or anyone else, Blake, and I will make sure they lock you up in the dungeons of Tith and I will personally incinerate the key."

I was fuming, but I couldn't breathe. I tried to wrench myself free of his grip as his acid started to burn my throat. I couldn't get out of his grip.

"The dungeons of Tith are enchanted. No dragon has ever escaped from them. I will leave you there to rot."

I saw the truth in my father's eyes. "Okay, Dad." I choked. "I believe you."

He let me go. "Get your shit together, Blake. And don't ever make me come here to sort it out again."

I nodded. I had never seen my father like this. He was dark, too, but he was always so weak.

He looked out the window. "Have you turned?"

I kept quiet.

"Have you turned, Blake?"

"I don't know. Part of me is darker, but apparently I still feel some fear." Just felt it now.

"Then there is still hope."

He looked away and strode out of the infirmary without looking back.

I shuddered. I didn't think that I would ever fear my father again, but every bone in my body, every scale that covered me, trembled.

The beast didn't like that.

❧

A COUPLE CLAIMINGS ENSUED. I didn't care anymore.

I developed insomnia. I was scared of falling asleep. If it wasn't that fucked-up dream where I was sewn up all wrong, it was one where I got claimed by what apparently was light. I hadn't dreamt either of them, but I was dead tired.

I went to see Irene again. She was the only one who made me feel calm. Gave me what I wanted and fucked me the way I needed. A part of me still cared for her, but it was different now.

Everything was different.

Every time Lucian spoke about setting a date for his next attempt, I wasn't afraid for him anymore.

I just wanted to kill.

I had two more claimings. I wanted to kill them, to feed my darkness, but the authorities stopped the claiming before it got that far.

And then one night, I dreamed it.

It wasn't one of the two dreams I feared. It was another. I was hopelessly lost, mentally lost. I felt alone, scared, afraid.

The wind didn't blow. There was no sign of darkness. The Colosseum wasn't in sight, and neither was the desert.

I was afraid; this was the opposite of my usual dreams. It was peaceful. I was underneath a tree. I was lying on a bed, soaking up the warm sun. My body ached from too much sex. She stirred in my arms and I looked down at a redhead.

It washed over me like a tidal wave.

I grabbed her softly and my lips lingered on her freckled skin. I started to break down. A part of me hated it.

She woke up. There were tears in her eyes. I wanted to ask what was wrong.

"You don't love me."

"What?" I asked, confused.

"You don't love me."

"Baby," I said as alarm rose in my chest. What was wrong with her?

"You don't love me. You don't love me. You don't love me." She started to cry. Then she screamed and I woke up.

The old numbness came back, but a tear escaped and trickled across my cheek.

She was right. I didn't love her.

I never did.

I didn't belong to anyone, and I never would.

&.

"WHAT IS GOING on with your back?" Tabitha yelled one morning.

"Don't," I warned her.

"Who are you seeing, Blake?"

"It was nothing."

"You are unbelievable."

"You don't like it? There's the door, precious." I pulled my T-shirt over my head.

She wasn't going to tell me what I could and couldn't do. There were already rumors that we were an item.

"My brother still wants you to call him. Just speak to him. He's driving me insane." She pulled on her pants and walked out my room, wearing only her bra.

I shook my head. Phil could rot for all I cared.

The past few months had been a cruise, to be honest. Irene supplied my stash now. I just had to try and hold on.

I didn't feel that dark.

I always thought that when I went dark, I would want to free Goran and would die trying to do, or incinerate my world and rule the rest. That sort of thing.

Maybe my father was right. I still feared and with fear, I didn't know. Maybe the sign of my capitulation to darkness was there would be no fear.

I was fear.

But I still feared.

I got dressed and made my way to one of those boring fucking classes again.

Tabitha was next to me. Her hand moving up my leg and then she touched me. I closed my eyes. It felt good.

When the bell rang, I pulled her into a closet and fucked her brains out.

See life wasn't that bad. Well, not yet.

TWENTY-5

BACK IN THE COLOSSEUM. Cheers echoed against the walls. Dull sounds vibrated through my scales. Everything that I was shivered. Ugh fuck, not this. Please.

I knew what was going to happen once that gate opened. It was going to be a knight wearing pure white armor, and the sun's sharp rays would reflect on it, robbing my sight.

Everything about this night scared me to death.

The knight had a weird ability, one that made him replicate into an army. And although it was against dragon law to claim a dragon through multiple riders, this one didn't count.

I stared at the gate, as if by some miracle I would gain an extra ability that could incinerate the knight with nothing but my baleful stare. My heartbeat became audible. Everything around me went super quiet. It was just me and the knight—or should I say knights?—behind that gate.

The gate opened with a loud screech, and then I heard the clang of armor and the reflection of metal in the sun blinded my sight.

I woke up.

Sweat dripped from my face. Lucian was still asleep across the room. The clock on my bedside table read midnight.

Why was I dreaming this shit?

I struggled to shake the feeling. For some reason it was harder getting harder after each dream.

I shifted my legs off the bed and rested my head in the palms of my hands. My elbows rested on my knees and I took huge breaths to calm my nerves.

It didn't work. Something was wrong tonight.

A tap came from the window. I froze. I looked up slowly and saw nothing but the inky depths of night. Even that felt wrong.

I pushed myself from the bed and slowly approached the window.

It felt as if the wall backed away from me and it took forever to reach the damn window.

I finally reached it and looked out. Something was definitely not right; I stared up at the sky and couldn't even see stars.

My heart beat fast, hard. I heard it, something which wasn't possible, but here I stood, in my room that wasn't my room, staring into a starless night. I began to wonder where the hell I was.

A rumble of some sort vibrated through everything I was, and…

I jumped up in bed. Again.

The first thing I saw was the moonlight reflecting in my

room. A breeze fluttered the curtains. Every single hair on my arms stood up.

I still felt it. The vibration. It was humming through my scales hiding deep underneath my skin. My jaw muscles pumped and I ground my teeth. I only realize then that my hands were in balls of fury.

Soft voices came from way below in the courtyard. I tiptoed to the window.

Lucian stirred as I pulled the curtain back. Down below, Matt was carrying a body. Constance was voicing concerns and Master Longwei guided the way to the infirmary.

On any other night, I wouldn't have paid any attention to this, but something within me reacted with pure instinct.

I had to find out what the hell Matt was doing here. He lived on the other side and only came to Paegeia... well, when something brought him back. Only the most important matters. I simply had to know what was so important this time.

I strode over to my dresser, yanked open a drawer, and put on a shirt. My jeans were still on the floor of where I'd kicked them off this evening, and I pulled them back on.

"Blake," Lucian said in a sleepy voice. "What the hell? Where are you going?"

I looked back at him. "Go back to sleep. This doesn't concern you."

I shouldn't have said that. In fact I shouldn't have said anything. My tone was filled with alarm and he knew me too well.

"Blake, what is it?"

"Go back to sleep, Lucian," I said, trying a calmer tone, it looked as if it worked. Then a voice—Mia's—rang out below. I could hear it clear.

Apparently, so could Lucian; his gaze snapped to the window and he got out of bed. He gave me a quizzical look as he looked down on the courtyard of the main entrance. "What the hell is Matt doing here?"

I pulled on my shoes as Lucian dressed. I didn't wait for him. I didn't want him to come, to figure out what had brought Matt to Paegeia before I did.

Lucian would. He always put two and two together so fast. I hated that. I pushed the call button for the elevator and just my luck, tonight it was taking its time. I was contemplating taking the stairs when the elevator opened. It was almost closing with me inside when a hand appeared in the door and the elevator doors opened again.

My lungs expelled.

"Seriously, you couldn't wait two seconds?" His tense posture made it clear just how unhappy he was.

"Bite me," I grunted, hardly audible.

The ride down to the seventh floor felt longer than usual. I kept staring at the numbers. My nerves stood on end. Who was the person Matt had brought in and why did they have this effect on me? Was he linked to me, somehow?

My mind almost went there. But then again my father

would've known. I needed to see Irene. She must know something.

The elevator finally dinged and the doors opened. I walked out first and wished I could just say something so that Lucian would go back to our room.

Seven floors down I tried to shake him, but he was just as fast as I was and kept up easily.

Just face it, Blake. Lucian is here to stay.

On the last set of stairs opposite the girls' staircase, I found Mia hurrying toward the main entrance, back to her dormitory, which was close to Irene's wing.

"Blake." She sounded surprised. "Lucian." Her body inflated as if she was annoyed with the two of us coming to investigate. "What are you guys doing here?"

"I saw Matt." I squinted at Mia, who for some reason couldn't look me in the eyes.

"What is going on?" Lucian asked.

"Nothing. Just some dragon spawn they brought in from the other side. I don't have all the details yet, but her father didn't make it and Matt has no idea who he was."

I squinted. "If they lived on the other side, they should've been regesterd?"

"Exactly my point," she said. "Go back to bed, I'm sure Master…"

"Blake," Master Longwei's voice came from around the corner, just exiting the hallway. "What are you boys doing here?"

"Couldn't sleep," I lied.

Lucian's eyes fixed on me. It made me feel uncomfortable.

"Why is Matt here?" I insisted.

"He brought a girl from the other side."

"A girl?" Lucian said.

"You boys should mind your own business," he admonished. "You should get back to bed, both of you."

They were all hiding something.

Irene's voice filled the hallway from the lobby. "No, Matt, I would've known."

"Come on Irene," Constance spoke. "The resemblance…"

Then Matt spoke. "I can't help but to think that somehow…?"

Irene didn't let him finish. "She isn't who you think she is. There is no way. You said it yourself: her father was a dragon."

"I think you two should get back to your room now."

I squinted at Master Longwei. "What is it that none of you want to say?"

"Oh no," I heard Irene speaking.

"Blake is here," Matt said absently while Master Longwei stroked his face, not answering my question.

"Go back to your room. I mean it, Blake. We will speak about this later."

Matt's eyes found mine as he exited the hallway. It was written all over his face. Confusion, excitement, hope. He looked at the ceiling and back to Master Longwei and I knew what he meant. I had to wait for him on the roof of the boy's dorms. He will speak to me later.

I spun without saying a word, but Lucian still wanted to know more about the dragon spawn. I didn't wait for him and retreated to the elevator, back to the top, the roof, where I would get some answers.

§&

I WAITED for about forty-five minutes. I knew it was forty-five minutes because I kept checking my watch every five seconds.

Matt's head popped through the opening that led to the roof. He saw me sitting on the edge and climbed up. He reached me in a few seconds and came to sit down next to me, both our legs dangling from the roof.

It was silent for a few seconds and then I couldn't take it anymore. "Who is she, Matt?"

He stroked his face hard, the exact same way Master Longwei had tonight. "I don't know, Blake. All I can tell you is that her father wasn't an idiot. I didn't even know about their existence until he called me this morning, saying that he needed to speak to me urgently, that the matter was of great importance and that he couldn't discuss it over the phone. How he knew my number, knew my name and what I was, I have no idea."

I squinted. "They weren't registered?"

He shook his head and took a deep breath. "Fox and his colony were after him."

I stared at him, my mouth agape.

"Yeah," he agreed. "I bet Fox saw them a mile away, and I would give anything to know what he knew."

"Knew?" He'd used past tense.

"Her father died minutes before I got there. His face was badly burned, and Fox was a heap of torn limbs. Copper-Horns are gentle creatures, but you don't mess with one. Especially when it comes to family."

"Okay so she is a dragon spawn?"

Matt nodded.

It still didn't explain why I woke up, why my body reacted the way it had.

"One that carries the mark of the riders, Blake, and a very dark one too."

I stared at him again. Dragon spawn weren't riders. Sure, they were human, but they carried dragon DNA. Although they didn't have dragon forms, it was against dragon law for one to claim a dragon. They were never born with a mark either, not to mention a dark one.

"I don't understand. Her father is a dragon? Is that the reason why Irene…"

"No," Matt interrupt. "The reason why Irene is shaken up is because of who she looks like."

I waited for more and he took a while. "I need to know, Blake. You need to be straight with me. Honest. Please."

I hated when people begged.

"Did your father ever mention Queen Catherine being pregnant?"

I leaned back on the heels of my hands. "What?" Had I heard him right?

"Do you know if Queen Catherine was ever pregnant? Did they lie? Dragons remember every detail of their lives. What can you remember?"

I thought about it.

She wasn't pregnant, but there was a time when she was on her self-discovery quest... No, it couldn't be.

I shook my head. "No. I remember nothing like that. Why are you asking me this?"

He took another deep breath. "She looks like them, and no, not just a part of her reminds me of him. *She looks like him.* Like he was her father and the queen her mother."

"Do you even hear yourself? You of all people should know that no human can pass the Wall, so it doesn't matter what she looks like, Matt. She wouldn't have made it past that wall."

He nodded and closed his eyes.

When he opened them, he look straight down to the ground thousands of feet below us. "I kept telling myself that, Blake. But you haven't seen her. They say a dragon always knows."

"Matt, c'mon. You don't believe in that mumbo jumbo, do you?"

"I'm not Chromatic, Blake. You need to tell me..."

"No. You think I want to turn evil? You think I want to

know that one day I might incinerate my world, kill the people I love? Fight whoever is brave enough to kill me, which will probably be the one guy who would be able to tame me? No. I promise you this: if they had a child, my father would've known, I would've known, and I wouldn't be the dark mess that I am now and I would've had hope. She is a dragon spawn. The Wall would not have let her leave if she wasn't."

Silence fell again. Why was I lying to Matt?

TWENTY-6

MANY PEOPLE HAD SHOWN up from all over Paegeia over the years, sprouting rumors and speculation that they were the king and queen's children. Many. Not once had they been royalty. Not even close.

This was the same. This girl, whoever she was, was a dragon spawn, nothing more.

I found Lucian waiting on the couch of our small living room.

I sighed. *Here it comes.*

The sound effect of bikes racing played from the TV screen. A controller was lodged in Lucian's hand and his thumbs jabbed the buttons like there was no tomorrow.

"Where were you?" he asked without taking his eyes off the screen.

"So what, you're my mom now?" I asked sarcastically.

He put down the controller hard on the coffee table. "Who is she, Blake?" He stood up and pointed toward the window. "You were not awake. You fall asleep before me. Now tell me the truth?"

"What are you talking about?" I pretended I had no idea what he meant.

He huffed. "You know exactly what I'm talking about."

"Lucian, please. I heard voices, got up, and went to look and saw Matt. She is dragon spawn, that's all. Matt wanted to speak to me because of Fox. I swear."

His eye twitched. I never knew what it meant whenever his eye twitched. It twitched for many reasons. When he was tired, didn't buy a stupid excuse, or if he was hiding something in return.

His body relaxed and then he looked at me again with softer, kinder eyes. "So what did Matt say about Fox?"

"He's dead. Her father was a Copper-Horn and killed him in the process."

"Fox is dead?" Lucian sounded just as surprised as I felt. I nodded.

"Must have been some Copper-Horn."

"He must." My words were barely audible.

"Still," he said. "What is she doing here?"

I sighed. Like I said, Lucian was smart and always asked questions. "She was born with the mark of the Dragonians," I said, wishing he would just let this go as I knew where this road would lead.

"What? But she is dragon offspring."

"From what I gathered, her mother was human and her father a dragon."

"Still, dragon offspring never carry the mark of the Dragonians."

"She does," I said as if it was not impossible.

"Wicked." He grinned.

I fell on my bed and stared at the ceiling. Whenever Lucian said *wicked*, the conversation was over. Motorcycle sound effects blared from the speakers again.

I missed the old days. When I was still me, still sane and good, and he was still my best friend. I wanted that so bad again… But then, why had I lied tonight when Matt asked me to be honest with him? That a dragon knows his or her rider... I told him it was mumbo jumbo, that I didn't believe in it.

Why had I woken up? Why had I lied to Lucian? Was she who Matt thought she was?

No, she couldn't be. Again I thought about the time Queen Catherine had gone on a self-discovery quest to enhance her hearing.

A cold finger traced along my spine. She was part of a Dent. She didn't need to go on a quest to enhance her hearing; she could hear just as well as her dragon.

Then why had she left for five months?

ஃ

THE NEXT DAY the whole school was talking about our visitor. By the end of the day, the stories had grown. Some said her father was an ex–military man who hid out because he was on Paegeia's wanted list. Others said he was one of Fox's ex-members, which was how he'd managed to kill

Fox. I didn't listen to half the stories, but by the end of the day Master Longwei had to step in.

He called us all to the auditorium and in less than thirty minutes every chair was filled. I took a seat next to George, and saw him shaking as one of the first years walked away. He clearly didn't like her that much.

I couldn't help but snigger. "That girl confess her undying love for you or something?"

"What?" he asked, squinting.

"First year, short brown hair, fights like a dude?"

"Oh." He shook his head as if he had no idea what the hell I was talking about.

I let it go. I wasn't imagining things. Why did I get the feeling that George was hiding something?

Tabitha suddenly plopped down into the chair next to me along with one of her Green-Vapor friends, Susan or was it Sarah. I could never tell the two apart. The girl was excellent when it came to making up stories, and lied through her teeth to get out of any situation, but then again, that was what Green-Vapors were known for.

Tabitha gave me a kiss as my eyes caught Irene walking in. Irene gave me that one-raised-eyebrow look. The one that made me feel like I was going to be in the doghouse if I didn't break the kiss.

I turned my head away from Tabitha's face and smiled. Tabitha didn't make a big fuss. I wasn't the cuddling type and it was easy to hide from her that she was merely a cover-up so I could see Irene. I loved Irene and didn't care if she was a three-hundred-year-old Moon-Bolt.

It was never a bad thing to have someone close to you who can see the future. She would know when things got too dark. Or when the end was near.

The lights in the auditorium dimmed. Guys made dumbass mating sounds around us. Master Longwei walked onto the podium and grabbed the microphone, telling us to keep quiet. Right then grabby hands pulled my face and my lips found Tabitha's. I didn't know what it was about her kisses—hers and Irene's—but whenever the two of them started to kiss me, the beast was temporarily satisfied.

I didn't listen to a thing that Master Longwei said, except for the few words that slipped through the raging hormones here and there. Like *Fox* and *dead*, words that got the beast's attention.

And then just like that Tabitha stopped kissing me. *Why?* When I opened my eyes, my lips were puffy from all the kissing and my hormones were cranked up. The lights were on. Tabitha sucked in her lips as she waved goodbye.

Meet me tonight? she mouthed.

I nodded with a smile spreading over my face.

I found George grinning at me like an idiot. "You didn't hear a thing Master Longwei said, did you?"

"Nope," I said and he just laughed as we made our way out the auditorium.

I CLIMAXED. The beast inside of me felt satisfied again. Jumping from Tabitha to Irene like a bee pollinating flowers, or deflowering as Brian would call it, was a game the beast liked to play. I sounded like Brain but it was so not the moment to think about him.

"That was amazing," Tabitha said in a tired voice and I grinned.

"Amazing is my middle name," I joked.

She laughed sweetly in my ear, which she gently nibbled. It drove me insane the way only Tabitha could. This was getting confusing. Like, what the hell was Tabitha doing to me? At the same time, I felt bad for Irene.

I chuckled and pushed her back onto the bed, pinning her down.

Her legs twirled around my waist as I stared down at her. "You know what your sucking and nibbling does to me, young lady," I grunted playfully, pressing her harder into her bed.

She screamed with laughter as I dug my mouth into her neck and pretended to rip her apart.

It led quickly to hard, pounding sex. Afterward, she collapsed in my arms. We fell asleep.

Usually when I was exhausted, I didn't dream. But ever since the new girl showed up with Matt, I had nightmares each night.

The suffocation of the Colosseum. The crowd making me feel small. My normally silent heart pounding in my ears. The screech as the gate opened, and the sound of metal marching inexorably toward me, thousands of knights in white armor, and the sun's blinding reflection. Everything then fell silent. The type of echoing nothingness that made me feel like I was drowning in it.

I woke up at the chirp of the alarm in my ear. Six-thirty. I'd slept for like twenty minutes. My eyes felt raw from the lack of sleep.

Since the girl had arrived, I hadn't slept well. *Why was she doing this to me? Why her? Why was I so worried, she is a dragon spawn?*

I didn't like any of this. I didn't like the way I was reacting to her, to some creature who didn't even know dragons existed—or at least, that was what Lucian told me the day after Master Longwei called us to the auditorium. He said that Constance didn't know if her mind was going to perceive our reality.

Typical. Lucian already knew what she looked like; he was a real knight in shining armor. More like a royal pain in my ass. He'd already asked Constance if there was anything he could help with. So noble of him.

I stroked my face hard. Why this girl?

She didn't even know that our world existed. Probably didn't even have enough balls to face a dragon. How had her father hid it from her all these years? Why did he hide it from her?

The more I thought about her, the more I wanted to know who she was and what it meant for me. She was dragon spawn bearing the mark of the riders.

I'd thought Matt was overreacting that night when he said she looked like the king and queen, but over the past few days, I was starting to worry. Just a little.

Mia, Professor Gregory, Sir Edward, and even Professor Pheizer, they all had the same look. They were trying to contemplate how the girl had made it to the other side.

She couldn't look that much like the king and queen. I had to see her with my own eyes. I had to know. I had to get this over with, so I could fucking carry on with my messed-up life.

If I saw her, I would know the professors were wrong.

She would be just another dragon spawn.

I had no true rider.

WENTY-7

"So, Blake, would you mind sharing your input on why…"

"Excuse me," I interrupted Professor Pheizer. She never asked me for my input and I wasn't going to start giving it now. "I'm not interested in input. Well, not in class, that's for sure."

Sniggers traveled through the students as they got I was saying. Professor Pheizer's cheeks turned bright red.

"That was uncalled for. Fine, please leave my class if you are not going to participate."

I stared at her while packing my bag. I hated this class anyway. She was all for Dragonians, dragon bonds, and whatnots. It was wrong. Humans and dragons should never mix like that.

To my surprise, Tabitha started to pack her bag, too, throwing a wrench into my plans to seek out a certain Moon-Bolt for the rest of the afternoon.

"Stay," I grunted and saw confusion with a little hurt fill her expression.

I ignored it and walked out of Professor Pheizer's class.

"I know you think his behavior is so wretched, but that is the attitude of someone who is not going to get far."

I tuned her out. Everyone was still jostling for my better half. I was going to become dark. It was time that the rest of the world knew it too.

Just then, an electric surge went through my core. It turned my stomach and nausea overpowered me. I looked around to see if I could spot Lucian. He hadn't made me feel like this in a long time. It had died slowly after the Arianna incident. But here I was, feeling it again. The innate, disgusted rejection of his purity.

I swallowed hard and sped up toward the tower by the boys' dormitories. Purple flowers stuck out from green leaves of the thick ivy that ran up the length of Irene's tower. There was something magical about that tower, not to mention how magical the dragon was inside that tower. I felt aroused just thinking about the next hour.

I pushed the door open and the more stairs I climbed, the quicker the feeling dissipated. I didn't feel sick anymore.

I went to knock on the door when it suddenly opened and Irene grabbed me around my neck, pulling me inside the room.

Our lips touched feverishly. The kiss was fast and hard. My hands were needy. I lifted up the long blue dress that perfectly hugged her body.

She ripped off my shirt and I didn't even worry about not bringing an extra with me.

I just wanted her. She was making my head hurt with want.

Pulling off each other's clothes was vigorous and when we were naked, Irene jumped on top of me, slamming into me hard.

I bit her shoulder. The feeling of being inside of her was driving me more insane.

My grunts and Irene's soft moans satisfied the beast's demands. I shielded us from the rest of the school. Not that her tower wasn't soundproof, but her window was open.

She always needed fresh air. Well, she was going to be begging for it soon.

※

WE FELL, spent, on her bed.

Two fucking hours. I had no idea how humans were done so fast.

Irene gave me her tired laugh as she lay on my shoulder. She smelled of violets and warm sand.

The Moon-Bolt sense always came through the strongest after our sex-capades.

I loved her more than anything in this world and for some reason I knew this wasn't going to end well. I could feel Irene's eyes on me. I opened mine, looking down at her. She was resting her chin on her hand, leaning on my chest.

I gave her my famous lopsided smile, which she returned with a vague one. "What is it?" I asked. "And if you say we can't do this anymore, well, I might just end you."

She laughed. "It's not that."

"Is it about a certain Snow Dragon? I told you before, she is just cover."

She smiled. "I'm not worried about the Snow Dragon either." She sat up with her back facing me. Something was really bothering her.

I pushed myself from the bed, propped up on my elbow, and kissed her shoulder. "Please tell me what is bothering you."

She sighed. "Master Longwei. The entire fucking Board of Directors." She got up, pulling on her robe. She went to the table where her fine china tea set was displayed. She opened the teapot's lid and took out a joint.

"What about them?" I didn't have to ask. I knew what it was about. The new dragon spawn.

"Her father was a dragon. She is dragon spawn. Her mark is just a birth defect. She isn't who they think she is."

I narrowed my eyes. "We talking about the new girl Matt brought in?"

She nodded.

"Who do they think she is?" I played dumb.

"Really, you haven't heard?"

I chuckled. "I'm not always occupied with what the grownups are talking about, Irene," I joked.

She laughed and came over to the bed after she lit the joint.

I took it from her the minute I could.

"She doesn't even look like them. I don't know what everyone is so worked up about."

"Look like who?" A part of me wanted to hear her say it, say King Albert's name, Queen Catherine's. She sighed.

"Like Al and Katie." She called them by their nicknames.

"They think this girl is my rider?" I let my voice sound sarcastic.

She laughed. "Yeah, I didn't even think about that. The offspring of that royal line being your foretold rider. You feel anything?"

"Like what?"

"C'mon, Blake. A dragon always knows."

"I doubt that mumbo jumbo."

"I knew the minute I saw Tansee. I actually felt it before I ever realized it."

"Felt it?"

"Yeah, she put me on edge. My entire body felt wrong."

My teeth ground hard. I didn't like that. So this was real. A dragon did know.

"She isn't who they say she is. The Wall. If she was royalty, then how the fuck did they get her to the other side? The Wall would've incinerated her."

She waved away a cloud of grayish smoke. "I know, but why did Tanya leave?"

"You know why she left."

She gave me a look as I took a drag. "No, I don't."

My left eyebrow rose and I blew out the smoke. "You didn't see it?" I asked, surprised.

She gave me a you-know-I-couldn't-see-anything-about-them look. "Sorry, forgot." I sighed and smiled. "My dad told me King Albert didn't like Tanya so he told Catherine to choose. It's why she hated his guts after a while, why they were so far from each other the night of the betrayal."

"He asked her to choose between her relationship and her dragon?" She sounded shocked.

I nodded. "She chose him and Tanya left."

"That's horrible. He had no idea what he asked of her."

"So, don't worry. You're right. This girl's not who they think she is, and they'll discover that sooner or later."

"I can't even pick anything up from this one." she added.

I didn't like it. All the fucking signs were there. The way I'd felt ever since Matt brought her in. And today. Why today? Was she close and I just didn't see her?

My stomach grumbled and Irene laughed. "You need to eat. Go."

"You sure?" I said in a seductive voice.

"Yes, I have a session with Lucian after lunch. I need to get your scent out of here before he rocks up."

I narrowed my eyes. "I hope it's a foretelling session and not the kind of session we just had."

She hit me with her pillow. "For heaven's sake, it's Lucian. Prince of Tith. Helmut would kill me, not to mention what Maggie would do."

I laughed, grabbed her by the robe, and pulled her closer for one last kiss.

&.

I WAS one of the first people in the cafeteria. I was ravenous. I needed to eat and heaps of it. I found an open table outside, needing fresh air to clear my head.

Irene's scent no longer clung to me. The shower I'd just taken made sure of that.

The school bell rang and it was officially lunchtime. In less than fifteen minutes, the cafeteria would be overflowing with students grabbing their meals.

I finished mine in record time. What could I say? I'd worked up an appetite. Tabitha was the first to join me. George and Brian were next, and soon people occupied tables all around us.

"So my brother asked when are you going to call him," Tabitha babbled. "He's been waiting for ever. What is going on with the two of you, anyway? What does Phil want with you?"

I took a sip of my Coke and then I felt it. The nausea had come back.

I took a deep breath. "None of your business."

"Seriously? My brother is bad news, Blake."

I started to laugh with George and Brian, which annoyed the hell out of Tabitha.

"Why are you laughing?"

"Blake is bad news too, buttercup," George said in a way-too-flirty tone I didn't like.

My gaze snagged on the girl from before and George's entire demeanor changed without even looking at her.

Oh my fucking scales! The girl was his rider. He was hiding the exact same thing I was trying to hide too. Was she also making him nauseous?

Then my eye caught on a newcomer. I couldn't help but stare.

"Damn," Brian said. "That's the new girl?" He asked and took a deep breath in.

Sun-Blasts. I shook my head. I knew what he was smelling for. I was tenth Sun-Blast and the scent of her virginity hit me like a tidal wave, without sniffing like a crazy idiot.

"Ahh," he said. "As intact as they can come. Not even tampered with."

I couldn't help but laugh.

"You are such a pig, Brian," Tabitha said.

"What? It's the truth. Brian is what Brian is, and I would like to play a little bit with that."

"Disgusting."

I couldn't help it but to laugh again. Brian was hilarious.

I could feel her eyes on me. Why I had this effect on all the fucking girls was beyond me. I hated it. It made the beast grunt and hiss. I tried hard not to give us away, that half the professors here were right about her.

She was royalty. I didn't have to look at her to know it. She was the spitting image of her father, King Albert, but there was something about her that was also Queen Catherine. Bright blonde hair, light green eyes. She was their long-lost daughter and I didn't care at this moment how she'd gotten her out. They were the king and queen of Paegeia and they'd wanted that girl with every ounce of their beings. It was why Tanya left. It must have been the reason.

My dragon side hated everything about it.

I wished that she could just stop staring.

George said something funny again about the girl torturing him which made me laugh again. Fucking idiot. How long had he known what Rebecca Johnson was to him? I only knew her name cause she was my sister's best friend—Becky.

Suddenly, Tabitha's hand, well her middle finger to be precise, covered my face and the entire table laughed. If that didn't make the new girl look away, well, then nothing would.

Becky laughed, which made George flinch.

Everything about her was making him insane, like this spawn who was supposed to tame me.

"Don't pay her any attention," I heard Becky say. I hated to eavesdrop but this one I needed to keep tabs on. Nobody could know who she truly was. It would be the end of me. "She's a bitch. You're not the only one who stares at him with googly eyes and a drooling mouth."

"Who's he?" she asked and it sent little shudder through my skin. It made me feel stiff, as if I hadn't stretched my wings for a long time.

Their conversation carried on, making introductions I didn't want to be made. I tried to pay attention to the one at our table instead.

Then my eyes caught her looking at the sky. It had Becky's attention too. She asked why she kept looking at the sky.

"It's stupid. You'll laugh." She sounded nervous.

"I might, but I can't help it. You're hilarious." Becky replied. *So she was funny. Just like her father. Don't, Blake. Just don't.*

"I keep waiting to see... a dragon."

I froze when she said it. She truly had no idea. How was that possible?

Sammy's hyena laugh pierced through the cafeteria. "She's hilarious!" my sister said.

Brian looked at her with those puppy-dog eyes.

I kicked him underneath the table. "Forget it," I warned him.

"Easy," he said. "Brian knows the girl is Blake's family. Brian is just getting his fix."

"And that is where it is going to stay. I'll kill you if you so much as think of touching my sister."

"Brian would never touch Blake's sister."

He sounded like an idiot. But he was an idiot who could put a genuine smile on my face.

"Good. Don't forget it," I warned, playfully this time.

Then the new girl presented me with the perfect plan. Sammy tried to explain what she was and the spawn shrieked. Her voice filled with fear. She was afraid dragons.

"Oh, shut up," Becky yelled as we all guffawed. "Eat your food."

"Sammy, you should take her to Constance for the serum, before she goes mental," Tabitha said, making everyone around the table laugh again, this time cruelly.

Sammy flipped Tabitha off. "Suck on that, bitch."

Tabitha jumped up from her seat the same time I did. Why couldn't the women in my life just get along? It would make my life so much fucking easier. Tabitha was gorgeous and smart, but she always come in second when it came to Sammy. Sammy was advanced already as a dragon and would beat Tabitha, scales down. I guessed it was the perk of growing up as the Rubicon's sibling.

"Forget it. They are wasting their time. The cause is a hopeless one," I whispered in her ear. She smiled.

Sooner or later the spawn would break, and with George's help, I had a feeling it was going to be real soon.

I SAT for a couple more minutes listening to them chatting. Trying not to eavesdrop too much, I actually cringed when Lucian introduced himself. What was it with this fucking guy?

Then it hit me. Sammy, Becky, and this spawn. If they were going to end up being friends, it would mean that I was going to see her a lot over summer break. *No, no, no, no, no. This cannot happen.* She needed to break, and she needed to break soon.

"George, can I see you for just a second?"

George smiled as if he could read my mind already. Or maybe he'd just seen glimpses of what I wanted to do. He was a Moon-Bolt, after all. He got up without saying a word and we went to my locker. "What's the plan?"

"Easy: scare the living crap out of her."

He grinned.

"In your dragon form."

His grin slipped. "Blake." He rubbed his neck. "I know you were busying with Tabitha that day in the auditorium, but scaring her as a Moon-Bolt... Her dad was killed by one."

"Dude, she doesn't belong in our school. She's a mix-breed. Just do it. I'll give you *Silent Trapper and Underdog.*"

His face broke into a huge grin. "It's not even due out for another couple of months. How the hell did you get your hands on it?"

I smiled. "Rubicon perks. Do we have a deal?"

"Fine, and let me guess, this is all my idea?"

"You sure you can't read my mind?"

"Haha. Better go wrap up that game, Blake."

"You got it. And as soon as possible. Like, now, if you don't mind."

"For real?"

"The sooner the better," I mumbled, sauntering away.

I did not want to miss the look on her face. She would be begging for the serum after this.

TWENTY-8

THE BELL finally rang and lunchtime was over. The hallway filled with students rummaging through their lockers. A normal afternoon.

A smile spread on my face as I saw George shifting into his dragon form.

Tabitha had almost reached me and she had to sidestep to get out of his way.

I heard sniggers, chuckles, and laughter. I had a feeling all of them knew it was aimed at the spawn.

Tabitha rolled her eyes. "Please tell me you had nothing to do with this."

"Me? Why would you think that?" I spoke through a huge grin, arms folded, watching George make his way to the entrance of the hallway.

"Is Sammy really a dragon?" I heard the new girl asking. They were close. I felt it too.

Becky chuckled. "Yeah, Fire-Tails are babblers, but they're also the kind of dragon you can ask to incinerate a body when in need."

Three, two, one. Becky appeared first and then a smile

spread over my face as the spawn froze, craning her neck to look at George.

Everyone sniggered.

George did his part. He growled, spitting on her face. The growl echoed off the walls and it was bound to reach the teachers.

More laughter erupted.

He stomped his paws, causing a rumble in the floor. She was going to piss herself. A tear rolled over her cheek and some of the laughter died away.

I enjoyed every minute of it. It disgusted me to think that someone in this fucked-up universe had given her the power to tame me. She was weak and my dragon would never yield to her. I would crush her the minute she faced me.

"Dammit, George, this isn't funny!" Becky screamed. At least she wasn't scared of him. I bet it made him even more furious.

"Make him stop!" Tabitha's sharp voice was coated in horror.

I gaped at her. "I thought you wanted this. She doesn't belong here, Tabitha."

"Make him stop now!" she ordered me.

I hated she did that. Nonetheless, I whistled before she could put two and two together and figure out that I was truly the one behind this.

George turned around and ran back in our direction, morphing back to his human form.

I stared down at Tabitha. "Don't ever tell me what to do again," I grunted.

I'd done my part. Hopefully Constance would give the new girl the serum and in a few weeks, everyone would forget about the girl with the dark mark, the girl who looked like King Albert.

As I was walking, something strong connected with my body and I was pushed into the wall.

Lucian's face was inches from mine. "Why did you do that?"

"Get off me." I pushed him away.

"Who is she to you, Blake?" he demanded and everyone close by stopped and stared at us. I didn't like the attention.

"Nobody, idiot." I laughed. "I told you before, she is dragon spawn, born on the other side of the Wall," I said the last part slowly so all of them could hear it. "I wasn't the one scaring the living crap out of her."

Lucian chuckled. "No that was your buddy, George, who would do anything you asked him to do." He pointed his finger at me. "I'm watching you."

I narrowed my eyes. "Is that supposed to scare me?" I shouted at his retreating figure.

"Yeah, if she turns out to be the one, Blake, your days are numbered."

I laughed again. "Whatever, dude."

I turned around and my grin disappeared fast. *Shit.* He was the last person I wanted to dig into this. If he discovered the truth and told someone like Master Longwei, it wouldn't matter how good my lies were. I had to make it clear to him that she wasn't the girl they all thought she was.

During Art of War, news started to reach the professors regarding what happened after lunch. Mia wasn't very happy. "Please tell me you weren't behind it, Blake."

"Mia, it was a fucked-up prank, okay? What do you want me to say? I didn't think it would cause her to have a fit," I lied. I wanted her to lose it.

She grunted and smoke actually escaped her nostrils. "Dammit, Blake. Why? You heard what Master Longwei said about her and what happened that night. A Moon-Bolt dragon killed her father. How could you…"

"Just stop. It's not my fault that she was unaware of the existence of dragons. Her father should've told her. She doesn't belong in Dragonia Academy, Mia. She is dragon spawn. Have you all forgotten that?"

"Out," she pointed to the door.

"Fine," I dropped the sword I'd been clutching. "If it carries on like this, Wyverns will soon be attending."

"Out!" she yelled again and I left.

I hated how fast news spread through the school. I knew Master Longwei was going to have a talk with me, too, as soon as it reached him.

I should've just played dumb, pretended it wasn't me, but it would just made them more suspicious. I never hid the shit I did. Okay, that was not entirely true. Nobody knew about the killings and the fight club, and Irene, and now this new girl.

I took a huge breath and decided to go back to Irene. I needed to clear my head. The walk from the dome to the tower wasn't a long one.

I was about to knock on her door when she yelled to enter. I opened the door and found her sitting by the window, a cup of chamomile tea in her hand. I hated the scent. She also had a joint.

She didn't embrace me or even smile as I entered. "Why did you do that, Blake?"

My face fell. "Not you too."

"Is she who they say she is?"

"Do you hear yourself?" I asked. My tone sounded strong, believable. "She was living on the other side, Irene." That part really was really starting to annoy me. I knew that they'd found a way to get her through the Wall years ago, but the others didn't. Now they just forgot about it, like it wasn't a big deal. "Dammit, I thought you agreed that she doesn't belong here. She is a runt, born with something that resembles the mark. Nothing more. If someone doesn't stop this, I don't even want to think about who they are going to let in next."

"Okay, calm down," she said and got up. "It's just the Board—all of them—wants answers. They had a huge meeting during lunch and then your little stunt, well, I guess you can see where it is heading. I know you might not like the fact that Longwei is giving a pass for runts, but it doesn't look good if you are behind pranks like that."

"I am behind most shit that happens in Dragonia," I countered. "It never bothered anyone before."

"Yeah, well, they don't see this girl as just anyone. She could be the princess, Blake, your rider."

"Oh, please. I came here to spend some time with you and now…" I shook my head. "It was a mistake, I shouldn't have come."

I strode to the door.

"C'mon, don't be like that!" She called after me.

I didn't stop. *That was stupid, Blake.* Stupid. Now everyone was going to be on my case. I should've just ignored the fucking spawn.

I pulled off my clothes as I reached the entrance of the tower and shifted into my dragon form. The only place that could cool me off was a forest on a mountaintop.

❦

I LAY on my back staring at the sky. *How? How did they get her past the Wall?* I knew they were smart, but I didn't think they were that smart.

I shouldn't speak to anyone about her; I shouldn't even ask my father what he thought. It would just raise red flags.

My mind wandered back to my dream and the meaning of it. The white armor, what did that represent? Royalty?

306 | ADRIENNE WOODS

The quantity, that my days of running free were growing shorter? I sighed.

I pushed myself up and rested my arms on my knees as a feeling I hadn't experienced in a long time filled my gut. Regret.

What if Constance did give her the serum? What then? My chance of becoming good again was gone forever.

No! The beast roared in my mind. *There is no hope. Darkness is our only destiny. Get the spawn out of your head or I will make her disappear.*

I closed my eyes. I hated these thoughts. They were mine, even though I felt like Brian whenever my good side's feelings differed from my dark side. It was a constant battle. I was so tired.

Then embrace what you are and give in to the darkness.

"No!" I yelled and birds in the surrounding trees shot into the sky as my voice echoed off the mountain.

I needed to pull myself together. Needed a distraction. I took out the notebook from my back pocket and started to write.

Darkest days, dreary night,
All I seem to do is fight.
Endless days against the world,
Only darkness inside can behold.
A feeling so strong awakens me,
The Descendant's here, it cannot be.

Hope's light ignites inside me,
The rider is here to set me free.
Soon to be a powerful Dent,
All my deeds would make amend.
Dreary nights will no longer be,
Until I saw the he is a she...

THE BEAST inside my head roared. He was furious at the words I'd written down. Making amends? What the fuck?

You are mine, mine. We belong to the darkness. I swear I will kill her, Blake. Get this fucking girl out of your head or she will no longer be. Don't you ever cross me. If you tell her, I will kill her.

"Okay," I spoke to myself again. "They are just words, stupid words. I don't want to be claimed."

I could still hear its fury.

I felt like a fucking loon. Speaking to myself in third person. But I felt it was the only way to hold on.

 TWENTY-9

I WENT BACK to school just before the final bell of the day rang. Thank heavens this day was over.

I felt weird whenever I got close to the spawn, and it was hard controlling it. Not to give anything away. To act normal. It was as if my skin had shrunk a size or two and was too small for my body. I couldn't breathe properly with a slight twirl in my stomach.

As I walked past other students on my way to the lobby, suddenly I was yanked back. My shoulder blades connected with the wall hard.

Tabitha trapped me with her beautifully sculpted body. Her ice-blue eyes were narrowed, looking deep into mine. It was as if she was searching for answers—where I had been and what I was hiding. Questions about the spawn.

Her boldness just turned me on. I liked it when women took charge. Her lips pressed hard on mine.

She grunted softly as I kissed her hard and I pushed myself off from the wall and pushed her against it. Our lips never left one another.

She was driving me crazy. My hand tangled up in a

piece of her shirt. I realized we were not in the confines of my room or hers, but right beneath the stairs. Still I couldn't stop touching her.

Then something hard smacked into me with strength. Dragon strength. I took a few steps back from Tabitha and saw a pissed-off Sammy all up in my personal space.

She was beyond livid. "You're such an asshole, Blake."

I chuckled, taunting her was easy. News did spread fast.

"Dad will hear about this," she threatened.

My father could not know about it. Not ever. "It was a joke, Samantha!"

"A joke? 'Larry and Brent walk into a bar' is a joke, Blake, not what you and George pulled this afternoon."

My eyes twitched and in the corner of my eyes I realized why I had a sudden aching need to turn into a dragon. I expanded my glare and found the spawn, still standing, still trying to cope with this reality.

She looked away. Weak. She was weak.

I looked at my sister again, my nostrils flaring. How could she be friends with her? I wanted to yell at her that this was against our dragon code. She was a runt—well, at least that was what everyone was supposed to think. My sister was never supposed to be friends with her.

"Didn't you hear what Master Longwei said about Elena the other night?" Samantha carried on. "I guess not. You were probably too busy thinking about Medusa's naked body."

Tabitha lunged at Sammy, but my reflexes were much faster. I pinned her back against the wall with one arm.

"I'm going to kill you, Samantha. Your mouth is way too big."

"She's not worth it, babes. Calm down," I said and moved closer to her ear. "It's worthless to use all that strength on them. I rather you used it on me, up in my room."

Tabitha's smile appeared.

"Disgusting," Samantha muttered. "At least I'm not a coward."

"Sammy," Becky said through clenched teeth.

Tabitha's jaw muscles pumped. I tried to calm her but she glared at my sister instead of me.

"Your sister has a big mouth, Blake."

"Yeah, and she is much stronger than you think, Tabitha."

She smiled. "What? You don't think I can take your sister?"

"Oh no, not that. It's just... my sister grew up as my sibling. When it comes to fighting, as crazy as I am about you, I'm afraid you will lose."

She grunted. "We'll see about that." She stalked away.

"My room in ten minutes." I grinned.

"Oh, why don't you ask your sister, if she is so perfect?"

Fuck! Typical. What was the point of being honest if it was going to bite me in the ass? I sighed and walked past the staircase to the main entrance.

The trapped feeling started to fade slightly as I walked up the stairs to the seventh floor. Well, at least I had a sign for whenever the spawn was close by. I could just head off in the opposite direction.

They could never find out who she truly was. Ever.

§

WHEN I OPENED THE DOOR, I found Lucian still here. It was Friday; he usually went back home over the weekends unless... *Don't even think about her.* It didn't matter why he was still here.

I walked past him to the bathroom.

I could feel his eyes on me, the way he was already trying to put two and two together about who the spawn was.

I locked myself in the bathroom door, needing something to calm the beast. I felt on edge. My body reacted to everything that was happening and it was out of my control.

I lift the bathroom tile and pulled out the powder. I was almost out again, and if I wanted more from Phil, well, I knew what it was he wanted. It didn't sound so bad anymore.

I had a gig on Saturday; maybe Ty would have some, or maybe he could get me some. I could always count on him. Still, I need my own stash.

I took out the powder and cut it in a long, thin line. My father would shave me clean if he knew I was using to keep the darkness at bay. I needed to be in control, to forget, to feel normal even for a few hours.

I bent over the basin and snorted the powder through my nostrils. It burned. Fire spread to my head, giving me a mother of a headache.

I had to control the noises coming from me. I needed to control the pain. I needed to be in control. Then the fire finally vanished and a soothing feeling spread. It clouded my mind. A warm sensation started to soothe my aching muscles.

I felt tired, so tired. I hadn't slept lately.

I walked out of the bathroom. I could feel Lucian's eyes on me. I pointed weakly at him. "Don't you dare judge me. I'm doing whatever I can to hold on."

Tears glistened in his eyes. I didn't need his pity.

The entire room started to spin. I literally crashed onto the bed. And the rest was one big fucking blur.

I remembered music, whether it was in my head or not, I had no idea. Maybe Lucian had thrown a party. It would be a first for him.

I remember screwing. Tabitha? How the hell? Was I even part of all these things? Fuck, why was I speaking to any of them? Was I enjoying myself? Telling things I shouldn't be telling?

And then the loud singing overpowered my head. It sounded like a thousand bugs baking in the sun. That deafening sound that made my skin feel too tight. Was she close by?

I hated the comedown, the agony of feeling so alone. Weakness. It was the worst.

I opened my eyes and the buzzing noise that had drowned out everything else finally turned down. It was just a buzz now.

Snow-white hair covered my chest. I sighed. Tabitha. I hated not remembering having sex. Sex was one of the things that calmed the beast. I didn't think that this would happen. She'd said to go ask my sister. Gross, she was my sister, and the time of screwing siblings so the dragon race don't die was so over.

If I knew it was going to turn to this, I wouldn't have used my last Fire-Cain.

I pulled my arm from underneath her and pushed myself up on the bed with my legs touching the floor.

I had a mother of a headache and my healing ability was still shitty. Why did the good ones always take the longest to develop?

Beer cans littered the floor. Fuck, what had happened here last night?

I hated being so out of it. I'd had no control. I can't even remember what I'd said. Had I spoken about the spawn?

I sighed. *Calm down. It's why you took Fire-Cain last night, to calm down.* To forget about the spawn, to just be free even if it was just for a few senseless hours.

Whatever the damage, it could be fixed.

THIRTY

AFTER I TOOK MY SHOWER, I spent the entire day in bed. My head was still pounding, and I was still so out of it. At times it felt as if I was awake. If people were coming and going from my room, I didn't even register.

It felt busy; the background noises started to irritate me, but I couldn't do shit about it as I was so out of it.

I hated the day after. The crash. It made me feel insignificant, weak, alone, unworthy. Things I hated.

At length, I opened my eyes. I felt better, but still like shit. I lifted my head as the sun was going down.

The room was clean. Tabitha? A part of me loved her, and a part of me hated her. She was so pathetic just like Snow Dragons were. She was merely a toy that I could play with whenever I was bored.

I found a note on my bedside table.

CALL PHIL.

I pressed my eye sockets hard with my thumb and forefinger. He wasn't going to take no for an answer or let me ignore him.

My stomach grumbled. Time to have dinner. I got up, took another shower, and got dressed.

The note was still taunting me from the bedside table. I put it in my back pocket and left.

Junk food, burgers, fries, pizza... I guessed someone other than Miss Know-It-All had gotten the riddle this time.

"Good evening, Blake," Chef greeted me.

I grunted my hello. Why he still kept trying to get me on his good side was beyond my knowledge. I'd never known Copper-Horns to be liars. The spawn's guardian was a Copper-Horn, and she had no idea what he was. He was a liar. If one Copper-Horn was a liar, others could easily be liars too.

I grabbed a burger and a plate filled with French fries and two sodas. I was glad that I was one of the very first students here and prayed I wouldn't catch the spawn on my way out.

It was hard enough not to wring her little neck, not to mention the feeling she brought with her.

I bit into my burger and as I closed my eyes, I saw Queen Catherine's eyes on me. Her glares. It wasn't because she didn't like me. It was because she knew her little girl was going to be my rider.

What had happened? Why did they feel the need to take her to the other side? How had they gotten her out? I needed to find out.

I devoured the rest of my burger and half of my fries when the trapped feeling overpowered my core again. My skin crawled as a cold shiver ran up my spine. How on earth was she doing this to me? She wasn't worthy. Not one bit.

When the swirl to my core came, I almost felt like barfing up my food. I tried to control it, tried to relax my face muscles, to not show that I felt sick. Too many questions that I didn't want to answer.

They walked in, chattering about their day. She'd gotten clothes from a trip to Elm.

I took a huge breath. *C'mon, Blake. You can control this. It's not so hard.*

I felt tired and just stared at the fire that was coming from the lantern that was sitting in the middle of the table.

I played with the fire, while concentrating on something else besides the spawn. It seemed to be working.

The Wall. How had they gotten her past the Wall?

I found her eyes on me again, boring into my soul as if she knew her destiny lived inside of me. I had to get out. I got up, dropped off my plates, and left out the side door, farthest away from them.

The feeling started to vanish the farther I got from her.

I still had Tabitha's note in my pocket. Maybe it was time to call Phil.

៛

GETTING AWAY from everyone was the best. I loved going to the mountains just to think, to fight with myself, to hold on.

I transformed back to my human form the minute I reached the spot, and didn't even bother putting on clothes.

If I had it my way, I would embrace my form and walk naked every day.

I took out my phone that was still in my pants pocket lying on a heap next to me. I dialed Phil's number on my Cammy and waited for his face to pop up.

"What took you so long?" he said. Not *Hi, bro, how are you doing?* Nope, Phil wasn't the kind of guy who gave anyone choices. He knew I needed the fights to keep the beast calm and he knew eventually I'd need more Fire-Cain.

"One fight," I said, "and you'd better make the payment worth it this time. Oh and Phil," I said and waited until he met my eyes. "Stop telling your sister to call me. I will call when I need you, not the other way around. Remember who you're dealing with."

I disconnected before he could say anything back.

꩜

THE WEEKEND WENT FAST, and by Monday I got a note from Irene to come and see her. She hadn't left me a note for a long time and a part of me wasn't looking forward to speaking with her.

I put the note in my nightstand.

The first few periods went fast and I'd made the choice not to go see Irene when Sir Edward stopped me during transformations and sent me to her.

"What's the use?" I was adamant. "I'm still going to end up on the other side." Meaning I would become dark.

"Just go see her, Blake. It's mandatory."

"Fine," I grunted. I transformed back and walked out the Colosseum without a shred of clothing on. I pulled on my pants as I reached her tower.

She opened the door. She didn't look happy; she look drained.

"I don't want to fight," I grunted. "So if you are here to fight over stupid things, I'm gone."

"I don't want to fight either." She let me in.

I didn't give a crap why she looked drained or tired. I just wanted her. And the Rubicon always got what he wanted.

THIRTY-1

FOR SOME REASON the more I tried to forget about the spawn as the week went by, the harder fate pushed us together, or made it hard not to think about her.

She was everywhere. I thanked heaven that my reflexes were fast so she didn't really see me.

Brian started talking about her during lunch. How she reminded him of a popular actress. He claimed that behind those too big shirts and jeans was no doubt a goddess. All that while speaking in the third person, of course.

All Brian was after was one thing, and it had nothing to do with her personality or who she reminded him of.

Then my roommate joined in. It happened on Thursday night, when I caught him speaking to his mother over his Cammy.

"Nope, not this weekend. Maybe another?"

"So let me get this straight," she said haughtily. "You don't want to come home?"

"Mom, I'm tired of all the traveling."

"Are you sure it has nothing to do with a certain new girl?"

"No, I just have a lot of studying to do, okay?" He glanced up, realized that I was in the room, and quickly changed his tune. "I have to go, I'll see you next week. Promise." He switched off his Cammy.

"Staying during weekends now?" I said. I felt irritated. *WHY?*

"I just don't want to go home. Is that a crime?"

"Nope, but I wonder if your mother wasn't onto something…" I tried to take the sting out of my words by adding a smile.

"You have a problem with that?" Lucian snapped. I'd touched a nerve.

"I was just joking. It's nice to see you trusting girls again."

"Shut up. Maybe you forgot who was behind my not trusting girls anymore."

"She was wrong for you. I did you a favor."

"A favor? I could've married a friend. Now I loathe the girl I have to marry."

"That is just horrible," I said, sneering. "Being a prince is so hard."

"Bite me." He got up and left.

Yeah, sometimes the truth hurt and he was right too. I was the reason behind their breakup.

But I was still wondering why he was all of a sudden wanting to stay over the weekend. Was it her, the dragon spawn?

I found myself leaving Irene's tower early in the morning three more times that week. I hid from my aunt as she took out the Swallow Annexes each morning. Fuck, I'd forgotten about that.

I really had to be more careful when it came to Irene.

&

FRIDAY NIGHT FINALLY ARRIVED. It was weird entering my room and finding Lucian without his bags lined up ready to go home. As if the week wasn't hard enough with him here, he was messing up my weekends too.

"Please, promise me, no drugs this weekend."

"You're not my mother," I said.

"No, but I don't like the things you do when you're on it, Blake."

"It's the only way." I sighed. "Why can't you get that?"

"It's Fire-Cain. You're going to destroy your life, Blake. I'm sorry I still see you as one of my friends. Stop using, or I will tell Master Longwei and get you expelled."

"Oh?" Rage bubbled up in my chest. "And who is that going to help in the end?"

"Just stop. I'm sure booze can help," he said.

Furious, I took a quick shower and when I got out, he was gone. There was a knock on the door as I toweled off.

I smiled. I knew who that was. Irene never came to my room, so it could only be a certain Snow Dragon.

I opened the door and found her leaning in skimpy shorts and a bright yellow tank top barely covering her breasts. I pulled her in by her shirt and she laughed as our lips found each other.

She touched my chest with ice-cold hands. It was doing something to my blazing hot temperature. Slowly, I started to relax and cool down. Her kisses were a breath of fresh air —or better yet, a cold breeze. She was my opposite... and it felt more and more like I could become addicted to her.

My towel disappeared from around my waist and her shorts were next. And in less than a minute, I was transported to paradise.

❦

WE WERE STILL GETTING busy when the door of the room opened. Tabitha shrieked and hid underneath me, pulling the covers around us.

"Please don't tell me that this is going to carry on the entire weekend."

I laughed softly.

"Hi, Lucian," Tabitha said.

I rolled off of Tabitha to find Lucian wearing swim shorts and a T-shirt. He'd come to pick up his towel.

"You going somewhere?" I asked, squinting.

"What, you're my mother now?" he chirped.

I deserved that. I pulled my mouth, which made Tabitha laugh again.

He walked out.

It was dark outside and I couldn't believe that Lucian was actually going to the lake, unless... *No, don't you dare think about the spawn.*

"Come here," I grunted and pulled Tabitha's body on top of me.

We carried on where we'd left off. When we were finally done, we played games. George came over and it was the two of us playing *Silent Trapper,* the game he'd won doing a lousy job pranking the spawn.

She was supposed to lose her mind, not cope.

It was getting late and there was still no sign of Lucian. Why was I so worried about him all of a sudden? We weren't really invested in each other's lives anymore, not since when we'd been best friends, brothers.

I took a deep breath and déjà vu hit me hard. The door opened and Lucian walked in. He was as white as a ghost.

"Dude," George said.

"Are you okay?" Tabitha asked.

He shook his head and went to sit on his bed.

"What happened?" Tabitha wanted to know.

So did I, but I wasn't going to beg him.

He looked straight at me. "You ever see someone Ascend?"

Please don't let it be the spawn, please, please. "What?" My throat was dry and I swallowed hard, dreading his answer.

"Have any of you ever seen someone Ascend right in front of you?"

George and Tabitha shook their heads. I just stared at him. "Someone Ascended?"

He nodded mutely.

WHO, IDIOT? My mind screamed at him.

"Rebecca Johnson."

George froze. He grew ashen. I knew exactly what he was hiding.

"You okay?" I asked George.

Lucian butted in. "You knew?" he asked George, sounding pissed off.

"Don't. I don't have to say shit to you." He grabbed his jacket and stormed out, game forgotten. The door slammed behind him, making Tabitha flinch.

"He is Becky's dragon, isn't he?" Lucian pushed.

"Just drop it, Lucian."

"Why? Why on earth didn't he say anything, Blake? How long?"

"How long what?"

"How long has he known?"

"I don't know. I only recently put two and two together that Becky was his rider."

"How long did he know?"

"I don't know. I told you I recently figured it out myself."

"How, Blake?" he asked, his nostrils flaring. "Let me guess, since the day Elena was brought in?"

"Here we go again." Annoyance welled up. "She's not my rider. My rider is fated to be of royal blood. Do you for one second think that Queen Catherine and King Albert would give up the only thing they had ever wanted without telling my father about it? Huh?"

He's face fell.

"Answer me!"

"Okay, it's just all the craziness happening lately and now tonight. I've never seen anyone struck by lightning and shake it off as if nothing happened to them."

"Seriously?" Tabitha sounded awestruck. "She just got up and shook it off?"

"All I can say is if she hadn't Ascended, she would've been dead."

Just then his Cammy rang. He took it out of his pocket and flinched. By that look I knew it was one of the 'rents. He walked into the bathroom before he answered it. Queen Magerite's voice shouted from the other line.

"I'm glad I'm not him," Tabitha said.

"Yeah, sometimes it's awesome to just be normal," I joked.

It grew very quiet and I knew exactly what was brewing in her mind. "Don't. Please. I meant every word I said."

"Then why is he thinking she is linked to you?"

"Because." I sighed and decided to try a different technique. "You know how all the professors are with her? Trying to help her cope with the shock of learning about our world? She reminds them of King Albert."

"She looks like him?"

I nodded. "That, and she apparently has a very dark mark. Put those two together and some of them have concluded that she is his heir."

"She's not?"

"No, a dragon always knows, Tabitha. I have no true rider."

She nodded. "You think maybe there could be someone out there?"

"No, there isn't. The Wall would never let a human pass."

"I'm sorry," she said softly and lay her head on my shoulder. "I feel bad for George, though. It was like he knew and just didn't want to say anything. Why?"

"Would you? If you knew who your rider was, would you say anything?"

She looked into the middle distance and shook her head.

"Exactly. He didn't either. It's a Chromatic thing, I think."

She laughed. "Thank heavens you are half and half then."

I smiled. If only she knew how strong my Chromatic part was. If she only knew.

THE NEXT DAY I was on edge. Not because of the spawn, but because of the night to come.

Fight night.

I was going to slip out around six and fly to Phil's place. From there we were going to do the spell. I would transform and fight as a rider. To the death.

A lot of people hated what was going on at the fringes of the black market. Fights like these were illegal, but they also put the Fire-Cain I needed in my pocket. And the beast wanted bloodshed. I was betraying my own kind, fighting to the death, but a kill like this kept the beast away for at least two weeks.

I needed to control my acid tonight, and only my acid. If the system found out that I was the Rubicon and not a human, there would be dire consequences.

Around five, I took a shower and got ready. I pulled on my robe and slipped to the roof of the boys' dormitories.

I transformed, jumped into the air, and flew as hard as I could to get behind the clouds and out of the authorities' sight.

A hard thirty minutes later, I came in hard on the opening of Samuel's mansion.

Tonight I was going to fight one of this year's best Night-Villains.

"Blake!" Phil got up from the couch and greeted me at the gate where I'd just transformed back into my human form.

"You ready?"

"No, not really, but I've run out. You have my stash."

He lifted his hands. "Don't I always?" He tapped my face hard, riling up the beast. "You under control?"

"Yeah." I glared at him. *No.*

He smiled. "Let's go and make some money."

THIRTY-2

I HAD TO ADMIT, the identity Dimi worked up this time for me was a cool one. My name was going to be Grey. I had skin the color of mahogany and a cloud of corkscrew black hair.

Grey hated dragons because one killed his father and violated his sister and mother when he was only ten. Years and years of therapy didn't fix our poor Grey, and that was why he was in the ring tonight, facing a dragon who resembled the one who had killed his family.

Avenging them was the only thing on Grey's mind right now.

The chest and arms of Grey were covered in intricate tattoos, hiding the mark of the Rubicon. His muscles were ripped and ready for violence.

Just don't show your other abilities, the beast said, *and kill him fast. One kill, Blake.*

I followed Phil and Dimi out of the locker rooms. I watched the last few minutes of the fight before mine. The fight was hard.

The stands were packed with grimy spectators, everyone

cheering for their favorite. People with surreptitious gestures and a habit of looking over their shoulders. The place smelled of blood, fried meat, bourbon, and cigarette smoke.

I felt it once, thought it was going to rip my skull apart and was surprised that my spelled disguise didn't waver.

The dragon in his human form had gotten hold of the human. He had him in a death grip. A couple people standing close to me couldn't watch and turned their heads.

This was it. The dragon was going to win this round.

I couldn't see the death blow, but I heard it. It broke his neck. Bones shattered and the crowd went crazy.

A hand slapped me on my shoulder. "You ready?" Dimi asked.

"Let's do this." I followed him to the ring.

The staff was busy dragging out the dead body and the emcee lifted the dragon's arm in victory.

Big bloke. He was one of the big three. A Sun-Blast—he answered my question by spouting red and blue flame from his lips into the sky. It wound the crowd up even more.

The dragon left the cage and the walls of the cage started to rise.

People had about ten more minutes to make their bets for the next fight. Tonight, odds were one to thirty-five. Nobody knew me—they weren't supposed to—and the Night-Villain was a favorites in this tournament. If they know that I was Hansel in disguise or Blake in disguise, it would've been a different story.

"For our next fight," the emcee intoned dramatically, "I present the mighty Night Crawler!" He listed the dragon's stats. He wasn't that big, but his stats were staggering. I wasn't even that big yet.

The Night Crawler hated Dragonians; he saw them as intruders in his world.

The feeling was mutual.

The crowd cheered as the Night Crawler showed off his strength.

Then the emcee called me up. Grey Templeton. I didn't know how Samuel came up with these names. He started to give my stats. How much I weighed, my so-called ability, where I was from, and so on.

I felt bad for this dragon. If he truly knew who was concealed behind these tattoos, he would shit himself.

༄

THE FIGHT WAS ACTUALLY HARDER than I thought, but he wasn't fast.

I was fast. I went straight for the wings and his mane. My knuckles were raw by the fifth round.

By the tenth round, the beast inside me was roaring, enraged. I'd toyed with my opponent too long.

For a split second, I let it take over. The darkness filled me. Everything went black.

When I came to, blood was everywhere. I looked at my

hand and saw the Night-Villain's wing. I shuddered and threw it paces away from me.

He was literally dismantled.

The screen on the far wall said round twelve. The beast had fought him for two rounds. It had felt like two seconds.

My entire body vibrated.

The spell was wearing off. Although the emcee wanted to announce my victory, I left the ring, zombielike. I was dazed and tired.

In the locker rooms, I took a shower, trying to remember what the hell I'd done in that ring during the last two rounds.

How the hell had I ripped his wing off? Images of blood pooled on the floor, the same blood I was washing from me now, filled my mind.

I got out of the shower and wrapped a towel around my waist. The spell was still holding. I was still Grey.

The door opened and Samuel strolled in with two of his buddies flanking him. He slow-clapped. "You surprised me today, big guy." He grabbed both my shoulders and squeezed.

"Twelve fucking rounds! You gave them the show of a lifetime." He grinned broadly.

I wished I shared the same enthusiasm, but I didn't. I was weak tonight. I had to give in to the beast to end it. I had to give in to the darkness.

"I have to admit," Samuel said, eyeing me in the mirror.

"I thought you'd met your match, but those last two rounds..."

"Stop it. I don't want to hear this. Just give me my cut. I gotta go."

"Grey, c'mon. You need to fight again. The people love you."

"My stash, Samuel!" I said through clenched teeth.

"Fine." All enthusiasm evaporated. He handed me a bag of Fire-Cain.

"Call me when you need me," Samuel sang.

⁊⦿

I TOOK a cab a few miles out from the Abysmal, far from everyone who witnessed the fight. The driver dropped me off. I disrobed, transformed back into my dragon form, darted into the air, and flew back to Dragonia Academy.

I landed hard on the roof and pulled my clothes back on. I tucked the Fire-Cain in my hoodie pocket.

I opened the door and was glad that Lucian was asleep. I didn't want to answer his stupid questions about where I'd been and why I looked like shit.

I locked myself in the bathroom and turned on the faucet.

My hands were raw. My knuckles bloody. It had been really bad tonight; I could see the white of bone. I ground my teeth as I lowered both hands into the warm water.

Sharp pain zagged through the wounds. I concentrated

hard on my healing ability, but it never worked on command. I had no fucking clue how it was supposed to work.

I wrapped both my hands with a clean bandage from under the sink—we always had to keep them on hand—and went to bed.

I wished I could sleep, but half-remembered images of what the beast had done to that Night-Villain played through my mind.

It would give me nightmares knowing that I had taken another life. Knowing that I was weak, that I'd given in to the darkness.

At least the beast would back off just a little giving me time to breathe, time to feel normal again.

At length, I drifted away.

In my dreams, I was forced to relive the fight. Including the parts I had blacked out for. I wasn't ready for this. My point of view was weird; I was someone watching from the sidelines, apart from myself.

I looked at Grey in the ring. He was tired. The screen showed round ten. I wished I could just leave but it didn't work like that. I had to see this. This was my doing and there was no escaping it.

Then it happened. The beast took over.

It changed Grey's face. His eyes became shallow, dark, emotionless. So stark, it gave me a chill. He jumped up, unnaturally fast, stomped on the Night-Villain, and somehow wrenched his wing around his neck. He squeezed with all his might.

The Night-Villain pounded hard against the wall, slamming Grey's body, trying to get him to let go. Finally he got hold of Grey and threw him off. Sparks flew as Grey—my —body connected with the cage.

Still, Grey didn't stay down. He went for the dragon again and again. Each attempt a failure, or was it? The beast's intention was to find the Night-Villain's weakness.

The bell chimed. Round ten was over.

Round eleven was more or less the same. I was kicking ass. Samuel and the shady spectators were cheering me on. Dimi was concentrating as hard as he could. His lips barely moved.

The bell chimed. Round eleven in the bag. The Night-Villain was still intact.

I watched Grey. This round was it. The beast had found the Night-Villain's weakness. It was ready to transform this fight into murder scene. His back was to the Night-Villain.

A small smile tugged on Grey's face. It was a game to him, that was it, a stupid game. I was the one who had to deal with his actions. Hatred rose in me like hot bile, but I couldn't move, trapped, forced to watch my sick reality play out.

Then he looked straight at me in the crowd. "This is why you are weak. You are weak. I should be in control," he said.

I was frozen to the spot.

"Watch and learn, pup."

The bell chimed. Grey launched himself at an impossible speed toward the Night-Villain. He dodged from all the dragon's blows. He skidded in between his legs before jumping up behind him.

The Night-Villain had no idea what hit him as balls and balls of acid rained from his hands. Grey started shredding off wings and tearing into the Night-Villain's flesh with his bare hands.

The gore was unimaginable. Body parts were discarded to the floor.

I couldn't watch, but I heard the wing being torn off and the howling and screeching of the Night-Villain. This was too much. It was unnecessary. It was beyond cruel.

It was evil.

Grey screamed and it was over.

Some spectators cheered. Others vomited right on the spot.

Grey screamed his victory scream, went to the still hulk of the Night Villain's corpse, and tore off his arm.

I jumped up in bed. Morning light was seeping into the room, the wind gently blowing the curtains.

Nausea feeling crept into my gut. I ran for the toilet.

I could never let the beast take over again like that. Ever.

I could never return to that ring.

I had to be strong.

THIRTY-3

I SLEPT ALMOST all day Sunday. I didn't want to speak to anyone. I only got up in the late evening when I started to feel like I was starving.

When I got back, Lucian was sitting on his bed. He looked different; something had happened.

"Where were you last night?" He looked pointedly at my bandaged hands.

"Drop it, Lucian. It has nothing to do with you."

"Let me guess, more measures to keep 'it' under control?" He sounded sarcastic. "Look at you, Blake. It's not worth it. You're stronger than this. You have to fight this without losing yourself in the process."

"Losing myself?" I chuckled and shook my head. "Are you blind? Am I the only one seeing this? This *is* me fighting, Lucian!" I yelled the last part. "If I don't do fucked-up shit, the beast will take over. I don't expect you to understand any of this. It's not you who has to live with the consequences. Let it go."

He stared at me for a while longer and then he turned around and walked out the door.

Good riddance.

I put on my earphones and listened to music as I wrote in my journal. I spilled my feelings on the page, what I was actually trying to fight, which wasn't the beast anymore, but the spawn.

I must have drifted away again, as I had the white-knight dream. It somehow always overpowered any other nightmares, even the horror of the Night-Villain's death. The dream of me getting claimed by thousands of knights suffocated me. It was killing me. It was worse than killing anyone.

On Monday I kept to myself. Around lunch, I tentatively rejoined the world. I gave myself a day to sulk, just one day, and then I moved on.

I ate like the beast I was and as I was finishing, George plopped onto the chair in front of me.

"I can't fucking believe this." He was annoyed, frustrated.

I really didn't have the time or patience to deal with his shit too. "What can't you believe?" I said, humoring him.

"Can you believe Irene is making me fight Becky? Seriously, just because she saw some girl getting electrocuted by the lake doesn't mean it's my true rider."

"George." I shook my head. "Everyone knows. No matter how hard you try to fight this, it's over. They know she's your rider, and worse, she is more than just your rider. She is your Dent. Something that hasn't happened in a fucking long time."

"What?" George sounded shocked.

"You are fucking screwed, okay? Make peace with it."

"Make peace. Would *you* make peace with it?"

"It's not my ass on the line," I said.

"Aw, man," he started.

I cut him off; I just couldn't. "I don't have the inclination to deal with your shit, too, George. If you don't want her to become your rider, then kill her in the ring. It's as easy as that."

If you had to kill to not get claimed, well, the Colosseum was the only place you could do that.

Over following days I avoided everyone. Stayed away from Irene, even though my dragon was aching for her, and I stayed far away from the spawn.

I saw her one night in the cafeteria. Lucian was sitting next to her. They were laughing, as the nauseous feeling in my stomach intensified.

What was this? Was it a sign? Was my body trying to tell me that she was worthy of claiming me? Not today, obviously, but one day? The only one who had this effect, or something similar, was Lucian.

I got up from my pillow and walked over to their table. Lucian would understand. He would know why I hadn't said something sooner, but I couldn't live like this anymore. I just didn't have the strength anymore.

I stopped and all of them looked at me. My sister narrowed her eyes. Becky raised one eyebrow and looked awkwardly at Lucian, who squinted. "What is it, Blake?" he asked.

"I can't do this anymore," I sighed.

"Do what?"

"You're right about everything."

He frowned. "I don't understand," he said.

I shook my head. It was weird how the beast was so calm. It must be her. It had to be her. "About who she is. A dragon knows, Lucian."

He's eyes grew round. He got what I was saying and looked at the spawn.

She had no idea what I was talking about.

Lucian asked hesitatingly, "We need to tell Master Longwei. Why are you telling me now?"

"Because I can't do this anymore. I can't hold on anymore." I'd given in. "I want it to be over."

"Okay," he said and looked at the spawn.

"What?" she smiled awkwardly.

"We need to go to Master Longwei—Blake, me, and you."

"Why me?" She swallowed hard and sounded confused, even scared.

"Because you are the one."

"What?" she yelled. "No, no, this has to be a mistake."

"There is no mistake," I snapped. "A dragon always knows, just like George knows Becky is his rider. He just didn't want to say it. I'm sorry I didn't say anything sooner. It's complicated."

"Lucian." She shook her head. "I can't do this. Please, don't make me do this."

"It's going to be okay. Trust me."

She looked like she was going to cry, I shouldn't have told her. Everyone in the cafeteria was watching. All the dragons, all the teachers. They couldn't believe what I was saying.

Just then, I woke up.

I was breathing heavily. Part of me still felt glad that I'd finally told someone, it had meant my struggle was over. *Why did I dream this?*

'Cause this is your life, Blake. You are mine and not the Prince of Tith's, not this little insignificant girl's. Neither one will save you. You are mine, mine, mine.

The darkness was back, and it was only Wednesday. *Four days.* Murder had only kept the insanity away four days. It was getting harder to keep the darkness away.

I sighed. The beast was never going to let me tell anyone. It was never going to allow me to get claimed.

The darkness was going to suck me in, and that would be the end of me.

⚓

I WENT to see Irene again. She didn't ask stupid questions like Tabitha and Lucian. Being with her actually helped, but it wasn't enough anymore.

We used Fire-Cain again, only a little, and I passed out in Irene's arms.

She shoved me out of her tower around three that morning, and I took more Fire-Cain when I got to my room.

Why wasn't Irene enough anymore?

I passed out on the bed again. I missed the entire day Thursday. The only thing that I registered was being woken up.

In the distance I could hear someone speaking over a microphone. It was a dull, distant sound.

"Blake." My body shook and I realized that someone was trying to wake me up. "Blake." The voice was louder, more insistent. Another shake. "Dammit, Blake, wake up!" A hand slapped my cheek. I opened my one eye and found Tabitha standing next to my bed.

The light was blinding. I shut my eyes.

"What is wrong with you?" She yanked open my bedside table's drawer. "You used again!"

"Get out." It was barely a whisper.

She carried on screaming. Tiny knife jabs against my skull, her voice was annoyingly painful.

"Get out!" I yelled.

The door slammed after a while and I fell asleep again.

I only emerged again Friday. The weekend wasn't much different. Lucian was finally going home for the weekend, not that it mattered to me at all.

The Fire-Cain worked better when it was diluted with water. I mixed water with the white powder. The parts were measured to perfection, a milky liquid. I pulled it up with a syringe and pushed the needle into my bloodstream.

In less than a minute, I could feel my mind being clouded. In less than an hour, I would either be knocked out or wouldn't remember what hit me.

If this was the only way the darkness would stay away, then I would do it every single day if I had to. It wasn't going to take me. I would rather die than become its prisoner.

 THIRTY-4

A HAND SLAPPED hard against my face.

Tabitha, I crunched on my teeth.

But I couldn't open my eyes. I was weak. Too weak. I didn't like this feeling. I shouldn't. I didn't want to die.

I'd jinxed myself.

Then fingers pried my eyes open and a light shone brightly into them. I could hear voices but so far away. As if I was lying in a bath of water.

Arms lifted me. I felt the coldness of the floor against my back. Water on my face.

I still didn't react.

This was bad. Real bad.

I didn't know if it was day or night. How many days had passed? What was going on around me? This wasn't something new. I'd gone through it a couple of times already, but never quite this bad.

"Blake," wailed a shrill voice. I felt something inside of me. It was moving, making me sick. Then my body reanimated and I threw up. A lot.

"BLAKE." Master Longwei was heavy with disappointment. We were in his lushly furnished office, surrounded by tapestries and the solemnity of the headmaster's position.

I didn't want to look at him. He didn't understand. He wouldn't; he was a Metallic. They don't need anybody to help them stay good. Not the beatings, not drugs, nothing. "Lucian tells me that this was not the first time you overdosed on illicit drugs."

"Lucian has a big mouth," I muttered.

"If it wasn't for Lucian fetching help, you would be dead right now. You want to be dead?"

I didn't reply.

"What am I going to do with you, Blake? I have to report this."

Report it. They would lock me up. My father had already threatened me. It was the only thing that the beast feared. Not being able to be in the sky, to feel the wind. My sight blurred. A tear fell over my cheek.

"Speak to me. I want to help, but I can't if you don't open up."

"I can't," I said. I wiped my cheek with the back of my hand and folded my arms across my chest.

"You want to be locked up, Blake? For your own safety?"

"No," I roared. "I'll get my shit together. Please don't report me."

He nodded. Thought hard for a bit and then nodded again. "Fine, but I am going to need your cooperation. You must earn back my trust and stop using Fire-Cain. That substance kills dragons. The next time I catch you with it, I will lock you up myself and throw away the key. Do you understand?"

I nodded.

"Your aunt wants a word with you." He waved his hand for me to go.

I got up and left his office.

Master Longwei was one thing, but my aunt was another. She was my mother's twin.

⚘

To say that Constance yelled was an understatement. I'd never seen her lose it. She was always so together, always handled situations with poise and grace. This, this was something she struggled to handle.

I let her get it out of her system. When she was done, she actually looked tired.

"For the next three months, you will come and take a drug test every single morning," she said. "Have I made myself clear? Otherwise, I will tell your father, Blake, and let Robert deal with you."

I huffed. "You'd let them lock me up, Constance?"

"If that is going to save your life, then yes!" she yelled. "I'll see you tomorrow morning at seven."

I pushed myself off the chair; it skidded backward. Maybe it fell over, but I didn't care.

Fuck. How the hell was I going to tame the beast now? These idiots had no idea what the fuck they'd just unleashed on me.

❧

IRENE WAS the last person I had to deal with. She cried and she raged. She demanded to know if she wasn't enough anymore.

"I don't want you to die, Blake, but I need you to fight," She begged. "We've been monitoring the Fire-Cain. What happened?"

"I had more."

"Dammit, Blake. Where did you get it?"

"You know where."

"I thought you were done with the fights. It will only push you over the edge faster. What don't you understand about this?"

"I'm sorry, okay? I struggle. I…" My vision became blurry again.

"It's the darkness, isn't it?"

I nodded.

"I can't see anything anymore. Not even a glimpse."

I hated that because I knew it wasn't just the darkness; it was her.

"I'll try harder," I promised dully.

"You'd better. I'm not going to lose you."

She kissed my lips. I just wanted more.

For the next two months, my life was a living hell. Constance kept to her word. She would be waiting in her office for me at seven every morning. There she pricked my finger and tested my blood for drugs.

Of course there was some still in my system the first few weeks, but the number of nanograms per milliliter grew smaller and smaller. I, on the other hand, was getting crazier and crazier as the beast was getting restless.

I hated everyone. Lucian for doing what he did best. Master Longwei for threatening me with the council. My aunt for threatening me with my dad. Irene for caring too much.

I didn't care about any of them anymore. I didn't even care what day it was. Then Master Longwei called my name over the intercom with a couple of others.

I grunted. Although I wasn't in the mood to go to his office, I was obligated. He meant it when he said I had to earn his trust back.

In fact, he'd had me cleaning up his messes. First I had to fix up the library, which was extremely boring, except when Tabitha relieved some of the tension. Then I had to fix one tower behind school. It was old and was held together by termites. I had to make it stronger. Hard labor was what would keep me sane, or that was what Master Longwei and my aunt thought.

When I got there, I found Cheng, Arianna, and Lucian in front of the office.

"Seriously?" Arianna looked at Lucian, not impressed. Her arms folded in front of her. "You know she is only going to get hurt in the end, Lucian."

"We'll see about that," he said.

What the hell were they talking about?

Arianna chuckled. "She is a dragon spawn, a commoner who is going to lose her mind eventually. They can never perceive of our reality. In short, you are wasting her time and yours."

"The spawn?" I asked and realized it sounded a bit possessive. All of them looked at me and I let out a mirthless laugh. "You and the spawn." I put two and two together real quick. A few weeks ago Lucian had asked me a ridiculous question. He wanted to date the spawn. Why he'd asked for my permission… and then it hit me. He was on to me.

"She has a name. You two make her sound like some sort of plague. And yes, she is actually a very interesting person." He scowled at me.

I lifted my hands in defense, mocking him further and covering for my slip-up.

"And you—" he looked at Arianna—"I would rather die than marry someone like you."

The faint smile on her face vanished. I snorted.

"Enter," Master Longwei said from the other side of the

closed door. We all walked into his office. We found him sitting behind his desk.

Lucian, Arianna, and the geek sat on the chairs while I took a post against the wall. I folded my arms.

"What is this about, Master Longwei?" Arianna asked in her supercilious princess tone. I hated that tone. But she didn't like the spawn either, so she was still okay in my book.

"It's about the new student."

And then he just had to say it. Her name. I wanted to walk away. I was about to tell him to shove Dragonia up his ass, but then my mother's face jumped into my mind. I had to try for her. What would she say if she found out about my addiction?

So I stayed.

"What about Elena?" Lucian asked.

"She is struggling extremely hard. One thing I can say in her favor is that she doesn't give up easily." He looked straight at me. As if he knew that I knew and wasn't telling.

I didn't like that, not one bit. I looked away first. How should I act? How would I act if it was anyone else but the person I suspected of being my true rider? Unfazed. But I was.

"So, I said I would see what I could do to help."

"I don't get it," Arianna said.

"Not everyone can have both brains and beauty, princess," I said scathingly.

She shot me a withering look.

"Enough, Blake." Master Longwei shot us both a look, mine was harder than hers. "I need you to help her get the basics down. You are all the best in a certain field and if you help me, I will make sure that you get extra points on your end-of-year exams, which, I might add," he looked at me again, "some of you need desperately."

I shrugged. *Pretend not to care*: that was the new motto. She was merely dragon spawn.

"So what?" Arianna asked. "We have to train her?" She sounded confused.

"Yes, with enchantments, princess, as professor Deisenberg told me you are advanced in your class."

She straightened, smiling. She would freeze when push came to shove.

"As for you, Lucian," Master Longwei said, "Art of War. Teach her to be a warrior."

I didn't like the way he said warrior. It was like he was speaking code, telling Lucian to train her to claim the Rubicon.

"Cheng, bring her up to date with Paegeia's history."

I squinted. Enchantments, Art of War, History. He was trying to get everyone else to put two and two together about who the spawn was.

"Blake," he said.

"No," I spoke without thinking.

Master Longwei's eyes twitched and his mouth opened partially. "I don't think you have a say in this one."

"I'm not going to teach her to speak Latin. Teaching a

mere human, less than that, dragon spawn, how to speak Latin is impossible. You know it."

"Try," he said. "That's all I'm asking."

"You are wasting our time. The Viden is right. You should listen to her."

Shut the fuck up. You idiot.

I took a deep breath instead and gave him a not-impressed, couldn't-care-less look.

"I see about wasting your time, Mr. Leaf." He rose and glided toward me. "And what would you do if I thought I was wasting *my* time, let's say, with you?" He looked me straight in the eyes, invading my personal space.

"Fine. I'll try," I mumbled.

"Good." He sounded like himself again. "That's all I wanted to hear." He went to sit back down and handed us each a piece of paper. We had a fucking schedule now. "You may go."

I was out first. I crumpled up the piece of paper after seeing something like Thursday in the library.

Lucian mumbled something about me needing to take things seriously, but I didn't stop to listen.

I couldn't believe that I was going to teach the spawn how to communicate with the beast.

§

THAT WEEKEND I used the Fire-Cain that I'd hidden from

Master Longwei. Constance wasn't here and Julia was hardly a dragon.

It would knock me out until next Sunday. Then maybe I wouldn't have to teach the little shit a thing.

The entire weekend I was out of it. I had no idea what the hell was going on around me.

I snapped out of it on Monday. I don't know how it happened. A dose like that usually kicked me out for a week.

I was either getting very strong and dark, or the spawn had something to do with it. Something that was unexplainable to everyone except professor coo-coo with her fascination for bonds and whatnot.

The next few days zoomed by. The more I wanted to go and get more Fire-Cain and just skip Thursday altogether, the harder fate started to push. It was as if she was already starting to count off the days until my claiming.

I wasn't anybody's lamb or property. I was the Rubicon, not some pathetic little girl's lapdog.

I ran into George. I actually stopped and gawked at him and Rebecca Johnson walking hand-in-hand, all giddy, laughing at each other's jokes.

When the hell did this happen? I knew she'd claimed him, but when had this happened?

They were talking about a saddle being made. I was speechless. He'd become her lapdog. He'd sworn he would never belong to her. He hated her, for crying out loud.

The Dent wasn't real. A tidal wave of incoherent

emotion rushed through me. It wasn't real. It was merely a spell. A spell that forced us to love and protect them. Enslaved us.

I was seeing the proof with my own two eyes.

George Mills had hated every inch of Rebecca Johnson and now? Now they were talking about what color hair their children would have.

The Dent was not real. It was a treachery of the highest magnitude. And I was the only one who knew the truth.

THIRTY-5

By the time Thursday rolled around, I wasn't myself at all. To be honest, I hadn't been myself since the spawn made her appearance, and I needed to change that. I need to carry on the way I always had, without feeling. I didn't even know what this feeling was. All I knew was I'd never felt anything like this before and I couldn't explain it, but I DID NOT LIKE IT!

And now I was sitting like an idiot in the library of all places, waiting for her to arrive.

I wouldn't have come. But Lucian had begged me. I hated when he begged. I closed my eyes reliving that afternoon yesterday

"Pleeeease, she needs your help, Blake."

"You have no idea what you're asking of me, Lucian."

"No, I do," he said. "I know that, deep down inside, you are still there. You still care. My friend is still in there. And I will never give up on you. Please, just help her. Maybe—who knows?—it might be good for you to help someone else for a change."

I relented. He was so hopeful. I wasn't, but I hated to disappoint him.

I felt it before I saw her. The tightening of my skin, the cold finger rushing up my spine, my skin crawling. My stomach lurching. I didn't know how the hell I was going to get through this. I took a deep breath, cleared my head, and tried to calm my stomach.

She finally entered the library and looked around like an idiot. She shuffled toward me. She didn't even walk with confidence. What the hell was the universe thinking, pairing this witless, meek creature with the mighty Rubicon? Eons later, she reached my table.

Nothing. She said nothing. Just stared.

I wielded a shield around us, one she didn't even seem to notice.

"Io, Elena," I greeted her. A basic Latin greeting.

She at least snapped out of her staring—but went straight to frowning.

"I told Master Longwei that this is a mistake," I said in Latin, fast too. "But he really thinks I can teach you Latin. Honestly, I don't want to teach you anything. I want you to fail. You don't belong here, no matter what the universe…" *Easy, Blake. You are not the only dragon in the library.* Though my insides were snarling, but my words came out as if I were merely bored.

"You have nothing to say in reply?" I mocked her. "I think it's time for me to …"

She shook her head with vigor. "What?"

"Yeah," I said, still in Latin. "I'm wasting my time. Good day, Elena." I nodded my farewell, glad that this was over.

"Blake, please!" she cried.

An invisible force made me stop. I tried to take another step forward but I couldn't. What was this?

"I really need your help. I don't want to fail."

I tried to move, but nothing. I couldn't panic, not here. Plenty of amused onlookers were watching us.

This was the Dent, this fucked-up bond. ALREADY?

"Please," she begged again.

A growl left my mouth. She hadn't even claimed me yet and part of me was already yielding to her. The beast didn't like it one bit. He was roaring in my head. She was an insignificant little spawn but she had this strange hold on me.

Calm down, Blake. Calm down. Hide it. I took a deep breath and struggled to calm down. One thing was clear: I was going to teach her Latin whether I wanted to or not. "Fine, but if you cry, I'm done."

Latin. *Let's see how hard I can push.* If dragons and magic hadn't broken her, maybe Latin would.

❧

THE LESSON WAS HARDER for me than it was for her apparently. By some miracle, she didn't cry.

The minute my hour was up, I was gone. I mumbled

something about not being late next Thursday. I had to get away from her. My stomach could only handle so much. I threw up the minute I reached the bathroom down the hall.

When I left my stall, a couple of guys looked at me funny. "I must have eaten a sick deer or something," I grumbled. They chuckled, leaving it there.

I found Lucian on the bed. His eyebrows rose as I fell on the couch and switched on the TV. I felt better.

"See, that wasn't so hard, now was it?" Lucian cajoled.

"She's not getting anything. Her pronunciation is atrocious. I'm wasting my time."

Lucian chuckled. "Nobody is perfect in Latin, Blake. Well, except you. Give her time. She's picking the other things up quite quickly. I would love to see her claim a dragon one day." His gaze was steady on me.

"What?" I glared.

He smiled. "Nothing."

Lucian knew. He'd always known. I had to change that somehow.

❧

ON FRIDAY, Lucian didn't leave. He was sulking. If she wasn't who I thought she was, I would probably sleep with her just to piss him off, but I couldn't. Who knew what fucked-up shit the Dent would do?

Tabitha stayed with us and Lucian was somewhere else.

It was weird how I didn't like that. A part of me hated

the fact that he'd gone after the spawn. That she was with him.

She wasn't his.

I didn't want her, but she wasn't his.

It was probably a dragon thing. It was upsetting that she made me feel like this.

The redhead popped in my mind. The last time I'd dreamt about her, she'd been bawling because I didn't love her. Why had she been a redhead in the dream?

I used. Tabitha used too and we screwed each other's brains out the rest of the weekend.

Sunday, late afternoon, Lucian got in. "You've got to be kidding me," he remarked when he saw Tabitha's naked form sprawled across my bed. He stared at me.

"Leave if you don't like it."

"I'm not going anywhere, Blake." He rolled his eyes. "I live here, remember?"

I didn't care if he disapproved. Sex was what I needed and lately the beast didn't really worry who I got it from. Irene, Tabitha... just as long as it wasn't the spawn.

Just then a siren rang out. It was ear-splitting—and unprecedented.

"What is it?" Lucian shouted over the alarm.

Paegeia was in danger.

I slapped Tabitha on the ass. She woke up. The fear on her face as she registered the strange siren was real. It was a Snow Dragon thing. She dressed frantically as Lucian left.

I had to admit, the siren was making my scales vibrate

too. For some reason, I didn't want to be in this room. I wanted to be somewhere else.

Lucian would find her.

Why did I keep having these unwelcome thoughts? I didn't want to be claimed, but... what? So confusing. "Hurry up," I growled.

"I'm coming." She pulled on her shoes and we headed out into the hall.

Outside, we followed the flow of students down the stairs to the auditorium. Everyone was abuzz with speculation—"What's going on? What does this mean? Did someone die? Has there been a disaster?"

I pursed my lips and said nothing, yanking Tabitha along in my wake.

Once inside the auditorium, I searched for her. I found Lucian and she was right next to him. My scales eased up marginally.

I didn't tune in to their conversation. I didn't want to hear her fears. I couldn't. I shouldn't worry. Why did I worry? This was freaking me out.

My eyes found Irene's. She squinted. I looked away. She couldn't put two and two together now. I couldn't survive without her. And she might abandon me if she suspected I had a Dent with the spawn. I took a deep, uneasy breath. When I looked at Irene again, she was speaking to Sir Edward.

They had no idea why the sirens were going off.

I had to keep myself sitting on the chair to stop myself from running up to her.

Fuck.

I hated this. I hated feeling this way. This was seriously fucked up. All I could think was that Lucian wasn't protecting her well enough.

Stop it, Blake.

Maybe it was a Dent thing.

It sure as hell wasn't me.

THIRTY-6

"THE KING of Lion sword has been stolen." Master Long-wei's voice echoed over a microphone.

"What?" Tabitha whispered in shock next to me.

The King of Lion sword. My mind spun out of control. It didn't matter what the theories were, the fact that the legendary sword was gone was a problem. If Goran ever made it out of Etan, that sword was the only weapon that could defeat him.

How? Was he behind this?

I didn't give a crap about Elena now.

I only wanted to get that sword back, but I had no fucking idea how.

"Did you hear that?" Tabitha sounded petrified.

"Calm down." Irritation sharpened my voice. I hated the way Snow Dragons acted in times of need. Damn cowards.

Everyone was talking at once, an anxious cloud of chatter. I couldn't make out what they were all saying, but it boiled down to the same concerns I had: That sword was critical to Paegeia's survival.

"Silence!" Master Longwei's voice roared. "There is no reason to panic yet. Members of the Royal Council are searching for it as we speak. However, we must keep guard for any sign of danger. Dragonia will be one of the first places they attack in the event of war."

You sure about that, old man? The thought flew through my mind. I was the Rubicon; I had the Pink Kiss. They were going to see their asses with this one.

"We will have watch groups in place first thing tomorrow morning," Master Longwei said. He rattled off names. I was obviously among them.

Why, why, why, does he always call on me? Dumb question. Because I was the Rubicon.

Everyone got up at his dismissal. My eyes caught on Elena and Lucian kissing.

"I'll tell you what I know, okay?" he said to her and she nodded.

I looked away. I walked through the back door after Brian took Tabitha and led her out the same way as the rest of the student body. I found Cheng, Lionel, James, and Lucian in Master Longwei's office.

Cheng's eyes rested on mine. He was a Crown-Tail and thought too much for his own stupid good. He could easily ferret out my secret.

What if she figured it out? She'd been learning history with Cheng. But no. She wouldn't. She wasn't brave enough to even consider claiming a dragon, not to mention me.

"We have to guard the school until the sword is found. I

meant it when I said they will come to the school first. Eliminating you, Blake, is one of the first things they will do."

"Or try recruiting him," Lionel interjected.

I gaped at him. So did Lucian and Master Longwei.

"What I'm saying is, it's not like he's been peaches and cream this year."

I scowled. "I'm still here, aren't I?"

Lionel shook his head somewhat sadly.

I swear some of these Dragonians think they're the shit.

Master Longwei carried on. School would be cancelled for the next few weeks until the Council and the king's guards found the King of Lion sword. King Helmut and King Caleb had both sent out search parties to accompany the Council.

My stomach knotted. I hadn't felt this much unease in such a long time.

Irene's name was mentioned and I froze. "She's what?" I asked. *Be cool, Blake.*

"Irene is in charge of putting the watch groups together, Blake."

"What groups?"

"Everyone is being paired up for watch duty."

I started to chuckle. "Even me?"

"If danger comes, you can shift and do what it is you do, while your team member can alert the rest of us to the attack."

The way he put it didn't sound as insulting as I originally took it. "Okay, fine," I said grudgingly.

Please, don't let it be someone pathetic.

I couldn't visit Irene that night; Eddie and Greg were with her for hours. My mind went there: a threesome. She wouldn't. They wouldn't. *Stop it, Blake, Irene isn't stupid.* Well, that wasn't entirely true, either. She'd got mixed up with my shit, hadn't she?

ᔕ

THE NEXT MORNING, all the watch assignments were hung out on the wall. Hung magically overnight by the faculty.

Everyone was still asleep.

I went to the wall outside the cafeteria and found our names. There were five groups. The group leaders were Lucian, Lionel, James, Cheng, and myself. Then individual pairings were listed within each group.

Sammy was in Lionel's group. She was paired with Lucian's friend, Dean.

Brian was paired with Brittainy. I remembered the joke Tabitha had cracked in the beginning goody-two-shoes Britt being able to lead me down a good path. Such a long time ago.

Tabitha was paired with Lucian.

George was paired with Becky.

I froze. *No, no, no, no.* I found my group and looked at who was with me. The spawn.

My eyes skimmed the names. No one was paired with

the same species. All of the teams were Dragon and Dragonian. I knew what this was.

Irene had seen it. Maybe not crystal clear. But something about danger, this level of danger, unleashed her power. She had seen something.

Irene had paired all the dragons with their riders, whether they were already claimed or not.

I didn't like it one bit.

Sammy was going to be Dean's dragon. My father would just love that.

Lucian was a snow wielder and one day he would claim Tabitha. That thought should've infuriated me, but it didn't.

I wouldn't be alive anymore when that happened. Rubicons didn't reach advanced age. I wasn't going to roll over and get claimed. I'd rather die a dragon intact than one tamed. Especially by that weakling.

I stalked away before people started to wake up and I had to encounter any vapid discussion of the pairings.

The knowledge that she was going to guard the front gate with me for more than eight hours was already making me uncomfortable.

How was I going to hide this secret? It was who she was, what she represented. It was making me feel trapped, full of loathing.

The mere thought of her made my stomach roil. She would never be enough. If Lucian couldn't tame me, she wouldn't be able to either. She wasn't enough.

&

I ENDED up in Irene's tower again. She was ill at ease, a ball of nervous energy. "What if something happens and they catch you here?"

"Relax." I stroked her silky hair. She was in my arms as we shared a cigarette. "I'm getting quite good at hypnotizing people."

She hit me on the chest. "I'm serious."

"Me too. I would do anything to keep us a secret until the right time. Once I'm free from Dragonia, I can do whatever I want and see whomever I want."

"That's unless someone claims you. Then you need to stay longer."

"No one will claim me." I tried to sound depressed.

But she was right. If danger came and the authorities found me in her tower, they would fire Irene.

The next day Master Longwei called me in again. Every time he did that, I was scared someone had seen me leaving Irene's tower. Then again, worse, what if the Council had found the sword destroyed?

I knocked on his office door.

"Enter."

I let myself in.

"Sit down, Blake," he said and I took the chair in front of the desk. "I'm sorry to ask this of you, but you have another drug test."

I closed my eyes.

"Your aunt believes this crisis we're in might trigger some... needs."

"She thinks or you do?" I snapped.

"Blake," he sounded stern. "This is our arrangement. You said anytime we want, we just have to let you know. Remember?"

"Fine. I just don't know what you'll do if you find drugs in my system. You gonna lock me up while we are in danger?"

"We've handled far worse threats before your time, Blake," Master Longwei said without batting an eye. "I'm sure this can be sorted without you too." Cocky bastard.

"Whatever," I grumbled.

"Your aunt is waiting for you. She is going to call me in twenty minutes if you don't show."

"I'm going," I whined. *I'm trying for crying out loud.* I wanted to scream that part, but it was no use.

He was right; I'd agreed to this. The last time popped into my head. Shit, I was going to test positive. I was so screwed.

I did as I was told and went straight to the infirmary. There, I found my aunt speaking to Julia.

She caught my gaze. "Don't give me that look."

I held out my arm. "Just do it and let me be in fucking peace."

"Language!"

"You think for one second I give a shit about my language?"

She gave me a withering look. She took my finger and pricked me harder than usual. She could be so evil sometimes.

"I will dispose of it as usual after I'm done. You have my word."

"If only you believed mine," I snapped. I jumped off the bed and walked out the infirmary.

"He's really pissed off," I heard Julia say.

"I don't care in the slightest. He's being a baby. Being clean is what he needs. And I will demand random tests until I'm certain he is."

"I'm just saying," Julia said.

I tuned them out. So I'd broken my aunt's trust. Who gave a shit?

∮

No DRUGS SHOWED. My healing ability saved my ass, it must be that.

Soon it was time—my turn on the watch schedule.

I was all knots.

I even packed a flask of coffee. What was I doing? I wasn't much of a coffee drinker and I didn't need surplus energy either. I filled my flask with vodka. Why was I doing this? Trying to make her feel comfortable? I shouldn't care. She was a useless spawn.

At nine Master Longwei turned up at the wall.

I'd just relieved the previous pair after a brief recon flight.

The beast was dissatisfied. It made me feel a little like my old self again, but not entirely. The human part of me wasn't very human anymore.

"Find anything?" Master Longwei wanted to know.

"No, no change. Did the Council?"

Master Longwei shook his head.

It had been three days already. The window was closing. What if they didn't find the sword? It was written all over my face and it was on Master Longwei's too.

"Okay, stay safe."

"I will," I assured him.

"And please ensure Elena's safety as well."

I sighed. It was like he knew who she was, like he was just waiting for confirmation.

"Blake."

"Fine, whatever."

The spawn was somewhere nearby. I took a deep breath. My skin crawled. A cold finger rushed up my spine. On cue, my skin pulled tight and my stomach wrenched.

Why did she have such a strong physical effect on me? Was it to push me to tell the truth? *It will never happen!* I silently yelled. *Never.*

"And if he transforms, don't freak out," Lucian advised her. Always with her.

She didn't respond.

Maybe I should transform. Maybe it would scare her

shitless. After all, I was the biggest, ugliest dragon at the Academy. Maybe I should finish what George couldn't.

Don't. She would wonder why. Girls did that and I most definitely didn't want her to even think there was even the most remote possibility that I liked her.

Master Longwei cleared his throat. "Say goodnight, Your Highness."

They both giggled. Fucking giggled. I huffed. His daddy was going to love this new girl. It was going to fuck up all their arrangements. Lucian would never marry Arianna now. I knew him. He thought he loved this one.

Even if she didn't belong to him.

The nausea intensified. I took a deep breath. She was close. I stared at the horizon, trying to focus on whether anything was out of the ordinary.

Whoever had stolen the sword wouldn't move it. Not now, not while the trail was still fresh. No, they would wait. At least, that was what I would've done.

"Hey." Her voice was hardly audible. Pathetic. Nothing about her had confidence. How the fuck was she going to claim me? I wanted to laugh but didn't.

She sat down finally and silence filled the space around us. It was silent for a long time. My gaze was alert.

Then I thought about her again. The redhead was supposed to be a blonde. The blonde sitting right next to me. No, I wasn't going to believe that.

"There's coffee in the flask when you feel tired."

"No thanks. I'm fine."

Polite. I huffed softly. "It's the perfect night to watch." Words just streamed out of my mouth. "I hope you don't mind my choosing this time." *Shut the fuck up.*

She didn't answer or look my way. She just sat, knees tucked up with her arms clutching them tight. Her head rested lazily on them.

I took a deep breath.

Just shut up.

I felt her eyes on me.

Don't look.

"I guess I understand why you chose it."

I looked.

"Your senses are most alert at night, right?"

Most alert? "Something like that," I mumbled. I couldn't believe that the corners of my lips were tugging upwards.

Most alert.

Silence settled again. She wasn't much of a talker. Thank heavens for that.

My mind wandered. Who had her father been? I'd searched for a Herbert Watkins but couldn't find anything this side. Had he known King Albert?

I shouldn't be this intrigued by her. *Just leave it.*

"Will they wake?"

I stole another peek at her. She was staring at the stones behind her.

"Who, the stone dragons?" I wanted to laugh. So Cheng had told her. "They are not like Grimdoe, and they have no reason to be. To be honest, I think it's just an old wives' tale told to get naughty children to go to sleep."

"With the sword missing..." Her voice grew slightly more self-assured. "They've got all the reason in the world to be awake."

I shrugged. *That was hardly a disagreement, little spawn.* I was disappointed again. She had no worth. No fight in her. Zero backbone.

I glanced back at the infirmary and took out my packet of cigarettes.

"You smoke!" she practically yelled.

"Shh, Elena," I snapped. I tuned in to see whether Constance had heard. She would insist I stop smoking next. It was the only thing I had left.

When no one stirred, I blew gently on the tip of my cigarette. A friendly red cherry appeared and I took a drag.

She gasped. I pretend not to hear.

I blew out the smoke. It trailed back in her direction. *Seriously?* Everything was pointing to what Elena was, even the smoke of my cigarette. *Pathetic.*

She coughed. I felt her eyes on me again as I stared at the horizon.

It was silent once more.

Nothing fucking happened. I lit one cigarette after the other. Around three, Elena fell asleep. I stared at her sleeping figure for a long time. At one point she muttered something that sounded like *blueberries.*

How was she going to claim me? She wouldn't. She

wasn't. She would never be worthy of me.

It was the biggest joke of all time.

Why didn't she know her own identity? Did her father know, the man who raised her? How had she crossed the Wall? It was questions like these I needed answered. They were driving me insane.

I saw Master Longwei's figure and tossed my cigarette butt off the cliff. I shoved the pack, or what was left of it, back in my bag with the flask still filled with coffee.

Two students—a fifth-year dragon with his Dragonian —relieved us.

Elena woke up and rubbed her nose.

"I guess there was no emergency," Master Longwei said, smiling.

I glared at her. Some partner she was. Without a word she turned around and left.

"Blake?" Master Longwei asked.

"I'm going." I pulled off my shirt and pants. I opened my arms and dove off the cliff. Wings and scales ran down my body and in a few seconds, the dragon had taken the human's place.

"Is it just me, or is he getting bigger by the day?" someone mumbled.

"Let's just hope Lucian succeeds soon," Master Longwei said. But I could tell he wasn't sure about that anymore.

Was it because of my size?

Or because of the girl?

THIRTY-7

I STAYED in my room with Tabitha over the next few days until it was our turn to go on watch again. Nearly two weeks and they hadn't found the sword again.

The second time we stood watch, Elena hardly spoke to me at all. She showed up toting the queen's axes. I wanted to ask her where the fuck she had gotten them.

What was this? Really, it was as if destiny was trying to push us together.

I could see fear in her though. She was twitchy and breathed heavily. I really wanted to know how strong that fear was. Was she shit scared or scared shitless? On a scale of one to ten, shitless would be an eleven.

It was probably the latter. She wasn't worthy.

By three she was asleep again. I left right before she woke up for my flight. When I came back, the next team had already taken up their post.

"Let me guess: nothing," the dragon said.

"Nope."

I went back to my room. I was tired. Why was she on my mind so much lately?

I'd done so well, and now... I needed Fire-Cain. I needed Irene.

Tabitha tried her best the following week to make me forget. She even snuck in weed and we smoked. My aunt was testing for Fire-Cain, not weed. We drank, but for some reason, I didn't get wasted.

I was always on edge, alert, watching the news. The sword was long gone.

The third time the spawn and I guarded Dragonia came faster than I expected. The sword had been gone for almost two weeks.

She didn't greet me tonight. She didn't speak. She was reading up on something. She didn't look scared anymore. She saw this as some kind of book club? What was going through her fucking mind? I wanted to grab that book and take a peek.

Her eyes almost caught mine as she looked up.

Ask me something. Anything.

Nothing.

She put the book in front of her shirt. She was mental. When I looked at her again at four o'clock, she was conked out. She was driving me nuts.

I left minutes before the shift changed. I found Tabitha in my room again.

Later that day, Master Longwei summoned me again. He looked worried. Irene was with him.

My heart galloped. Although I couldn't hear it, I could feel it in every fiber of my being. Had someone seen me earlier leaving her tower? *Shit.* This was it. I doubted I could hypnotize Master Longwei.

"Sit, Blake," Master Longwei said.

I pulled out my chair and perched on it, ready to sprint away if need be. *Don't speak. Deny if you have to.*

"Irene saw something," he said gravely.

I froze. "What?" I asked. "When?"

"She saw the sword being destroyed."

It's not about us. Dizzying relief plowed into me. "Where?"

"That's the one thing I didn't see. It was messed up. I can't explain it." Irene's voice broke.

I felt so sorry for her and wished I could just hold her in my arms.

"That's not the only thing she saw."

Oh, fuck.

"She saw you destroying it."

&

"You saw what?"

"That's not to say that you are going to destroy the sword, Blake." She sighed. This was the spawn. She could never see the royal family. The spawn was the same. King Albert's blood flowed through her veins.

"It's just that you are going to be a part of its destruction."

"I am not," I said loudly.

"We aren't saying it directly, Blake," Master Longwei interrupted. "Now you might have seen something and decided not to act."

"You think I wouldn't act on something I thought was out of place? I'm not that dark yet, Master Longwei."

"We aren't saying you are," Irene said. "We need you to be honest with us. If you see something that is out of place, anything at all, please tell us."

"Yeah, jeez." I formed a fist and released it and reformed it. "I would never destroy that sword." They didn't say anything. I got up. "Anything else? You seeing me destroying Paegeia too?"

Hurt filled Irene's big blue eyes. "I didn't mean it like that."

"Blake, a bit of respect." Master Longwei's tone was flinty.

"With all due respect sir, both of you just accused me of destroying the sword."

"Not you. Your actions. There is a huge difference."

Silence spooled between us as I stared at him, my jaw clenched.

"You are free to leave."

I nodded and left.

THE REST of the day I flew around. Why had Irene seen that? *I would never. Would I?*

I hadn't seen anything that was out of place either.

I went back to the Academy, my stomach grumbling. I dished up and sat inside the cafeteria. Tabitha spoke, but I just couldn't stop thinking about what Irene had seen.

"I need a word." Lucian's voice broke through my thoughts.

I frowned as he sat on the pillow opposite mine.

He look ashen, as if he'd seen a ghost.

"What do you want?"

He wielded a shield. I could hear the small popping sound. "It's Elena. She's fucking crazy but I have to go with her."

I frowned. "Huh?"

"She thinks she can find the sword."

I chuckled.

"It's not funny, Blake. You don't know her. She has a very strong mind and once it's made up she doesn't turn back. She wants to seek the sword's location in the Sacred Cavern."

My eyebrows rose. Was this a dream? "You serious? The spawn wants to find the sword?"

"Stop calling her that. She is much braver than you think."

I didn't like that. But this, this I had to see for myself. "All right. When does she want to leave?"

"Tonight. Bill is guarding with Dave at the front gate. We are going to leave from the tower at the east side."

The tower I'd fixed earlier this year. "You forgot one thing, shift change isn't at ten tonight. It's at eight-thirty."

He shook his head. "No, I didn't forget. We are meeting the girls around that time at the tower."

"We?"

"Yes. George, Becky, and Sammy."

I pursed my lips. "My sister is going?"

"She won't back out, Blake. Don't ask her."

"She could get herself killed."

"She won't. We need her, unless you are going to transport Elena and me."

My eye actually twitched.

"Yeah, I didn't think so. Meet me in the room around eight."

He got up. Beside me, Tabitha watched both of us with huge eyes.

"What is up?" Brian asked.

"Nothing, eat your food."

"Brian's not stupid, Blake. What is the Prince of Tith planning?"

"Not the prince. Someone who should've been locked up a long time ago."

"Elena?" Tabitha asked.

"Drop it."

"Oh no. What is going on?"

I wielded my shield.

He checked out my shield, impressed.

"They are leaving tonight for the Sacred Cavern. Lucian and Elena think they can find the sword."

"Are they fucking insane?"

"No, apparently they have a bit of backbone," I snapped at Tabitha. "You don't have to come."

"Hell no. I'll be there." She tossed her hair, haughty. "I'll just get some things ready." Without even a pack on the cheek, she was gone.

"Righteous. Brian likes this idea."

"It's stupid, dude. She's going to get herself killed." I didn't like the idea as much as I thought I would. She wasn't worthy.

"I'm in." Arianna plunged onto Lucian's empty pillow.

"In on what?"

She cocked her head and gave me an I'm-not-dumb look. "Your pathetic excuse for a shield is weak, Blake. Impressive that you can wield one, but not impressive enough."

"You heard?"

"Yes, and you are going to need me. I'm the best at enchantments."

I glanced around. The sound of everyone else's voices faded.

"*That* is how you wield a shield," she teased, gliding away.

"So the prince and the princess." Brian smiled.

"Dude, keep your mouth shut. And be in my room at eight."

I got up just as Becky, Sammy, Elena, and George walked into the room.

She still made my stomach turn. I tried to ignore it, but it wasn't getting any easier.

I went to my room. I need to get my tent and prepare. Lucian was already packing too. His tent was on the floor with sleeping bags and everything.

"You mind carrying this bag? I don't think Sammy is going to be able to."

"Sure," I said woodenly.

He paused. "What is it?"

"It might be more than just us."

He closed his eyes. "What did you do?"

"Nothing. Brian and Tabitha want in and Arianna overheard."

"You're kidding."

"Don't worry. She only overheard 'cause she has the ability to penetrate my shield."

He frowned. "You can wield a shield?"

I shouldn't have said that. "Sort of. Not a good one apparently."

"So they know we are going to the Sacred Cavern, right?"

"Yeah. All of them are as sick as your girlfriend."

"She's not sick. She really believes she can do this."

"Why?" I chuckled again.

"I don't know. I think it's sort of in the same as me believing I can claim you."

This girl was going to get herself killed. It wasn't such a bad thing, it meant I'd be free.

Just then I realized what was happening. Irene's vision. My actions were going to destroy the sword. We were not going to recover it.

We were going to be the reason it was destroyed.

Well, it was one vision that had to change

THIRTY-8

WE ALL WORE BLACK. Even Arianna.

"Ouch!" Brian yelled when he saw her. She scowled.

Lucian shook his head as he picked up a smaller bag and walked into the elevator.

Tabitha smacked Brian.

"Ouch! You are so mean to Brian."

"Because you are an idiot."

I smiled. The elevator closed. I prayed that nobody ran into us. We passed the hallway easily and waited for the shift change.

As Professor Gregory and Sir Edward did their rounds, Arianna did some sort of vanishing spell. Her nose almost bled, but I had to admit, I felt better having her there.

"We should go," Lucian whispered. We all made a run for it.

I could hear human heartbeats.

So this was what she had been reading up on. The Sacred Cavern. Planning this right under my nose. And here I'd thought she was scared.

"What the?" Sammy breathed. She heard our footsteps. They all looked up at us.

"Lucian?" The spawn sounded unimpressed.

"I had no choice, Elena."

"So, are we going to do this or what?" I asked. I sounded so pissed off. I was. When the fuck had she gotten a backbone?

"Three more minutes, Blake, then we can be off. You guys should get ready," Lucian said.

I dropped the bag and started to take off my clothes.

Tabitha did too. A smile tugged at the corner of my lips. She was lean and sinuous and confident and curvy in all the right places. She smiled at me too.

We stripped down to our underwear and we all handed our clothes to Arianna.

The spawn was still fighting with Lucian. She was so naïve. She had no idea what awaited all of us, not just her. She would've never succeeded alone.

We all jumped onto the ledge.

I climbed onto the wall. My talons had already come out and I crawled higher as she kept scolding Lucian.

"Arianna?"

"She heard Blake and me talking and wanted a piece of the action," Lucian lied. It wasn't entirely correct, but I guessed that he didn't want to get into all the details regarding his ex right now.

"It's not a game, Lucian."

I was surprised to hear her say that. So maybe she did

know what to expect. I tuned out and transformed as I clung for dear life to the tower.

Tabitha and Brian both changed below me.

George came next. He was such a lamb now. Becky was on his back already. His precious. He'd changed so much. He used to hate her and now he was all up in her ass. Literally.

Lucian and the spawn finally showed. Her heart hammered like crazy when she saw us. Still pathetic.

I let go. Tabitha and Brian followed. We ascended as fast as we could into the air, to get above the clouds.

It was going to be a long stretch to the Sacred Carvern. If we were lucky, we would get there by morning.

I prayed that nobody would die on the trip. It would be just what I needed. More blood on my hands.

The siren hadn't gone off. All five dragons were in the air. That was a good sign, but I couldn't believe how gifted Irene was. She didn't suck things out of her thumb. She'd seen this, what we were doing, and a part of me didn't know if we were going to succeed or not.

She couldn't see that Elena would be the one to destroy the sword, doubtless for the same reason she struggled to see my future.

The darkness she saw was Elena's wall. It happened when my father had become a part of the lives of King Albert and Queen Catherine too. Irene still couldn't see his future. Just darkness.

Was this Elena's doing?

THE FIRST RAY of sunshine was on the horizon when our destination came into sight. We'd all flown straight through the night to Tith.

Tabitha was tired. She'd started breathing hard since four o'clock in the morning. Not to mention Sammy, who was carrying two humans.

At last we descended.

Almost there, Sammy. Hold on.

I broke through the roof of clouds and the first thing my eyes caught was Lucian's home. The castle had seven towers and lots of fertile land for harvesting.

"My dad is so going to kill me," Lucian said.

Forty-five minutes later at the most and we were there. The mountain that led to the Sacred Cavern finally came into view.

I landed first and disappeared into the woods to change. Brian was second, then Tabitha.

Sammy hadn't landed yet. Finally, I heard her loud touchdown. She was beyond tired.

"That's it, girl, you did great," Lucian said as he petted her.

She wasn't a pet.

Becky was still struggling to remove George's saddle and Lucian went to help her.

"Can I have a towel?" Sammy spoke tiredly.

"Towel!" Becky yelled and ran past the spawn to fetch the towel that Arianna had.

"Chill, drama queen." Arianna let go of the towel.

Becky didn't reply, just held it in front of Sammy's body as she transformed back into her human form. My little sister barely had the strength to stand. I broke into a run when I saw her heading in the direction of the ground and caught her just in time. "Dad's going to kill me for letting you come with us." I shouldn't have let her come.

"Dad's not here, so shut up," she teased tiredly.

I smiled at her. I too could barely keep my eyes open. I took her to a nearby tree and let her sit down with the towel covering her.

I touched Tabitha's chin and winked as I passed her. She smiled, too exhausted for anything else.

I chucked Tabitha's clothes to her.

"We need to rest." I looked at Lucian as I pulled on my jeans.

"We all have to rest, Blake."

He helped us put the tents up and in no time a camp was pitched.

Tabitha and Arianna went to look for some wood while Brian was busy with a fire. George was the best at hunting and fishing. We agreed to have a quick bite and then rest.

Becky sat with Sammy. I could feel the tension between them and Elena.

It doesn't concern you, Blake. Just ignore it. I disappeared into my tent.

"Elena, you need your rest," Lucian called from inside their tent.

My skin crawled. I still didn't like it.

🐚

TABITHA FINALLY CRAWLED in after scavenging for wood with Arianna.

"Lazy bum." She kicked me.

"What? I erected the tents." I smiled.

She crawled down next to me. "Please don't. I'm way too tired."

I chuckled. "That makes two of us." I closed my eyes.

When I woke up, thanked the heavens I didn't dream of anything fucked-up. I could smell the roast.

Outside, Brian was already busy with the food. He loved camping. Four small animals, rabbits it looked like, were skewered onto sticks. He gently blew on them. Perks of being a Sun-Blast.

"What about that little Pink Kiss flavor? Brian is dying to taste it."

I chuckled. "I'm afraid there would be nothing left when Blake is done with it."

"Damn," he joked. He looked around. "It sure is beautiful up here."

"Sure is." I imagined the gorgeous trees up in flames. I recoiled and pushed the image back.

I was a coward. She was right here. She could claim me. She could end this. Yet I didn't want it.

I heard Lucian and the spawn's soft laughter coming from their tent as they both stirred. "That's creepy," Lucian said.

I shook my head. I couldn't wait for food. I needed more than just a rabbit.

"There are some elk about two miles down." Brian was dead-on with what I was thinking. "That look on your face is how Brian looked about two hours ago."

I chuckled. "Thanks, Brian."

I took off my clothes and jumped into the air. I needed real food, not a little rabbit. In my dragon form, I devoured two elk and came back. I had a small piece of the rabbit Tabitha set aside for me.

"You need more food." I was worried about her; she looked wan.

"I'll fish when we wash up tonight."

I frowned. "You can fish?"

"Ha, ha." Flirting, she slapped me hard on the ass and went into the tent to get a new set of clothes and her towel.

We left right after I finished the rabbit and made our way to the stream below.

Lucian and Elena were finishing up and on their way back. They talked about silly things. They weren't taking this seriously.

"We need to talk about what we are going to do." I was right in front of them.

The spawn slipped and my reflexes almost reached out for her, but Lucian already had it covered.

"We take it as it comes," Lucian said.

"Excuse me?"

"We don't know the rules with this one, Blake. What do you want to go over?" He snapped.

"You bring me here only to tell me we have to wing it?"

"I didn't bring anyone here. You wanted to come." Lucian passed me, shoving his shoulder roughly into mine. What the fuck?

She almost slipped again and Lucian steadied her. She was so clumsy.

A pathetic mannerism. A human trait.

I got that feeling again. She wasn't worthy.

"Let's go," Tabitha said. I walked with her to the lake. She tried to take my mind off everything, but I was on edge.

I needed a plan. I couldn't go into something blind. Was *she* like that? If so, we were complete opposites.

After a bath in the lake, we went back. I didn't want to go to the Sacred Cavern anymore, but what kind of dragon would I be if I chickened out now?

Around eight I grabbed my backpack from Tabitha. "It's about an hour's walk to the Sacred Cavern." I said. "I suggest we get a move on."

"Would Brian do me the honor?" George held a manmade torch in Brian's direction. Brian blew on it. The torch caught fire instantly. He lit two more and gave me one as I took the lead.

"Your Highness," Brian joked.

"Ha, ha," Lucian said sarcastically.

I moved swiftly through the forest. My hearing picked up everything within a mile radius. Rodents had made their homes beneath our feet, and could hear them scurrying to flee us, as well as the more subtle sounds of owls waiting for their turn to hunt.

"Fuck," Tabitha yelped as a mouse ran in front of her.

I chuckled.

"It's not funny," she whined.

A ruckus arose at our rear. It was Arianna and Lucian. When were they going to kiss and make up? His father was never going to let him marry dragon spawn. Well, someone they believed to be one, anyway.

"Because what you are doing, Elena, isn't brave at all. It's stupid. And if any of us dies tonight, it's on your head."

"Wait here." I shook my head and approached the three of them where they stood quarreling.

"Arianna, you begged to come with us tonight, so shut your pie-hole," Lucian snapped.

"You guys, enough!" I yelled. "Nobody was forced into coming tonight, Arianna, though I happen to agree with you: this is a suicide mission. There's nothing we can do about it now, so all of you shut your traps."

Brian and George chuckled. Even Sammy rolled her eyes.

Fucking humans. I returned to the front of the group.

It was quiet the rest of the trip. Nobody said a word

when we finally exited the woods and found a huge stone staircase that led up to a yawning cavern.

I looked up at the sky. Fog obscured the entrance to the cavern. Two massive wooden doors led to the unknown.

This was it. We were going to do it. I climbed the steps, trusting the others to follow. In twenty minutes to a half an hour, we reached the top.

"Welcome to the Sacred Cavern," I bellowed in a theatrical tone. Tabitha and Arianna, who were right behind me, giggled.

"Becky will speak to you again, Elena," I heard Lucian said.

So the two besties were fighting. Was it because of tonight, her crazy mission?

"You sure about that? I said some pretty mean things to her."

"They were true. She'll only become part of the Royal Council if she gets a bit more of what you have."

He made her sound so brave. I tuned out as he cooed to her, either giving her the strength not to run away or maybe he was just that pathetic. A walking cliché.

Becky and Sammy gasped when they finally reached the summit.

I held out my hand for Brian and George. They helped the girls up.

"Thanks," Sammy smiled at Brian.

"Brian is at Sammy's service."

I slapped him behind the head.

"Ow," he rubbed his head.

"Don't even think about it."

Sammy laughed, glancing at me, her protective big brother.

I took out some water bottles from my backpack. Becky and Sammy's backpack toppled to the ground as I opened a bottle. I took a few gulps and handed it to Tabitha.

My eyes caught on the spawn struggling with the last step and I reached out. She looked at me with King Albert's eyes and accepted my helping hand.

Her touch made my stomach crawl. I really didn't like the way she made me feel. It felt so wrong.

I lifted her up with one pull and extended my hand for Lucian again. "So what's the plan, big shot?" I thrust a bottle of water into Lucian's hand. Why did I feel so pissed off at him?

He took the bottle, opened it, and gulped down half before handing it to the spawn. "We all go and face whatever comes our way together," he said as if that was the plan all along. Not that it was a plan at all.

We held each other's stares for a few beats. Then my eyes shifted to everyone else. They'd all contemplated this. It was the only way.

"All of you agree?" I asked. Everyone nodded, including the spawn.

Tabitha was the only one who seemed as if she was going to pee herself.

"Tabitha?" I asked in a low voice. She didn't answer or look up. "Babes, are you in?"

Her eyes glistened. *Oh fuck.* "I can't do this, Blake."

Arianna sighed. "Just leave her here. I doubt anything will happen, and if there is any danger, she can fly away."

"Arianna, take a hike," I snapped at her.

"We can't afford to fight." Lucian stepped in. "We need Arianna inside. She's the best at enchantments, Blake. Use your head."

"Fine." I looked back at her. "But you stay as far away from me as possible. Get that?"

Arianna shrugged and raised her upper lip in a sarcastic sneer before turning her back on me.

Why was I so upset? It was all Lucian's fault.

"Ready?" Lucian asked. We formed a line and approached the door.

Wings flapped and a hulking figure came down hard. My reflexes kicked in and I was half transformed before I stopped myself. I knew this dragon. They called him the Keeper. He wouldn't allow us to pass.

The spikes on his head looked like a crown. Two long whiskers ran down his mouth. His scales were a dark auburn and his snout was long and pointy.

"Stop. You cannot enter." His words rumbled through the stones. It made me think about my dream with the knights again.

I bowed as low as I could and everyone followed my example. "My name is Blake Leaf. I'm the Rubicon and we must enter. All of us. Lucian the Prince of Tith, Arianna the Princess of Areeth, Becky, her dragon George, and my sister, Samantha." I didn't introduce the rest; it was enough. "The King of Lion sword is missing. We need to find if it's still retrievable. The only way for us to find things that don't want to be found is by looking in the Millpond."

"There is no we in this, Rubicon," the Keeper rumbled. "There is only one."

"Understood," I said, though my mind was spinning.

Lucian was whispering to the spawn what the Keeper had said, because the exchange had been in Latin.

"What are the rules?"

"Not many. Choose one. It cannot be dragon."

My throat closed. Dragons were not allowed?

The dragon spoke again. "Call me when you have made your choice." The dragon flew away.

I straightened cautiously. Everyone stood straight. Shock was evident on every face.

"This was a waste of time, Lucian," I snapped.

"We just have to choose one person," Lucian countered.

"Yeah? Who's going to do it? You heard what he said: no dragons." I was hostile. I had to go in there. Why couldn't I go in?

No one said anything.

"I'll go," Lucian said. "There's no other choice."

Elena stopped him. "You can't."

"What?" Lucian and I asked at the same time. The others just stared. Was she really that stupid?

"No man has made it back. Only women."

I laughed. "So what you're saying is that men can't do this?"

"Yes," she barked at me. Authority was in her tone.

I did not like it.

"Elena, you don't know that," Sammy interrupted. Our gaze broke.

"I did my research. Five made it out. They were all women."

Sure they were, and most of them queens too. I looked up at the sky. What was this? Another fucking test.

"So you want to tell me it's between Arianna and Becky?" Lucian had made up her mind for her—and Sammy too.

"And me, Lucian," she said firmly. Was she for real?

Lucian's face lost a bit of color at her words. "No, Elena..." He stopped. "I meant to say that you don't have nearly enough training to face whatever waits behind those doors."

"I'll go." Becky stepped forward. George pushed her back. "Are you insane? You head what he said, Becky. No dragons."

"So..."

"Becky, are you still... intact?" Elena interrupted.

"What does *that* have to do with anything?" She shoved George aside and was ready to get her shit going with the spawn.

Girl fight.

"Everything. You have to be a maiden."

We all froze.

"Becky?" George demanded her to answer. But it was written all over her face. "You've got to be fucking kidding me."

This was getting fun. A smile tugged at the corners of my lips.

"They were all maidens. I think that means somewhere in there is a Sun-Blast."

Brian had a huge grin on his face.

I looked over at Arianna. "Well, Arianna, that means you are screwed." Both Brian and I chuckled.

Lucian gave me a look.

Arianna gave me the finger.

I winked and pretended to send her a kiss.

"I can't fucking believe that you slept with someone," George said in a disgusting tone.

"Oh, come on!" she yelled. "It was a one-time thing, and a huge mistake."

"George, not now," I begged playfully. George grunted.

Elena was the only human who could pass through those doors. Our eyes met.

"So what you're saying is that only you can enter these doors?" I wanted to laugh. But maybe, just maybe, she wouldn't come out and I'd be free from her at last.

"No. Listen, we tried," Lucian interrupted. "You simply can't go through those doors."

Listen to him, pumpkin, I thought sarcastically.

"We can't back out now. We're so close." She was determined.

"Elena, I don't know what's behind those doors," he wheedled. "If you don't finish in a certain time, you'll never come back."

"I know."

"What if you have to fight a dragon? You don't have enough training. This is crazy."

"Please don't start. I need to do this." She was serious.

I took a deep breath as they bickered.

She gestured to the queen's axes hanging from her waist.

"Elena! You don't know what you're saying." Tears glistened in his eyes. Lucian really loved her. I glanced over at Arianna. She looked like she had eaten something sour.

"I'm the only one who has a chance of making it out. Please, have a little faith in me." She cupped his face with her hands.

I had to suppress a growl. No, this wasn't happening. She wasn't worthy. I took a deep breath as they started to whisper sweet promises. *Make her stop.*

"Lucian, let her go. You always say if someone believes they can do it, they can," I said in Latin.

He regarded me coolly. It was as if he knew. He knew my agenda. That I wanted her to go in and never come out. He returned his attention to her. "You'd better come out, you hear me? Otherwise I'll blow this cavern apart," he said with a waver in his voice.

She nodded. They grabbed each other again. I looked away.

"Come back," he said.

She started to make her rounds with a few parting words for everyone. This was it. She was really going into the cavern.

She spoke to my sister first. "Don't change anything and have faith, okay?"

Sammy hugged her tightly. "Just come back, please."

Next was George. "Good luck, Elena."

"Take care of my girl, okay?"

Becky didn't look at her. She was so spiteful over whatever they were fighting about.

I shook my head. "It is going to take a miracle for you to make it out alive," I said and sighed. "But if you do, you'll have my respect."

She looked at me weird and huffed. She didn't buy it.

"I guess Brian will see whether Master Longwei was right about Elena's mark." Brian chuckled. "You're one crazy chick for doing this and it's driving Brian nuts."

"Brian!" Lucian and I scolded him.

"What? It's the truth."

She narrowed her eyes as Brian shrugged.

You couldn't take him anywhere.

"Good luck," Tabitha and Arianna said.

I called the Keeper back.

He landed with a buffet of wind and a shaking of the earth. "Have you decided who will enter the cavern?"

"Yes," I said, "but there is a tiny problem. She cannot speak the tongue of the dragons yet. Is there a way you might lend the ability to her for a short while?"

The Keeper considered this for a moment. Then shook his scales. I knew what that was. He'd granted my wish.

"Only for a short while."

"Did you understand him, Elena?" She would've if he'd granted it.

She nodded, seeming thunderstruck.

"Thank you, Great Keeper," I said.

Elena got up.

I saw the tears glistening in Lucian's eyes. I'd snatched one love away from him and I was going to do it again. But she had to go. She didn't belong here.

"What is your name?" the Keeper asked her.

"Elena Watkins."

"Elena Watkins, are you prepared to accept the consequences if you fail to complete what the cavern holds?"

"Yes." She sounded so confident. How had this happened? A few months ago, she was ready for the serum. Now she was ready to give up her freedom for the greater good.

"Good. Let the games begin." The Keeper flew away.

A huge shudder, more like an earthquake, made all of us lose our balance. When it stopped, one of the wooden doors was halfway open.

Lucian pushed past me and grabbed her waist. "Come back to me," he whispered.

They shared a kiss so passionate, it made Brian grunt. I bumped him but couldn't look away either. I didn't know Lucian could kiss anyone like that.

Arianna regarded them with an unreadable expression. *Yeah, how much do you miss those times, princess?*

Elena finally broke the kiss. She marched to the door.

This was it. In three seconds, I would be a free dragon again.

I watched her take that first step into the cavern when Becky yelled.

"Elena, wait!" She pulled her back. "You know I would do this if I could, right?"

She nodded. Becky grabbed her around the neck.

I groaned. *Such drama queens.* I was tiring of this extended goodbye. *Get on with it already.*

"You kick some ass, and you come back to us. I'm so sorry about earlier."

"It's okay, Becky. I'm sorry too."

They finally broke their embrace and the spawn quickly slipped through the door. "Wait for me for two days, please. If I'm not out by then, go home."

The door closed.

"No! Don't you dare!" Lucian yelled and beat against the door. But it was too late. "No, this isn't happening!"

"Lucian." Becky hugged him from behind.

"She doesn't believe she can do this, Becky." He sounded shaken. "If she did, she wouldn't have said that."

"Calm down."

Lucian didn't listen.

I felt like freedom was right in front of me. "She wanted to do this without our help. She seems to know what's in there. I don't know how, but it feels like she does. We need to have faith."

"Have *faith*? That is all you have to say?" He shook his head. "I'm going!"

"Where?" Becky and Sammy yelled.

"This is nuts," Arianna said.

"To get dynamite." The whites of Lucian's eyes were showing. "I meant what I said."

The door rumbled again and all of us paused as the doors lumbered open again.

A figure emerged.

Becky gasped as she grabbed her.

"Ow!" Elena yelled, touching her arm.

What the actual fuck?

"What happened? Becky asked.

Elena winced. "My shoulder."

"You got hurt?"

She nodded.

"And they let you out?" Becky asked again. She pulled Elena away from the doors.

Lucian was cemented to the spot, staring at her. His eyes were as round as mine.

Elena cocked her head, clearly bemused . "No! I had to finish."

"You... finished?"

"Elena, you just went in a minute ago." I was still scrambling to figure out what the fuck was going on.

"Huh?" A confused frown solidified on her face.

Then Lucian darted toward her and grabbed her tight.

"Ouch!" she exclaimed loudly.

"You dislocated your shoulder? How?"

She shook her head.

I huffed. She wasn't going to tell a soul what was behind those doors.

Lucian kissed her all over and this time I really didn't like it. I looked away and ground my jaw.

"We must push your shoulder back."

"Wait," Arianna interjected. "You said you finished?"

"Yes," Elena said firmly. "I know where to find the sword."

No one said anything, trying to process this. It was impossible.

"It still exists?" Brian and George said in unison.

"You really finished?" Lucian laughed. It was a gleeful, disbelieving sound. He thought she could walk on water. *Fucking royals.* Made me sick.

The flapping of wings descended on us again and I prostrated myself on the ground as before. Everyone bowed in to the Keeper with me, but he stopped Elena.

"Not you." He bowed his head. He stayed like that for a short moment and straightened. "Well done, Elena Watkins."

She didn't need to bow. He deemed her worthy to stand in his presence. *Hear that? She is worthy!*

A book appeared out of nowhere. The Keeper pushed it in her direction.

I know how she must feel at this very moment because a part of me felt it.

She opened it and patted her pockets. "Does anyone have a pen?"

We all chuckled; no one had brought a stupid pen.

"You don't need a pen, Elena," the Keeper said. "Give me your hand."

She hesitated. Damn, Lucian and I hesitated on her behalf.

Her arm trembled in his paw. Then a big claw slashed her wrist.

My instincts had me wanting to get up and rush to her defense, but I couldn't. From the looks of things, Lucian couldn't either. We were held in place by a higher power.

Blood splashed everywhere. The floor, her pants, the pages, everywhere.

Then the book closed. A thin laser appeared out of his claw.

What the fuck? I'd seen it all now.

He made a circular motion with his laser paw over her hand. It looked like she didn't feel a thing. When he was done, she twisted her wrist, staring at it.

Who was she?

She's your rider, Blake.

He showed her the book, closed it, and that was that.

When he left, Lucian was the first one to scramble up and reach her. They shared another passionate kiss.

I wanted to throw up. "We need to move," I said, breaking up their little moment.

"She's hurt, Blake," Lucian and Becky said at the same time.

"We have to get the sword now or this will all be for nothing."

Lucian got all in my face. "What don't you understand? She is hurt. She needs to rest."

"Don't fight. It's no use!" She yelled, looking disgusted.

"What do you mean, it's no use?" I asked.

"I don't know where it is right now," she barked at me.

"Then when, Elena?" Anger filled me from toe to head.

"Tomorrow night."

"We have to wait a whole night?" My arms flew up in the air. *What the hell?*

"Deal with it," Lucian growled. He lifted her in his arms.

I growled this time but it was misunderstood.

"Calm down. You will get your spotlight tomorrow," Tabitha cooed. If only it was that.

We reached camp in no time. The others helped make a fire and brewed coffee. Lucian and George pushed her shoulder back into place. He gave her his belt to bite on.

I could heal her, but I wasn't going to. She screamed and

I cringed. Pain was something I'd had my fair share of. I decided to go for a flight.

I didn't want to be here. If I stuck around, I would say something and regret it. But as I took flight, the wind beneath my wings helped me ponder everything that had taken place. Something in me had shifted tonight when she came out of that cavern alive.

She was the sixth person—woman, queen—in history to survive the Sacred Cavern.

She was worthy.

Hopefully by tomorrow, I wouldn't feel this way anymore. It would all wash away.

THIRTY-9

I CAME BACK LATE. The camp was quiet.

Brian was the only one still awake. "You okay?" he asked.

"Yes, just tense. It's the King of Lion sword."

"Yeah, I know. We're going to make history, Blake."

I smiled. "But who would've thought a dragon spawn born with the mark would do that?"

He looked in the direction of the cavern. A smile lingered on his face. "She makes Brian crazy. She doesn't make Blake crazy?"

"Not that crazy, no." This was a patent lie. She was driving me crazy, every inch of her.

He laughed. "Brian had a rough night tonight. He needs to go and crash."

I chuckled. "Goodnight, Brian."

"Night, Blake."

I went to take a seat at the edge of the trees.

Looking at the stars, I took out the poetry notebook I used when I wasn't using my journal.

I had no words tonight. The words I had... the darkness

would kill me if I wrote them down. It would kill her. I couldn't. *I can't.*

But I found myself gazing at the sky again and my mind started to wander. What would happen if I marched into Lucian's tent now and confessed?

Confessed who she was, confessed how she made me feel. How she'd made me feel tonight. Confessed that she was my rider.

Oh starry, starry night, you are the only one that sees this.

I found a pen in my backpack. I'd had one all along. I opened my notebook and steadied myself with another long look at the stars.

Oh starry, starry night,
Your moon gleams so bright.
But this darkness inside me won't stop to fight.
I know what is right and I know what is wrong,
But how do I tell the truth... through a song?
Oh starry, starry night, but I can't.
It won't be fair, it won't be right,
Even if she proves to be worthy, proves that she has all the might.
The beast will never yield to her light.

So fuck the words and fuck the song. I'd show them in due time, when I was dark, lost, and totally gone.

I did own a heart, and it was strong.
The beast will never let me be.

> *The darkness will never set me free.*
> *And through this choice, it won't be so bad,*
> *That she never knew the real me.*

Through the corner of my eye I saw her. She'd just emerged.

I'd made up my mind. It wasn't fair to her. She would go crazy if I told her the truth.

And I was sparing her from a lot of things. Not just the royal duties she didn't know she had, but from darkness and nightmares.

She reached me. I couldn't look at her. Scared that she would see the truth in my eyes.

I buried my notebook under my ass.

"Do you mind?" she asked.

"Sure." I shrugged. "Whatever."

She sat against the tree opposite me.

None of us said a word. She wasn't a big talker. That much I'd figured out from our nights guarding Dragonia.

"It was really brave what you did tonight," I said.

She huffed softly, still not looking at me. "I guess anyone in my position would have tried their best."

I snorted and smiled, sort of. "How's the arm?"

"Hurts like hell."

My smile grew. I should heal her, but I felt weird again. It was strange around her.

I stared into the night again. It was quiet, deadly quiet, until she sighed. It looked as if she wanted to get up and my mouth popped open again. *Why?* "You're wrong about everyone being able to do what you did."

"Blake, please. I did what I said I would do." Her expression was fiery. *Was it always going to be so intense between us?*

"That's exactly my point. What people say they'll do and what they actually do are two different things, Elena. I learned that the hard way." The words just spilled out. *Great, why don't I just tell her who the hell she is?*

She looked away. "I always do what I say I will."

"You don't get it." I chuckled. "You could have asked to see *anything*."

"And your point is?" She was starting to get annoyed.

"You have no idea why your dad died? Or why that dragon was after you? The pond would've even shown you where your mom is." I looked away the minute I said it. I wasn't supposed to know, but Irene told me that her mother had left.

Fuck, fuck, fuck, fuck.

I could feel her eyes on me. "How do you know about her?" He voice was softer than usual.

"Just forget it."

To my surprise, she did leave it. Tears glistened in her eyes.

Dammit, Blake. Are you ever going to give her a break?

"It doesn't matter. The past isn't going to save us. I went into that cave to find out about the sword and I did." even as she spoke, I had a thought: if she'd asked to see her mother, it would've shown her Queen Catherine.

She would've known the truth.

Whoa, that could've backfired badly.

I realized I needed to answer her. "It's brave of you to have given up that opportunity."

She rolled her eyes, pissed off. She looked away and I could swear there was a little shake of her head. "You guys were brave for coming with me."

"We're dragons, Elena. What kind of Rubicon would I be if I chickened out?" A smile toyed with my lips.

"Still, it was very brave."

I sighed. I want to tell her so badly. "You have much to learn."

"So everyone tells me. Thanks for asking that dragon to give me the gift to understand Latin. I would never have been able to go through it without that."

"Tell me about it," I mumbled.

She gave me a sarcastic smile, though it disappeared fast. "So, you guys really don't understand English when you're in your other form?"

I squinted slightly. *Other form?* "No, dragon is what I am. My true colors show when he comes out. I don't have to hide the way I feel." I took out my packet of cigarettes from my back pocket and lit one.

She started to cough the minute my smoke blew in her direction again.

So many signs and she didn't seem to see one of them.

"So you are aware every time you end up hurting someone during a claiming?"

I nodded. Shit, I was open with her. Was it part of the Dent? Would I tell the truth if she asked me that question? It scared me.

"You don't care?"

"It's not who I am," I spoke the truth again and released a long breath. "I don't know how to explain it to you. A part of this form doesn't want to be a dragon and it clashes when I'm one. It's hard to explain."

"*Dr. Jekyll and Mr. Hyde*," she said.

She learned really fast. "Exactly. The only thing that we've agreed on lately is this mission." So it seemed.

"Is it why you and Lucian are no longer friends?"

He'd told her. Of course he'd told her.

I looked back at Lucian's tent. "I knew he would tell you about us."

"You didn't answer my question."

I pursed my lips as her eyes lingered on mine. She wasn't going to back off. "Yes, Elena. The older I get, the more I want to be a dragon. The more I'm a dragon, the less I will stay human. Which means I'll end up losing this." I gestured to my good looks. "Believe me, I did Lucian a big favor."

"How can you say that, Blake? It's selfish to make that kind of a decision on someone else's behalf."

She was infuriating me. "It's not that easy," I shot back. "I know Cheng gave you the breakdown of what I'll turn into if I'm not claimed by a certain date. That part of me grows stronger every single day. My human form can't fight this. It's just too much. You have no idea how much it hurts when I'm forcing myself to do the opposite of what *it* wants." *Stop it, stop it, stop it. Don't say anther fucking word. Idiot.*

"Will it change if Lucian claims you?"

I started to laugh. If only she knew how close the one person who could claim me was. "He will never claim me."

"He could, Blake."

"You live in a dream world. I'll become evil, and it's something I struggle to make peace with, but sooner or later, I'll have no choice." She needed to stop asking these questions. I didn't want to tell her the most important part.

"You don't have to," she said. "You have to fight it, Blake. Don't give up."

"You think I'm not trying?" Anger made my hand shake when I went to ash my cigarette. "I'm seeing the Viden on a daily basis just for one ounce of hope. Just so you know, I haven't found it yet, and to be honest, every time I leave that fucking tower, I become happier. That's not a normal reaction," I lied. I lied and I wasn't withering in pain. I could lie to her.

Good.

"She did predict your true Dragonian being born."

What? Think, Blake. Don't say the words. Just don't. Lie.
"My Dragonian didn't get a chance to take a single breath.

Goran made sure of it the night he killed the king and queen."

"You don't know that," she said as if she knew; she believed it. She didn't know. Couldn't. Right? "What if he's been born and no one knows about it? Like maybe not with Queen Catherine."

He, she'd said he. She didn't know a thing. *You need to answer her, Blake.* My mind tried to remember what she'd said.

"Are you implying that the king committed adultery? The king loved the queen; he would never do that."

"How do you know that?"

"Because his dragon would have known." She needed to stop asking these questions.

"Oh? And you know Sir Robert?" She sounded sarcastic. She didn't know. How?

"Yes, he's my father."

Her eyes widened. She didn't know. "Your father's *the* Night-Villain King Albert claimed?"

Yes, your father claimed mine. "My dad knew everything about them. He would've told me if there was even a shred of hope. There is none, Elena. I've got no Dragonian."

I sounded the way I should sound. Dejected. No hope, no future. A great lie to throw her off. A stupid lie.

"Just try to give Lucian a chance to claim you, Blake."

My jaw muscles tightened again. "I can't. I'm already giving everything in me not to kill him." I'd had enough of this. I took one last drag of my cigarette, got up, and flicked it away.

I didn't even say goodnight, just went to my tent and lay behind Tabitha. She was so cold, always cold.

But I thought about Elena. I didn't call her a spawn anymore. She wasn't a spawn, she just couldn't know that. I heard her scurrying around the campsite for a few more minutes and then she went back to Lucian.

We shouldn't have had that conversation tonight. I felt disgusted for the way I'd lied and for the way she'd made me feel. I closed my eyes and prayed that by tomorrow, wanting her would be gone from my mind.

FORTY

I WAS RIGHT. By the next morning, I felt disgusted with my weakness from the night before.

She made me sick.

I didn't need a Dragonian. I wasn't a stupid lamb like George. He gave Becky everything she wanted.

I left the tent early. I found Lucian by the fire. We exchanged some words. Before I could stop myself, I asked, "Why did you tell her?"

"What, that you were my best friend?"

"I'm not weak."

He frowned at the red embers. "I didn't say you were."

"I can't do this. I'm not built this way."

"You'll get the chance to shine tonight, Blake."

I looked at his tent.

"If she's making your nervous, go take a flight and calm down. You are not going to take this one too. I won't let you."

I chuckled. "You seriously think that I want your spawn? C'mon, Lucian."

"Take a flight Blake. Cool down."

I was glad that he'd misinterpreted me. Still, he wasn't completely off-base. He knew that I wanted her, even if I didn't.

She didn't belong to him. He was going to feel pretty stupid when he realized the truth. If he hadn't already. Lucian wasn't stupid. He didn't forget.

I flew. I had to calm down. By the time I got back, I felt better. I was glad I hadn't told her, and I felt stupid for writing those words. Unfortunately, the dumbest ones made excellent songs.

Around midmorning, I saw Brian flying in my direction. He landed and morphed back. "Mountain of Ekwardor. We have to go soon if we want to make it on time."

"That's where he is?" So she'd told them without me there.

Brian nodded.

Without delay, I flew behind Brian. We both landed with a thud. He morphed back first and I followed. Elena looked resolutely in the other direction.

A wicked smile lit my face. She wasn't comfortable with the nakedness. I climbed into my pants and pulled my shirt over my head.

I couldn't believe that I'd been so weak last night.

Tabitha handed me a plate of squirrel roasted on the open fire. We dug in. As we ate, my eyes met Elena's for a few short seconds. She wasn't as intimidating as she had been last night. She looked away first.

After breakfast I spoke with Lucian as he started breaking down his tent. "So where do we go?"

"Ekwardor. He's going to destroy the sword tonight in the volcano," Lucian answered.

"He? Who is it?"

"Don't know. Elena has never seen him before." Lucian sounded irritated.

"Let me guess: we *wing* this one too."

"Yeah, and if you've got a problem with that, you're free to leave."

"Lucian?" Elena said.

They just stared at one another..

"I hope you're right about this, Elena." My voice was harsh. I zipped up my backpack and started to shed my clothes again.

Brian was right; the mountain of Ekwardor was a push. We needed to leave now.

❧

IT WASN'T AS FAR as it had been coming to the Sacred Cavern, but it was about half the distance, which was still quite a ways. We landed on Ekwardor around three in the afternoon.

There was a volcano just up ahead. I hoped the place looked familiar to Elena from her vision in the Millpond.

Sammy landed with Elena and Lucian on her back. Elena started looking around everywhere.

We got dressed as they started to speak about the plan. I needed a plan. I was not going to wing it this time.

Irene's foretelling wasn't going to come true. We needed the King of Lion sword.

"Elena, what side of the volcano is he coming from and when?"

"The vision showed nightfall. We're in exactly the right spot."

"Are you sure?" Arianna asked. She was just as annoyed with the two of them as I was.

"Positive. If I'm not mistaken, the volcano is just ahead, about two miles." She pointed. Brian sprinted down the path. Sun-Blasts loved volcanoes.

"Okay, we have to corner the Dragonian here." I drew a rough map on the ground. "We can't let him get past the P.O.N.R." Short for Point of No Return.

Elena whispered something to Lucian and he answered fast.

"Where's the sword, Elena?" I asked.

"He was carrying it close to him. It was covered with fabric and bound with string."

I touched my chin. She knew exactly where it was. It was her task. "So we have to find a way to snatch it from him. I doubt that he'll be compelled—"

"You're wrong," she interrupted.

No, please. I sighed. This might just become a suicide mission if Goran was involved. I stared at the ground. I couldn't let him know what I looked like. "Are you sure?" I coughed and my voice almost broke. None of them knew what that meant.

"The guy marched into the volcano and melted away . I would say he's compelled."

Melting away? Becky mouthed. Elena nodded.

"What is it, Blake?" Lucian saw straight through me.

"It's not good." I paced, thinking hard. "If Goran controls him, he'll see everything, including us." The danger in my tone was real. I couldn't hide it anymore. I tried to come up with a Plan B, but I couldn't. It was insane just thinking about it. We couldn't show our true forms.

"Is that bad?" Elena asked.

"It's very bad, you crazy lunatic!" Tabitha yelled. "You've led us to our deaths."

"Tabitha, back off!" Becky said with a growl. Sammy cussed, calling her a fucking coward.

"Tabitha's got a point, but we've made a choice," I said to stop the quarreling. "We can't transform, Lucian. We have to fight in our human forms. Elena, to get back to your question, yes, the mission just turned suicidal. If Goran does compel the Dragonian, we are going to fight him indirectly. None of us is ready or trained for that."

They all fell silent as it clicked.

"Blake, I will change!" Sammy sounded terrified.

"Sammy, if Goran controls the Dragonian, he'll see through his eyes. If he knows we're dragons, he'll use magic. We will all die. We have to stay hidden. Let him think we're humans."

"I can't control it yet!" she shouted frantically. She was still so young.

"You can't change, Samantha!"

Tears rolled down her cheeks. "I really suck in Transformation class. I always turn when it gets too scary."

"Try," I pleaded. I couldn't lose her. I couldn't face my mom if anything happened to Sammy.

She nodded and Becky's arm curled around her shoulder.

"I can't fight Goran, Blake," Arianna started too. *Fuck me.* I didn't care if I had to compel this one. She was going to fucking stay. I walked over to her and cupped her face in my hands. "Don't think of it like that. You're the best with enchantments and spells. We need you, Arianna." My tone was soft and by Tabitha's growl I knew she didn't like it. But we needed Arianna.

"He's right, Arianna," Lucian seconded. "Don't do anything stupid. If Goran knows that you can do counter and reversal spells already, he'll take you out first."

Arianna started to panic. *Thanks, Lucian.*

"You have to stay calm," I ordered her with her face still cupped in my hands.

"We'll have to hide, wait for him until he's surrounded. We can trap him, and if we need to fight, so be it," I said to the group as a whole. If only I believed it myself.

"Blake, who will get the sword?" George asked.

"Elena has already proven herself ready for something like this. Lucian said you have crazy fast reflexes?"

She stared at me with huge unblinking eyes.

I stamped my foot in frustration. "Ugh! For crying out loud, what is it?"

"I can't do this, Blake."

"Elena? You're the only one who knows where the sword—"

"It's not that! My arm is killing me. I won't succeed with only one arm."

I glared at her. *Fuck, now I have to heal her arm. Lucian is not going to love this.* He was going to ponder this like a little bitch.

"Fine!" I walked toward her fast.

She retreated.

"Just relax!" I grabbed her arm and pulled her closer. I didn't know what to feel with her being this close to me. It didn't feel right. I unbuckled the belt that was holding her shoulder in place. *Don't Ascend!*

I found her eyes on me, judging me.

"Don't look at me."

She turned her head to look at Lucian. I could feel his eyes on me, boring into my soul, and knew he was cussing me out silently.

I closed my eyes and concentrated on my healing ability. Heat radiated from my hands. I could hear her silent scream. Her eyes were on me; I opened mine. "I said don't look!" I yelled.

Her head snapped back to Lucian. The warmth grew hotter. It didn't stop.

She finally screamed in pain.

"Blake, that's enough!" Lucian yelled. He pushed me away. I lost the energy—like, it bottomed out immediately. I found myself kneeling on the ground.

"What the hell did you just do?" Elena screamed.

"I'm sorry. I'm still learning how to control it," My tone was strained. I tried to control my energy, or what was left of it. I could feel it climbing again. It was going to be fine. I could sleep later and build up my energy again. She didn't Ascend. *Thank you.*

"How do you feel?" Lucian asked.

"I'm fine."

"Do you think you'll be able to get the sword now?" I asked again.

She rolled her shoulder around and then nodded. A weird expression was on her face. Doubt? Annoyance? I couldn't tell.

"Why didn't you heal her arm earlier?" Lucian lashed out.

I turned around and my index finger was in his face. "Don't start with me."

George and Brian stepped between us. We'd been here too many times already. "C'mon, guys, not today. We need to align to beat this." They whispered.

"Lucian, drop it," Arianna said. "Her arm is healed. So please, can we just get back to the mission? I really want to go home alive, and we need a solid plan."

Lucian's jaw was set. He was furious. He glared at me. "You stay away from me."

I started to laugh.

"Blake?" Arianna said, and gestured for me to carry on.

"Fine," I said and refocused on my crude drawings in the dirt. "Once Elena gets the sword, Sammy, you morph and get Elena the hell away from here. The rest of us will take care of the Dragonian."

"Okay," Sammy said in a faint whisper.

"Please, just try not to blow your cover until then," I begged again.

"I said I will try."

"It might work," Lucian said after a long silence.

"Of course it will," I said.

The conversation changed over to who would team up with whom after Sammy and Elena were gone.

Brian would obviously try to distract the Sun-Blast, while Becky and George tried to kill it.

Lucian, Arianna, and I would deal with the Dragonian.

The faster he died, the faster Goran would lose the connection. We could save the sword and go back to live our lives in peace... at least, until I went dark.

"What if his Sun-Blast comes after us, Blake?" Elena asked.

I hadn't thought about that.

"Don't worry about that, Elena." Brian winked at her. "Brian's got it covered."

"Brian, he might be fully grown," I said.

"Brian doesn't care. He's going to struggle to get past Brian."

I laughed and had to slap that hand. He was so ready for this. I really hoped he was.

"Idiot," Becky said in a singsong tone, rolling her eyes.

"That's good, Elena," Lucian whispered.

"What?"

"You're starting to think like a Dragonian in battle." He smiled reassuringly.

I did not like that.

We carried on with the plan of taking the Dragonian out. We had to kill him; there was no other way to break the connection.

"Don't worry, Elena. I'm really fast. I'll get us to safety, even if it's the last thing I do," Sammy said to Elena.

What about this plan didn't work for her? She looked so unsure. I couldn't be the one to get the sword. I didn't know where it was. Elena was the perfect one. She could do it. I knew she could.

❦

WE WAITED PATIENTLY for the Dragonian and his dragon to land.

I guarded the entrance and tuned out completely when Lucian start telling Elena more things about me. It was as if he was preparing her silently for what she had to do.

Fuck, what if that was the reason he'd trained her?

I saw the outline of the dragon finally and sprinted down the path to my hiding place, a bush opposite Lucian's.

Please let this work. I was fighting on the good side. Maybe for the only time too. I needed this victory.

We waited with bated breath as the dragon and his compelled Dragonian landed.

They walked slowly. Way too slowly. They already knew we were here. They could smell us.

The Dragonian's arm was already broken. Yet he waved for his dragon to go. I hadn't bargained on that. Neither had Brian. He was going to follow Sammy.

A new plan formed in my head.

I'd have to go with. I needed to kill the dragon and make sure my sister and Elena were safe. My stomach coiled up in knots.

Then Sammy moved. *Fuck!*

He heard a branch snap. He stopped and looked around. Then he started to run.

We leaped into action. Elena was going for it just as Arianna was intoning a spell.

I saw Elena get the sword, but then he turned around. He spoke softly, calmly. Elena froze. Petrified. Her hood fell over her face. Something was wrong.

FORTY - 1

EVERYTHING HAPPENED SO FAST.

The Sun-Blast swooped back overhead and the Dragonian tossed him the sword.

I was already moving fast to get him into a headlock.

Brian leaped into the air after the Sun-Blast.

Arianna shouted the spell and the Dragonian said the counter-spell.

George, Becky, and Lucian were struck with what whatever paralyzing effect Elena had been. They were all frozen on the spot.

As I grabbed him, I was blasted ten paces away.

All in a matter of seconds.

We were going to die. We were no match for Goran.

Sammy turned. Thick roots and branches clawed her in. They pulled her down and I thought that my nightmare was going to come true.

I couldn't see Elena's face. She was the nearest to me.

Sammy, relax, I wanted to tell her, but the pain that racked my body was unreal. I wanted to scream but didn't. I wasn't going to give him the satisfaction. *Not today, not ever.*

The Dragonian started to laugh, praising his masterpiece of a trap. The sound was otherworldly. Goran's voice through his vocal chords. How he'd trapped us all in a mere minute, maybe less.

He crouched down next to me. He laughed. "You really think you could stop me, boy?" His eyes flickered. He knew it was me.

I grunted. The pain of his touch was unbearable.

"I'll kill you one day," I swore through clenched teeth. "If it's the last thing I do!"

Goran laughed. Then he stopped just for a second and lifted up my sleeve, revealing the mark of the Rubicon.

"My, my, my. How exciting," he said in a flat tone. His laugh pierced me again. It made my skin crawl. "The Rubicon trying to save the day. It doesn't suit you, Blake Leaf."

I growled. This couldn't be happening. I wouldn't give up. Not now.

"You're so full of anger," Goran whispered. "I revel in the knowledge that deep down inside, you like it too."

I hated the fact that his words were real. I did secretly want to become his dragon. The darkness in me resonated with his. We were the same.

"You won't kill me, boy. You want to know why? Because when you turn, you'll be mine." He laughed again, as if this was his favorite game. "Just imagine what we'll be able to do together. No one will ever get in our way."

"I'll kill myself before that happens!" I roared.

"Wanna bet?" Goran mocked me. The Dragonian whose body he was compelling stood up from his crouch. "However, you'll hate me now because I'm going to kill all your friends, one by one."

No, please, don't do this. Please. It's your fucking nephew.

"We can't have brave little teenagers running riot when I finally break free from that disgusting hellhole you love so much. Which one should I kill first?"

"You fuck!" I spat through the pain. *Be a man and kill me.*

"Blake!" Lucian scolded through gritted teeth.

"Eenie, meenie, miney, mo." He pointed at each paralyzed person in turn. He landed on Elena. *No, no, no, no. Please, kill me*, I begged. I had wanted her dead and now, it was going to come true if help didn't come soon.

Lucian roared. He'd lost it. I knew the feeling. "Leave her alone, you freak!"

Goran ignored Lucian. He walked straight to Elena.

Please, help, I begged a greater power. Any form, any form of a distraction. *Please.*

Lucian started cussing. Begging his uncle to kill him. But Goran wanted to kill Elena. He didn't know who she was, but he would the minute he saw her eyes.

There was no mistaking them.

He'd smelled her, the same way Brian had that first time. "Not a dragon," Goran said. He lifted her hood with the tip of his dagger.

His face froze when he saw her.

Elena, look at me, I begged. She was trapped in his hands. I tried to get up. I strained against invisible bonds with every bit of strength I had. His eyes were dead. The connection was not very strong, but I couldn't move. I was pinned to the spot.

Lucian, stop cussing and try to break free. I didn't say it out loud. He needed to take control. I was sure he could see the eyes. They were gray.

Why couldn't I free myself? I felt it right within my reach. I grunted. *Break! Just break something and get out of this.*

Lucian still spat a stream of curses.

I looked at Goran again—or the Dragonian who was his puppet. I only saw Goran pulling the strings. The eyes turned from grey to black again.

Then the arm with the knife thrust the dagger into Elena, over and over again.

Time stopped.

He looked straight at me. He was killing my only fucking chance and he knew it. I could hear the knife going in and coming out. In again, and out.

He started to laugh.

Lucian was beyond himself, screaming and cussing. It

didn't even sound like him anymore. It was the sound of his soul shattering.

I watched her blood splatter onto the ground.

Over her axes.

I just need that axe, that's all I needed.

Then Goran stopped and whispered, "You tell your mother I send her my love and a gift. Condolences to whatever your name is."

Then I heard it. A dragon.

The dragon was swooping in. A scale was slightly out of place. Brian. His claws came out and he picked both Elena and the Dragonian up.

A distraction. The paralyzing spell broke.

Elena immediately toppled toward the earth.

Lucian caught her.

I shook free and shot my pink fire at the Dragonian. Brian dropped him just too soon and he landed with a thud.

Elena's axes were right next to me. Her blood was on them. I hoped this theory that I had was true. That the blood of Albert's bloodline on the weapon would transform it into a King of Lion weapon. One that could destroy evil.

I threw an axe with as much force as I could muster.

He intoned a spell, and I froze. But the axe had already hit him.

"Fight, Elena!" Lucian cried.

Arianna's spell connected with something that she couldn't control and caused an explosion.

The earth vibrated. The Dragonian fell to the floor with the axe lodged in his torso.

Work, please, I begged silently.

Arianna gasped. I saw it too. The axe was making the Dragonian turn to ash. Slowly.

"Blake!" Arianna couldn't take her eyes off it. "What does this mean?"

"Nothing," I lied. "They are Queen Catherine's axes, found in the pantheon. They carry a bit of the king's blood. It's what saved us."

"How did you know it was going to do that?"

"I didn't!" I yelled. Half-true. I grabbed Elena's other, blood-free axe and pulled the other one from his disintegrating flesh. The Dragonian was still alive. "I'll never be yours," I growled at him. His eyes finally went dead.

"Elena, stay with me!" Lucian roared and cried.

No, she couldn't be dead.

"Lucian, we need to get her to a hospital, now!" Becky cried.

No, she wasn't going to die. Not today. *She'll die when I chose.* I grabbed her while the two of them were still quarreling and jumped off the mountain.

Tith was the closest. I just had to make it to the hospital there. I sped up, faster and faster, pumping my wings like I had never flown before.

Elena was clutched in my palms.

My scales burned from the wind that screamed against them.

My sight zoomed in... too much, because I saw Dragonia Academy.

My scales still burned.

Elena was dying in my paw.

I pushed harder.

Without her I was nothing. I was evil, I didn't have a fucking chance. I wasn't going to become his. Not his.

I pushed faster.

Then a wall was right in front of me. I couldn't stop. I tucked Elena close to my heart and crashed through the wall. I skidded to a halt.

I prayed she was okay.

I had no idea where I was. Then I heard Constance's voice. No fucking way.

"It's Blake, Master Longwei!" my aunt yelled.

I opened my eyes.

"Can you hear me?" She spoke Latin.

"Help," I said.

I couldn't open my paw. She was dying. She couldn't be dead.

"Help her."

My aunt looked at me weird.

My eyes closed and my paw finally opened.

FORTY - 2

MY SKIN FELT tight when I opened my eyes.

I was in the infirmary. My mom and dad were next to my bed. Sammy was also here.

"Ugh," I grunted.

"Blake," my father said first.

Then came my mother's voice in that strong British accent of hers, which was at the moment filled with alarm. "What were you thinking?" It was weird that neither me or Sammy spoke like her. We could easily imitate one, but we didn't speak with it. I shook my head to rid it of the stupid tangent. Why was I thinking this?

"It was the King of Lion sword," I croaked.

"You could've died."

"I didn't."

"You saved a girl's life." My mother smiled.

Fuck. I shouldn't have done this. *Why did I?* "I would've done it for anyone, Mom."

"It doesn't matter." She kissed the top of my head. "You will always be my hero. You make me so proud."

"Was it *him*?" my father asked.

"Yes, it was him. He's waiting."

His face was grim. "He won't get you. I promise."

I hoped he could keep that one. A dragon's promise was a binding oath. I was the only dragon who could break a promise. I was different. Stronger.

"So is it gone?"

I rubbed my temples. "The King of Lion sword?"

He nodded and so did I. I didn't want to tell them, but remembered Arianna and there wasn't time to compel her.

"There is another weapon we can use. The queen's axes."

"What?"

"They were here, Dad, at the Academy. They're not lost. They put fake ones in the museum."

"Are you sure?"

"They had her initials. I don't know where the gloves are, but it's an Alex Rhodes. I didn't think it was like the King of Lion sword, but when I struck the Dragonian, he turned into dust. Just like when the sword killed evil."

"They exploded?"

I lied by nodding. It was my word against Arianna's.

Where are they now, Blake?" my father wanted to know.

"Ask Constance. They were in my paw when I crashed."

My father left. Mom stayed, stroking my forehead. "Constance told me your heart almost exploded. The tips of your scales burned, Blake."

"Scales heal, Mom. Please don't make a huge deal out

of it. I had to save her life. She stole the prince's heart. It was the least I could do."

I looked around. Elena wasn't in the same room as me. Must be in the one closest to Constance's room.

She nodded. "My hero," she smiled and I closed my eyes.

§⁂

IT TOOK about two days until I was all healed. My dragon form was a different story. My scales were going to take time.

Victory was what they'd printed in all the papers. And *bravery*. Everyone in Paegeia clamored to hear the tale of how nine courageous Dragonians and dragons had found the sword.

But only eight returned.

Brian.

I flipped out when Constance told me. I punched a wall. Tears even threatened to consume me. I screamed and raged and bellowed and broke things.

Master Longwei wanted to know every detail of the events that had transpired. I refused. "Not my story to tell."

The other seven said the same. We were a united front of silence.

My father was livid. I thought he was going to skin me alive. But when Sammy stood by me and also refused to talk, he stormed out.

King Helmut was just as upset. "Is it true?" I hear Lucian's dad ask him.

"About what?" Lucian asked.

"The girl, son."

"Dad, it isn't the fourteenth century anymore. I can choose who I love. She's my choice." He pointed in the direction of the infirmary.

"Her? The dragon spawn they brought in?" King Helmut spluttered.

Lucian grunted. "Stop calling her that. She has every right to be here just like me and Blake and Becky, like everyone else. She saved the day, Dad, and I know you don't see it, but I promise you that I will never marry Arianna."

"Lucian, you will lose everything."

"Then so be it. I won't give her up." He stomped away.

In shock, King Helmut wandered off in the opposite direction. He had no idea I was near.

Lucian really loved her.

I closed my eyes.

This was what Irene saw. She said it was true love.

This was fucked up.

I was going to break his heart again. I should just let them be. I was nobody's lamb anyway.

My darkness returned slowly as the victory and adrenaline from finding the missing sword wore off. I was back to my old self.

"Why did you save her?" Lucian asked one day on his way to the infirmary.

"Seriously? I thought you were happy."

He chuckled. "You think I'm stupid?"

"Not this shit again," I said, pretending one more time.

"What is she to you, Blake? Please, I need to know."

"She's nothing, Lucian. Nothing, fucking nothing. I saved her for you!" I yelled.

He nodded. He came over and hugged me. "I owe you." He sniffed once and took his leave.

I blew out hot air. I hoped he'd leave it now.

&a.

BRIAN'S FUNERAL CAME NEXT. It was devastating. He was the only dragon who have hatched in his family. The only spawn. His parents were bereft.

The ceremony was held in the cathedral in Elm and from there we went to a sacred hill. The seven of us were there, Elena was still out.

I hated funerals. They were so sad to watch. But this one was a thousand times worse. He'd saved us all.

I gave a speech too.

"Blake hates funerals," I spoke softly and everyone chuckled fondly at my third-person homage. "King Albert was the first to believe that dragon is dragon, no matter Metallic or Chromatic. With the right influence, Chromatic is just as noble and as righteous as the Metallic. Brian, you proved that. By dying to save all of us. If it weren't for you, for your distraction, today there would be nine caskets, not just one."

A few strangled sobs followed this.

I continued, "You were right that night when you said we were going to make history. You did it. You proved that Chromatics can be just as noble as Metallics, and you were only twenty years old. I'm sorry I wasn't strong enough, but I promise you, your star will guide me to become better, braver. I will fight. I will fight until I cannot fight anymore. Blake is going to miss Brian a hell of lot more than Brain thought. Goodbye my friend."

As grief squeezed a vise around my heart, all the fire and lightning breathers stood in a semicircle around the burning altar that carried Brian's casket.

The priest said a few words about how we all returned to the air and became guiding stars in the end.

All of the things that I didn't believe in.

Then we all lit the altar with our abilities. It started to burn. Sobs overwhelmed the cracking of the fire. Brian's mother wailed. His father looked hopeless and empty, holding her in his arms.

Guilt and grief warred within me. I was sorry to have abandoned the fight. But I had to save Elena. He'd died so a princess could live. And who knew? Maybe one day a reckoning would come.

I returned to Dragonia Academy after I gave them my condolences. I wanted to leave before they could blame me.

Sammy, Lucian, George, and Becky stayed behind, along with a couple of the other students that had attended.

Back in my room at Dragonia, I lay on my bed staring at the ceiling.

Brian's death was on me. All of it. If I'd told authorities who Elena was, none of this would've happened.

None of it.

But I couldn't tell. The beast wouldn't let me. Besides, I'd killed Brian. She would hate me if she ever discovered the truth.

🐉

SHE FINALLY WOKE UP. She finally told her story.

Lucian was elated that she had recovered, but the fact that his parents didn't approve of their relationship ate at him. He wasn't going to give Elena up.

I saw it, and I hoped she would fight too.

He was worth it.

Still, her tutoring carried on. She needed the extra lessons. Arianna dedicated herself to teaching her for real. She even mused for a while that Elena was a lost princess.

But I insisted that was impossible. The Wall. It always boiled down the fucking Wall. Thank heavens for that, oh and that a dragon always know. That one saved my ass too.

Thursday came faster then I hoped. I wasn't sick anymore like I used to be in her presence. It was weird.

We went over a couple of conjugations, and she repeated them okay.

"Thank you," she said. I ignored her. I carried on with pronunciation lesson.

"Thank you, Blake," she interrupted again, louder this time.

I squinted at her. She just stared at me, guileless and sincere. *Let it go, Elena. Just let it go.* I repeated the phrase we were studying.

She sighed. Just when I thought she wasn't going to thank me again, she said it one more time.

"Stop it, Elena. There's nothing to thank me for, okay? I would've done it for anybody in that group." Harsh. Good.

She narrowed her eyes. Maybe I'd gone too far. "What happened to 'you've got all my respect when you get out of there?'" She wiggled in her chair, making her tone deeper. Was that supposed to sound like me?

I huffed. "To be honest, I didn't think you *would* get out of there. So, I lied. Sue me."

Her mouth fell open. "I thought dragons lived by their promises."

"Those rules don't apply to me."

Her nostrils flared and I was ready to continue our lesson when her shoe connected hard with my shin. She stormed out of the library.

"Elena!" I rubbed my shin hard and cussed.

She didn't look back or say anything.

My hand burned to zap her with the Pink Kiss. I'd be

glad to watch her burn. But she wouldn't burn; she would Ascend. So I left it. I just rubbed my shin.

I never thought she was going to do that. What had happened to her? A few months ago, she was this timid little thing who wouldn't dare, and now she was kicking me.

She wasn't scared of me anymore.

I didn't like that.

Not one bit.

ABOUT THE AUTHOR

Adrienne Woods lives in South Africa with her Husband and two beautiful little girls. She writes full time and has recently finished her 18th Novel.
If she isn't writing she is teaching her bulldogs to stop eating the furniture.

Want to know more about Adrienne and her books.
www.authoradriennewoods.com

Get your pre-order now on all major online platforms for only 99c and sent.

Made in the USA
Coppell, TX
13 July 2021

58879698R00270